PAPAL WHISPERS

PAPAL WHISPERS

Stephen Cartmell

The Book Guild Ltd
Sussex, England

This book is a work of fiction. The characters and situations in this story are imaginary. No resemblance is intended between these characters and any real persons, either living or dead.

The Book Guild Ltd,
25 High Street,
Lewes, Sussex

First published 1998

Set in Baskerville
Typesetting by
SetSystems Ltd, Saffron Walden, Essex

Printed in Great Britain by
Antony Rowe Ltd, Chippenham, Wiltshire

A catalogue record for this book is
available from the British Library

ISBN 1 85776 335 1

Voor Dorrit – met liefde – bedankt voor je steun en je onuitputtelijk geduld.
Stephen.

‘The compulsive quest for certainty is not the expression of genuine faith but is rooted in the need to conquer the unbearable doubt.’

Erich Fromm, 1942

1

Bishop Costello sensed that the time had come. Alerted by the footsteps outside his dimly lit office, he turned his head towards the door. The padding feet, so often a sign of reassurance and certainty, now suggested a growing urgency as their pace quickened. The sudden flurry of activity left no doubt of its meaning. Even the telephones in distant rooms appeared to be more shrill, as if demanding immediate response. He was a man who trusted his instincts and he knew that the summons would not be long in coming.

Despite his anticipation, the bishop was startled when his own phone rang. Drawing a deep breath he allowed it to ring four times before he lifted the receiver and awaited the inevitable message.

'Thomas?' asked the caller in no more than a whisper.

'Yes.'

'It's Giulio.'

'I was expecting you.'

'Sadly, I suppose you were. How are you?'

'Fine. Fine. What news do you have?'

'It's nearly over, I'm afraid. You will be in for a busy day. The *Stampa Estera* are already blocking every line into the press office.'

'I'm sure they are. Is the Holy Father suffering much pain?'

'No. I feel it will be a peaceful end. God be with you, Thomas.'

'And with you, Giulio. We will need his support and guidance.'

Bishop Thomas Costello was no stranger to death. His early work as a youthful priest in a number of English parishes had made him familiar with man's inability to accept that life on earth was finite. He had witnessed the whole gamut of reactions to the apparent unfairness of mortality. The void left by the passing of husband, wife, child, friend or associate was often tangible in those left behind. Common amongst them all was a sense of anger at the disruption to their certainty, the forced revolution in their lives and a questioning of a fragile belief which rested on continuity and order. And yet, as the Holy Father lay on his death bed, Costello struggled with his own guilt at sharing none of the emotions he had so often witnessed in others. He harboured no great desire for the end of this present papal tenancy but the possibilities for change filled him with an excitement which he knew was inappropriate to his position. It was a concealed elation which taunted his convictions but confirmed his judgement.

The call from the prefect of the pontifical household had resurrected the doubts with which he had struggled over the last few years. He knew they were reservations shared by the prefect and though Giulio had been the bearer of bad tidings, Costello thought he sensed a certain animation in his tone. As the pope's 'gatekeeper', Mgr Giulio Palazzini controlled and regulated all private audiences and was a conduit to all information passing between the Holy Father and world outside. Because of this powerful position Palazzini was feared by many of those within the gossiping Vatican inner circle. A story had circulated some years before that a visiting cardinal had once written to a friend, as a postscript to his letter: '*Timeo non Paulus, sed secretarium eius*' – 'I don't mind Paul, it's his secretary who scares me'.

Bishop Costello could understand this reaction in others. But surprisingly he had built up a firm friendship with this aging Benedictine, who had always impressed him with his sharp intellect and unbridled faith. It was true that Giulio did not suffer fools gladly but his occasional sharpness came from a desire to fulfil his task with precision rather than any desire to demean his fellow clergy. Thomas Costello was by now in his early fifties, but Palazzini still viewed him with favour, as a representative of youthful Catholicism and the growing movement towards ecumenicalism. Even now, in his dotage, Palazzini longed for a healing of the rifts which had weakened the church so destructively and had led to the gradual hardening of Catholic orthodoxy. He sensed, in his young prodigy a shared belief that the present pope represented perhaps the last hurdle, before Christian churches were given another chance to re-establish their unity. The succession to the dying pope would be all-important.

Bishop Costello struggled to collect his thoughts as he glanced out at the sharp spring sunshine. The death of winter and the rebirth of spring struck him as being symbolic of impending events. From his office high above the Piazza San Pietro, he was able to catch a glimpse of the Mole Adriana, an imposing mass which dominated the skyline of Rome. It had been built as a mausoleum to former emperors who, in common with the present supreme pontiff, were unable to secure immortality. Now it was merely a curious relic to be pawed and poured over by the swarm of tourists who annually choked the streets of Rome. Although it was only early in the day, they could already be seen bustling across the Pont Sant' Angelo, driven by their schedules and pre-planned itineraries. Thomas Costello knew the bridge well. Habitually, he took a brisk morning walk before breakfast, often along the river bank to the Palazzo Di Giustizia, over the Ponte Umberto and returning to the west bank via the Pont Sant' Angelo. The view from his office window was restricted, yet it was still possible to make out the baroque angelic statues which decorated the bridge, their eternal postures welcoming humanity to the fortress gates. It always pleased him that, on a sunlit day, and even from this distance, he was able to see the glimmer of the Tiber. It was a river which had snaked its way through history, witnessed the birth and death of empires and seen Christianity established on its tree-lined banks. As he contemplated the wide city landscape he quietly prayed that the river would witness a peaceful revolution in the church he loved so dearly. It had given him everything and yet robbed him of so much.

The phone rang impatiently, breaking his growing pessimism.

'Bishop Costello?'

'Yes.'

'*Osservatore Romano* on the line for you.'

'Thank you.'

'Thomas? It's Giovanni.'

'Giovanni. I hoped it would be you.'

'This is no time for a sub-editor, Thomas! What's going on? There's an awful lot of rumours flying around the press room. I hoped you might be able to keep me up to date.'

'I will, Giovanni, I will. The *Stampa Estera* are already chasing us for any gossip on succession.'

'So he's on his way then?'

'I can think of more delicate ways to describe the death of a pope, Giovanni!'

'I'm sorry. Forgive me, but I think it's essential that we are the first to report the story. We may even be able to put a block on any wild rumours of election. I know the paper's a bit of an irritant at times, but we do have our uses.'

'I agree, Giovanni. I agree. Don't worry. You'll be the first to know when things really come to a head. Leave it with me. I won't let you down.'

'Fine, fine. I'll be at my desk all day. Make it a personal call. It's going to need some discreet handling.'

It had begun. As a member of the Secretariat of State, Thomas Costello had been given the responsibility to provide the pope with press summaries from national and international publications. Like many fellow members of the Vatican bureaucracy he was a bishop without a diocese, a small cog in the huge machinery of Catholicism. But this duty had been of little significance over the past few weeks. Pope Paul VII had now become incapable of any coherent thought. The press releases had stressed that the Holy Father was 'comfortable' despite his severe illness, but Thomas was aware that he had been tormented with pain during the preceding weeks. The stroke which had suddenly afflicted this once formidable and vibrant man had led almost immediately to total paralysis and pitiful blindness. It was enough to test even the strongest faith. From Giulio's news, it was clear that the torture was approaching its end. He was about to find relief from his constant suffering.

As Giovanni Oliveri's call confirmed, the world was no longer interested in the present incumbent, but in his successor. Bishop Costello reflected that it is the fate of all leaders to be forgotten before they die. Temporal posts are ironically eternal, the power lying in the title and not in the holder. Great men and women are soon dismissed from this earth, their history often revised as inconsequential rather than effectual. Though not a journalist Thomas Costello realised that the pope's obituaries had already been written. That he had been accused, tried and sentenced well before his body grew cold. History had been revised even before history had been written.

For the next three hours Bishop Costello was forced to fend off a barrage of enquiries from journalists and television companies. He felt they were like carrion waiting to pick at the bones of papacy. Glancing down into St Peter's Square he noticed that the crowds were beginning to grow. Television crews jostled with clergy, sightseers and pilgrims to gain space for an exclusive shot. What did they expect? Did they want Pope Paul to come to the window and wave a last farewell? He knew that the death of another was a great comfort to those who remained. To outlive the powerful guarantees the survivor a brief taste of supremacy.

The bishop's door suddenly opened.

'It's over, Thomas. God rest his soul and grant him eternal peace.'

'Amen to that, Giulio. Thank you for letting me know.'

Mgr Giulio Palazzini stood at the entrance, his hands trembling slightly but displaying no other visible emotion. The heavy oak doorway framed this small but erect cassocked figure. Thomas imagined this very scene had been played out centuries before and the image presented by the prefect seemed like a glimpse into history.

Palazzini moved towards the bishop's desk, pulled a chair from near the window and slumped into its green leather back. At closer quarters Thomas could see that the prefect looked exhausted. His usually tanned and full face had become drawn and lined with tiredness. His hair, once shining with health, now seemed dull and unkempt. Even the voice had lost some of its authority, his speech punctuated by his irregular breathing.

'May I suggest you contact *Osservatore Romano* as soon as possible. I feel we need to be very prudent in our response.'

'I told Giovanni I would call him first. How do you suggest I handle the inevitable questions of succession?'

'With great diplomacy. We must be very careful.'

'Of course.'

'There must be no hint of a successor waiting in the wings. We both know there are certain members of our holy church who harbour ambitions but it is better left unsaid. Better simply to state that God will guide our cardinals' hands in their election.'

'I pray to God He does. You look tired, Giulio. You should rest.'

'In time, Thomas. In time. There is the funeral to arrange. I will rest when the Holy Father is at rest. Now I must protect the dead from the living.'

'Indeed.'

'The mourning period will give us a little time. For the next two weeks we must try to dampen all speculation. It will serve no one's cause.'

'There are some ambitious factions, Giulio. It may be difficult.'

Palazzini smiled knowingly.

'The conclave has always stamped on open ambition, Thomas. We must watch for those who are diffident in public yet harbour a desire for power.'

'You have someone in mind, Giulio?' queried Costello.

'Perhaps, Thomas. At least those who declare their purpose are honest about their dishonesty.'

'But not to themselves, I think.'

'You may be right, Thomas. Man is a master of self-delusion. It is a universal frailty.'

Giulio straightened himself and moved forward in his chair.

'I must go; there's much to do,' he said suddenly, hesitating before he reached the doorway. He turned towards Costello, his face shaded in the darkness of the entrance. 'Listen to those who don't speak, Thomas. Others will speak for them.'

Mgr Palazzini shuffled from the room to resume his work. Thomas could hear him beyond the door, responding to enquiries from minor Secretariat staff. The authority in his voice appeared to return immediately, his strength revitalised by his sense of duty. He was flattered that Giulio felt able to briefly drop his guard in his own company. It reaffirmed what a staunch ally he had in this humble and godly man.

The phone rang yet again.

'The *Stampa Estera* for you, Bishop.'

'Ask them to come back to me in five minutes.'

He knew that he could now waste no time. The last thing that Thomas wanted was for the *Stampa* to start chasing unofficial sources. He had always maintained good relationships with the Foreign Press Club and it was important to maintain their respect. But, as he had promised, it was vital that he first contact Giovanni. The *Osservatore Romano* still represented the official voice of the Vatican and it was best to nip gossip in the bud before it blossomed into rumour. He knew that tomorrow's papers would be full of text and comment which falsely based their reporting on 'official sources in the Vatican,' none of which would have any validity. He had to stop the press setting the agenda and fuelling the inevitable in-fighting.

Bishop Costello had known Giovanni Oliveri for many

years. Although Oliveri was about to retire, he had lost none of his vitality and inquisitiveness. His appointment as editor of *Osservatore Romano* had come within six months of Costello's appointment to the Vatican Press Office. They shared a sense of having learnt their trade together. Though *Civiltà Cattolica* remained its chief rival, *Osservatore Romano* had become the official mouthpiece of the Vatican. To edit such a newspaper was a difficult task which could only be handled by a man who combined a journalist's instincts with a politician's cunning. The tightrope which Oliveri had to tread so carefully was to convince the Vatican bureaucracy that he remained in their pocket, whilst satisfying his readers that the paper remained unshackled and free to express uncensored opinion.

The established reputation of Giovanni Oliveri had been built during the Second Vatican Council in the early sixties. Under Pope John XXIII the church was attempting to renew its faith and return its message to the people. Orthodoxy and centralisation had increased the impotence of its teachings. This liberal pope was determined to welcome more than just the faithful into his flock. The ramifications were felt throughout the Christian world and inevitably polarised the opposing factions within the Vatican. This drawing of battle lines allowed Giovanni Oliveri to come into his own. By a deft use of his theological knowledge and an ability to employ subtle logic he managed, in a series of leader articles, to placate the warring camps. More importantly he gained the trust of both the readership and the Vatican hierarchy.

He became noticed, not least by Thomas Costello, who had read Oliveri's work in his seminary studies. Even though he was not to meet Giovanni for another fifteen years, Thomas had followed his rise to editorship with acute interest. He had watched Oliveri ride easily on the swells of orthodoxy which perpetually rise and fall within Catholicism. But he also knew that even Giovanni had great difficulty in restraining his opposition to the present Pope's doctrinal and authoritarian practices. It had come to a head when the *Osservatore Romano* was granted a private audience with Pope Paul in order to produce a written transcript of the interview. Oliveri had been given the responsibility to pose a number of prepared questions, but was denied use of any tape recording equipment which meant having to brush up on his now defunct short-hand skills.

The interview ranged from questioning Pope Paul's views of sacrament, infallibility, birth control – a whole list of central issues which had dogged the church for centuries. Giovanni received responses which were no more than he had expected though he had been shocked by what he could only translate as a complete lack of compassion. Pope Paul made it quite clear that obedience to the *magisterium*, the Church's teaching authority, was paramount. It was not open to question. However, it was the pope's response to the growing evidence of mass starvation in Africa and Asia which most disturbed Oliveri. The pontiff could offer no practical comment, maintaining that his duty lay in the spiritual rather than temporal world. 'Let them eat the word of God, Signor Oliveri. It is all I can offer.'

Though the *Ossavatore Romano* had thought it best not to include this quote for fear of public response, Bishop Costello had been told the story at a Vatican press dinner when Oliveri's tongue had been loosened by chianti. Costello was equally appalled and a little disturbed by Giovanni's indiscretion, but it had sealed their friendship. He thought of that conversation as he rang the *Osservatore* and prepared to release the news to the waiting media.

'Giovanni?'

'Thomas! He's gone then?'

'Just after two-thirty. You're the first to know.'

'Thanks. It's good of you. Have you phoned *Civiltà* yet?'

'They'll be next. I have no choice.'

'I suppose not. Who's making the funeral arrangements?'

'Giulio.'

'He'll do it well.'

'He will.'

Thomas Costello knew this was no more than a preamble to Giovanni's real interests. He steeled himself for the next question.

'Who's it going to be then, Thomas?'

'You know I can't answer that, Giovanni, even to a good friend. You know the official line.'

'Guiding hand of God, *etcetera, etcetera*?'

'Correct.'

'Can we meet? Off the record? I bet the knives are out already!'

'It could be difficult. There's a lot to do.'

'Come on, Thomas! You'll need to get out of there at some time. We all need a break. Meet me at Sebastiano's around eight thirty. You know the place. Just off the Piazza di Spagna. We'd better keep well away from the Circola for the time being. Too many wagging tongues.'

'I'll try, Giovanni, but I can't promise. Things are difficult.'

'I know. I know. See you at eight thirty!'

'You're incorrigible, Giovanni!'

'I know,' answered Oliveri with a sigh.

It was only early April, yet Thomas Costello noticed for the first time the warmth in the evening air. His day had been punctuated by continual calls and guarded responses, dominated by the need to fend off questions of succession. Disguising his personal opinion was a skill he had developed since joining the press office. He preferred to think of it as diplomacy rather than lying, though it still left him feeling uneasy. It was the chance to escape this world of half-truths which made him decide to join Giovanni for dinner. Like the confessional admissions he had so often heard behind metal grilles, he too had a desire to unburden his true feelings to someone who listened without condition.

In anticipation of the looming crisis Costello had missed his morning walk along the river. He had the seniority to use the Vatican chauffeur service but had decided to go on foot and enjoy the freedom of solitude and the anonymity of the city streets. He felt a need to collect his thoughts and review his strategy for the days ahead. Heading quickly out of St Peter's Square, now teeming with tearful mourners, he crossed the river at the Pont Pric Amedeo, across the Corso and into the narrow streets leading to the Palazzo Montecitorio. It was far quieter than the last time he had walked through the city. As a mark of respect, a number of restaurants had closed for the evening, their faded shutters fastened tightly on the windows of the ochre-faced apartments which flanked the pavements. Small groups of women huddled in the shadows chattering in hushed tones, their men a few metres away but more animated in their discussion.

Familiar as he was with the area, Thomas Costello soon realised he had taken a wrong turn, his pre-occupation with the sights and sounds of the city blurring his purpose. Before him stood the statue of the elephant dominating the Piazza della Minerva. Above it towered the obelisk of wisdom, borne upon the elephant's sturdy back. It was a sight which Bishop Costello had seen many times before. The Accademia Pontificia, the school for Vatican diplomats, had provided his route into the Secretariat of State. It was from these windows that he had often gazed down and wondered at the incongruity of Ferrata's sculptured beast.

Realising he was going to be late, Costello quickened his step towards the main thoroughfare of Via del Tritone. His sedentary life had affected his stamina and he arrived at Sebastiano's restaurant breathless and sweating under his heavy jacket.

Giovanni was waiting by the entrance, with the habitual cigarette in the corner of his mouth, blowing smoke into the night air. Thomas coughed as he inhaled Giovanni's toxic cloud.

'That's a filthy habit, Giovanni. You really should stop.'

'Don't chastise me, Thomas. We've more important things to discuss.'

'I'm sorry I'm late. Believe it or not I lost my way. Shall we go in?'

'We'll have to ring. Sebastiano has closed for the night. He's a good Catholic you know! But he's agreed to throw something together for us, and we can talk in private.'

Giovanni pushed the cracked, white porcelain bell. A moment later, Sebastiano opened the door, greeting Giovanni like a lost friend. The restaurateur seemed to fill the entrance, his starched, white apron offering no disguise for a body which had obviously sampled the entire menu. But curiously Thomas noticed that his hands had a surprising delicacy. Yet his character was in his eyes – sharp, attentive and framed by lines of pleasure. Here was a man who loved his profession as a *bon vivant*, assuring himself of his clients' allegiance through an animated passion for life.

Being the only customers in the restaurant seemed strange. Sebastiano had prepared a table at the back of the room away from the prying eyes in the street outside. Two candles illuminated the whole area, casting exaggerated, dancing shadows onto the walls, as they approached the small, round table. Thomas Costello smiled to himself as he thought of its resemblance to the intimacy of the confessional.

They sipped aperitifs and briefly exchanged pleasantries before Giovanni checked to ensure that Sebastiano was busying himself in the kitchen. He leaned closer to Bishop Costello.

'So what do you think?'

Thomas smiled at such a vague question but knew that it was an invitation to unburden his thoughts.

'I'm not sure.'

Oliveri did not attempt to reply. He had learnt from his years in journalism that the best way to gain information was to say nothing and simply to maintain eye contact. Thomas repeated his reply.

'I'm not sure.'

Oliveri said nothing.

'It's not easy, Giovanni.'

Oliveri glanced across the table, waiting for his old friend to win the battle with his conscience. He watched Costello tapping his spoon rhythmically on the white table cloth, searching for guidance from the monotony of its sound. Occasionally his eyes caught Giovanni's stare but avoided any hint that he was ready to declare his hand.

But as Oliveri had suspected the dam soon broke and within an instant the drip of information became a torrent. By the time Sebastiano served the cannelloni, the barriers of formality were broken. They were now both defenceless but their personal trust and respect allowed them to enjoy their vulnerability. Costello desired the comfort of Oliveri's ear as much as the journalist desired the bishop's inside information. Costello began to play his cards.

2

Giovanni's decision to avoid the Circulo proved to be a wise choice. Within days of the pope's death the Vatican had resumed its reputation as the village of gossip. The 'informal Vatican' was in full swing, every street corner, café and restaurant providing a meeting place for hurriedly-made alliances amongst the papal staff.

The Santa Marta Club, known simply to the inner circle as the 'Circulo', remained, as it had done for decades, at the hub of the chattering wheel. Only a few minutes' walk from St Peter's Square, it allowed for the rapid transmission of any scandal or indiscretion. More importantly, at a time of papal succession, it had, as a clandestine Vatican structure, the ability to smell out ambition. Now, as the gate-keeper of information, it was keen to open its doors to the constant flow of whispered intrigue and to control its release into the corridors of Vatican power.

Within three days of Pope Paul VII's final breath, Mgr Giulio Palazzini had set in motion the arrangements for the funeral circus. Despite the rise of orthodoxy during this pope's tenure there would be a coming together of the great and good of the world's religions, republics, democracies and dwindling monarchies. In many ways Giulio was in his element. A born organiser and delegator, the pieces of the jigsaw fell easily into place. The various protocols for the burial of popes had been handed down over the centuries and there was little room for modernity within the establishment. If anything, Pope Paul would be laid to rest in a far more traditional manner than his recent predecessors. Perhaps nothing symbolised his intolerance of modernism more than the reinstatement of the papal triple crown which was to adorn his coffin. The pontiff had viewed it as a reaffirmation of his power over earth, heaven and hell, a symbol dismissed by Pope John Paul I whom he had always despised. Even though this former pontiff had only held office for 33 days he had been gradually demonised as a man who had instigated the rot in the timbers of Catholic tradition. Despite his reservations, Giulio knew that he could not deny the present Holy Father his final wish to bear the crown to heaven.

Within the Santa Marta Club there was little talk of heaven. Matters of a more temporal nature dominated their conversations. There were the usual bids for preferred positions within the basilica on the day of the funeral, but as Thomas Costello and Giovanni Oliveri had assumed, it was the election of the next pope which provided the focus of attention.

Fr Ciro Ferrara walked briskly down the Via Sant' Uffizio towards the Piazza Santa Marta. The early taste of summer had continued, bringing office workers out on to the piazzas and into the pavement cafés. He was unable to deny himself the pleasure of seeing young women displaying their femininity. As a young priest he remembered the pangs of guilt which overwhelmed him when such thoughts invaded his mind. But now older and, he liked to think, wiser, he was content to revel in God's work and enjoy briefly his own masculinity. He had always viewed his enforced celibacy as a minor irritant rather than a suppression of any sexual drive and at the age of 78, such inner control was now rarely needed to salve his conscience.

As he entered the stone-walled *trattoria* of the Santa Marta club and glanced around for a familiar face, he smiled at the sight laid before him. There would be no temptation here, he thought. Three long, linen-covered tables stretched out along the ill-lit room. Before him were the retired bishops and cardinals, priests whom preferment had passed by and those, like himself, who had never really sought advancement. But he also saw the authority which lay in their union. Here sat the eyes and ears of the Roman Curia, the power behind the papal throne.

'You look amused, Ciro!'

'Nothing more than a passing thought, Salvatore.'

'Come and join us, we're just about to eat.'

It was a fortunate encounter. Bishop Salvatore Molare would almost certainly be Cellini's man. Here was a cleric, like many others, who had entered the Secretariat not through achievement but rather by proving to be a thorn in the flesh of the church establishment. Now in his eighties, Molare had once been a young rising star in the Florence diocese and destined for high office. However, his unconcealed austerity had proved his downfall. Earning a small retainer from the *Civilta Cattolica*, he had published a small number of articles questioning the wisdom of Pope John XXIII's papacy, particularly the shift towards ecumenicalism. He became a 'difficulty'. Within weeks the mechanisms of the Vatican state churned into action. Molare had been plucked from his diocese and given a minor role within the Secretariat with special responsibilities for internal finances. Robbed of his power base, Salvatore Molare's fire had been doused by the establishment. The tactic of inviting your enemy to dine at your table was a well worn strategy.

Fr Ferrara reflected that Salvatore's invitation had a certain irony given the purpose of his visit to Santa Marta.

'I think you know most of the people here, Ciro. Come and sit next to me. We can order right away.'

Ciro nodded a greeting to the fifteen ecclesiastics gathered around the long trestle table, which was already heaving under the bread and carafes of wine delivered before his arrival. It was obvious that the conversation was well under way, though Salvatore was kind enough to ease him into the discussion.

'How are the non-believers, Ciro?'

'Like the poor. Always with us, Salvatore.'

Molare let out a chuckle of approval.

'You haven't lost your sense of humour, Ciro!'

'It's the only way to survive.'

'But the department. Is it still as busy as ever?'

'As ever. As ever, Salvatore. Like your own office, we're waiting to see what happens.'

'There'll be change for us all, Ciro.'

Molare drew closer to Fr Ferrara, reducing his voice to a whisper.

'Between you and me, the whole Vatican's in a state of panic. Nobody knows which way to jump. Look at the faces around this table. They're like headless chickens.'

The conversation had indeed regained its volume since his late arrival. Faces had become flushed, fingers were pointed, arms waved in disapproval of rejected opinion.

'I can't see beyond Cellini, can you, Ciro?'

Salvatore Molare had declared his hand early, presumably to test out Ciro's reaction. He paused and gave Molare an answer which gave him no ammunition.

'I should think you're right, Salvatore. There's no real alternative. Has the college already assembled?'

'Not formally. As you know, the period of mourning must be completed first. But the *feel* is definitely for Cellini.'

Molare laid great emphasis on the word 'feel'. This was his way of letting Ferrara know that he was in the company of a man who had his finger on the pulse of the electoral process.

The mention of Cellini's name appeared to galvanise the assembled clergy. Though a few reservations were voiced it quickly became obvious that consensus had already been reached. Ferrara watched as Molare manipulated the discussion by adopting the rôle of devil's advocate.

'And what of Lombardo? He is sure to be given consideration. And we mustn't dismiss the chances of Woeters or even Reardon.'

The mention of Cardinal Reardon promoted general laughter around the table.

'I am quite serious, my friends,' retorted Molare. 'There are factions in the Curio who may well promote his interests.'

Ciro Ferrara imagined that exactly the same list of probable contenders for the papacy was being bandied around many others of Rome's *trattorie.* He had little doubt that Cellini was the most likely successor. As the delegate for the pontifical representatives to the Holy See, Cardinal Eugenio Cellini had spent the last two years not only writing the majority of the pope's speeches, but also constructing papal policy. He would provide a continuation of the status quo, a seamless thread between one papacy and the next. His rise had been steady rather than meteoric. Having attended a local seminary in the southern Italian town of Lecce he had gone on to complete an unremarkable doctorate on 'The iconography of the Trinity from the Reformation to the early part of the twentieth century'. It proved to be a treatise which, as its title suggested, achieved no more than the gathering of dust on the shelves of Catholic seminaries, its pages rarely disturbed by any but the most studious clerical scholars. Even during his post-doctoral studies at the Catholic University of the Sacred Heart in Milan, there seemed little evidence that he was destined for high office.

His break came, however, with the election of Karol Wojtyla, the first non-Italian pope since the Dutchman, Adrian VI. Though it was constantly denied, Pope John Paul II gathered about him a coterie of Polish confidantes to establish a defence against the predominantly Italian Curia who threatened to dominate his papacy. Eugenio Cellini had been blessed with a Polish mother and this proved enough to gain him access to the reorganised Secretariat. Though he felt himself to be pure Italian, it suited his purpose to broadcast his ancestry, and to great effect.

Fr Ferrara, like many others, had always resented Cellini's opportunism. He had watched him hang on to the tails of the papal robes and it was apparent that he was simply waiting for his final preferment. Now Ferrara was forced to listen to a group of men campaigning for this unprincipled cardinal. Rather than emphasise Cellini's credentials, which they viewed as unquestionable, they had begun to castigate his possible opponents. He listened intently as each possible candidate was set up as a target for their joint amusement.

'Cardinal Reardon? An American pope? A black American pope! It's unthinkable!'

'Cardinal Woeters? A Dutch reactionary! God forbid!'

'Cardinal Lombardo? A good man. Italian. But too old. No energy. He'd be in the pocket of every minor interest-group!'

They were dismissed in turn. Molare had succeeded in whipping them up into a frenzied mob, intent on achieving their collective aim. History was being repeated, thought Fr Ferrara. The unofficial episcopacy of Santa Marta was fulfilling its electoral role. Battles lines were being drawn, opposing camps identified, intelligence systems set in place. It would only be a matter of hours before the college of cardinals was given a verbal transcript of this and other similar meetings which were taking place throughout Rome. Every gathering would contain its own messenger.

On the pretext of pressure of work, Ciro Ferrara left his lunch companions before the coffee was served and whilst his head was still clear. His objective had been met and he felt it important to delay no longer than necessary. It was now four o'clock and the earlier clear skies had given way to gathering clouds. Rumbles of thunder could be heard in the distance and he noticed people's steps quickening to avoid the coming showers. In contrast, Ferrara maintained a steady pace, intent on collecting his thoughts and committing to memory all the views he had heard around the tables of Santa Marta. It was imperative that he should judge the mood correctly.

St Peter's Square now glistened as the spring rain sent tourists scurrying for the cover of the porticos, their Tuscan columns standing guard over the piazza. Caligula's obelisk, erect in reality, could be seen as a crooked reflection, pointing its image towards the distant river. Glancing briefly up towards the facade of St Peter's, Fr Ferrara mumbled a small prayer to the statues of the apostles. They appeared to stand in judgement over all those who entered the basilica.

As the sun disappeared once more behind the pink rimmed clouds, his gaze shifted to the right of St Peter's. Rising behind the porticos he could see the Apostolic Palace and a number of lights beginning to flicker on as the growing shadows began to seep into the Vatican offices.

Hurrying now, Ferrara crossed the piazza and made his way towards the small cluster of buildings which stood to the side of the church of San Damaso. By the time he arrived the inner courtyard had become grey and rather forbidding, any former sunlight now blocked out by the surrounding buildings. But he stepped out with great certainty. It was a route he followed instinctively, its familiarity hastening his movements.

The large oak door gave way easily as he turned the elaborate iron handle. Above him, and now highlighted by the light in the hallway, was the stained glass above the transom bearing the words *Segratario di Stato.* He was entering the engine room of the Vatican, the power base of the Curia, the heart of Catholicism.

Ciro Ferrara had always been amused by the smell of this building. Given its famed position in the hierarchy of Rome, he had expected, on his first visit, many years before, to be met with the odours of candle-wax, incense, even the scent of humility. Instead he had been met with the aroma of certainty, organisation, bureaucracy, the click of typewriters, the hum of computers and the stench of cleanliness. He often felt there was an absence of spirit and a strange inhumanity within these walls.

Climbing as quickly as he could up to the third floor, Ferrara knocked softly on the door of the office which lay at the very end of the long corridor. A simple wooden cross was mounted on the doorway and he touched it briefly before entering the room.

'Ciro! Come in. Come in. Tell me your news.'

Bishop Thomas Costello sat at his desk, a mountain of paper covering the surface and even more documents scattered across the floor. Ferrara felt pleased to see such apparent chaos. It was a characteristic which he had always viewed as a common bond and a welcome challenge to the controlled sterility of the Segretario.

'Let me make a quick call, Ciro. It'll give you a chance to regain your breath. I'll order some tea.'

'You're still very English, Thomas!'

'It never leaves you, Ciro!'

Costello rang his secretary and told her to hold all incoming calls.

'Just one more Ciro. This won't take a second.'

Ferrara watched Bishop Costello tap out only three numbers on to his phone. He realised it could only be an internal call and Costello spoke very briefly.

'He's here. Five minutes? Fine.'

It soon became apparent that it was appropriate for the messenger to delay his news until the other guest arrived. Costello quizzed him about his work in the department, about his nieces and nephews and his attendance at the funeral. It was a sincere questioning but Ferrara realised it was no more than a necessary postponement. After a few minutes the door opened behind Ciro and he turned to see the figure of Giulio Palazzini. He stood and greeted his old friend.

'It's been some time Giulio. How are you?'

'Well, Ciro. A little tired, but well.'

Ferrara studied the face of Palazzini. He did not look well. Instead, he appeared gaunt and grey, and gave all the signs of a man under intense pressure. The tension was visibly lined into his features. They had, years before, and as young men, attended the same seminary in Turin. It was disturbing to see such a decline in a man he remembered so fondly for his drive and sense of purpose. He remembered how it had been Palazzini above all others, who had rekindled his faith when, in a moment of inner crisis, he had considered leaving the church. As far as he knew, Giulio's own belief had never once faltered and it was this obvious resolve, intellect and integrity which had probably guaranteed his rise to the highest ranks of the Vatican staff. Thomas Costello could see the sadness in Ciro's eyes and knew that, like himself, he was shocked by Palazzini's apparent physical weakness. But his mind was still sharp. 'I suppose they talk of nothing but Cellini? Am I correct, Ciro?'

'Without doubt, Giulio. They talk of nothing else.'

'And the other names?'

'Dismissed, Giulio. They can see no further than Cellini.'

'As I thought. All blind to the truth. What do you think, Thomas?'

Costello sighed slowly, tapping his fingers lightly together and looked across to Ferrara. 'We must be careful. What's the feeling in Santa Marta?'

Ciro Ferrara recounted his experiences over lunch, the conversation with Salvatore Molare, and the possible but vilified contenders. He made it clear to Costello and Palazzini that the majority of clerics viewed the election of Cellini as a foregone conclusion. There appeared to be no way of stopping his promotion to the highest office and his support seemed to be growing by the minute.

Bishop Costello and Mgr Palazzini sat quietly as Ferrara delivered his tale of the Santa Marta. Occasionally one of them would interject for a matter of detail but for the majority of the time they allowed Ciro to hold the floor. There was a pause of such pregnancy at the end of his report that Ferrara felt uncomfortable and forced to speak.

'It doesn't look too good, does it, my friends?'

'Thomas?'

Palazzini glanced across at Bishop Costello who was now staring out of the window, lost in thought. He turned and faced back into the room.

'Lombardo. It can only be Lombardo. It's our only hope.'

'I tend to agree,' responded Palazzini, with a smile.

Ciro Ferrara looked startled. He could hardly believe what he was hearing.

'You can't support Lombardo!' he protested. 'I thought we were looking for change!'

Costello interrupted quickly, intent on reassuring his ally. 'I assure you, Ciro, we *are* looking for change. I beg you to trust our judgment.'

But Ferrara was determined to have his say and pressed

on with his rejection. 'Completely ineffectual. He's old. Nearly as old as me in fact, and no less doctrinaire than Cellini. We might as well return to the dark days of Pius XII. Cellini would pull his strings from the day he stepped into office.'

'We know that, Ciro,' answered Palazzini. 'But, as Thomas says, he may be our only hope. A move at this stage for any of the other candidates would only harden the resolve of Cellini's supporters.'

'But it makes no sense, Giulio,' retorted Ferrara, now standing, and beginning to pace the room. 'If you accept my criticism of Lombardo, as you say you do, how on earth can you lend him your support? Surely you can see it's a nonsense.'

'On the surface,' interrupted Costello, gesturing for Ferrara to re-take his seat. 'Let me assure you, Ciro, we are still totally committed to progression. There's no question of allying ourselves with the present stagnation.'

'And Lombardo's your answer?' laughed Ferrara, his voice now shaking with agitation.

'Have faith, Ciro.'

'Faith I have. Understanding I do not.'

'Then patience, Ciro. That's all I ask,' smiled Costello.

'And if it goes wrong?' quizzed Ferrara.

'Then God help us all.'

The three men sat for another hour, deep in conversation. Their strategy had to be carefully constructed and their promotion of Lombardo seen as unquestionably beneficial to the church. Their only hope of influencing the College of Cardinals would be through the arteries of the Curio, never more than a heartbeat away from the decisions of the establishment. They had embarked on a dangerous and very high risk game in which Cardinal Cellini had already established a significant lead.

3

'Well, fuck me sideways!'

'Charming.'

'They've gone for the fucking Dutchman!'

'You've got a lovely turn of phrase, Anthony. What Dutchman?'

'The new pope. They've elected Cardinal Woeters.'

'Really?'

'Sure as shit. It's true. I've just caught it on a news-flash. The scheming bastards have really screwed up Cellini. He was an odds-on favourite.'

'Was he?'

'Don't you read the papers, Robert?'

'I only write them, Anthony. I make a point of never reading them.'

'It'll put a bomb under Religious Affairs. They're always desperate for a story.'

Robert Paine watched the assistant editor tear across the press room. He marvelled at how Anthony Reynolds had lost little of his enthusiasm, even after 40 years in journalism. He was coarse, irreverent and demanding, but had maintained the respect of his staff through his sheer professionalism. Journalists thought of him as the best editor the industry had never had. Too honest for his own good was the general consensus amongst the news hacks. He possessed what his fellow journalists would have called 'edge', the very quality which Paine knew was absent from his own character.

To all outward appearances Robert Paine's career had been highly successful, having moved fairly swiftly from the tabloids into the more substantial broadsheets. His time in the States, on secondment to the *Washington Post,* had established a certain reputation. The series of articles he had written on the rise and fall of the Democrats had received plaudits from almost all his contemporaries. Students of politics considered his erudite analysis of the American and British electoral systems to be essential reading. Now, as political editor of the *Sunday Times* he was at the pinnacle of his career.

And yet he always sensed there was something missing. Inwardly he lacked the inner fulfilment which he desired so much. What the form of this contentment might be had always eluded him. As a committed agnostic he was plagued, like all other atheists and agnostics, with the suspicion that religious faith might be a useful asset. But he doubted that his problems lay in spirituality. Instead he simply harboured a sense of personal failure, a feeling that he had far more to give than had already been achieved.

His mind jolted back to Anthony's news of the pope's election. In an increasingly secular world he doubted if the choice of some obscure Dutch cardinal would provide much more than passing interest. It had now been over two weeks since the funeral of the last pope and the media were hardly giving the election blanket coverage. The public still preferred to feed from the trough of scandal, wayward politicians, royal sleaze and disgraced sporting heroes. Religious affairs do not sell newspapers and this was the bottom line for all editors who hoped to keep their jobs. But he also knew that as far as public interest stories were concerned, Reynolds was famed for his keen sense of smell. There was bound to be a good feature waiting to be written if Anthony had shown such excitement.

Robert Paine tried hard to concentrate on his current article, now further delayed by Reynolds' interruption. The submission deadline was four o'clock and he was beginning to feel the pressure. He glanced at the small black travelling clock which always sat on top of his word processor. It still gave him another couple of hours, but so far his piece lacked the bite he was looking for. European single currency issues were still dominating the political scene, even after all these years. He had just returned from a dreary lunch with a small number of back-benchers who bellowed their indignation and xenophobia at anyone who was willing to provide them with a free meal. They knew they had lost their battle but were intent on giving the final Bill as rough a passage as possible. Paine was suffering his usual problem of concealing his own loathing of nationalism behind the required veil of objectivity, and at the moment was struggling to strike the right balance.

It was then that he remembered the letter. He had been so consumed in his article that, even in his brief conversation with Anthony, it had completely slipped his mind. Paine reached for the phone.

'Alex? It's me.'

'She's fine.'

'Sorry?'

'Rachel. Your daughter, Robert.'

'Oh God! Yes. Sorry. Did everything go OK?'

'Yes, no problems. The doctor says everything's fine.'

'That's good news. Look, could you . . .'

'That is why you rang, isn't it, Robert?'

'Yes. But there's something else.'

He heard his wife sigh audibly. There was no hiding the fact that he had forgotten about Rachel's appointment. She was in the early stages of pregnancy and about to supply them with their first grandchild. He cursed his own insensitivity as he heard the irritation in his wife's voice.

'What is it?'

'There's a letter on my desk, Alex. Italian stamp. Rome postmark. Could you see if you can find it?'

'The one from your old college chum?'

'Yes, that's it. I think it's on the bureau. Probably under that pile of bills.'

'Do you want it now?'

'If you can.'

'Hang on.'

He heard his wife's steps as they hurried from the kitchen towards his office and could imagine her disappointment in his assumed lack of concern for his daughter. In truth he was probably far more anxious than Alex, and had spent most of his married life trying to avoid being over-protective to his children. The only way he was able to prevent himself from becoming a neurotic parent was to blank his family out of his mind altogether. The submersion in his work gave him a constant and welcome distraction. He heard the receiver being lifted from the wooden kitchen table.

'Got it.'

'Great. Could you fax it through for me, Alex?'

'Are you in for supper?'

'I'm going to try and make it for seven. See you later. I must go.'

Paine could understand his wife's sharp response. They had been married in their early twenties, two young reporters on a large provincial newspaper in Southampton. Alex had welcomed the arrival of their two children, but he always sensed that she bore resentment in having to forego a promising career and sit back and watch her husband's progress. He also knew that she probably possessed the greater of their two talents and may well have become an eminent journalist in her own right. Sadly, Alex had never been able to shake off the inherited morals of her own parents and had settled for the rôle of dutiful mother. Now, with the children established in their own careers and relationships, the embers of her old ambitions were still glowing. But it was all too late. Contacts had gone. Styles had altered. She was left with no more than the odd morsel of freelance work and a large amount of suppressed bitterness. It had rankled greatly when, in her forties, the resurrection of the past had seemed a possibility. The feelings of ennui still remained but had gradually mellowed as the realities of middle age tempered her desire for success.

Within a few minutes Robert Paine heard the familiar chunk of the fax machine. He watched the paper, at first slowly, and then more rapidly, curl its contents onto the desk-top like a wave breaking on the shore line. Never failing to marvel at a technology whose workings had always remained a mystery, he reached over, unravelled the document, and re-read the letter he had received two weeks earlier.

4th April 1999

My dear Robert,

I'm sure you'll be surprised to hear from me. Forgive me for not writing more regularly. The pressures of work are a constant distraction – poor excuse I know. How's Alex and the children? I remember you saying that Rachel was to be married. That must be a couple of years ago now. It's so long since I've seen them all. I hope they're all prospering and enjoying good health. They all seem to have grown into fine adults. Did Peter follow his father's footsteps and go into journalism?

I'm sure you're very proud of them all.

You'll realise that since the recent death of the Holy Father I have been extremely busy. I'm constantly caught between the demands of the Vatican and keeping you press people happy. You're a determined lot, Robert! I suppose that's what prompted me to write. It's good to feel you have friendships in the 'real' world outside the Vatican walls. To be frank it can seem a little claustrophobic and parochial at times – even infantile. In times of crisis we all seem to revert to our childhood!

I suspect the election isn't going to take too long. The College of Cardinals will be in full session within a week's time. I don't know if you're familiar with the procedures, Robert, but it follows a fairly well-established ritual. It's certainly no time for a tourist visit – the Sistine Chapel will remain under lock and key until the white plume signals their decision. You'd perhaps be surprised by the secrecy which surrounds the conclave. Believe it or not, all phones into the chapel are disconnected and every entry to the small voting area remains guarded at all times. If nothing else the discomfort of 'imprisonment' tends to focus the collective mind! Without giving names away (I haven't forgotten you're a journalist!) there appears to be only a small number of possible successors and I suspect the cardinals in their wisdom will avoid any radical changes. We shall see. The Holy Spirit will no doubt guide their judgement as he has always done.

I will obviously give my full support to whoever gains election though I have to admit that some change might not be a bad thing. Pope Paul VII was a good man in many respects but had some very entrenched views in terms of opposing modernisation and church unity. You'll not be surprised to learn that I had some difficulty in promoting his conservatism! But I won't bore you with the details, though I'm sure you'd be interested in the political element. There are an awful lot of people positioning themselves at the moment and trying to back the right horse. (Don't quote me, Robert! I have to trust in your confidentiality!)

I read your piece in the *Times* last week. It was extremely good. I still have the job of monitoring the world press and always look out for your articles. I share your views on the benefits of continuing the expansion of the European Union. I wish I could lay out my own arguments for church unity with such clarity. Your mind is as sharp as ever, Robert. I give way to the sin of envy every time I pick up the paper!

Before I forget, I had a letter from Izzy not long ago. We've tried to stay in touch (like ourselves, not always successfully). She seems fine and very busy. Still 'messing about with optics and telescopes' as she put it. Apparently she decided not to marry again but says she is happy enough. Sadly the tone of her letter left me in some doubt. Do you ever hear from her? I'm sure she would appreciate a letter if you ever have time. I've put her address on the back of this letter in case you have lost contact.

We must make an effort to meet, Robert. It's been too long. I rarely leave Rome these days but if I am ever in London I'll make a point of letting you know. If you are ever tempted by a trip to Italy it would be wonderful to see you. I have many friends in the city who could put you up in your usual style!

My regards to your family.
God bless you all.
Thomas.

Robert Paine now realised why he had failed to make an immediate link between the news of Cardinal Woeters' election and Thomas Costello's letter. His old friend had given very little away and only hinted that a revolution within Catholicism was a possibility. There had been no mention of Cardinal Cellini. He could only presume that he represented the conservative choice which Thomas had suggested was the likely outcome. The wisdom of the cardinals had obviously taken an unexpected course.

But it was the news of Isobel Griffin which had probably most distracted him from the affairs of the Catholic Church. She had been passing through his mind regularly since Costello's letter. It was not the re-emergence of some long lost love, but a reminder of his academic roots and late adolescent development. For some reason, which he could not pinpoint, Robert Paine gained comfort from recalling old friendships. They had been days of certainty, energy and optimism. In his present state of self-doubt their memory provided a safe escape from the present inner turmoil.

He recalled their meeting on a bitterly cold January morning, in the late 1960s. There had been no more than nods of acknowledgement as they fought to shield themselves from the strong north-easterly wind. He smiled to himself as he remembered Izzy suggesting that what they were about to do was probably a very big mistake. But despite the icy conditions they had taken to the water with the rest of their team. He chuckled again as memories of their first breakfast together flooded back in surprising detail. They were all shivering uncontrollably, using the brimming mugs of tea to warm their frozen fingers and yet bristling with excitement. It was their first common bond.

With characteristic bravery, it was Thomas Costello who

first admitted that he had a deep-seated hatred of water, but he had been relieved to find that both Robert and Izzy shared his apprehension. None of them was particularly athletic but all had agreed to join the college rowing team to challenge their own fears and escape the tedium of constant study.

His train of thought was suddenly interrupted by the telephone.

'Peter here. Have you got a minute?'

'I'm just finishing my piece for tomorrow's edition. To be honest, Peter, I'd be grateful for a bit more time.'

'Say about five o'clock then. My office. It won't take long.'

Paine agreed to the request but his mind was still wandering. He was trying to fathom why the relationship had worked. They had been three people with nothing in common apart from Trinity College and their intellect. Thomas Costello had been raised in the East End of London, the only son of an immigrant Italian plumber and an English mother. Isobel Griffin could hardly have been more different. She was thoroughly public school, estate agent father, solicitor mother and very 'home counties'. Though Robert shared a private education his upbringing had been quite dissimilar. His own father had died in a car accident when Paine was only three years old, leaving his mother as a young and grieving widow who never remarried. At the time of his premature death, his father had been a rising star of the Conservative party, at home amongst the patriarchy of the Macmillan era. He had been a self-made industrialist, making component parts for the then flourishing armaments industry. Fortunately for Robert and his two elder brothers, he had the foresight to marry well. Robert's mother was from good Scottish stock and in his late thirties they had all benefited from the inheritance of many acres of woodland in the highland borders. Despite early widowhood, his mother had never had problems with money but the loss of a husband and father had left its mark, impoverishing the spirit which had always been her major strength.

He knew in his heart that his present depression, his entry into journalism and his specialism in politics was a reflection of a constant desire to please the father he had never known. For many years he had harboured the faint knowledge that the lack of paternal affirmation had condemned him to some never-ending quest, in which every success only seemed to confirm his sense of inadequacy.

Looking quickly up at his travel clock, Paine realised he could afford no more distractions. Hurriedly pushing Costello's letter back into the inner pocket of his jacket, he returned to his article on the single currency. He felt strangely refreshed and the editing of his work came easily, in stark contrast to his earlier struggles. But it was a close thing. Although he had missed the deadline by about half an hour, experience told him that the print room would give him at least an hour's leeway.

Quickly tidying his desk, Paine grabbed his jacket from the back of the chair and headed off for his meeting with Peter Finlay. They had established a good relationship built on a mutual respect for their shared professionalism and he assumed it would be no more than a casual briefing to consider next week's parliamentary agenda. As he strode through the various departments he watched as young journalists bent over their word processors and secretaries scurried between departments. He was aware of the constant dull chatter of computer keyboards often drowned by the shouts of superiors demanding copy. It had a vibrancy and excitement which, despite his growing tiredness, never failed to lift his spirits.

He knocked on the editor's door, not waiting for a response.

'Robert. Thanks for coming. I've invited Anthony along. He'll be here in a second.'

Peter Finlay was one of the new breed of what were once known as Fleet Street editors. A small and rather wiry man, he nonetheless carried an air of authority. He was what his mother might have termed a dapper dresser, and his hair, whilst presentable within the official circles in which he mixed, was unkempt enough to give a hint of rebellion.

Anthony Reynolds entered with his usual bluster, dominating the setting with his sheer presence.

'Hello, Robert. Sorry Peter, got held up by those fucking motoring correspondents. Bloody amateurs!'

Reynolds' inclusion immediately raised Robert Paine's interest. It was highly unusual for him to be present at minor policy meetings and there had to be good reason for him to give up even a minute of his hectic schedule. As usual, Finlay wasted little time on pleasantries and came quickly to the point.

'Anthony tells me there's a big shake-up in the Vatican. What's your reaction, Robert?'

'Well it's not my area really, Peter.'

'Yes, I know that, but tell me anyway.'

Paine tried to collect his thoughts. He was tempted to reveal his contact with Thomas Costello but felt it would be a betrayal of their friendship. The letter had revealed very little detail but he knew that if the editor got wind of his access to a Vatican insider he was likely to push very hard. He decided to play the rôle of interested observer and gave a very general response to Finlay's question.

'From what Anthony says it sounds as if they've managed to manoeuvre Cardinal Woeters into the post. Apparently it was all sewn up in favour of the other chap.'

'Cellini?'

'Yes, that's it, Cellini.'

'How was it managed, do you think?'

'God knows, Peter.'

'I hope he does,' chuckled Reynolds, now slouched in his chair with hands clasped behind his head. The editor continued his questioning.

'Anthony thinks we need to know. He senses there's more to this election than meets the eye, and I trust his judgement.'

'But it's not really my area, as I said, Peter.'

'We think it might be.'

'Really? You know me. I'm more of an old Westminster hack. Good old political dishonesty.'

Finlay shuffled in his chair and leaned forward towards Paine. It was a sure indication that the real purpose of the meeting was about to be revealed.

'Look, Robert. As far as Anthony and I are concerned, this election of Woeters seems to have far more to do with politics than religion. There's obviously been a stitch-up and the big players in the Vatican have been wielding a great deal of power.'

'Well it seems that way from the little I've heard so far.'

Paine was conscious that he had also shifted forward in his own seat, in anticipation of his editor's demands. He had half guessed what was coming next.

'To be frank, Robert, I'd like you to take it on. It would be a fresh challenge. If you know about anything, you know about power, about political in-fighting, about insider pressure groups. No one knows more about the arm-twisting that goes on in the Whip's office. My guess is that the Vatican hierarchy isn't much different.'

'You're probably right, Peter. But I've got a hell of a lot on at the moment with this single currency issue. There's also the chance of a snap election. It could be a busy twelve months.'

'We can handle it, Robert. Ian Aitcheson's a fine reporter and he could do to take a bit more responsibility.'

'You're not trying to get rid of me are you, Peter?'

Robert Paine delivered his question with laughter in his voice but a slight hint of panic in his eyes.

'No, no,' responded Finlay quickly. 'There's no question of that. We simply want the best man for the job. I think you know me well enough by now, Robert. If I had the slightest desire to promote you to the dustbin, I wouldn't pussyfoot around. If Anthony's hunch is correct this could be one of the most important jobs you've ever taken on. You know your work has my total respect.'

'Well thanks for that, Peter. Just for a second I thought . . .'

'No bloody chance, Robert,' interrupted Reynolds.'We're not about to sell off the family silver, you're too fucking valuable.'

Now reassured, Paine relaxed into their conversation. In many ways he was quite flattered and excited by the prospect of getting back into some form of investigative journalism. He also suspected that Reynolds had been the prime mover in suggesting this change of direction to Finlay. Despite all his bluster, Reynolds was a perceptive man who had sensed some time ago that Paine was becoming a little disillusioned, and this sudden Vatican upheaval had provided him with a perfect way of helping out an old friend.

The three men chatted for over half an hour, trying to construct a strategy for extracting information from the guarded Catholic establishment. It was difficult at times for Paine to conceal his friendship with Bishop Costello but he managed to hedge round any details of how he would take on his task. He left them with an intentionally vague reassurance that he would be able to come up with something and would report back in a few days.

By now it was six o'clock and he remembered having promised Alex that he'd try and make it home for supper. The traffic would be horrendous at this time of night and he realised it was going to take him at least an hour to get out of the city and into Richmond. He scrabbled his papers together and rushed down to the underground car park and out into the evening rush hour.

It had been a challenging day. He felt suddenly tired and yet somehow revived. His mind whirled with a mixture of apprehension and renewed optimism. If he had been asked at that instant how he felt, he would have been incapable of giving a coherent response.

As he approached the Marble Arch roundabout he noticed the brake lights of the car in front suddenly brighten. It had begun to rain heavily and the red lights seemed to diffuse in his streaked windscreen, making it difficult to judge the distance between the two cars. There was a sudden jolt and the sound of metal crumpling under the impact. His now taut safety belt dug hard into his chest and Paine could feel himself sweating heavily.

To the great indignation of the drivers around him he stopped his car and got out to check the damage. Horns blared out around him, a few drivers shaking their heads in mimed disapproval.

A middle-aged woman stood by her car, obviously shocked but seemingly uninjured.

'Sorry, I was miles away,' said Paine. 'We'll need to exchange details. Don't worry, I won't quibble over liability.'

'Shame. I only bought the car yesterday.'

This woman obviously wasn't going to make a fuss and seemed more embarrassed by the growing queues of traffic than the damage to her car. She looked vaguely familiar to the journalist, not so much in terms of her appearance, but the way in which she dealt with the situation. It was a problem, but a minor crisis and inconsequential. She was evidently a woman who had her priorities and emotions under tight control.

The rain was even heavier by now and they went through the formalities as quickly as they could. Robert Paine jumped back into his car. The damage was fairly minimal and apart from a dent in his right front wing and a cracked headlight, he had no problem in continuing his journey. But there was something about the woman's behaviour which made him search his memory. He went through a whole catalogue of possibilities. Newspaper staff, parliamentary researchers, friends of Alex, even members of his golf club. None of them seemed to fit. It was then that he recalled the slight hint of dismissiveness in the woman's eyes. He had only ever seen that look once before. It was an expression shared by Isobel Griffin.

He remembered a very brief affair, which they both knew was inappropriate to their friendship. It had amounted to little more than the natural culmination of a cheap but amusing meal and two bottles of an even cheaper burgundy. Its novelty had been the shared lack of intention and he recalled Izzy simply replying, 'Why not?' when he asked her to stay the night. Their bodies had gone through the mechanical process of love-making but the physical climax was accompanied by an emotional indifference which was obvious to them both. Their giggling and teasing was not a sign of their sexual pleasure in one another but a masking of their shared embarrassment. But it was the look which Izzy gave him in the morning which now cemented his memory. There had been no sign of regret or disenchantment, simply the drawing of a veil over a mistaken episode, a minor crash on a long sexual journey.

In a strange way the short but unsuccessful liaison confirmed their strong friendship. There had been a certain honesty in Izzy's response and it had cleared in an instant the potentially muddy water. Though left unsaid, there was an understanding that Thomas Costello should remain ignorant of the event. No benefit could have been gained by pricking the bubble of intimacy which the three friends shared and valued so much.

Approaching Hammersmith Bridge, the traffic ground to a halt. It was already seven o'clock and he imagined Alex looking hard at the kitchen clock with a growing irritation. Her imposed domesticity had seen her revert to the obsessive punctuality which she used to ridicule in her friends. Rummaging in the glove compartment he searched blindly for the mobile phone keeping a close eye on the distance between himself and the car in front. With one hand he tapped out his home number and waited for the ring. The weather was really closing in and Paine could see lightning forking through the distant sky.

'Alex? It's me. Can you hear me?'

'Just. You're very faint.'

'It must be the storm. Look, I'm stuck on Hammersmith Bridge. Hell of a traffic jam. Should be home in about twenty minutes with a bit of luck. Sorry. Can't do a thing about it.'

'OK, Robert. As long as I know. It's only a casserole, it'll keep.'

'Any messages?'

'Just one, I think. Thomas Costello.'

'You're joking!'

'I'm not. It was his letter I faxed to you, wasn't it?'

'Yes it was. Did he leave a message?'

'He just told you not to call. Seemed quite adamant. Said he would write.'

'Extraordinary!'

'Why? What's happened, Robert?'

'I'll tell you when I get home. I'll be as quick as I can.'

Paine's head whirled with a chaos of thoughts. Why should Costello ring today of all days? It was only an hour since he had his conversation with Finlay and Reynolds. There couldn't be a connection between the two events, it was beyond all reason.

The traffic began to nudge slowly forward only to stop yet again after a few yards. He could sense the frustration in the other drivers who were blowing their cheeks and tapping their steering wheels in the monotonous rhythms of impatience. But Paine was now too pre-occupied by his wife's information and was glad of the time to think. What was Costello up to?

Paine still remembered him as a youthful philosophy student. They had only met on three occasions since their college days, the last time over nine years ago. Intermittent letters and the odd call had allowed their friendship to continue, even though they had gone on such different paths. Looking back, it was hard to see why the three of them had struck it off at all. The accident of meeting in the rowing club was an unlikely stimulus. Their social and academic backgrounds were more likely to divide than unite them. They didn't really have much interest in each other's subjects. Thomas was consumed by philosophy, Izzy excited by physics and Paine remembered having trudged through economics. He recalled with a wry smile that Isobel had suggested that economists were like virgins giving advice on sexual intercourse and after years of observing ineffectual chancellors, he thought she probably had a point.

But they had come together nonetheless. They sparked in

one another a comradeship which none of them had ever experienced. Perhaps it was the shared humour. The unspoken but shared basic values. Whatever it was, it was indefinable. It was a friendship built on trust and a mutual admiration for the qualities held by the others which they were unable to locate in themselves. It was this bond of fellowship which both he and Isobel had been so intent on preserving after their short affair.

Paine recalled with some affection the day his tutor had told him that Thomas, Robert and Isobel had been christened the trinity of Trinity College. It had remained the nickname of this triangular relationship till the day they left Cambridge and yet now, some thirty years later, the triangle seemed to be reforming. It felt unnerving, yet strangely inevitable.

4

It was well after eight o'clock by the time Paine turned into the gravelled drive. The suburbs of Richmond provided a welcome relief from the buzz of the city and the tensions of his journey. He would have preferred a house in the country and still harboured a desire to escape one day into the Scottish borders. But his ambition and the practicalities of everyday life had so far denied him this latent dream. Instead, he had been forced to settle for the relative tranquillity of south-west London. His generous salary and his late father's estate had allowed him to live in some style. The Edwardian red-bricked building had become Paine's adult comforter, a safe haven from the stresses of life. Set in almost two acres of secluded land, it was well-hidden from prying eyes. The small copse which lay at the rear of the unmanicured gardens allowed both Alex and himself to live out a fantasy of rural living.

As he turned the key and entered the hallway he felt drained and depressingly middle-aged. He called out for Alex.

'In the kitchen!' came the reply from the far end of the hall.

Dropping his briefcase, he headed for the sound of Alex's voice.

'Hungry?' asked Alex with a welcoming smile. She had fought off the indignation which had threatened to consume her. There had been many ruined meals in their long marriage and she knew it was unlikely to change.

'Maybe later, Alex. I'd love a drink first, if that's OK?'

Paine slumped in the kitchen chair as Alex opened a bottle of red wine. She could see the tiredness in his face and instinctively recognised the signals that her husband wished to talk.

'What's going on, Robert?'

He glanced at her, surprised at her directness but grateful for her intuition.

'Come on. Get it off your chest.'

'You sound like my mother,' he laughed.

'Men love being mothered. Dependent till death, so my grandmother used to say.'

'Perceptive woman.'

'She was. What's the problem, Robert?'

Paine hesitated momentarily, his expression responding to Alex's lightly-veiled accusation of childishness.

'God knows! It's been a strange day.'

Alex waited. Like many husbands and wives, they had developed a set routine of conversation. She knew that Robert hated to be interrogated and that the best way to elicit information was simply to push the door open and retreat. In her own days as a full-time journalist she had felt much the same way. Her golden rule had always been to question lightly and listen hard, letting her subjects set their own pace and craft their own tale.

After a few moments' silence, Paine began to relate the details of his conversation with Finlay and Reynolds; his fear of being sidelined; the new job he had been offered and the coincidence of Costello's letter. At what she judged as an appropriate moment, Alex pushed the door open a little more.

'You told them about Thomas Costello?'

'That's the problem, Alex. I didn't, and it puts me in a really difficult situation.'

'But you hardly know him now, Robert. You could hardly be accused of betraying a friendship.

'We go back a long way.'

'You didn't even reply to his letter, did you?'

'No. I did mean to. You know how it is.'

'I remember him visiting when we lived in Chelsea but it's

a hell of a long time ago. You're hardly bosom buddies any longer.'

'I don't know, Alex. His letter. His phone call today. There's something odd about the whole thing.'

'Well sleep on it, Robert. I'm sure it will all seem clearer in the morning. You're obviously very tired. Do you want to eat?'

'Not really Alex. I'm sorry.'

'Ah well, at least the dog will be happy. You can always come upstairs and take advantage of my sumptuous fifty-year-old body.'

Robert smiled in admiration at his wife's constant ability to snap him out of mental self-indulgence.

'Serious?' he heard himself say.

'Genuine offer,' laughed Alex, unbuttoning his shirt in a teasing manner.

'Why not? I've got to eat something,' answered Paine, biting her fingers gently. Thoughts of Isobel Griffin invaded the intimacy as they locked up the house, switched off the lights and headed for the bedroom.

Paine slept heavily. The mixture of wine, sex and exhaustion proved to be a successful cure for his insomnia. The shafts of light which greeted his waking told him that the storm of the previous evening had now cleared, leaving a bright spring morning. He turned over and reached towards Alex only to find the bed empty. Sliding his feet across the mattress he could still feel her warmth in the sheets. She had been right. Though he knew his dilemma wasn't resolved, he was soon aware of a greater clarity in his thinking and a sense that he would find a solution before the day was out. With this new sense of optimism Paine drifted back into light sleep, only to be woken minutes later by Alex.

'Would you like some tea, Robert? I thought we'd spoil ourselves.'

'Love some. Thanks.'

'You may need it.'

'What do you mean?'

'Look what's just dropped on the mat.'

Alex handed him the letter. He immediately saw the airmail sticker and the Italian stamp.

'It's from Thomas, isn't it?' queried Alex.

'It must be!' answered Robert, now sitting up in the bed. 'This is ridiculous. He only phoned last night.'

'Is there a posting date on the envelope?'

'Twentieth of April.'

'It's the twenty-fourth today. He must have written it days before he called last night. Open it. See what he has to say.'

Paine hurriedly tore open the envelope and looked to the end of the letter.

'Yes, it's Thomas all right.'

'Read it out, Robert.'

Looking at the top of the letterhead, Paine could see that the letter had been written on the nineteenth of April and posted a day later. He wondered what could have possibly happened between Costello's decision to write and last night's phone call, which promised yet another letter. His investigative reasoning was now fired by such a bizarre chain of events and he sensed his energy rising as he began to read out loud to Alex.

> My dear Robert,
>
> Two letters in as many weeks! I realise it makes little sense and I haven't managed to rationalise my own actions. There has been so much happening in my life during the past few months that I hardly know where to begin. What remains a mystery to me is why I feel so compelled to write to you. Let's just say that God works in mysterious ways and it's not always best to question His purpose. I realise it is not a faith we share, Robert, but I'm also sure you would have an equally difficult time finding rational reasons for all your own motives.
>
> You'll recall that in my previous letter I told you that the College of Cardinals was about to assemble. As I'm

sure you will now know, this resulted in the election of Cardinal Johannes Woeters who has become Pope Adrian VII. From my comments you'll also realise that this has caused quite a stir in the Catholic community as he was one of the least likely candidates to succeed to the papacy. He is only the second non-Italian pope since Adrian VI (from whom he takes his name) and I thank God for his election.

At this point, Robert, I must plead yet again for your confidentiality. I know church affairs are no more than a minor interest for you but as I said before, your journalistic instincts are probably as alert as ever. If you feel this letter compromises you in any way, do let me know. It's a risk I feel compelled to take.

I will try to keep my 'tale' as simple as possible – the Vatican is notorious for its complexity. Let's just say that when a pope dies the danger lies not in his passing but in the vacuum which it creates. For a short time the power of the church is no longer with the papacy but in the hands of its bureaucracy. This creates tensions as people vie to assert their influence. I suppose it would be much the same if your own editor suddenly resigned. What is at stake of course is the future direction of Catholicism, and even a non-Catholic such as yourself will be aware that there has been an ever-rising tide of orthodoxy since Pope Paul VII took office. Please don't misunderstand my intentions. I accepted his election as God's purpose, but remained concerned over his translation of the doctrine of infallibity in such an overt manner. In essence, the power of the church had become re-established in the hands of the pope and an international network of what some have termed as sycophantic cardinals and bishops. The laity (the true heart of the church) had been forced into the submissiveness they had encountered under Pope John Paul II.

I can hear you thinking: what right have I to try and guide the hand of God? I have none. But we are all blessed with the divine gift of free will, to form opinion, to decry what we see as misjudgement and error. It is God who will make the final decision through his cardinals. But before that occurs, we, as his servants, have a duty at least to inform that decision. If God rejects that opinion he will surely guide our hand rather than be guided himself.

Before I tell you the details of the election you perhaps need to know a little more about the inner mechanisms of the Vatican. When I spoke earlier in the letter of a powerful bureaucracy I was really talking of the Roman Curia. For simplicity you could think of it as a 'royal' court which acts in the name of the incumbent pope. Its tentacles stretch far out into the Catholic world, operating through a series of secretariats, councils, tribunals and minor institutions. I myself represent one of those tentacles(!) though I have recently found myself thrust into a new rôle. (I will tell you more of this later in the letter.)

Suffice it to say, the Curia represents the major decision-making structure in the Catholic church, though this can lead to a misunderstanding. The Catholic church is not a democracy. Apart from the word of God, the pope enjoys absolute power. There exists no temporal court who may sit in judgement upon him. The Curia can only ever hope to temper that power, to influence the pronouncements which become set in ecclesiastical stone At best, they can only act as ineffective regulators of power but in the final analysis all power lies with the pope – if he wishes to use it. And here lies the problem faced by the present Curia. Our recently deceased Pope Paul VII insisted on the total retention of papal power, and in doing so alienated large sections of the Curia.

By a series of careful placements and preferments, he succeeded in reducing their influence by promoting his own men into prime positions within the various Secretariats. At the same time, he surrounded himself with a cohort of supportive cardinals who would guarantee

> election for his chosen successor. This was of course – as you will have seen reported – Cardinal Eugenio Cellini.

Robert Paine stopped reading and looked up at Alex.

'Cellini. That's the name Reynolds mentioned when the news first broke. He makes the pope sound more like a politician than a man of the cloth.'

'You should read Trollope.'

'I have. But this is more like bugging the Whip's office. It's a far cry from a vicarage tea party.'

'What else does he say?' prompted Alex, impatiently.

Her husband continued, glancing quickly through the letter to see how much was yet to be revealed.

> You can imagine, Robert, that a great many members of the Curia found the prospect of Cellini's promotion quite unimaginable. He was seen most damagingly as a careerist and no more than a clone of the existing pope. It seemed likely that he would diminish the status of the Curia even further and reduce them to a rubber-stamping bureaucracy.
>
> It is here, however, that I should try to divorce myself from this motive for rejecting Cardinal Cellini. It was never my proposal to run with the pack, in such a self-interested manner. My intentions have always been to consider the needs of the church before my own ambitions. Forgive this apparent piety but I mean this with all sincerity. I saw a chance, not to return Catholicism to the Curia, but to return it to its membership, to the body of our church. It was an opinion shared by a number of my closest colleagues, most notably the Prefect of the Pontifical Household, Mgr Giulio Palazzini. We could see no other course of action than to promote the interest of Cardinal Johannes Woeters. Given his history of Dutch radicalism, it at first seemed a futile ambition, and yet we felt driven towards an attempt at least to hamper the seemingly inevitable

election of Cardinal Cellini. At first the problem seemed insurmountable.

I think you might enjoy the resolution, Robert! To put you more in the picture, there appeared to be four main candidates, three of whom were really thought to be 'making up the numbers'. As I say, Woeters was considered too radical. Of the other contenders Cardinal Lombardo was really too old and ineffective, and Cardinal Reardon, dare I say it, black and a non-European – worthy, but an unrealistic proposition. I think by now you may be guessing at our strategy. I seem to remember Margaret Thatcher suffering a similar fate when her party was split in two by a stalking horse. To cut a long story short, we put all our support behind Lombardo.

It had to be done with the utmost discretion. You know the sort of thing, Robert. Non-attributable sources, words in the right ears. The late pope had not really mustered his defences as well as he would have liked and there was still a strong phalanx within the Curia who bore some deep-seated resentment. We were also fortunate in conscripting Giovanni Oliveri, the editor of *Osservatore Romano* who, by some carefully crafted articles, began to raise some doubts regarding Cardinal Cellini's election. I'm sure I needn't detail the rest. By the time the College of Cardinals went into *purdah* the voting was bound to be split. Obviously I was not party to the discussions which took place: we could only sit nervously and await the outcome. What we did know is that if there was a fairly equal division, the only possible beneficiary would be Cardinal Woeters. As they say, Robert – the rest is history.

Unfortunately I have to add a sad postscript to my letter. Only a few days after the pope's election, my good friend Giulio Palazzini suffered a massive stroke whilst attending mass and died within minutes. He had seemed unwell for some time but I have no doubts that the stress of the election precipitated his death. It was still a terrible shock and I will always value his friendship and wisdom. I hope he is now at peace in God's arms.

But he left a legacy, Robert. Only three days ago I was called to the Holy Father's offices to be informed that I was to become the new prefect in place of Guillio. He had apparently left letters in his will which recommended me for the post. It is obviously a great honour though somewhat daunting. To be at the centre of affairs, however, is exhilarating, especially as I anticipate some fairly fundamental changes over the next few years.

The pontificate is in good hands, Robert. I am sure of that. Pope Adrian VII is undoubtedly a man of compassion and vision. I only hope he has the fortitude to stand up to dissenters. It will be no easy task – the demands on any pontiff can be quite extreme. Even at this early stage the Holy Father has not found it easy and has been plagued by numerous headaches which I am sure are a result of the arduous responsibilities of his post. In some way it is encouraging to see such a man displaying such mortal weakness!

I must go. Forgive me for such a long letter but there was so much to tell you. If you do get a chance I would love to hear from you and hear your own news.

God bless you.
Thomas.

Robert Paine turned to his wife with a look of disbelief.

'God! It's bloody dynamite,' was all he could muster in response to Costello's letter. 'He's just presented me with a loaded pistol.'

'And you're going to use it?'

'How can I? I've still got some morals. But he's taking a hell of a chance.'

'There's a postscript, Robert. What does it say?' queried Alex, just too far away to decipher the neat but tiny writing.

'Oh, he just asks if I've written to Izzy. He asked me in his last letter.'

'I didn't really read it. Is that Isobel Griffin?'

'Yes, that's her. The other member of the trinity, as they used to call us. You remember her, don't you?' he asked casually.

Alex did remember her. Unknown to Robert, her name had played on Alex Paine's emotions since the day they had met. She had always suspected that there may have been a physical relationship between the two of them but had always avoided confronting Robert with the question. In truth, it was very low on Alex's list of priorities. What had always concerned her was that Isobel Griffin had in some way gained access to a part of her husband which had remained inaccessible to herself. Robert's tales of this so-called trinity had always unnerved her despite his constant reassurances that it was no more than platonic, a friendship built on an affinity of intellect, humour and companionship. Until the recent events she had almost forgotten Thomas Costello, and yet now, as she thought of Isobel Griffin, she sensed a growing resentment against both his old friends. She had raised Robert's children and forfeited a promising career. Robert's time and attention was supposed to be her pay-off. She wanted him for herself. The sudden resurrection of Isobel Griffin and Thomas Costello seemed to threaten that desired stability.

Her husband interrupted her train of thought.

'I'll have to write.'

'To Isobel?' she asked abruptly.

'No. To Thomas. He says he doesn't want to compromise me and yet he's put me in an impossible situation.'

Alex decided to resist challenging her husband on his relationship with Isobel. There would be more appropriate moments. It was obvious that Robert was totally preoccupied by Costello's news. With some resignation, Alex feigned indifference and tried to ease her husband's concerns. She forced herself back into her maternal rôle.

'Of course Thomas doesn't realise you've just been asked to look into the papal election. He obviously sees you as a safe confidante, even though he knows you're a journalist.'

'That's all well and good, Alex, but Finlay's going to be chasing me for an article within a week. What do I do? Simply ignore the information he's just handed to me on a plate?'

'I don't know,' answered Alex, now beginning to see the real difficulties faced by Paine.

'I'll have to call him and make it clear that I've got a conflict of interests. It's only fair to me, and to him, come to that.'

There was a pause in their conversation until Alex remembered Costello's phone call from the previous evening.

'There's a problem, Robert.'

'What's that?'

'Don't you remember? Thomas almost pleaded with me to make sure that you didn't return his call. He said he would write. For all I know he could be posting another letter at this very minute.'

'God! This is getting ridiculous. If it was that urgent he could have faxed me.'

'Perhaps he's frightened of security or something.'

Paine laughed at his wife's last remark. There was a danger of their imaginations getting out of control.

'You make it sound like a cheap spy novel,' he chuckled. 'My tea's gone cold. Shall I make some more?'

They decided to spend the morning in bed, a rare opportunity to relive the habits of their early married life and for Paine to switch off from the difficulties he now faced. Though it remained unspoken, it allowed Alex the chance momentarily to lay claim to her husband. She was a strong woman but she also knew that the re-emergence of Isobel Griffin had exposed her Achilles heel.

They drifted into sex as easily as they later drifted into sleep, the warmth of the bed and the absence of any constraint heightening their desire. Yet Paine was surprised by the intensity of their love-making. He sensed a certain passion in Alex which he hadn't experienced for many years. There was almost a fierce determination in her actions, a desire to please him at all costs. He found it exciting and yet disturbing, but was unable to guess at her unstated motives.

They slept until well after eleven o'clock, only woken by the whining of their labrador who was desperate to escape into the garden.

'I'll go,' mumbled Paine reluctantly.

He returned to find that Alex had slipped back into a deep sleep. Climbing carefully in beside her, he lay with his hands cupped around the back of his head. He could understand why depressives so often take to their beds. The maternal warmth, the illusion of safety, even the raising of the bed from the floor all seem to detach you from the need to face the world, to take decisions, to face reality.

But Paine was not depressed, he only feared depression's arrival. What he desired most at this moment was to confront his present problem.

'Alex?' he whispered, touching her gently on the shoulder.

'What is it?' she answered, stirring herself and blinking through half-closed eyes.

'I know what I'm going to do.'

'What?'

'Take a break.'

'Take a break?' she answered, gradually becoming more alert. 'You mean give up your job?'

'Yes. It's the only way.'

'For how long?'

'Oh, I don't know. Three months or so. Ian Aitcheson can cover the political stuff and I'm sure they'll find someone to scratch around for a decent Vatican story. That'll let me off the hook and I won't need to betray Costello's information.'

'You mean you wouldn't even mention it to Finlay?'

'That's right.'

'Are you sure?'

'I think I am. I could do with a break anyway. Let's call it an interlude. I've felt so tired recently. We could even spend more time together.'

Alex smiled.

'I'll take that with a pinch of salt. But if you're sure, then do it. It's not as if you haven't earned it. That paper's certainly had its pound of flesh. Look at it as an opportunity, you've still got a lot to give.'

'Good existentialist advice,' laughed Paine. 'I knew Sartre would come in handy one day.'

'You never got beyond the first page!' mocked Alex.

'Page two if you must know. Enough to see me safely through a dinner party,' answered Paine, parrying his wife's teasing and enjoying his self-mockery.

Paine shaved and showered quickly, racing to avoid his indecision and now more willing to accept his own mortality. He knew that ringing Finlay would not be easy but he felt excited by his own sense of relief. As he picked up the phone he had no idea what he was going to say to his editor. He was put through immediately.

'Peter?'

'Yes, Robert. What can I do for you?'

'I'm going to take a sort of sabbatical, Peter.'

'A sort of what?'

'Sabbatical, Peter. I realise it's a bit sudden but I really need to take a break.'

There was a pause as Finlay absorbed Paine's message.

'Is there a health problem, Robert?' he asked finally.

'On the contrary, Peter. I feel quite rejuvenated to tell you the truth, but my instincts tell me it would be a good move.'

'Sure?'

'Positive.'

'You're happy for Ian to take over?'

'As you said, he's a fine journalist. He's got enough contacts to keep the ship afloat.'

'And the Vatican story?'

Paine struggled for a response. 'I really can't see it developing,' he lied. 'I'm sure the religious affairs boys can handle it.'

'Anthony's not so sure.'

‘Trust me. They’ll be fine.’

He was surprised by his own abruptness. Unconsciously, he realised that the most likely way to gain an acceptance of his request was to present Finlay with a *fait accompli* and reduce the chances of being dissuaded. The conversation was far shorter than he had expected.

‘Well, that’s it, Alex,’ said Paine, returning to the kitchen where his wife sat in her dressing gown, reading the morning paper. She looked up.

‘How did he take it?’

‘Well, thankfully he did make some attempt to change my mind. I’d have been offended if he hadn’t.’

‘You’re an egomaniac!’ laughed Alex.

‘I know, I know. But seriously, he was very supportive in the end. Gave me the usual guarantees and wished me well.’

‘How long?’

‘He seemed happy with the idea of three months, but I didn’t set an exact date.’

‘So what happens next?’

‘Lunch, I think. What else?’

5

'Let us speak in English, Thomas. It will be our little relaxation.'

'If you wish, Holy Father.'

'It would please me. Italian is a beautiful language but it tires me. You don't speak Dutch do you, Thomas?'

'I'm afraid not, Holy Father.'

'Then English it shall be. It is my second language and your first, I think. Your father was English?'

'No. My mother, Holy Father.'

'Good. Good. That is settled then. What day lies ahead, Thomas?'

Bishop Costello opened the leather-bound file and hurriedly searched for the pope's itinerary. He handed a copy to the pontiff and ran through the major appointments.

'There's the American ambassador at 10.30, the apostolic delegate to Angola at 11.30, and of course mass at four o'clock. You will see that I have also included a number of small meetings with various members of the Secretariat.'

'We thank God for the Angelus, Thomas. It may be my only moment of peace in the day.'

Costello smiled at the pope's dry humour, but it was taking him time to accustom himself to such a relaxed exchange.

'I apologise for such a busy schedule, Holy Father. I'm afraid it's unavoidable. Some of the meetings were arranged months ago by my predecessor.'

'I understand, Thomas. The transition is bound to be difficult. Do you have the briefing notes for the ambassador?'

Thomas Costello handed over the details of the American's personal background, his views on Catholic matters, his standpoint on current international issues. His old press office colleagues had done a thorough job in constructing a detailed document which allowed the pope to avoid any embarrassments during the audience.

He imagined that the American State Department had found their own briefing a great deal more difficult. Pope Adrian VII was still an unknown quantity. Though they would have been aware that he represented a liberal shift in church policy, the Americans would be uncertain as to how far this might extend. If they had been privy to Costello's experiences over the last three weeks it would have sent shock waves as far as the White House.

Within days of Costello's promotion to the Prefecture he had become a confidante and sounding board for the new pope. Initially, his conversations with the pontiff had fired him with excitement and anticipation. There was no doubt that he was a man driven by the need for change, just as Thomas and his old friend Palazzini had hoped. But they could never have anticipated the pace of those changes.

Shortly after Woeters' accession, the number of directives coming from the papal office grew rapidly. At first they were concerned with minor bureaucratic issues, such as the timing of long established meetings, the opening of lines of communication into the Secretariat's office and a reduction in the number of formal meals within the papal enclave. There were a number of raised eyebrows but in general the Vatican staff welcomed the more *laissez-faire* atmosphere. Little did they realise that Pope Adrian VII had done no more than light the fuse of subsequent revolution.

Yet Thomas Costello did not share their naïvete. In his privileged position as prefect he quickly realised that he was witnessing the seeds of turmoil being planted in every corner of the Catholic church. Though only a small step beyond meddling in bureaucratic trivia, the pope's next directive sent warning bells ringing through the dioceses and offices of his bishops and cardinals. Not only did he demand a complete breakdown of the church's finances, but also a comprehensive assessment of the responsibilities held by all his senior clergy. It was the declaration of open government. But far more was to follow.

By the end of the second week the pope insisted that there was to be an immediate change in the election of bishops. It had become custom for recommendations of candidates to be made through the Vatican, with the pontiff making the final selection. Pope Adrian VII abolished this precedent at a stroke and announced that the church hierarchy in each country could now freely appoint their own bishops without reference to himself. There had been strong protests, on the grounds that such a policy would open up the chances of state political pressure being exerted to elect 'appropriate' candidates. The separation of church and state had always been viewed as a paramount safeguard.

Given the intricate processes involved in implementing such changes, news of the pope's dramatic change of direction had yet to filter down to the church membership. The press officers within the Secretariat were concentrating all their efforts on damage limitation. Editorials within the Catholic press were limited to speculation rather than hard fact. The bureaucratic machine, if only as a matter of self interest, were filtering and censoring the flow of information. But they knew they were constructing a very fragile dam against the inevitable speculation.

Costello returned to his office, leaving the pontiff to prepare for the day's meetings. His task of protecting the pope from incessant interruptions was becoming harder by the minute. Within the Vatican walls rumour was rife and the officers of state were now beginning to try and second guess the next directive. Their initial optimism was gradually turning to fear and it was an emotion which the prefect was starting to share.

He was becoming racked with self-doubt. It was not a loss of confidence in his ability to fulfil his new role, but a loss of faith in his own judgement. The election of Johannes Woeters had been built on Costello's positive expectations, yet the events of the last few weeks had begun to erode that certainty. The defeated Eugenio Cellini, whilst giving public support to the Holy Father, was now re-grouping his forces within the Curia, aware not only of the pope's ability to take a step too far but also of his apparent fragile health. Cellini was contemplating a second chance, a pious vulture casting a shadow over the papal office.

Costello glanced out from his window. His promotion had denied him the view he had enjoyed across the city and down to the Tiber. Now he was restricted to a small glimpse of the Vatican gardens, deprived of the morning sun and the bustle of St Peter's Square. He felt as if the walls of the old city were beginning to close around him and he was overcome with a gnawing depression which was beginning to sap his energy. The thought of Cellini waiting in the wings, ready to snatch victory from defeat, was too awful to contemplate. It could only mean the end of all his hopes for the rejuvenation of Catholicism and would probably guarantee his own removal to a minor South American bishopric. He was sure that by now Cellini would be aware of his hand in Woeters' election, and he was not a man to forgive his enemies. Nor was he a man to miss the signs of illness in the man who blocked his path.

Johannes Woeters had entered the election in a robust manner. There was no indication that his health may have presented a problem. He was considered, like many men in sedentary occupations, to be slightly overweight. But he was a big man, well over six feet tall, and his ruddy complexion suggested an iron constitution. For a man in his early sixties his face carried very few lines and his whole demeanour of frankness and friendly openness showed that he had retained his Dutch roots. Yet within days of his election he had begun to age rapidly.

At first, as Costello had told Robert Paine in his earlier letter, the decline was assumed to be no more than an indicator of the stresses and strains of office. The pope had been intent on dismissing his growing tiredness and occasional headaches as a temporary malaise and refused to call his doctors. But the world demands intimacy with its public figures and a denial of any rights to seclusion. The walls of privacy were soon breached. The revived gossip in the Santa Marta feasted on the scraps of information readily furnished by their allies in the Curia. There was talk of the pontiff cancelling meetings at short notice, constantly missing meals, and there were signs of an uncharacteristic short temper when orders were not followed to the letter. Costello was filled with foreboding. As a young priest he had witnessed the rapid decline of John Paul I, who died within 33 days of taking office. He feared that history was about to be repeated and with similar consequences.

The Vatican press were soon hounding the prefect for daily bulletins of the pope's condition, and it became increasingly difficult to cover up the severity of the growing illness. Giovanni Oliveri called him constantly from the *Osservatore Romano*, aware that their connivance in Woeters election was in danger of going horribly wrong. He also confirmed that Cellini was already plotting amongst his friends within the Curia and that Thomas should be careful to whom he spoke. There was even a suggestion that the internal Vatican telephone exchange was no longer secure and it would be better to have future meetings face-to-face.

It was Oliveri's phone call which had prompted Costello to call Robert Paine. He realised the implications of his last letter to his old friend and he couldn't be sure that Robert would respect his pleas for confidentiality. If the staff in the press office knew of his contact with a journalist outside the Vatican circle, there would be enormous repercussions.

Thomas Costello now sat at his desk weighing up all the possible outcomes of the Holy Father's sweeping changes, the pope's increasingly poor health, and his own foolishness in having written to Robert. He still felt unsure about his motives for contacting Paine in the first place. It had gone against all his instincts and yet he remembered having felt compelled to put his thoughts on paper.

It had become his practice to still scan the world's press, just as he had done in his old post. He was still driven by an interest in world affairs but he was now most concerned to see if Robert had made use of the information he had been sent. What he now found so odd was that Paine's articles seemed to have disappeared from the *Times* altogether. He noticed, as he shuffled through the edition which lay before him, that the parliamentary sketch appeared to have been written by someone called Ian Aitcheson.

The small green light which sat on Costello's desk suddenly illuminated. He thought of his good friend Palazzini who had installed the device before his untimely death. For a brief instant Costello wished that it was a summons from the grave rather than the Holy Father. He felt in desperate need of Palazzini's guidance and reassurance.

Gathering together any papers he felt might be useful he left his office and headed for the papal rooms only a few yards down the corridor. He tapped quietly on the door.

The pope sat, white-robed, by an open fire, his shoeless feet on a small stool. Costello felt the heat of the room as soon as he entered and began to sweat heavily. It was already May and it was over a month since he had lit a fire in his own apartments.

'Sit down, Thomas.'

'Thank you, Holy Father.'

'May I ask a favour of you, Thomas?'

'Of course.'

'I would like you to call me Johannes.'

Costello was stunned by the request. He knew that the pope enjoyed informality but what was now being asked was unprecedented.

'I would find that very difficult, Holy Father,' he replied hesitantly.

'I know that, Thomas. It would only be in our private meetings, of course.'

'Of course,' stuttered Costello.

'You must remember, Thomas, that when God called me to be the Bishop of Rome, I took on the title of Pope Adrian VII. It is not always easy for a man to give up his childhood. Even in my position we are all equal before God. I am sure he would not deny me the small luxury of retaining a little of my past.'

'I'm sure he wouldn't, your Holiness.'

'Johannes.'

'Johannes,' echoed Costello with difficulty.

'Thank you, Thomas. I am grateful.'

Costello looked across at the pope. He already seemed tired and drawn. On the small table beside his chair he noticed a glass of water and a small packet of pills which had been partially hidden under the briefing notes he had given him earlier.

'Now Thomas,' continued the pope, 'we have a little time before we meet the ambassador. I wanted your opinion on a number of matters.'

'Yes, of course.'

'Let me come to the point. What are your thoughts on papal infallibility?'

At first Thomas Costello could only smile a silent response. Even for this pope, his sudden question on such a profound issue was startling and totally unexpected. It was a question which had torn the church apart for many centuries, creating schisms that remained unrepaired.

Woeters could see Costello's discomfort and tried to ease him into a response.

'Forgive my Dutch bluntness, Thomas! I am not testing your faith in any manner. Please believe me. I only seek to make use of your intellect. To seek your guidance. No more than that.'

Costello hesitated. He was not concerned so much with the question as with the motive for this inquisition, and he offered a non-committal response.

'You are our guide, Holy Father,' he replied, unable to adopt the pope's first name as he had been asked. 'You are the supreme pastor, the vicar of Christ.'

'And who guides the guide, Thomas?'

'Our Lord, of course, Holy Father. You are Peter's successor in whom he placed his faith.'

'And who gives me supremacy, Thomas?'

'God grants it through your election.'

'To me alone?'

'There is only one pope, Holy Father.'

'And my congregation? Am I to sit above them? Direct them? Have authority over them?'

'Only to unify and confirm the faith and morals of Catholicism.'

Woeters paused for a moment, looking into Costello's eyes as if to test his honesty and yet with a gentleness that put his prefect at ease.

'And if I, in all my panoply of office, were to make a declaration that the body of the Church was unable to recognise as a reflection of that faith and morality, would my proclamation retain the status of infallibility?'

Costello hesitated once more. The pope was driving the conversation forward at an extraordinary pace and the prefect again wondered what motive lay behind their debate.

'It may be proof of error, Holy Father. The whole body of the church is surely blessed with the same spirit through the sacraments.'

'So the church belongs to its members?'

'I believe it does, Holy Father.'

'And such a belief diminishes my own authority?'

'If you will forgive my flippancy, Holy Father, you still retain the casting vote and therefore your authority over the church.'

'And I can trust my own judgements, Thomas?'

'Within limits, Holy Father. Beyond morality and faith your free will will expose you to mortal error.'

Woeters paused yet again to consider Costello's response.

'In the realm of faith and morality I am denied free will?

'Your hand is guided by God, Holy Father. You are invested with his authority.'

Johannes Woeters stopped talking and gazed into the fire, his hands together as if in prayer. After a few moments he turned back to face Costello.

'I think my authority has gone, Thomas. And I welcome it. It is time to impose upon myself, and the church structures, a self-denying ordinance. It is time to place the people back into the hand of God. Do you understand what I am saying?'

'Not entirely, Holy Father.'

'You will call me Johannes one day, Thomas,' said the Pope kindly. 'We will talk again. Now we had better attend to the ambassador.'

They walked together in silence. Costello felt dazed by their conversation. In essence it had resolved nothing and the Holy Father's final statement had been so ambiguous that it left him feeling agitated and frustrated. The meeting with the American ambassador came as an unwelcome intrusion and Costello had to fight an inner sense of resentment towards the emissary.

As they entered the ornate study library, the American party stood to greet the Pontiff. They held the expressions which Costello had witnessed on many occasions. He appreciated that audiences with the pope were difficult for all visitors, whatever their social or political status. What they all shared was a desire to strike a balance between retaining their naturalness whilst adhering to the normal protocol. What inevitably occurred was an uneasy mixture of politeness, deference and timid bravado.

Costello listened as the conversation unravelled. The ambassador proved to be a skilled communicator, moving easily between the points of discussion. Occasionally he would throw in an amusing reminiscence which gained a supportive but nervous squeal from his wife, cut short by a sideways glance of disapproval from the story-teller. But most impressive was Woeters. He said very little but asked a great deal. As a former philosophy student, Costello was well aware of the pope's Socratic method and realised that his own recent conversation had mirrored this very style. Rather than make statements and give personal opinions, the pope did no more than ask a series of simple questions, gradually exposing the ambassador to a sense of his own ignorance and inadequacy. It was done with no apparent sense of malice, but Costello could see that by the end of the audience, the ambassador and his wife looked mentally and emotionally drained.

'What did you think, Thomas?' asked Woeters as the Americans left.

'A muddled thinker, Holy Father,' responded Costello.

'A politician,' smiled the Pontiff.

They waited quietly for the arrival of the Angolan delegate. Thomas Costello let his eyes wander around the opulence of the library towards Titian's painting of Christ's resurrection, which adorned the far wall. At its sides stood the statues of John the Baptist and John the Evangelist, given life by the glistening light from the Venetian chandeliers.

The delegate entered and gave the pope a detailed and informative analysis of the state of the church in Angola. His account of squalor, famine, persecution and poverty seemed in stark contrast to their surroundings. It added an uncomfortable irony to the pathos of the delegate's message and he sensed in Woeters' responses a certain anger, tinged with despair.

The meeting ran well over the allotted time, extended by the pope's demand for detail and a short break for the Angelus prayers at midday. By 1.30 Costello could see that the colour had completely drained from Woeters' face, and the slumped posture of his body seemed to diminish his size.

'Take lunch with me, Thomas,' he said, as the delegate left. 'I am in need of company.'

They returned to the pope's apartments and for a short time reflected on the morning's events. Costello was desperate to get back to their former discussion but knew that he did not hold the prerogative for such a move.

They took a light lunch with a little red wine. Costello could see the pope's energy returning though he still appeared pale and exhausted. Woeters noticed the preoccupation in his prefect's face and responded to his unspoken wishes.

'You are thinking of our conversation, Thomas?'

'To be honest, I was concerned how tired you seemed, Johannes.'

Costello was suddenly aware that he had used the Holy Father's first name and he quickly looked towards the pope for reassurance. Woeters smiled in acknowledgement.

'Thank you, Thomas. You will get used to it before long.'

'Do you feel unwell?'

'A headache. That is all. Would you pass me those pills, Thomas? They are on the table by the fireplace.'

Costello crossed the room and picked up the small silvery packet.

'Do they help?' he said, handing over the tablets and pouring a glass of water from the carafe on the table.

'They did at first, Thomas.'

'Not now?'

'A little. A little. They give some relief.'

'You should seek medical advice, Johannes.'

'They were prescribed,' answered Woeters simply.

'You were examined?'

'Sufficiently.'

'A second opinion? It can easily be arranged.'

'In time, Thomas. Let's not dwell on it.'

'I'm sorry. I didn't mean to . . .'

'No, no. It's kind of you to be concerned. But let's move on to other matters.'

'Of course.'

'Make up the fire a little, Thomas. I feel quite chilled.'

They moved back to the chairs they had occupied earlier in the day, Costello pushing his chair away from the fire to avoid the direct heat.

'You are troubled by our discussion, Thomas?' broached Woeters.

'Troubled? Perhaps,' replied Costello. 'Uneasy might be a more accurate description.'

'I was perhaps somewhat obscure?'

'You were, Johannes. I'm not sure where you were leading.'

'It is a development, Thomas.'

'That is also obscure, Johannes!' laughed Costello.

'True. That is true. But I am aware of the fallibility of my own thoughts. I must tread carefully.'

'Given what you have said so far, that would be judicious.'

'It would. But we must not fear our God-given instincts. They are His gift and we should not be intimidated by their possible consequences.'

'I agree.'

Costello waited for the revelation. He could sense that the pope was about to voice those instincts. There was a lengthy pause as Woeters contemplated his next statement, adjusting his robes and squaring his shoulders as if in preparation for a verbal joust. He turned to face his prefect directly.

'Tell me. What are your views on ecumenicalism, Thomas?'

As hard as he tried, Costello was unable to disguise his delight at such a question. Under Pope Paul VII he had been forced to sit back and watch the entrenchment of fundamentalist Catholic attitudes and the death of ecumenicalism. His resort to manipulating the election of Johannes Woeters had been driven by his desire to see these central matters resurrected in the church's dialogues. At last he found himself at the feet of power and conceivably in a position to effect the changes which he and Palazzini had so often discussed. He was determined not to miss the opportunity.

Measuring his words carefully, Costello laid out his case for a radical rethink in the ecumenical movement. Initially he limited himself to the conventional lines of a need for unity, a healing of the rifts in the Christian world, the possibilities of using compromise, not only to build bridges between Eastern Orthodoxy and the Roman Catholic faith but also to reach out to Protestantism. As he spoke he tried desperately to assess the pope's reaction, carefully moderating his arguments as he viewed the response.

Taking the occasional nod of the head as an affirmation of his opinion, he pressed on, exposing his enthusiasm with every added point. Woeters remained silent apart from a rare prompting question, gauged to tempt his prefect into unguarded honesty.

As he gained in confidence, Costello began to justify his strategy for reform, risking an attack on the structures of Catholicism which he considered had hampered the ecumenical movement. At one point he suddenly found himself quoting Antonio Gramsci, the Italian communist imprisoned by Mussolini, who had written so profoundly of the ability of institutions to defend themselves against the march of socialism by using their embedded structures like defensive trenches against the enemy.

'We are no different, Johannes,' he concluded.

'Perhaps we are not, Thomas,' responded the pope.

'I'm sorry. I sound like a Marxist now! God forbid!' stuttered Costello, fearing that he had perhaps overstepped his mark.

'Not at all, Thomas.' answered Woeters reassuringly. 'I take your point entirely.'

Costello sat back in his chair, reviewing his proffered case. Had he gone too far? Had he been too restrained? From the pope's reaction it was almost impossible to judge the impact of his delivery.

Woeters continued his silence and returned to gazing into the fire in a state of contemplation. Costello became uneasy and began to sense that this lull in the conversation suggested rejection and that he had perhaps over-exposed his own radicalism. Woeters turned back towards his prefect.

'But is it enough?' he whispered almost inaudibly.

'I'm sorry. I don't follow.'

'Can we afford to take such faltering steps?'

Costello was almost silenced by this unexpected response and voiced his fears.

'I was concerned that you would find my ideas almost heretical, Holy Father,' replied Costello, returning briefly to a more formal address. In some ways it seemed more appropriate, given the importance of their discussion.

'Not at all, Thomas. My greater concern is that you are perhaps a little too restrained.'

Costello could now do no more than raise a quizzical eyebrow and offer a small shrug of his shoulders. He searched for a reply without success. But Woeters saved him from further misgivings.

'Thomas. I would like you to do something for me.'

'If I can. Of course,' he replied, wondering what further surprises lay in store.

'I think we should go to England.'

'To England?' replied Costello with some incredulity.

'Yes, Thomas. I feel we should meet with Richard Munro.'

'The Archbishop of Canterbury?'

'Of course.'

'So soon? It's unprecedented at such an early stage of a papacy.'

'I realise that, Thomas. But delay is often the enemy of ambition.'

'You would like me to arrange it? For when, Johannes?'

'Next week would be appropriate.'

'Next week! I'm not sure that will be possible at such short notice.'

'All things are possible, Thomas.'

'I will try, Holy Father.'

'Leave me now, Thomas. I must rest before mass.'

'Is the press office to be informed?'

'Once arranged, I have no objection. Secrecy can only undermine our church.'

Thomas Costello's mind was in turmoil as he returned to his office. Despite his dealings in Woeters' election he was at heart a wary pragmatist, careful in his decision-making and not prone to emotive actions. He was surprised by his own reaction to the pope's dynamism, his desire to press forward, his disregard for convention. Yet, like many who have pretensions of radicalism, Costello still had to fight his inner conservatism. It was all happening too quickly. What was even more unnerving was that he had no sight of the end result.

What had the pope meant when he had suggested that Costello's analysis was insufficient, that they represented only 'faltering steps'? What more did he want? Why the sudden demand to meet with Archbishop Munro?

Costello needed some air, away from the musty confines of the papal offices. He needed time to think, to reassess, to play with the puzzle he had been set. Quickly checking his diary Costello found he had at least another hour before his next meeting, cancelled all his calls and rushed out into the afternoon sunlight. He had no conscious idea of where he was heading, but his feet automatically took him towards the river and down to the Palazzo Di Giustizia. The tourist season was now in full bloom and he had difficulty in finding the quiet solitude he so desperately desired. The banks of the river were packed with the bustle of sightseers taking picnics and searching their guidebooks for a renewed assault on the city's history.

Heading further down the river towards the Ponte Cavour, and aware of his limited times, Costello gave up his pursuit of quiet contemplation and decided to sit amongst the crowds. Even in Rome, a city used to the plethora of clergy, his presence amongst the casually dressed tourists promoted some quizzical interest. The prefect smiled and acknowledged their stares, amused by his knowledge that the majority were in Rome as voyeurs of religion. His arrival threatened them with an involvement they wished to avoid.

But after a short time his companions began to relax and ignore this dark suited figure. He wondered how many of them were Catholics. How many of them were good Catholics? How many of them were lapsed Catholics? How many of them knew that sat amongst them was the prefect of the pontifical household who minutes before had been with their pope?

Costello knew the answer to his last question. To these people, he was no more than another clerical figure, no more than a tiny symbol of Catholicism. In terms of their own lives, aspirations, experiences and fears, he was of no consequence. But he knew they were mistaken. Glancing around at the playing children, the tired parents, the indulgent grandparents, and young lovers oblivious to the world about them, Costello realised that he was about to become a major consequence in all their lives. He was still uncertain about how this might occur. The pope's final destination still remained a mystery but he sensed the enormity of the changes in which he was about to be involved.

Without thinking, he lay back on the grassed river bank, letting the warmth of the sun relax his mind. His eyes grew heavier and though he fought against it, he allowed himself to enjoy the sense of euphoria which envelops the body between waking and sleeping.

He dozed for only a few minutes, woken by the shadow of a passer-by. Blinking his eyes open, he at first had difficulty collecting his thoughts. He was aware of the residue of a dream and tried hard to recapture its content before it slipped back into his unconscious. But he failed to retain any detail, as he always did. All he could recall was a hazy image of water and a boat in which all the passengers sat strangely in line, one behind the other. Costello grappled to hang on to the fading image and the face which stared at him from the front of the boat. Closing his eyes once more he tried to reconstruct the mental picture, the mass of unconscious confusion. It came to him quite suddenly.

The face was that of Isobel Griffin, still young but filled with sadness. Costello forced his eyes open, startled by his realisation and her sudden intrusion. He knew what he must do next.

6

'What does he say, Robert?' shouted Alex from inside the shower.

'It's a hell of a long letter.'

'Give me the gist. I'll read it when I'm dressed!'

'Says he dreamt of Izzy Griffin and knew he had to contact me again.'

'Very improper for a bishop!' laughed Alex. 'What else?'

'Says he's coming to London. Wants to meet up.'

'Go on.'

'This is ridiculous, Alex. I can't talk to you in the shower. Come and have some breakfast. I'll tell you then. It's quite a letter. Hard to believe.'

Alex Paine dried herself quickly, threw on an old pair of trousers and a tee shirt. It was only early June but it was already very warm and an ideal day to get out into her beloved garden. She was still combing her thick, though greying, wet hair when she entered the kitchen.

'Coffee?' offered Robert.

'Please. I'll make some toast. What does he say?'

'Here, have a look for yourself. It's extraordinary!'

Alex took the letter and scanned over the pages. Her eye caught the name of Isobel Griffin within the first paragraph and she sensed the seeds of resentment already taking root.

'You're right. It's very long, Robert. I'll have to read it later. Give me the outline. I can't concentrate at the moment.'

She handed the letter back to her husband, determined not to reveal her true emotions. If she had voiced her petty jealousy, she knew that Robert would be courteous but dismissive. Since his self-imposed sabbatical they had re-established what had been a flagging relationship and she didn't want it spoilt by what she tried to rationalise as an illogical response to an old girlfriend's name. Alex prompted him into reply.

'Why's he coming to London?'

'He's accompanying the pope. They're coming to see Munro.'

'Good God! It's a bit soon to start tripping round the world, isn't it? He's only been in the post five minutes.'

'I know. It's odd. And Thomas seems to be up to his neck in the whole thing.'

Paine ran through the points of Costello's letter which detailed all the main events of the past few weeks. As he related the contents to his wife, he realised how lucky he had been in turning down Finlay's offer to take on the story behind the pope's election. Costello's latest letter would have set the seal on an impossible situation. At least now he owed allegiance to no-one but himself, and he could follow his own instincts rather than the directives of his editor. The major problem for Paine was that Costello's letter had yet again stirred his journalistic instincts. With the sort of inside information he was receiving, he knew that once the dust had settled there was a major article or even a book waiting to be written. It might even provide the legacy desired by all middle-aged men: a chance to be remembered, the chance to lay claim to a speck of history.

'You've got to use it, Robert,' interrupted Alex as he paused for a moment.

'One day I will, Alex. But not yet. I think there may be a lot more to come.'

'Maybe. But don't miss the boat, Robert. By the time the media get wind of the visit, even the tabloids will be chasing the story.'

Paine grunted a reply and returned to his re-reading of the letter.

'Apparently he's written to Izzy Griffin with the same information. I hope to God she keeps it to herself or I'll be up the proverbial creek.'

Alex tried to shift the conversation away from Isobel, afraid that her true feelings might surface.

'Why's he doing it, Robert? Why is he risking his position? To you. A journalist of all people!'

'That's the one thing I can't fathom, Alex. He just keeps repeating that he feels compelled to write to me and pleads for confidentiality. The whole thing's very strange.'

'He must trust you.'

'I suppose he does. That's the problem. How long can I justify holding onto this stuff? Pass the butter, would you?'

The door bell suddenly rang, followed by the sound of the door latch opening and steps coming down the hallway. The dog's tail wagged its welcome, aware of a familiar scent.

'Hi, you two! Still having breakfast?'

Rachel bounded into the kitchen full of the youthful vigour which Paine had seen in Alex when they had first met. She had the same thick hair as his wife and carried her femininity with equal confidence.

'Sorry, can't stop. I've got a doctor's appointment in half an hour.'

'Problems?' asked Robert, with a look of concern.

'No. Not at all. Just checking the baby's okay.'

'He is?'

'It is,' she answered pointedly. 'Just the regular check-up. No more than that.'

'Don't fuss, Robert,' interrupted Alex. 'It's normal practice. Sure you can't stop for a few minutes, Rachel?'

'I can't really. I only popped in to see if you could make it for dinner on Friday. Roger's had a promotion and wants to celebrate. Just the four of us.'

'That would be fine, wouldn't it, Robert?' asked Alex, looking across the table for confirmation.

'I don't see why not. Thank you, darling, we'll be there. You're sure everything's going OK?'

'I'm fine, Daddy. Really,' answered Rachel.' 'The only problem I've got is that Roger's going to have to travel a lot more. But the extra money will be useful.'

She crossed the kitchen and put her arms round her father, kissing him gently on the cheek.

'Don't worry, I'll let you know if there are any hiccups. By Christmas you'll be cuddling your first grand-child.'

'I can't wait,' smiled Alex, resting her hand on Rachel's shoulder.

'Got to go. I'll call you this evening.'

They heard the dog whining his disapproval as the door closed behind their daughter.

'God, she's lovely, Alex.'

'I know, Robert. Takes after her mother,' she laughed. 'I'm going into the garden. Are you coming?'

'I could fuck you in the fuchsias if you like,' answered Paine. He jumped up from his chair and made as if to chase after his wife.

'Nice alliteration, Robert. But no thanks. Come on, Toby!'she called.

The labrador shuffled to her side and Alex wandered out onto the sun-filled lawn, feeling elated by her husband's advances. Though she was sure it was unplanned, his timing had been perfect. The mention of Isobel Griffin and the short visit by her effervescent daughter had left her feeling highly vulnerable and sensitive to her fading looks. Though she had rejected Robert's vulgar suggestion with theatrical horror, she had been thrilled by his sexual teasing. She felt her confidence return and secretly hoped he might follow her into the garden.

The news broke in the press three days later, and from the style of reporting Paine could tell that his fellow journalists were totally reliant on Vatican press releases. The broadsheets made no reference to any inside sources and the tabloids gave the visit fairly scant coverage. Though the pope's visit to Lambeth Palace was seen as unusual so early in a new papacy, it was simply reported as a fresh initiative in papal diplomacy, a new broom in the Vatican.

Paine was badgered by Finlay for a couple of days, chasing any information that Robert may have heard on the press grapevine. At first, the concealment of his knowledge filled him with a sense of betrayal, but gradually his new found freedom allowed Paine to enjoy the role of conspirator. His involvement in the growing intrigue seemed to renew his sense of purpose and lift the depression he had succumbed to only a few weeks before. His spirits were lifted by anticipation, the energy supplied by the unpredictable. Alex could see this change and Paine was able to monitor his growing vitality in his wife's responses. They had rediscovered an element of their youth; teasing and attentive like young lovers, and he waited for Costello's call, with the adolescent excitement he had felt when he and Alex first met. The joy was not in the message, but in what it promised.

The days passed slowly, a hindrance to the unravelling story. Alex accused him of impatience and irritability but quietly enjoyed her husband's animated state. She tried desperately to occupy his interest, visiting art galleries, museums and renewing their love of theatre. But he was a distracted man.

It was more than six days since Costello's letter when Robert Paine and his wife returned from a West End show. Though he professed enjoyment, Alex had witnessed Paine's shuffling and squirming during the whole of the performance, a sure sign that his attention was elsewhere.

'You're not going to be happy until Thomas calls, are you, Robert?'

'Sorry. I suppose not. They arrived today, you know. Caught it on the early evening news.'

'Couldn't you call him?'

'Not really. There'll be a great deal of security round the palace. I'd better wait.'

'Maybe tomorrow?'

'Maybe.'

'I'm going to bed. Are you staying up?'

'No, I'll be there in a minute.'

'Don't forget I'm meeting Rachel in town tomorrow. We're going to do some shopping and have lunch.'

'That'll be good,' answered Paine without showing any real interest in her plans.

'Yes, I'm looking forward to it. I'll be leaving about eight, before the rush starts.'

Though tired, Paine slept fitfully and at seven o'clock woke suddenly, aware that he had been dreaming. He was lathered in sweat and despite having little recall of his dream he was consumed by a sense of fear. All he could remember was an image of Thomas Costello, in full bishop's robes, holding a baby in his arms, high above his head. Alex lay sleeping, her breath light and rhythmical as Paine crept out of the bedroom and down into the kitchen. He made some tea and sat for perhaps half an hour reading old magazines, intent on shaking off his nightmare.

'Are you all right, Robert? I thought you were making tea.'

Paine looked up to see Alex, already dressed, standing by his chair.

'Yes, I'm fine, Alex. Sorry. I came down earlier. Touch of indigestion,' he lied. 'I must have dozed off again. Are you off?'

'Yes, it's eight-fifteen. I'm already late. Will you be OK?'

'Fine. Fine. Really.'

After a quick cup of coffee, Alex Paine rushed off to see her daughter, leaving her husband still struggling fully to regain his rationality.

'Who do you know in Hawaii?' came Alex's voice from the hall.

'Hawaii?'

'Yes, Hawaii!'

'No idea.'

Alex ran back into the kitchen clutching the mail which had just been delivered.

'Got to go. Tell me tonight. Looks exotic!'

Robert Paine revelled in the sudden quietness of the house. It allowed him to enjoy the selfishness of being alone.

No demands. No deadlines. No pretence. Responsible to no one but himself. They were moments he valued, a return to the comfort of childhood.

The stark white letter stood out from the other brown envelopes as if demanding to be read. There was no clue as to the sender, no address on the back of the envelope. His own name and address had been typed, again offering no indication and yet he searched the envelope's surface like some amateur sleuth. It was as if he had to go through a ritual of discovery before tearing open the letter. Finally he gave in to his curiosity and began to read the contents.

> 14 June 1999
>
> Dear Robert,
>
> Well, here's a surprise! If you haven't looked at the end of the letter yet – it's me – Izzy. Shock, shock.

Paine *was* shocked. He quickly turned to the end of the letter to confirm his own disbelief. Reaching for his glasses with one hand he edged his chair closer to the reading lamp which sat at the end of the table. He found himself glancing towards the door to check that Alex had really gone and then continued to read.

> Did Thomas tell you I was going to write? He sent me your address in his last letter – he knows I always lose these things. How's life in the old sceptred isle then, Robert? From what I can gather Thomas will probably be in England by the time you receive this letter. What's going on? He's always stayed in touch – the odd postcard, Christmas card and that sort of thing, but suddenly I get this epistle and a general baring of the soul. I found it really odd. He tells me he has been giving you the same information. He must be mad. Doesn't he know you're a journalist? How's that going, by the way? I've been in the States so long I'm afraid I've lost touch with your rise to fame since your spell in New York. It's a pity we never got a chance to meet, but it's a hell of a

long way from Dakota! I don't really understand all this pope stuff – not really my thing. From what he says they sound like a real bunch of conniving bastards. So much for Christian ethics! It sounds as if Thomas could be a bit out of his depth. What do you think?

Sorry – I must stop asking you all these unanswerable questions. As usual I'm rambling and probably not making much sense. My students used to say the same! I daren't even think how long it is since we met or even wrote to one another. Yes, my hair is starting to go grey. For all I know you may be as bald as a coot! These things are best left in the memory.

By now you're probably asking yourself why I'm writing. You're probably asking why I'm writing from Hawaii of all places. I wish I had an answer. I suppose Thomas spurred me on in some ways – mentioned you a lot in his letter, said you might be in touch. But you're not one of the world's great letter writers, are you, Robert? I have to admit I'm just the same. All intentions and no action. But I've started this now and am determined to finish. Once you start it's really quite enjoyable.

Did Thomas mention the trinity of Trinity in his letter? He did in mine. Haven't thought about that for years. Quite spooky really. It seems such a long time ago. It's a pity we all drifted apart and yet here we are nearly thirty years later passing little notes to one another just as we did in college. Bizarre really. But a long time. I can't even remember which chapter you're up to in my life story. I'll give you a quick resumé. Forgive me if some of it's a bit old hat. I'll keep it short.

You'll remember that I left Cambridge and did my Ph.D. in spectroscopy – all that sort of stuff. At the time we managed to produce some fairly revolutionary work, and two or three of us got picked up by the Americans who were still shovelling dollars into their space programme. Happy days! Of course it's all moved on to fibreoptics these days but at the time the Cambridge group were hot property. To cut a long story short, I ended up working on field flatteners for astronomical telescopes – in North Dakota of all places! (Don't ask me what field flatteners are – it would take too long – let's just say they help us to get better images.) It was there I met Bill. Bright, handsome, extrovert, from a wealthy American middle-class family. Perfect! As it turned out he was also a complete shit.

It was a pity, really. It went well for about five years until we decided to have a family. Crisis – I didn't have the necessary equipment. All those early years popping pills, sweating over a missed period, fumbling with revolting condoms, and I need never have bothered. What an irony! But dear old Bill wasn't happy. He wanted children. His mother wanted grand-children. His brothers and sisters wanted nieces and nephews. His grand-mother wanted great grand-children. I tell you, Robert, it was like trying to conceive in a Harrods' window during the January sales. My gynaecological plumbing was given a listing in Dakota's tourist guide. The whole thing was bloody awful.

If you're still in possession of that sharp imagination, Robert, I'm sure you can guess the rest. Bill entered the sex olympics and won the gold medal. Screwed everything in sight apart from me – suppose he thought there was no point. But it was a long time ago. He disappeared thankfully, with one of his students from the university. They bred like rabbits, which was a bit hard at first but I've settled for it now. I did 'what came naturally' for a few years but it never amounted to much – I'll spare you the details, but it honestly wasn't worth the effort. A lot of sweating and no soul. Sorry, I'm rambling again.

The shrill sound of the phone interrupted Paine's attention to Isobel's letter. He hesitated at first and let it ring, annoyed at the interruption, but found it impossible to ignore. He answered it rather abruptly.

'Yes?'
'Robert?'
'Yes.'
'It's Thomas.'
'Thomas?' he queried. 'Thomas!'
'Hello, Robert. How are you?'
'I'm fine. Just fine. Where are you?'
'At Lambeth. I've only got a few minutes. Can we meet?'
'Sure. Yes. Of course. How long are you here for?'
'It would have to be tonight.'
'Tonight? It's a bit sudden, but I suppose I could. Where?'
'What about the National Theatre? One of the secretaries here tells me it's only a twenty minute walk. I could do with the fresh air.'
'Sounds fine. There's a little area just by the bookshop. Do you know it?'
'It's been a long time, Robert.'
'You can't miss it. I'll look out for you.'
'About six-thirty?'
'Fine.'
'I'm afraid I'll only have about an hour. I've got to attend a formal dinner at eight-thirty.'
'I understand. No problem. It'll be good to see you.'
'And you, Robert. Sorry. Got to go. It's very busy here. See you at six thirty?'
'At six-thirty.'

Paine replaced the receiver feeling numbed by Costello's call. He stared out to the trees at the end of the garden as if looking for respite amongst nature. The pieces of some obscure jigsaw were beginning to fall into place but he wasn't sure if he enjoyed the construction of the puzzle. He had often proudly boasted that there was not an ounce of superstition in his being, but he was now starting to doubt his own judgement. To receive Costello's call in the middle of reading Isobel's letter, seemed to go beyond his usual reason. He returned quickly to his reading, intent on maintaining his rationality. The letter continued, unaware of the interruption.

It's almost midnight now. I'm tired and smoking far too much. My bedroom's the only place I can indulge these days – the Americans make you feel like a social outcast every time you light up. I'm happy enough over here, but the puritanism can be bloody irritating!

I say 'over here' but you'll be puzzled by the fancy stamp – and fancy address! After Bill left, I stayed on in Dakota for a couple of years but it became more and more difficult, especially once his first child was born. I started applying for new jobs in the same field, but no joy. Ended up teaching physics in New York State – at Colgate University of all places. Can you imagine working for a toothpaste! It was more fun than I expected but not really what I had spent years training to do. To cut a long story short (again!) I was saved by the shuttle. NASA started to get increased funding and started to sling all sorts of hardware into space. By a stroke of luck my boss at Colgate knew a few people in the space programme and put my name forward. Hey presto – ended up in Goldstone, California. One of the perks is that I do get to travel. Not on the shuttle, thank God! But they do use me in a consultancy role when they start having trouble with what we call 'mapping errors' – again too complicated to explain, but it does draw on some of my old research, which is handy. It also gets me the odd trip to Hawaii. Sounds wonderful doesn't it? Well, it would be if I had the time. In truth I'm cooped up in laboratories most of the day and night, and though it's interesting work there's only a small team here and it all gets a bit insular.

I suppose I'll have to admit why I'm really writing. I told you at the beginning of this letter that Thomas had been in touch and it really stirred up the memory. You'll probably think the next bit's a little silly but I'll chance it anyway. Two days ago I dreamt of you, Robert. Isn't that sweet! But it was a bizarre dream – me at the end of a telescope and you constantly standing in front of me trying to obscure the image. I can tell you I got extremely annoyed and remember screaming at you to get out of the way. You know what dreams are like – crazy and it made no sense at all. But it did make me want to write – and here I am!

I hope you don't mind, Robert. I know what these letters can do – they have a habit of ruffling feathers. But what the hell – it's good to make contact again with both you and Thomas. Happy days!

I'll stop now. I've got an early start in the morning and my lungs can't take another cigarette. If you feel like writing, it would be good to hear from you.

With love,

Izzy.

Robert Paine blew a long sigh, folded the letter and placed it back into its envelope. Calling his dog from his basket, where he lay snoring, happily oblivious to his master's tension, Paine wandered into the sanity of his garden. He needed space and time to think, to absorb Isobel's letter and prepare for his meeting with Thomas.

Aware of Costello's tight schedule, Robert Paine arrived early and was fortunate to find a parking spot behind the theatre. His day had been frittered away, his concentration destroyed by Izzy's letter and the anticipation of his meeting with Costello. He could feel the tension in his body as he walked towards the theatre, his breathing slow and purposeful, intent on regaining his composure. As he wandered past the stage door a small group of young autograph-hunters gathered in the street hoping to add to their collection of forgotten stars. Despite being a warm summer evening, the greyness of the concrete-clad theatre gave a wintry pallor to the surrounding pavements and terraces. It was a building which seemed to rob the seasons. Paine had often thought of it as a modern palace caught in the permanent ice and snows of Narnia. Yet like the wardrobe of C.S. Lewis, the pleasure lay beyond the entrance.

Although it was only just after six o'clock, Paine glanced around the large foyer for a sight of Costello. He was concerned that after such a long time he might not even recognise his old friend, and he had not thought to ask what the bishop might be wearing. Feeling like a desperate bachelor on a blind date, he smiled as he imagined Costello making a grand entrance in ornate robes with mitred head and crook in hand. But there was no sign of him amongst the swirl of theatre-goers.

He headed across the floor towards the bookshop. Young couples defended their territory with overt intimacy and he was lucky to lay claim to the only free table which fortunately gave him a clear view of the main entrance. He sat quietly, trying to contain his excited anticipation, occasionally weakening and checking his watch. The strains of a string quartet punctuated his increasing nervousness. The piece seemed vaguely familiar but he was no connoisseur. He overheard the couple at the adjacent table mention Bartók and he would happily have given way to their certainty.

It was still only 6.15, and he was glad of the opportunity to collect his thoughts. He had left a note for Alex and felt sure she would understand his sense of urgency. Isobel's letter was another problem and not so easily solved. Alex had already been alerted by the Hawaiian stamp and would be certain to ask about its contents and who it was from. He knew that the best course of action would simply be to hand it over. There was nothing in Isobel's stories which could offend his wife, at least not in the lines themselves. It was what Alex might read between the lines that really bothered Paine. Izzy had a habit of being a little vulgar and her mention of ruffling feathers might raise some suspicion in his wife. He tried to reason that he had absolutely nothing to hide. He had always made a point of dismissing his relationship with Isobel as no more than a passing and platonic friendship. Was there really anything in Isobel's letter that might make Alex feel resentful?

He was still trying to resolve these questions when he caught sight of Costello. Before making himself known,

Paine watched as the grey-suited bishop searched the crowds for his presence. He had aged well, thought Paine. Despite the white hair, Costello's face had retained the youthful glow which he had noticed in other men of the cloth. It was a face which he thought reflected abstinence and healthy living, an unpolluted body and a well-nourished soul. Even from a distance he could see those alert and inquisitive eyes which he had first noticed at Cambridge. Paine still said nothing, waiting for Costello's glances to turn towards him and signal his recognition.

With a smile and a brief raise of the hand, the bishop walked towards his friend.

'Robert!' he said, grasping both of Paine's hands in his own. 'It's so good to see you!'

'And you, Thomas. It's been too long.'

'You look well, Robert. How's Alex and the children?'

'We're all fine, Thomas. Shall I get a drink? How long have you got?'

'Less than an hour, Robert. It took me a little longer than I expected. A fruit juice would be fine. We'll be having wine with dinner.'

'Still the controlled pragmatist,' thought Paine as he went over to the bar. The reaffirmation of Costello's character made his recent contact even more contradictory.

'This is quite a place,' said Costello as the drinks were placed on the table.

'You've never been here before?' queried Paine.

'I've been out of the country so long. London's changed a great deal.'

'For the worse, Thomas.'

The two men followed the prescribed rules of conversation, flitting between family news, the state of the country, memories of old friends and colleagues. But Paine was well aware of Costello's limited time and was eager to get to the heart of the matter. As their exchange of tales drifted aimlessly, Paine felt he could sense Costello's need to move away from the inconsequential. There was a sudden pause and Costello's eyes widened slightly as he leant forward in his chair. He let out a small sigh and looked Paine directly in the face.

'You will be wondering why I wrote, Robert.'

'To be frank, I'm surprised you trusted me so much, Thomas.'

'You think it was foolish?'

'Not at all. Risky perhaps, but not foolish.'

'You felt compromised?'

'To be honest, I did. It was hard to resist betraying your friendship.'

'I'm sorry. I'd no intention of . . .'

Paine interrupted him.

'It's no problem, Thomas. I needed a break anyway. It proved a blessing in disguise.'

'You're not working for the paper any longer?'

'Taken a sabbatical.'

Paine related the tale of his dealings with Finlay, his growing lack of fulfilment and the renewed energy he had found in Costello's letters.

'I may use it one day,' added Paine.

'Then it will be history, Robert.'

'But good history, Thomas. And in no need of revision.'

Costello smiled and seemed relaxed by Paine's loyalty and lack of threat.

'So what's going on, Thomas?'

The bishop hesitated, glancing round to the other tables as if checking for spies. There were only a few people left in the foyer by now. The plays in the various theatres had just begun and apart from the occasional latecomer running towards the ticket office, they had the place virtually to themselves.

'Where do I begin, Robert? It has all happened so quickly.'

'God knows, Thomas! From what you've already told me it sounds as if the whole Vatican is running out of control.'

Costello smiled with closed lips and shrugged his shoulders like a man resigned to fate.

'Not yet, Robert. But I can see it coming. I feel as if I'm sitting on a time-bomb.'

'And the visit?'

'Hard to say. I'm privy to most aspects of the Holy Father's thinking, but he's playing this one very close to his chest.'

'But it's ecumenicalism surely?' asked Paine. 'The press can see no other reason.'

'I'm sure they're right, Robert. But it's not so simple.'

'Meaning?'

'Meaning: how far does he intend to take it, and what's the motive?'

'You make it sound like a cheap detective novel!'

'Not intentionally, Robert,' smiled Costello. 'What concerns me is a much bigger issue.'

Costello paused again and Paine noticed that his friend's delivery had slowed considerably. He was weighing and measuring the value of each word before he spoke, as if terrified of their consequences.

'And?' queried Paine, eager to extract as much information as possible.

'I have to reiterate my call for confidentiality, Robert. I'm sorry to seem so untrusting.'

'I understand, Thomas. Really. It will go no further.'

Costello looked Paine in the eye once more, seeking to verify his own judgement.

'It's a matter of faith, Robert.'

'Faith in what?'

'The church, Robert.'

Paine gave Costello a quizzical look, trying hard to piece together the scraps of information he was being given. He found himself laughing as he gave his response.

'You're not telling me the pope doesn't believe in God, are you?'

'No, no. You misunderstand,' replied Costello, returning Paine's laughter. 'It's his faith in Catholicism which I suspect is in question.'

'You're not serious, Thomas!' Paine found himself laughing yet again, this time quite audibly. 'A pope who doesn't believe in Catholicism. It would make your church a laughing stock!'

The waiter who was now clearing the pre-theatre glasses glanced quickly towards him and prompted Costello to draw his chair closer and whisper his reply.

'It would, and I am deadly serious, Robert.'

'Good God!'

'Amen to that, Robert.'

Paine gently manoeuvred his friend into a detailed revelation of the events of the past few months. Costello obliged, at first slowly, but then with an increased rapidity as his trust grew. He was aware that he had reached the point of no return, and, like a prisoner who has finally succumbed to interrogation, the facts spilled from his mouth. As the story took shape, Paine began to realise the enormity of the implications. Pope Adrian VII appeared hell-bent on turning the Catholic church on its head. Costello related the new pope's views on de-centralisation, a diminution of cardinals' power, a liberalisation of restrictions on contraception and abortion, and a review of papal infallibility. He seemed to be committed to breaking down every known barrier to the unification of the Christian churches.

Once Costello had warmed to his task, Paine listened without interruption. He felt almost dumbstruck by the information he was receiving, his mind a whirl of detail.

'It's quite a story,' he finally said, aware of the inadequacy of his comment. 'Can't you get rid of him?'

'God forbid, Robert. He is the supreme pontiff. Christ's vicar on earth, Peter's successor. Chosen by God's delegates and therefore by definition by God himself.'

'But you were the architect of his appointment!'

'I gave God the plans; that is all.'

'You have no control over his actions?'

'God's?' queried Costello.

'The pope's!' laughed Paine, amused by Costello's earnest response.

'To a limited extent. But you must remember that once a pope is elected he is there for life. The holder of Peter's office has the final authority on earth in the central matters of faith and morals.'

'But you say he's beginning to question his own infallibility.'

'He is. But his own personal judgements of the limits of his papacy won't be shared by the church members. They feel obliged to follow his pronouncements.'

'You mean the more he decries his own infallibility the more infallible he becomes?'

'Ironically. Yes. It's a conundrum.'

'It's ridiculous! When's he meeting the archbishop?'

'Informally tonight, and then tomorrow he'll. . .'

A shrill bleeping noise interrupted Costello's response. Reaching inside his jacket the bishop pulled out a small black object which Paine recognised immediately as a telephone pager.

'Very high-tech!' he commented, surprised to see a cleric using such a device.

'The palace issued them on our arrival,' answered Costello. 'I'll have to phone in, Robert. I'll be back in a moment. Do you have any change?'

Paine rustled through his pockets and handed Costello a mixed collection of coins.

'There's a call-box just by the entrance to the Olivier Theatre. Over there, to the right.'

He pointed Costello to the phone and watched him scurry across the foyer floor. He had so many more questions to ask but sensed that a call for the pope's prefect probably meant the end of their conversation. It was only a few minutes before Costello returned.

'Everything OK?' he queried.

The answer was etched on his friend's face. He looked visibly paler than he had when they first met and his hands shook as he returned the unused coins.

'What is it, Thomas?' asked Paine, aware that the news must have been important.

Costello replied with a faltering voice and Paine couldn't help but notice the early signs of tears in the bishop's eyes.

'The Holy Father has collapsed.'

'Good God! On top of everything else. Are you sure?'

'Absolutely. He was found on the floor of his room only ten minutes ago.'

'Heart attack?'

'I don't know, Robert. The doctors are with him now. I must go.'

'Shall I drive you?'

'Thanks. But no. It will be as quick to walk. I doubt it's going to be public knowledge,' added Costello. 'Please be careful whom you speak to.'

'Of course. Don't worry, Thomas. I'll wait for the official announcement.'

Costello raced towards the exit, the pace of his steps displaying his anxiety. He turned briefly as he reached the door.

'I'll ring you, Robert,' he called. 'I'm sorry!'

Paine raised his hand in farewell, just as he had first signalled their earlier meeting.

7

The return to Lambeth took Costello on to the promenade which runs along the banks of the Thames. When he first stepped out of the theatre, the brightness of the sun had caught him unawares, forcing him to stop momentarily and shade his eyes. As he gradually became more accustomed to the light he began to walk briskly, his legs urged on by his racing pulse, but given strength by his growing anxiety.

Heading quickly under Waterloo Bridge, past the street musicians and homeless beggars, he broke into a run, at one point passing a struggling jogger who had staggered to less than walking pace. He could see the looks of amusement and puzzlement on the faces of the people coming towards him. The sight of a grey-suited, grey-haired, middle-aged man running past a jogger must have seemed incongruous. But he knew they could never begin to guess the motive for his actions. He would be explained away as a man late for his train rather than the holder of information which might potentially affect all of their lives.

Costello could not sustain his earlier pace and by the time he had reached Westminster Bridge he was sweating heavily and felt totally exhausted. He also felt consumed with depression and began to question his own actions. It was far quieter on the pathway beyond the bridge and he rested for a moment on one of the raised benches which look out across the river. The Houses of Parliament were now shaded, the building thrown into a stark and menacing silhouette by the dying sun. For a few seconds he watched the tourist boats ease their way through history, delivering their potted version of the rise and fall of the British empire to eager ears. Working barges were mooring up for the night and music from the floating discotheques could be heard drifting across the water. Life was going on, just as it always did.

Yet Costello felt like a Judas. When Paine had asked him if it were possible to jettison the pope he realised that his actions might justifiably be interpreted as betrayal. He was now torn between his love of Catholicism and his allegiance to Johannes Woeters. The proposed changes in the running of the church, and the pope's sudden meeting with Archbishop Munro, had clouded his judgement and weakened his desire for reform. Like many former radicals, a weakening of conviction was beginning to drive him to the safety of continuity, an escape from the freedom of change. But he knew that Woeters was essentially benevolent, principled in thought, and devoted to his belief in the tenets of Catholicism.

It was at this moment, as he looked over the ancient river, that his resolve strengthened. If the Holy Father survived his illness, he knew he must commit himself to Woeters' enigmatic mission, to display his faith in faith's revision.

Now rested and revitalised by certainty, Costello continued his hurried walk along the tow-path. It was almost eight o'clock when the towers of Lambeth Palace came into view, its dark and ominous flint-clad façade masking the frenetic activity which he knew he was about to encounter.

Aware that there may be a number of reporters outside the main gate hoping for a press statement on the pope's visit, Costello rang the brass bell of a side entrance which had been pointed out to him before he left for the National Theatre. It allowed him a discreet entrance into the palace via Lollards Tower. A voice came from the intercom at the side of the small timbered doorway.

'Yes?'

'Bishop Costello.'

'One moment, please.'

After what seemed an interminable wait, the door swung open.

'I'm sorry to keep you, Bishop. Paul Braine, Deacon to

the Archbishop. His Grace asked me to meet you and show you directly to his office.'

'Of course.'

They headed across the gardens and into the palace, both men comfortable with the silence between them. Thomas Costello followed Braine through the oak-lined corridors and up the simple staircase to the first floor. Paintings of former archbishops, dark and cracked with age, lined the walls and for the first time since his arrival, Costello felt like an intruder into a private protestant world.

He watched as the deacon knocked on the door of the archbishop's apartments and entered without waiting for reply.

'Bishop Costello, Your Grace,' said Braine, ushering the visitor into the room.

'Thank you, Paul. Come in, Bishop. Do sit down. This is a sorry business.'

'Indeed. I'm so sorry I wasn't here.'

'These things happen. You mustn't blame yourself.'

'How is the Holy Father?'

'Unwell, I fear. But in good hands. Our prayers are with him.'

'Thank you. Have you any idea what happened?'

'Not really. There is little we can do at the moment. Shall we first pray together, Bishop? I'm sure it is what the Holy Father would wish.'

He nodded his consent and they sat for a short time, heads bowed in contemplation. But Costello was distracted by his eagerness for information. Raising his head slightly he glanced towards the praying figure of the archbishop. They had never met before and he was surprised by the small stature of this leader of protestantism. Though bespectacled, he had the rugged looks of a farmer rather than the pallor of the intellectual Costello knew him to be. The cassock hid what he suspected was a rather portly figure and he found himself amused by its colour. Here was a Roman Catholic bishop praying with the leader of the Anglican faith who was dressed in the purple cloth which had once represented Roman power. It seemed ironic that the Reformation had led to the adoption of a symbol which seemed contrary to its own beliefs. The archbishop interrupted his thoughts.

'May God preserve and keep him.'

'Amen,' responded Costello.

There was a short pause whilst Munro collected his thoughts. He smiled kindly towards Costello and began to relate the events of the last hour.

'The Holy Father has been taken to St Thomas's hospital. We are fortunate it is so close.'

'I passed it only a few minutes ago. Do we have any idea what's wrong?'

'I spoke briefly to the doctor who was first called. He wouldn't really commit himself but seemed to think it might be a stroke. I'm sorry to be the bearer of such news.'

'Has the press been notified?'

'No. We thought it best to leave such a decision to yourself.'

'Thank you.'

'There were one or two reporters at the gate but they were told that the ambulance was for a member of staff with appendicitis. I hope the Lord will forgive our little white lie. There seems no point in whipping up hysteria.'

'I agree. We really need more details before we say anything. Can I see the Holy Father?'

'I see no reason why not. I'm told he has been taken to a private room in the neurological unit. You'll need to take identification, the security will be quite tight I should think. I'll ring and let them know you're coming.'

'I'm obliged.'

'Have you eaten yet?'

'Perhaps later. I would prefer to go straight to the hospital.'

'Of course.'

Costello raised himself from his seat, thanked the archbishop once more and headed towards the door. Just as he was about to leave Munro called him back.

'You should perhaps know that I was with him only minutes before his collapse. It was a fortunate chance that I left my glasses in his room and asked one of the staff to retrieve them.'

'You met whilst I was out?'

'He rang me soon after you left and asked for an unscheduled meeting. We must have spoken for about three-quarters of an hour. He has proved himself a brave and godly man.'

Costello stood silently before the Archbishop, unable to hide the puzzlement which now crossed his face.

'You must go, Bishop,' said Munro, touching Costello gently on the arm. 'My prayers go with you.'

It was no more than two minutes' walk to St Thomas's Hospital, its entrance fronting on to Lambeth Palace Road. On its façade in large letters was a sign bearing the inscription: 'Serving the Community 24 Hours a Day'.

'Like our Lord,' thought Costello, aware of his own irreverence. Climbing the large ramp which led to the main doors he noticed three or four cars parked discreetly in the roadway and two police officers barred his path into the hospital.

'Good evening, sir. Can I help you?' asked the taller of the two constables.

'Bishop Costello,' he replied, handing over his identity card.

'One moment, sir.'

The officer spoke into his radio and waited for a confirmation. Costello looked through the glass doorway. He half expected to see running figures, anxious faces, signs of urgency, and yet all seemed eerily calm. A nurse approached the door and as she pushed it open he instantly caught the smell of the interior. It never failed to evoke memories of childhood: the nauseous mixture of antiseptic and tangible fear. In that instant he could recall being carried by his mother, screaming, not in pain but in anticipation of the unknown. He had done no more than cut his knee on a broken bottle but his stomach still churned at the memory of being totally out of control of his own destiny. The nurses and doctors had been kind enough but offered no explanation of why he had to suffer the agonies of needles, stitches and the indignity of removing his trousers in front of strangers. He was amused to reflect on his childlike naïvete but it was a trauma he had never been able to shake off. As a parish priest many of his parishioners had expressed similar fears. He remembered having great difficulty in allaying their concerns when he too shared their terror.

'Bishop Costello?' queried the nurse.

'Yes.'

'Please follow me.'

She turned and led him with great certainty through the maze of corridors, the floors marked distinctly with red, blue and orange lines like some chaotic railway system. After a few minutes Costello was aware that they were following the yellow lines and that he was gradually becoming accustomed to the hospital's smell. They arrived at a door marked 'Strictly Private'. A young, stern-faced man guarded the door. He wore no uniform, but his hair was shaved in military fashion. He offered no more than a cursory nod of recognition.

'There's a small waiting room on the left,' said the nurse. 'Would you like a cup of tea?'

'No, I'm fine, thank you.'

'Doctor Goodliffe will be with you shortly.'

'Thank you.'

Costello sat on one of the old tubular chairs, its canvas seat torn and faded. The whole room gave him little confidence in the hospital's merits. Pale green paint was beginning to flake from the walls and the windows were so caked in dirt that he could hardly see into the courtyard below. On the small plastic table lay a number of out-of-date women's magazines and an ashtray with the butt of an old cigarette still lying in its centre. He felt a long way from

Rome and the relative luxury of the Vatican. The door suddenly opened.

'Bishop Costello, isn't it? Doctor Goodliffe. I attended the Holy Father at the Palace.'

'You're a Catholic?' queried Costello instinctively.

'Does it matter?' laughed the doctor.

'No, of course not. It's just that you called him Holy Father. I'm sorry. Hospitals make me a little nervous.'

'Don't worry. It's a difficult time. I am a Catholic, as it happens. This whole business has made me a little nervous too. But it's a great honour.'

'I'm sorry. It was a silly thing to ask. Can I see him?'

'Perhaps in a little while. He's heavily sedated at the moment and may not be conscious for some time.'

'Is he in danger?'

'He's stable. That's really all we can say at the moment.'

'Was it a stroke?'

'We think so, but we're not really sure. We're running some tests at the moment. We'll let you know as soon as we have anything.'

'But he's going to survive?'

'You can never be sure. But the prognosis looks encouraging.'

Costello felt the relief surge through him and quite unexpectedly burst into tears in front of the young doctor. For a few minutes he sobbed almost uncontrollably, bent over in his chair with head in hands. Goodliffe said nothing but held him gently by the shoulder.

'Forgive me,' said Costello finally, blowing his nose loudly and wiping the tears from his face.

'I think that's your job,' smiled Goodliffe, attempting to reduce the tension.

'So it is,' replied Costello, grateful for the comment.

'Good news is often harder to bear than bad. We can prepare ourselves for the worst.'

'You're a wise man, Doctor.'

Goodliffe didn't respond but allowed time for the bishop

to retain his composure. Even as a junior doctor he had experienced similar reactions in many of his patients' relatives who had braced themselves against the realisation of their fears. He waited for a few minutes until the bishop looked towards him.

'Mr Laidler has asked me to run through a few questions.'

'Mr Laidler?'

'He's the neurological consultant. We're very fortunate to have him at St Thomas's. He's probably the top man in his field.'

'So the Holy Father is in good hands?'

'To the best of my knowledge, there are none better.'

'How can I help?'

'We've already had the pope's medical records faxed from Rome but we need some up-to-date information.'

'So the Vatican knows?'

'We've played it down.'

'So what can I tell you?'

'I'm told you're in a position to be – what shall I say? – a confidante of the Holy Father.'

'I suppose I am.'

'Has he been unwell recently? Complained of chest pains? Dizziness? Pains in the arms? Muscle fatigue? Anything you could tell us might be a help.'

Thomas Costello rose from his chair and walked over to the window. Running his finger over the glass pane he thought back to the many meetings he had enjoyed with the new pope. The threatened revolution in the Catholic church had in retrospect perhaps made him ignore the obvious signs of illness. He thought back to the constant taking of pills, the frequent rest periods and the increasing sallowness in his complexion. He turned back towards Goodliffe.

'He has complained of headaches,' he said simply.

'Has he been seen by a doctor?'

'He has, but refused a full examination.'

'He took medication?'

'Only aspirin as far as I know.'

Doctor Goodliffe made a few notes in the brown file which lay on his knee.

'Anything else?' he asked.

'Not really. A little tired, I suppose. He seemed to need a great deal of sleep.'

'Thank you Bishop. It could be useful.'

The doctor closed the file and asked Costello to wait for Mr Laidler. As he turned the door handle he hesitated and turned back towards the bishop.

'By the way. Does the word "atu" or "utu" mean anything to you?'

'Not really. Why do you ask?'

'It's not important. Mr Laidler will explain. I'll have some tea sent in.'

Before Costello could respond, Goodliffe turned and left the room leaving his question hanging in the air and Costello feeling bemused. He paced up and down the small room scouring his mind for answers. Why had the Holy Father suddenly broken all accepted protocol and demanded an immediate audience with the archbishop? Did he know he was becoming ill? It was ludicrous that a doctor involved in saving a pope's life should choose to focus on the incomprehensible mumblings of his patient. Costello's meeting with Robert Paine also remained an enigma. However strong their friendship, it seemed impossible to clarify his own motives in exposing his concerns to a journalist. There appeared to be no logic in any of the mounting chaos.

His growing confusion made Costello even more desperate to see Woeters and he was becoming irritated by the delay. Continuing to examine every corner of this dingy room he glanced down at the fading magazines on the blue plastic table. It had been years since he had seen such material but the front covers were enough to confirm his belief that the world was becoming obsessed with physical immortality. They all seemed to promote better health, a better sex life, a trimmer body, how to reduce anxiety and even how to succeed in business in the next millennium.

They were a testament to a temporal and secular world and did little to raise Costello's spirits. He moved once again towards the window, but darkness had now fallen and all that could be seen were the blurred lights coming from the wards on the other side of the courtyard. With some relief, he heard the door opening behind him, and turned to see the nurse who had first shown him into the hospital.

'I've brought you some tea, Bishop. Mr Laidler will be with you any moment now.'

'Thank you. That's very kind.'

'I've a biscuit if you'd like one.'

'No, no. The tea will be fine.'

For the first time Costello noticed the nurse's strong Irish accent which for some reason made him feel more at ease. As she was leaving he thanked her again and turned towards the tray. There were two cups.

'Thank you, Mary', came a voice from the corridor.

The consultant bustled into the room carrying a thick wad of papers and a number of large brown envelopes.

'John Laidler,' he said, offering his hand and spilling papers on to the floor. 'I'm sorry to keep you waiting, Bishop.'

'Tea?' responded Costello, as Laidler bent to pick up the documents.

'I would love tea. It's been a long day as usual. Today a little longer than normal.'

Costello watched the consultant gather his papers together as he poured the tea. He was a tall man, probably in his early fifties, with a healthy complexion and thinning sandy hair. His body movements seemed unco-ordinated and chaotic, and his dress sense echoed this image. Yet Costello was absorbed not by what he saw but what he instinctively felt in this man's presence. He had been in his company for only a few seconds and yet the bishop felt immediately aware of the man's warmth and obvious intellect. It was a sensation he had rarely met, even amongst members of the clergy.

They sat together for a few minutes re-stating the events

of the last hour, the need for security and the general prognosis.

'I must be frank, Bishop,' said Laidler. 'From the results of the scans I've managed to do, I feel that surgery cannot be ruled out. To be frank, it has become a necessity.'

'I assumed it was a stroke,' responded Costello.

'We all did initially, but there are suggestions of other factors at play. Are you familiar with the physiology of the brain, Bishop?'

'I'm afraid not,' smiled Costello. 'Philosophy and theology is my limit. I envy your knowledge.'

'Then we envy one another, Bishop. I never got beyond Socrates personally. Always preferred hard facts, you see. Bit of a weakness in the medical profession.'

'Each to his own, Mr Laidler.'

'Quite.'

John Laidler began to rummage through the files and envelopes he had brought into the room, finally extracting what Costello recognised as a large X-ray negative.

'I'm afraid the light's not ideal, but it will serve our purpose for the moment,' said Laidler, holding the negative up to the bare bulb which hung above their heads. 'Can you see? Just there,' he added, using a pencil to locate a specific point on the blurred picture. 'There's our little problem, I suspect.'

Costello peered up towards the light.

'Not really,' he responded.

'There. Just on the edge of the cerebellum.'

'A tumour?'

'Possibly. But it's unusual to say the least. Without a biopsy we're working in the dark.'

'No alternative?'

'I fear not.'

'Do you need consent?'

'Under normal circumstances we would, but I presume it may be difficult in this case.'

'It would normally be the responsibility of the conclave of cardinals.'

'In Rome?'

'Yes.'

'I'm afraid we haven't time for such niceties, Bishop. It's likely his condition could worsen at any moment. Time really is of the essence. We have emergency powers of course but given the unusual nature of the patient I would prefer some formal consent.'

'Of course. You must go ahead. I will take full responsibility. May I see the Holy Father before the operation?'

'I see no reason why not, though you must realise he's still not regained consciousness apart from the odd word or two. Did Doctor Goodliffe mention he had spoken?'

'Not really.'

'But he asked you about "atu" or "utu"?'

'Is that what the Holy Father said?'

'That's all that he said, Bishop. It was no more than a murmur, of course, but fairly coherent. He repeated the word over and over again.'

'And you're sure that's what he said?'

'Not altogether. Damage to the cerebellum does tend to affect the muscles of the larynx and pharynx. There's bound to be a degree of distortion in the speech pattern. Do the words mean anything to you?'

'Nothing as far as I know. They could be Dutch, of course.'

'That was my guess. I rang a Dutch friend just before I came to see you and drew a blank on that theory. But I'm sure it's of no great relevance. I was simply curious. I must go and prepare for theatre.'

'I may see him now?'

'Of course. I'll show you the way.'

Costello followed as Laidler strode purposefully down the brightly lit corridors and through a series of doors. As they approached the intensive care unit he noticed an immediate change in their surroundings. Gone were the faded and dull interior of the waiting room. Instead, this section of the hospital gleamed with a clinical freshness and a sense of total order. It was like leaving the mayhem of an airport check-in area and entering the quiet and controlled atmosphere of the departure lounge.

'First door on the left,' said Laidler. 'I'll have to ask you to wear sterile clothing. Mary will sort you out. Try to get some rest if you can. I'll call the palace as soon as we have some results.'

'Whatever time?'

'Of course. I can only give you five minutes, I'm afraid. My anaesthetist will be here shortly.'

With this final demand Costello watched Laidler head towards the operating theatre, still studying his notes as he passed through the doors.

A few minutes later the bishop entered the pope's private ward. The green overalls, mask and hat he had been given to wear made him feel hot and uncomfortable. Catching sight of himself in the mirror at the side of the bed he was startled by his own appearance. He remembered the first time he had worn vestments. It was as though he was confronting a stranger.

He glanced around the room almost fearful of seeing the Holy Father in such a vulnerable state. The room seemed to be full of monitors, all bleeping their recognition of life but striking a terror into the observer. The inanimate caring for the animate, machinery created by man recreating its maker.

Above the bed, Costello noticed that someone had kindly placed a small and simple wooden cross. He guessed it may have been the Irish nurse and made a mental note to thank her before he left. With an audible intake of breath he finally braved himself to look down directly onto his pontiff. What he now saw was not what he had expected. Instead of a face racked with pain, Johannes Woeters looked better than Costello had seen him for some time. There was no tension in his face and the rather pale complexion was now infused with apparent health. He breathed quietly in a steady rhythmical manner. He looked like a man at peace.

'I am here, Holy Father,' said Costello gently. 'God be with you.'

Pulling over a chair he sat quietly, holding the pope's hand, watching the gentle rise and fall of his chest and the movement of his eyes below their closed lids. A tear ran down his cheek as he prayed silently and asked God to spare his chosen servant. It only seemed a few seconds before he was interrupted.

'I'm afraid you'll have to leave now,' said the nurse softly. 'The anaesthetist needs to give him a pre-med.'

'Yes, of course. I won't be a moment.'

Costello took the pope's hand once more and raised it to his lips. As he did so he noticed the pontiff's mouth open slightly. His eyes remained closed but he began to speak, at first inaudibly but for a few moments with greater clarity. Costello bent forward and put his ear close to Woeters' mouth. It was no more than a faint whisper but it left no doubt in Costello's mind. The word was quite distinct, each letter emphasised with care and clear in its delivery.

'A-i-t-u. A-i-t-u,' repeated Pope Adrian VII.

8

The explosion of light stopped Costello dead in his tracks, momentarily blinding him to the scene before him.

'How is he, Bishop?' came a shout from the right. 'Can you give us a statement?'

Flash-bulbs seemed to burst all around him, the whirr of motor-driven cameras filling the night air. It was hard for him to discern the number of figures in the crowd, but as his eyes gradually adjusted, the pack began to move forward, thrusting microphones towards his face. A young reporter had jostled his way to the front.

'Any comment, Bishop?' he shouted in a demanding tone.

Costello realised that someone must have leaked the information of the pope's illness. Whether it was from the hospital or Lambeth Palace he would probably never know, but he felt angered by this intrusion into what he felt was still a personal rather than public grief. He hesitated before responding.

'The Holy Father is quite comfortable and in good hands,' he said simply.

More shouted questions came from the throng of journalists who still fought each other for position.

'Is he on the critical list?'

'He's quite stable.'

'Is he having surgery?'

'I can't discuss details, I'm afraid.'

The questions continued unabated, pressing him for even the slightest morsel of news. Costello fended them off one by one and because of the unexpected arrival of the press he felt like a boxer caught on the ropes by his opponent. But he was a skilled diplomat. His time spent in the Vatican press office had trained him in the art of believable understatement and he still retained the ability to satisfy the media's hunger with no more than inconsequential scraps.

By now a member of the hospital's administrative staff had joined him at the exit. He touched Costello on the shoulder.

'Shall I call a taxi?' he asked.

'You better had. Thank you,' answered Costello, grateful for his intervention.

As he turned to re-enter the safe confines of the hospital another question was fired from the crowd.

'Why was the pope in England, Bishop?'

Costello turned back and hesitated for a moment.

'No more than a goodwill visit,' he responded. 'Forgive me, I must go.'

He turned again and hurried back into St Thomas's, glad to escape the prying questions.

But Costello knew he had made a mistake. He was familiar with journalistic questions and he was also aware how they measured the responses. His hesitation in answering the last question would have left no doubt in the mind of an experienced journalist that there had been a great deal left unsaid. Whoever had leaked the information of the pope's collapse may have said far more than simply reporting his sudden illness. It was now obvious, from the question asked and his own hesitant response, that the hounds would soon pick up the scent of intrigue.

The taxi came within minutes and he rushed into the black London cab without further comment. He felt exhausted by the added media pressure and slumped into the comfort of his seat. The cab smelt heavily of tobacco and though he had given up cigarettes many years ago the temptation to revert to their comfort still plagued him in times of stress.

His journey took less than two minutes and there were more cameramen and journalists gathered by the main entrance to Lambeth Palace. Their flash cameras fired into the cab as his driver sped through the timbered gateway.

It was nearly midnight by the time Costello finally entered

the palace hallway. The archbishop's deacon sat dozing in a large armchair, a small table lamp providing the only illumination to the room. He woke abruptly as Costello entered.

'You had no need to wait up, Deacon,' said Costello, approaching the waking figure.

'His Grace asked me to meet you on your return. He's in his study.' Paul Braine pointed a finger down the corridor which led off from the hallway. 'Could you spare him a few moments? I'm sure you're very tired.'

'It's not been the easiest of days but I'll be glad to speak with him.'

'Go straight in. His Grace is expecting you.'

Costello knocked and entered Munro's study to find the archbishop still alert and writing notes at his desk.

'Ah, Bishop,' welcomed Munro, removing his half-moon reading glasses and shuffling his papers to one side. 'How is the Holy Father?'

'It's difficult to say, your Grace. But the doctors seem hopeful.'

'Good news. Good news indeed.'

'We'll have more idea tomorrow. They're doing some tests at this very minute.'

'We can only pray, Bishop. Do sit down.'

Costello pulled up a chair opposite the archbishop's desk.

'You had to run the press gauntlet, I hear,' said Munro. 'I do apologise It's very difficult to keep these things quiet. I can't imagine how they found out. We have all been very careful to maintain our silence.'

'It could have been anyone,' answered Costello, aware of the Archbishop's embarrassment. 'Perhaps even a member of the hospital staff. These things can't be helped.'

'I suppose not, though it's hard not to feel responsible. You must be tired, don't let me keep you longer than necessary. I've had a tray sent up to your room. I don't suppose you have eaten?'

'That's very kind.'

Costello climbed the stairs to his bedroom, fatigue making

his steps heavy on the carpeted floor. Turning the key in his door he stepped into the darkness and was aware of his foot catching on something as he reached for the light switch. Looking down he noticed a neatly folded piece of paper which had obviously been put under his door whilst he was at the hospital. He bent down, unfolded the note and held it towards the light and began to read.

> My dear Bishop,
>
> Forgive my intrusion but I wondered if we might meet over breakfast. Perhaps at 7.30? His Grace normally takes breakfast in his quarters and it would be useful to have a confidential chat if it is convenient to yourself. I apologise for my rather secretive approach but I was uncertain what time you would return. I look forward to meeting you. May God's grace go with the Holy Father.
>
> My kindest regards,
>
> Robin Westgate (Bishop of London)

Costello slipped off his jacket and with the letter still in his hand lay back on top of his bed. In the space of five hours his world had been turned upside-down by a whole series of unforeseen events. Glancing through the note once more he could feel his eyelids heavy with tiredness and as hard as he fought he found himself trapped in its welcome web. He wished to escape from his turmoil and any ideas of following his normal routine of washing and changing seemed a hindrance to his deliverance from reality. The warm night air washed over him and he fell quickly into the oblivion of sleep.

Laidler's call came at four o'clock. Costello struggled to regain his senses as the bell rang incessantly. He had been sleeping fitfully, his mind a mass of confusion and yet oddly, given the pope's current plight, he was aware that he had yet again dreamt of Isobel Griffin. But most disturbing of all was a vague memory of viewing his own figure, as if in some out-of-body experience. He was just able to recall the image of himself standing in open fields, his face raised upwards. Even stranger was his faint memory of holding a small child, his hands supporting the infant high above his own head. He could feel the small beads of sweat running down his body as he reached across to the bedside phone.

'Yes?' he mumbled.

'Laidler here. I'm sorry, it's an unearthly hour but you did ask me to call, whatever the time.'

Costello rapidly came back to full consciousness at the sound of Laidler's voice.

'Of course. It's good of you to call. How is the Holy Father? Is he out of theatre?'

'All's well, Bishop. We've taken a small sample of tissue and we're running some tests right now. He's a strong man, you know.'

'So it wasn't a stroke?'

'I don't think so. In fact, it's hard to believe he was so ill only a few hours ago. You will be amazed by his recovery. He was chattering away the moment he came out of the anaesthetic.'

'Wonderful news. When can I see him?'

'Late morning would be best. We'll sedate him now. He may feel a great deal better but his body needs rest – just as mine does.'

'I understand.'

'Shall we say around midday?'

'That's fine.'

'We'll need to prepare some sort of press statement which you're happy with. You had a little bother, I hear.'

'I'm afraid so.'

Costello thanked Laidler once more and, in need of the bathroom, let his legs slide across the bed and on to the floor. He waited for a few seconds as his body responded to its new position. Taking a few deep breaths to counter the dizziness he felt from waking so quickly, he crossed the bedroom towards the tiny bathroom. Looking at the face in the mirror he could see that the previous day had taken its toll. The effects of sleep, anxiety and now sudden relief had left him looking old and dishevelled. He turned away, unwilling to confront his own image. Having washed and undressed, Costello slipped between the covers of his bed and finally fell into a deep sleep, uncluttered by his former dreams.

The alarm clock denied him the rest he needed and by seven o'clock he was forced to confront reality yet again. The welcome shower helped to revive his energy and as he towelled himself dry he glanced through the open bathroom door towards his bed. Still lying on the covers was the mystifying letter from the Bishop of London. He had been so tired the night before that he had given its contents very little thought. Why such an eminent churchman should take to leaving notes under his door remained unclear. What also disturbed Costello was why he seemed so insistent on meeting without the archbishop's knowledge.

Delayed by his over-long shower and his own unanswered questions Costello entered the breakfast room a little later than he had intended. Bishop Westgate rose to greet him as he walked towards the white-linen-covered table.

'It's good of you to meet me, Bishop,' said Westgate, offering his hand. 'I apologise for my seemingly strange behaviour.'

Costello reassured the bishop and responded to the inevitable questions of the pope's condition.

'You are visiting today?' asked Westgate.

'Around midday. The consultant suggested I should leave him to rest.'

'Yes, of course.'

The Bishop of London hedged carefully around the true purpose of their meeting, aware of the constant to-and-fro of the waitress who served their breakfast. It was not until they were brought coffee that Westgate broached the real topic.

'Are you aware that the Holy Father and His Grace have already had some informal discussions?'

Costello considered Westgate's question carefully as he realised it was only a precursor to the main event. He found it difficult to warm to this churchman who, despite his equal status, seemed to adopt a rather patronising air. He seemed a caricature of the English cleric, a rather pious figure from a Dickens novel.

'It was mentioned,' answered Costello warily.

'Do you know the extent of these discussions?'

'I'm not sure I follow.'

Bishop Westgate smiled knowingly, as if pleased to be the guardian of secrets.

'You don't know that they have been in constant communication since the pope's election?'

'Go on,' answered Costello, unwilling to divulge the limits of his knowledge.

'There have been letters. A number of letters.'

'Of what nature?'

Westgate paused and smiled once more, aware that he was gaining control.

'Let me pose you another question before I answer. There have been rumours that Pope Adrian VII is planning sweeping changes within the Catholic church. Forgive my directness, but is this true?'

Costello was now fully alert and began to choose his words with great care.

'Like any new incumbent, he wishes to put his own stamp on his papacy. This needn't imply revolution, simply an alternative route.'

'Mm,' came Westgate's non-committal response. 'There are some changes planned, however?'

'Inevitably.'

'What would your response be if I told you that Archbishop Munro is in the process of effecting changes to our ecumenical proposals that could only be described as revolutionary?'

'It would depend on the detail.'

'Quite.'

There was a long pause in their conversation as each man

sized up his opponent. They were beginning to play a hazardous game and one that reeked of conspiracy. Costello realised that the longer this conversation continued, the deeper he became embedded in an intrigue which he wished to avoid. Looking once more at Bishop Westgate he sensed an ambitious man, not unlike Eugenio Cellini, the cardinal frustrated by Woeters' election. Here was the same quick mind, the same schemer, the same willingness to breed doubt and uncertainty. Bishop Westgate chanced his trump card.

'I suspect both men are in danger of going beyond their elected responsibilities. Do you not agree?'

'I'm not privy to their conversations,' answered Costello guardedly.

Bishop Westgate sighed and shrugged his shoulders before responding.

'Prefect,' he began, laying great emphasis on Costello's official title, 'I realise that I place you in some difficulty with my observations, but I think you need to be aware – if you are not already aware, as I suspect you are – that the leaders of our respective churches are about to engage us all in a turmoil not seen since the pronouncements of Martin Luther. Surely you can see that?'

'You have no substantive evidence for such a claim,' retorted Costello, now shaken by Westgate's directness. 'I would prefer not to comment. You are making claims that could affect the very faith and doctrines of protestantism and Catholicism. It is, if you'll forgive me from saying so, a highly dangerous set of assumptions.'

'Precisely,' answered Westgate without hesitation, and obviously warming to their debate, 'but a danger not to ourselves, but to Christianity as we know it.'

'Perhaps it is God's wish, Bishop. Our church structures have been built by man. Perhaps it is time to question their foundations.'

'Perhaps, Prefect. But can we really risk destroying our churches in the process? It could put us back four hundred years. It could see minor denominations and irrelevant sects more than eager to pick up the pieces. They would offer heaven on earth to our disillusioned members.'

'I think that may be considered before any major steps are taken. The will of God is the will of God,' responded Costello, with growing assurance.

'But he also allows us free will, the power to choose, to contribute to our own destiny. All men are fallible, not only in their actions but also in their interpretations.'

'It is perhaps an issue which divides us, Bishop,' answered Costello rising from his chair to signal the end of their conversation and eager to stem the flow of conspiracy. 'We shall see,' he added abruptly.

'We will indeed,' said Westgate in a dismissive manner.

It was not the start to the day that Costello had anticipated. Apart from the distraction of Bishop Westgate's note, he had gone to bed buoyed by the news of the pope's apparent improvement and was looking forward to a day of relative calm. His breakfast conversation had left him feeling incensed by Westgate's arrogance. The Anglican bishop had confirmed himself as an enemy rather than the supportive ally Costello so badly needed. As a young priest he had at first carried a heavy sense of guilt when he felt critical of members of his fellow clergy. But as he matured and gained in experience, he began to realise that, like any institution, there are bound to be clashes of personality, whatever the shared goal. Now he felt no more than exasperation and a disappointment that, yet again, he was faced with raw ambition.

With time to spare before his visit to the Holy Father, Costello decided to enjoy the morning sunshine. Unusually for England, even in summer, the weather was warm and settled and he took his chance to take some light exercise before the streets became too crowded. Having collected his papers together he slipped out on to Lambeth Palace Road through the side gate he had used the previous evening. Walking quickly across the road he glanced back to the main entrance, a small gaggle of cameramen and journalists still searching for comment. They were becoming so desperate that they were even trying to elicit a response from the small queue who were lining up outside the Garden Museum which flanked the entrance to Lambeth Palace.

Walking quickly to avoid any possible recognition, he crossed Lambeth Bridge towards the west bank of the river. The city was just coming to life, commuters and tourists joined in a pursuit of their different goals. A newspaper stall on the far side of the bridge displayed its billboard of the pope's illness. Costello glanced at the various headlines in the newspapers displayed on the stand. The tabloids as usual went for the sensationalist approach. 'Dutch Pope on Deathbed', 'Cardinals on Red Alert', even 'No Dutch Luck for New Pope' screamed from the front page of one of the tabloids. Costello asked for a *Times* in search of more considered opinion, and unfolding the broadsheet he saw the evidence of his miscalculation and hesitation of the previous evening. 'Mystery Over Pope's Visit' read the headline.

Whoever had written this piece knew that the main story lay not in the pope's illness but in his sudden and unexpected visit to Lambeth Palace. It made it even more vital that the press statement he was to prepare with Laidler should be very carefully worded. The article contained little evidence of inside information though the speculation did focus on the probability of moves taking place within the ecumenical movement and an assumption that the Pope had suffered some kind of stroke.

By force of habit Costello skimmed through the paper in search of an article by Robert Paine. As he searched the columns of newsprint he began to feel ashamed of his lack of trust in his old friend. Only the previous day Paine had assured him of confidentiality, and before he had finished turning the pages he folded the newspaper under his arm and continued his walk. Turning right onto Victoria Tower Gardens, the towering structure of parliament stood before him, its many windows glinting brightly in the morning sun.

As he crossed the carefully mowed lawns he stopped briefly at the ornate monument which stood in the centre of the park. It reminded Costello of the papal crown, last worn by Pope Paul VI but dispensed with by later papacies. It had been viewed as a symbol of unacceptable power. Bending slightly to read the brass-plated plaque at the base of the structure, he was surprised to see that it had been erected to commemorate the anti-slavery society. It seemed to him ironic that lying in the shadow of parliament stood an edifice to a group of men and women who had at one time threatened its very existence. He realised in that moment that change and revolution, like man himself, had no more than a transient quality, a brief hold on time finally diluted in history. In some ways he felt it put Johannes Woeters' actions in perspective and that all upheaval, even in Christianity, must be viewed as no more than a ripple in man's spiritual evolution. The Holy Father was working on a much wider landscape than those who might oppose his views.

Costello sat for a time on the small wooden benches which lay within the monument, quietly mulling over its significance to his own position and sensing a growing confidence in his conviction to support his pope.

Still tired by his shortage of sleep, he allowed himself to doze in the warmth of the increasing heat. It was only a matter of minutes before he woke, but Costello woke feeling refreshed and renewed in his purpose. Rising slowly from his seat he headed across the gardens towards Westminster Bridge, now busy with tourists and police ushering the public into orderly queues. The Abbey stood to his left, made insignificant by the government buildings which surrounded the square. He had become so accustomed to the old red telephone boxes which he remembered from his youth that he almost missed the clear plastic booth which stood on the corner of the large grey Treasury building. He wished for the privacy of the old boxes but had no choice but to use its modern substitute. It reminded him of the giant hairdryers beneath which his mother would sit when he was a child. Costello smiled to himself as he punched out his chosen numbers.

'Robert? It's Thomas. I'm glad you're in. Can you hear me all right?' The heavy city traffic almost drowned Costello's voice.

'It's fine at my end. How's things?'

'So far, so good. I'm just on my way to visit.'

'That's good news and I'm glad you've rung. My phone's been going crazy this morning.'

'Trouble?'

'It may be, Thomas. I suspect someone's got wind of our association. Finlay's given me the third degree this morning.'

'I don't understand,' shouted Costello. 'We've been very careful.'

'Not careful enough. Finlay's convinced I'm holding things back and, as he put it, he smells a rat.'

'I saw the article this morning. It's no more than speculation.'

'I know, Thomas. But Finlay wrote that article himself and he's got the bit between his teeth. It's getting harder and harder for me to cover up.'

'I'm sorry. I didn't mean to put you in this situation.'

'I know. Don't worry. But I think you need to offer the press something before they start to set their own agenda.'

'I'm giving a statement later today.'

'You'd better think it through carefully. There are all sorts of rumours flying about in the press room.'

'I'll be careful.'

'By the way. Did you spot the reference to Cellini? Finlay threw his name into the conversation this morning but was pretty vague about his involvement.'

Costello failed to reply. The mention of Cellini had broken his train of thought. A young, denim-clad man paced up and down the pavement, impatient to use the phone. The bishop's anger at hearing Cellini's name showed in his face and transferred itself to the waiting youth. He stared back at Costello with what looked like hatred, raised two fingers and hurried off into the crowd.

'Thomas! Thomas!' came Paine's voice. 'Are you still there?'

Costello turned back into the booth.

'Yes I saw it, Robert. Cellini's shadow is never far away. It's not good news. I'll have to go. I'm sorry.'

'Stay in touch.'

'I will.'

The following hour passed in something of a daze. Costello wandered the streets, unsettled by Cellini's intrusion. Within the space of one morning Thomas Costello found himself out of control, on a rollercoaster of emotions. His rising spirit had been dampened by the very mention of Cellini's name.

As he approached St Thomas's Hospital he could see that the news reporters had maintained their vigil outside the entrance. Quickening his step, Costello waved their questions away, promising a full press statement later in the day. He entered the reception area and reported his presence to the main desk. His visit had been expected and he was shown directly to Laidler's office.

'Good morning, Bishop,' said the consultant, standing to greet Costello. 'Have you been given the mail?'

'The mail?'

'There are literally hundreds of letters, cards and faxes waiting for you. We even had a messenger from Buckingham Palace.'

'There was a planned, informal audience this evening. It's kind of Her Majesty to write. I'll attend to them later. I'm sure the Vatican machinery will have followed all the correct protocols by now.'

'I'm sure.'

'May I see the Holy Father?'

'Of course. We'll go straight away.'

As they walked the short distance towards the pope's private room Costello questioned Laidler closely. The consultant ran through the details of the operation and reaffirmed the pope's dramatic improvement.

'If you can come back to my office after your visit I may be able to give you a much clearer picture of his condition,' said Laidler as they approached the intensive care unit. 'We're expecting some preliminary results from the biopsy. Maybe within the next half-hour.'

Costello pushed open the door quietly, concerned that he might disturb the pope's sleep. But what he saw before him went far beyond all his expectations.

'Thomas. It's so good to see you,' greeted Woeters. His voice was strong and full of life. A turban-like bandage covered his head and monitors attached to his arm and chest still bleeped out their reassurance. But the pope no longer had the pallor of a dying man. Instead his face was once more full of colour and there was no hint of greyness beneath the eyes. Costello was truly startled by such a dramatic change.

'You look well, Holy Father,' he stuttered.

'Johannes,' admonished Woeters. 'I need mothering, Thomas,' he laughed.

As had become their habit, the two men joined in prayer for a few moments, giving thanks for God's deliverance and the comfort he afforded to the sick and the dying. They held hands as they prayed, sitting together in quiet reflection and re-forging their bond of friendship.

After a few more moments Woeters began to question Costello about the events of the previous evening. It quickly became apparent that the pope had little recall of his collapse and no memory whatsoever of his admission to the hospital.

'Has the Vatican been informed, Thomas?' asked Woeters, now returning to matters of office.

'The archbishop has been very kind. All is in order.'

'They had written me off perhaps?' smiled Woeters.

'Perhaps some,' answered Costello, immediately thinking again of Cellini.

'And the newspapers? Are they giving you a difficult time, Thomas?'

'We do need to give them a statement. With your approval, of course. I've managed to fend them off for the moment.'

'Of course. I've already given it a little thought. Perhaps later, when Mr Laidler gives his verdict. He's a good man, I think.'

'A caring man and very efficient.'

Costello tried his best to alleviate the pope's concerns regarding the results of the biopsy, and reassured him that he would take care of the cancelled engagements. Woeters could see the stress on Costello's face and held his hand once more.

'I'm in God's hands, Thomas. I am only one of his many servants.'

'Of course, Holy Father.'

Woeters lay back on his pillow and momentarily closed his eyes, attempting to regain his strength.

'Have you ever been in hospital, Thomas?' he asked, looking back towards Costello.

'Only for minor problems. Tonsils, appendix, that sort of thing. I have been fortunate to enjoy good health.'

'Until now I have shared your good fortune, Thomas. We take it so much for granted until God reminds us of our frailty.'

'Indeed.'

'I recall so little of last night and yet I have vivid memories of dreaming of my childhood. Perhaps the threat of having life snatched away drives you back to the safety of youth.'

Although Costello had enjoyed many conversations with Woeters during his time as Prefect, there had rarely been mention of his early days in the small coastal town of Doordrecht in the south of Holland. Now he spoke with affection of his early childhood spent by the canals and watching the cargo boats laden with goods heading slowly up river to the port of Rotterdam. He related how he had been the youngest of a family of six children, the son of a ship's carpenter who had been killed in the bombings of

1943. His mother, he recalled, never remarried and brought up her children without help, eking out a difficult living from the small bakery she owned with her brother.

'I can smell the bread even now,' remarked Woeters wistfully. 'They were happy days.'

'Do you still have family in Doordrecht, Johannes?'

'Only Paul, my elder brother. He still lives above the bakery on the Voorstraat, next to a sex shop of all things. It would have broken my mother's heart. There have been so many changes. I prefer to think of it as it once was – a close community, full of friendship and neighbourliness. Not now, I'm afraid.'

'Change is never easy,' comforted Costello, aware of the pope's growing depression.

The sound of the door being pushed open interrupted their conversation. Costello turned to find Laidler approaching the bed.

'Quite an improvement, Bishop. You'll be pleased with the Holy Father's progress?' asked Laidler in a manner suggesting that he was the bearer of good news.

'You have the results?' queried the pope with no hint of fear in his voice.

'It all looks very promising Holy Father,' responded Laidler. 'As far as we can see, there appears to be no sign of malignancy and the small growth was very localised.'

'I am truly blessed,' said Woeters with a sense of relief. 'You have removed this growth?'

'Totally. It was never my intention to do so, but once I could see that the tissue damage was so localised there seemed little point in subjecting you to further surgery.'

'There will be a full recovery?' interrupted Costello.

'I see no reason why not. The prognosis is good.'

'I can return to Rome?' asked Woeters.

'I would give it a few days but then it should be fine. You'll require further check-ups of course, but I can send your documentation on to the Vatican doctors. We can always liaise.'

'You have been very kind, Doctor,' said Woeters warmly.

'No more than my job, Holy Father. I'm glad I could be of some help. You really should rest now.'

'We have a statement to prepare,' answered Woeters, reluctant to lose Costello's company.

'Perhaps later. You really should try to sleep for a few hours.'

'I bow to your wisdom, Mr Laidler,' smiled Woeters.

Costello made his farewells and joined Laidler as he left the room.

'It has worked out better than I could have hoped,' said Costello as they walked down the corridor and into the main building of the hospital. Laidler stopped for a moment and took Costello's arm.

'There may, there just may, be a complication, Bishop.'

'There is something you haven't told us?' asked Costello, alerted by Laidler's serious manner.

'I didn't want to worry the pope at this stage. He needs to regain his strength. He may look well enough but any invasive surgery takes its toll, especially in a man of his age.'

'And?' demanded Costello.

Laidler hesitated, searching for the right words.

'Let me first reassure you that the growth definitely showed no signs of malignancy. The tissue sample revealed no hint of disease.'

'But?' Costello knew there was bound to be a *caveat* to the consultant's findings and pressed him for explanation.

'But,' he hesitated once more, 'there were signs of abnormality in the cell structure of the tissue.'

'What kind of abnormalities?'

'There lies the problem, Bishop. To be totally frank, I have never encountered its like before.'

'In what manner?'

'It's difficult to explain. Do you have any knowledge of cell structure?'

'I'm afraid not.'

'I'll try to keep it simple, but it's not easy.'

Laidler took out a pen and a white envelope from his breast pocket and began to draw a small diagram. He pointed to its detail as he began his explanation.

'Under normal conditions we would expect to see such a cell go through a series of activations and rest periods, depending on the transmission of impulses.'

He stopped and looked to Costello for confirmation.

'Please, go on.'

'What's puzzling us at the moment, is that the cells we located in the removed tissue appeared to have no resting potential, as we call it. They remained fully activated and, even more strangely, remained activated for a number of hours after their extraction.'

'You mean they had a life of their own?' asked Costello, trying desperately to follow the explanation.

'Not really,' laughed Laidler. 'We'd be into new paradigms of medical science if that were the case. I'd become a famous man overnight! It could well be no more than some sort of residual electrical stimulus, but we can't be sure.'

'But the cells are normal?'

'That's the enigma. I have consulted a number of eminent colleagues, and none of us has ever seen such a complex cellular formation, particularly in the axon branches.'

'Axon branches? I don't follow.'

'Let's just say they're the transmitters for all neural processes. They are far from uniform in make-up, but they do tend to follow a set construction. In this particular case, I have to say that they follow no pattern I have ever encountered.'

'And the next step?'

'We can only wait and see. Perhaps nothing. It's in the lap of the gods.'

'Or God alone,' smiled Costello.

'Forgive me,' laughed Laidler, 'an unfortunate turn of phrase.'

'One I have used many times myself,' responded Costello, aware of the consultant's embarrassment.

Laidler replaced the pen and envelope in his jacket and shook Costello's hand.

'Forgive me, I must go. I'm due in theatre in five minutes. I'll keep you posted. I'm sure it will be fine.'

Laidler scurried quickly away, leaving Costello stunned and bemused by this latest revelation. The bishop turned and began to walk towards the hospital entrance only to stop and turn back yet again towards the pope's room.

Costello peered round the door, edging slowly into the room. He approached the bed, careful not to let his feet disturb the silence. The pope lay quietly, apparently asleep, his hands clasped together as if in prayer. Costello moved closer.

'Johannes,' he whispered. 'Johannes.'

Woeters' eyes slowly opened as he sensed Costello's presence.

'Thomas?' he queried.

'Forgive me, Holy Father. There was something I meant to ask you.'

'What is it, Thomas?'

Costello glanced back towards the open door.

'Does the word "aitu" mean anything to you?'

'Say that again?'

'"Aitu."'

'"Aitu?" I don't think so. Why do you ask, Thomas?'

'You said the word over and over again last night, whilst you were unconscious.'

'"Aitu?" Are you sure?'

'Positive. You whispered it very clearly just before I left you last night.'

'It means nothing to me. Such a strange word.'

'Somewhere in Doordrecht perhaps?' pressed Costello.

'No. Definitely not. And yet it does sound familiar. You are sure it was "Aitu"? You're not mistaken?'

'I'm certain.'

The pope lay back on his pillow, visibly tiring by the second. Mention of the word had obviously disturbed him and he looked directly at Costello.

'Let's keep it between ourselves, Thomas,' said Woeters. 'I don't know why, but I sense it has some importance.'

9

'I can't persuade you, can I, Robert?'

'Not a chance, Peter. Until I took this break I didn't realise how really burnt out I was.'

'I know that, Robert. But how the hell can you pass up such a chance? I know you've got the contacts.'

'I know you know, Peter. I'd love to know who told you.'

'Sources.'

'Thanks for nothing.'

'Oh, come on, Robert. You're a journalist for Christ's sake. This could really put you on the map.'

'I thought I was already there,' laughed Paine.

'I'm talking about world maps not provincial guides.'

Robert Paine walked over to the table and sat down, keeping the portable phone close to his ear. He inhaled slowly.

'I'm resigning, Peter. Getting out.'

'Now you *are* joking.'

'I'm afraid not.'

'What the hell for?'

'I'm going to write a book.'

'Write a book? On what?'

'Catholicism.'

'On Catholicism? Do you know how many real Catholics are really out there?'

'Enough.'

'Enough to provide you with a pension?'

'This book might. I suspect it will have a much wider readership.'

Paine could hear Finlay's growing irritation, his quick speech punctuated with sighs.

'I feel I'm only getting half the story, Robert.'

'Maybe, Peter. I'm not sure I know the story myself.'

Finlay tried for another ten minutes before reluctantly accepting Paine's decision. He had felt from the moment of Woeters' election that Robert was sitting on a potentially explosive story. Of all his journalists, Paine had the knowledge and ability to expose the underbelly of Vatican politics. Aitcheson had done a good job filling in as a lobby correspondent, but the religious affairs people had hardly set the world on fire during the pope's illness. Their reporting had been efficient, well-researched, but no more than adequate. What he wanted was the sharp edge which Paine could have provided and he made this clear to Robert before surrendering to the journalist's ultimatum.

The idea of writing a book had been lurking in Paine's mind for some weeks, especially since the pope's collapse and his return to Rome. Finlay's call had been flattering but it also put an end to his prevarication. He was tired of resisting temptation and he now felt like a young schoolboy who gives in to his instincts and steals the sweets from the corner shop. It provided that exhilaration and element of danger which sets the pulse racing and fires the imagination. He had no idea how Alex might react, though he knew that she was well aware of his unsettled state.

It was now July and some three weeks since Costello had returned to Rome to oversee the pope's convalescence. Paine had persuaded his friend to stay in touch and they had managed to make a number of brief phone calls. It appeared that Woeters was regaining full strength, ploughing ahead with his reforms, and Thomas now appeared to be giving him full support. To all intents and purposes it seemed that this was the end of the affair. The press statement from Costello had been carefully crafted to draw a line under the whole affair, speaking of a gradual coming-together of protestantism and Catholicism and underplaying the state of the pope's health and the degree of change. From the media reaction it seemed as if the story had fizzled out altogether. It was high summer and the papers had shifted their concentration to Wimbledon, the test matches against Australia, Royal Ascot and trivial exposés of the rich and famous. The silly season of journalism had temporarily dampened public enthusiasm for religion.

But the pot was still boiling, and Finlay's call only confirmed Paine's instincts that he had merely touched the surface of a major story. After his initial meeting with Costello and the subsequent hiatus over the pope's supposed minor stroke, Paine decided to dig a little deeper into the reasons for Woeters' visit.

Using his network of contacts and carefully scanning the daily press, Paine gradually began to piece together a picture which revealed the Church of England to be on the edge of disarray. It became increasingly obvious that Archbishop Munro was a very active partner in the pope's revisionism and may well have instigated their meeting. Finlay had obviously sensed this, but had been driven down a cul-de-sac by Costello's careful management of the information. But there were other signs. Reports of clandestine meetings at the recent church synod, and ambiguous and guarded statements by high-ranking church officials, suggested that the Church of England was in no more a stable state than Roman Catholicism. What still mystified Paine was the identification of the real driving force behind this revolution. Munro and Woeters were without doubt in alliance, but what had brought them together with such urgency remained unclear.

What finally tipped the balance was Munro's recent and sudden illness. It set the seal on Paine's continued interest and probably prompted his decision to resign. It was no more than a hunch, but the single factor which alerted Paine's notice was the total under-reporting of the archbishop's condition. There had been a few scare stories which speculated about possible meningitis, mild heart attack, even cancer, but within days Munro was back in post and the papers returned to their concentration on summer trivia. And Paine recognised all the signs. This was no loss of interest by the press. The whole thing smacked of an orchestrated cover-up and a censorship of information. He knew instinctively that if he returned to the paper he would suffer the same constraints. In many ways the independent writing of a book provided his only option.

For the past two weeks Paine had struggled unsuccessfully towards an explanation. There seemed no reason why the two churches should try to conceal their dialogue. The ecumenical movement enjoyed majority support and, whilst the proposed pace of change was perhaps surprising, it was not wholly unexpected. There were bound to be implications and it was already beginning to stir up the anti-abortion lobby and a few fundamentalist groups from both churches. Even the hard-liners in Northern Ireland were beginning to express misgivings, but as far as Paine could see the unification of the churches might well offer more chance of a sustained peace. If the cover-up was being promoted by government it was hard to see the motive with such a secularised electorate. The two major parties had increasingly detached themselves from religious issues and the disestablishment of the church of England was gaining more and more support. He could think of no justification for the apparent secrecy.

If there was pressure being exerted from some faceless government department it made Finlay's call even more intriguing. Was it possible that his editor had forced his hand into resignation, knowing that a loose cannon was the only hope of getting to the truth?

Robert Paine was still struggling with this question when Alex came down for breakfast.

'What time are we leaving, Robert?' she asked, aware that her husband had been up for some time.

'About nine-thirty, I thought. It'll give us time to pop in and see Rachel before we get to the ground.'

'You look tired, Robert.'

'Not really. A lot on my mind, that's all.'

'Who was that on the phone?'

'Finlay – trying to persuade me back.'

'What did you say?'

'I resigned,' he answered bluntly, without adding an explanation.

'You did what?' responded Alex, obviously shocked by his sudden revelation.

'I resigned. Totally. Told him I'd had enough.'

'Good God! Are you sure you know what you're doing?'

'Positive.'

'Can we afford it?'

'We'll manage. I've still got mother's money. We can always sell some woodland in Scotland if it gets a bit tight. But we shouldn't have to.'

'What brought it on, Robert? I knew you were unhappy at the paper, but you've seemed so much better recently.'

'I know.'

'So why the sudden jump?'

'A hunch and a book, Alex. I know it doesn't seem much but I can't let go of the idea.'

'A book about what?'

Paine gave Alex enough detail to justify his decision without revealing the whole story. He wanted to maintain their improved relationship and he had kept her up-to-date with most of his investigations over the past few weeks. As always she had remained supportive, but this new twist had jolted her confidence.

'Do you have to resign? Your sabbatical's still got months to run and you'd miss the buzz of the office. I know I did when I had to leave.'

'It's risky, I know, Alex. But I feel I have no choice. Something inside me is telling me not to let go of this one. It feels a bit irrational but right, all the same.'

Alex Paine sat down next to her husband and put her arm around his shoulders.

'You don't think Thomas has told you the whole truth, do you, Robert?'

He turned his head towards Alex, responding to her intimacy.

'Well, to be frank, no. I think he's being honest enough, Alex. But if my hunch is right I don't think even Thomas knows what's going on. He's a big player without doubt and devoted to his pope, but I suspect he may be just as much in the dark as I am.'

'In what respect?'

'Too early, Alex. Too early.'

They left the house later than intended but still had time to visit Rachel. Her pregnancy was becoming more and more obvious, a small but prominent bump now showing as she lay back on the sun lounger.

'How's tricks?' asked Paine, kissing his daughter on the cheek.

'Off to the cricket, Daddy? Nice life!' she exclaimed.

'I've earned it!' laughed Paine in mock rebuke. 'Come on now. How are you?'

'Fussing again, Daddy. I'm fine. Really. You're such a worrier.'

They sat together for about half an hour, chatting about the weather, her husband's job and the miseries of pregnancy. Alex pressed her daughter about the sex of her baby. She could never resist asking the question.

'It's either a boy or a girl, Mummy. You never give in, do you!'

'You would tell me if you knew?'

'Is it important, Mummy?'

'Not at all. Only curiosity.'

'We have decided one thing, though.'

'What's that, darling?'

'We're going to have him or her baptised.'

'Why not?' interrupted Paine. 'I've always believed in taking out good insurance.'

'Daddy!' giggled his daughter. 'You'll be struck down if you're not careful!'

Minutes later they had left, heading across the city towards North London and St John's Wood. The traffic was light until they approached the ground, but there was no sign of a parking space.

'Try the press pass, Robert. It's worked before,' suggested Alex.

They approached the main gate at the east end of the ground and Paine waved his press card with as much confidence as he could muster. The attendant viewed him with a moment's suspicion but finally ushered him through and into the car park.

He could smell the freshly mown grass as soon as he stepped out of his car. It was a fragrance he had only ever encountered at Lord's cricket ground. It was unique to Lord's. It was the Lord's smell.

'God's gift to the English!' said Paine, sniffing the air.

'Steady, Robert,' laughed Alex. 'Don't go all nostalgic on me. Ardent nationalism doesn't suit you!'

'It is special, though. Don't you think so, Alex?'

'I suppose it is. Come on. We've already missed most of the first session.'

It was not the best of days for cricket. A stiff breeze blew across the ground from the pavilion end, chilling the sitting spectators. But the clouds were high and there was an expectation of a full day's play. Robert and Alex took their seats in their favoured Edrich stand, a hubbub of excitement and shouting contrasting with the starched correctness of the members' enclosure. Paine felt he enjoyed watching the crowd as much as he revelled in the play. There was still a good natured rivalry between the opposing supporters, not marred by the vulgarity and violence of football. By the end of the day, when the alcohol levels had risen, it would become fairly boisterous but he never sensed an element of danger. In his youth he had been as vocal as any of the crowd who sat with him at this moment.

He relaxed as the day unfolded, happy to watch the game's slow development, the civilised taking of lunch and tea. Alex took an interest, but was happy to tackle her daily crossword and pass the occasional comment when the crowd roared its approval or bellowed its criticism. They had been coming together for years, and like many long-term couples had settled into an understood routine of behaviour. There was great comfort in its certainty. It was not the tedium of predictability but the pleasure of simply enjoying one another's company, without the distraction of second-guessing your companion's needs.

The day passed quickly and as the breeze fell away they sat contented in the evening sunshine. As had happened to them many times before, they had formed fleeting relationships with other spectators, built on constant chatter, shared drinks, apologies when knees brushed against one another or the retrieval of dropped programmes. Paine glanced around the ground as people cheered a fallen wicket.

'Do you remember being stuck up there, Alex?' said Paine, pointing to the executive boxes which lined the top of the north stand.

'Never again,' smiled Alex. 'Stuffy and pompous.'

'I don't know why they bother,' came a voice from Paine's left. 'They spend most of their time by the bar.'

'Precisely,' answered Paine.

The man at his side was obviously a regular spectator. Paine guessed he might be a retired schoolmaster or solicitor, his former occupation betrayed by his organisation. He had come equipped with score cards, a hamper of food and a fine pair of binoculars which Paine had been allowed to borrow throughout the day. Paine stared back towards the boxes, shadowed under the huge white sail-like structures which had caused such a furore when they had first been erected. The architect had the temerity to dismiss tradition and erect a design which offended the more conservative members.

Paine's companion noticed him looking towards the structure.

'You like them?' he asked.

'The line of washing, you mean?'

'Is that what you call them?'

'I've heard it said!'

'My son calls them Arabian tents,' answered the stranger.

'It's a good description. I thought they were awful when they first went up. Too *avant-garde*. Unfitting somehow.'

'I suppose so. They were a bit revolutionary. And then they become part of the natural landscape. It's hard to imagine Lord's without them now. We reject these changes and then come to love them. It's strange how we adapt so easily.'

Robert Paine did not respond but looked once more at the tent-like covers. Alex turned to speak to him again.

'Robert? Are you all right? You look quite pale.'

'I've got it, Alex. I know what they're up to!' he whispered, putting his mouth close to her ear.

'Who's up to what, Robert?'

'The pope and the archbishop,' he answered, whispering his reply carefully. 'It's going to sound crazy but I think I know what they're trying to do.'

'Go on.'

'I'll explain later. Over dinner, perhaps. It's a bit public here.'

Alex Paine was burning for answers but their journey home was spent in virtual silence. Robert seemed totally preoccupied, hardly mentioning the day's cricket, and drove through the city in an apparent daze. She had offered to drive when Paine almost collided with another car on Tottenham Court Road but her suggestion was rejected with a dismissive grunt.

Alex had watched her husband changing over the past few weeks. She was happy to see him excited and focused on his new adventure, but she could also see that he was starting to become obsessive. His resignation from the paper had been something of a shock, made more disturbing by the fact that it seemed completely out of character. Ever since she had first met Robert, he had taken chances in his career, but they had always been carefully considered and not prompted by instinct. What she saw now was a man who was beginning to reveal a darker side, a man weighed down by some hidden drive and obscure motivation.

They arrived home at about eight o'clock, relieved to escape the growing tension of their journey.

'I'm sorry, Alex,' said Paine as he opened the door.

'Don't worry. You can talk to me later. Are you hungry?'

'Not really. You?'

'Me neither. I'll throw something together later. Let's have a drink first.'

'Good idea.'

A number of letters lay on the mat. Paine collected them together and carried the small pile of envelopes through to the kitchen.

'Anything interesting?' asked Alex, as she opened a bottle of red wine.

'Only bills and circulars by the look of it.'

Paine opened each envelope quickly, casting them to one side in a series of disappointments.

'What's that?'queried Alex, noticing that at least one of the letters had taken Robert's attention.

'Just a second.'

Alex watched her husband's concentration increase as he scanned the contents. His eyes creased into a smile as he turned the pages.

'Good news?' asked Alex once more.

'Well. Unexpected to say the least. What do they say? Every cloud has a silver lining?'

'They're usually lead-lined in my experience,' responded Alex with a chuckle, happy that the ice had been broken. They had always managed to talk openly and the silence of the car journey had left her feeling depressed and agitated.

'My Uncle Jamie's died. Do you remember him?'

'Vaguely. I doubt if we've seen him since our wedding. Who's the letter from?'

'Firm of solicitors in Inverness. The old stick has left me his cottage in the Boat of Garten.'

'Boat of where?'

'Garten. It's a small Scottish village, just on the edge of the Cairngorms.'

'Why you?'

'He was a bachelor. No immediate family. Suppose I'm next in line.'

'You'll sell it?'

'Not unless we have to. But it's come at a good time.'

Paine tried to visualise his uncle's cottage as Alex prepared their supper. His memory was vague and it was difficult to cling on to the fleeting images which flickered through his mind. Like many childhood experiences they had left him with only a residue of detail, events only captured as a series of emotions.

'What's it like?' asked Alex, determined not to let Robert slip back into silence.

'I'm trying to remember, Alex. It must be forty years since I was there.'

He glanced back through the solicitor's letter, looking for clues to his childhood. After his father's death the family had spent many summer holidays in Scotland. Even now he could recall refusing to walk another step when his mother set off on one of her notorious short rambles. It had not been unusual for her to convert a ten-minute-walk into a fifteen-mile-hike, even when Paine was only five or six years old.

'Is it in a nice setting?' asked Alex.

'Beautiful, as far as I can remember. I was just thinking about my mother's walks.'

'Ah! The famous walks,' answered Alex, happy to see her husband so distracted.

'She was as tough as old boots.'

'She was lovely.'

'I know.'

As he had grown into adolescence, Paine had come to share his mother's love of the countryside and, like many parents, had let history repeat itself. His own children had been subjected to the same treatment and he suspected that his new grand-child would have to fight the same battles with Rachel.

'Isn't that where you saw the ospreys?' queried Alex. 'I remember you talking about them when we first met.'

Paine looked across to his wife, startled by her memory and flattered that even such an inconsequential fact was still retained from their early days.

'You never fail to amaze me,' answered Paine with a look

of such warmth that Alex blushed like an emotional adolescent.

She had suddenly set his memory free: the soaring birds, swooping low down to the river and climbing rapidly over the heathers in search of prey. He could remember his mother's excitement as she trained her binoculars across the sky, almost shrieking with delight when the osprey came closer. And now he could visualise the cottage, set in the woods; the River Spey, once teeming with salmon, only a short walk from the small wooden gate which opened onto a wild unkempt garden. Behind the cottage loomed the Cairngorms, snowcapped, even in the height of summer. But it was the river which provided the clearest memory, the sound of its rushing waters cascading over the large stones which lay in its path. Paine could recall lying in bed in the early morning, listening to the rush of the river giving promise of a day spent playing on its banks and clambering amongst the granite boulders.

'Good days, Alex,' said Paine, casting off his nostalgia.

'Ready for supper?'

'Yes, if you are.'

They ate quietly at first, Alex careful not to confront Robert with any questions relating to his resignation. Brief comments were made about their day at the cricket, Rachel's pregnancy and even the re-decoration of their bedroom. But Paine knew his wife too well and could see that she was intentionally skirting around the main subject. The breaks in their conversation were unnatural, each pause a search for a new and contrived subject.

'I'm sorry Alex. I'm not being very fair, am I?' said Paine finally.

'Well, I'd love to know what's happening, Robert. All this church business and your resignation. It's a bit hard to fathom what's going on.'

'I know. I'm sorry. It's just that I'm a bit confused myself.'

'You said you had a hunch?' asked Alex, prompting Paine into explanation.

'You'll think I'm crazy.'

'Try me.'

Paine paused and looked blankly at the wall, trying to assemble his thoughts before laying out his case.

'It was the cover up of Munro's illness that first set me thinking.'

'Cover up by whom?'

'Good question, Alex. To be honest I've got no idea, but I'm damn sure there was a cover up. Church, government, God knows.'

'So what's the point?'

'The point is, Alex, if two church leaders meet to discuss ecumenicalism, then what's the big deal? We're all expecting it to happen, even hoping for it to happen. We're living in a fairly secular world, half the population haven't got the slightest interest. The Archbishop of Canterbury could declare himself an atheist and most people would just carry on watching game shows.'

'Bit cynical, Robert,' interrupted Alex.

'But true, Alex, most people couldn't give a shit.'

'I suppose so. But you're still not getting to the point, Robert,' pleaded Alex, now anxious for her husband to continue.

'Well, this is where it becomes a hunch. A wild one, I admit.'

'Go on.'

'What's our greatest fear, Alex?'

She paused before responding, unsure what answer was required.

'I don't know. Nuclear war? Aids? Cancer? I really don't know.'

Paine lent back in his chair and cupped the back of his head in his hands. Alex recognised this as a sign that she was about to be given the truth.

'The West is terrified of Islam. Frightened to death of it swamping Europe and America and destroying our whole culture.'

'Some of it wants destroying,' laughed Alex.

'I agree. But what you're talking about is a complete

undermining of the whole fabric of our society, our laws, morals, legal systems, institutions. The whole bag's under threat.'

'A touch extreme, Robert.'

'I know that, Alex, and I said it's only a hunch. But what do you do if you're under attack?'

'Well, defend yourself, I suppose.'

'Precisely. You build defences. The trouble with Islam is that you can't see your enemy. You're fighting shadows, fighting ideas. That's why the early Romans failed to subdue Christianity. They could kill as many Christians as they liked and enjoy the spectacle. But they couldn't kill the idea. You can't bomb Islam. There just aren't any targets.'

'So where do Woeters and Munro come into this? I'm not sure I see the connection.'

'I think they've been given the job of building the defences. Mustering the troops, raising the flag.'

'The flag?'

'The Christian flag.'

'I still don't see how that's going to help. What's the point?'

'Unity, Alex. Divide and conquer, unite and win. It's a basic military strategy.'

'You're not talking about one unified Christian church are you, Robert?'

'I am. The whole damn lot. Catholics, protestants, Greek orthodox, eastern orthodox, all the Lutheran spin-offs and minor Christian sects. Bring them all together and they can ride happily on the back of nationalism, justified as defenders of the faith. It wouldn't just unite the Christian element. It would drag in every agnostic and atheist in the so-called civilised world.'

'You make it sound like a Holy War!' exclaimed Alex.

'Maybe. But it would at least fill the vacuum.'

'Vacuum?'

'No cold war. Capitalism has gone global. We haven't even got a space race to fire us up.'

'Do we need one?'

'We need something. We need a cause. We need to belong. To something. Anything.'

'So we're all going to become born-again Christians? Now you are fantasising, Robert.'

'You don't think the rabble who joined the crusades believed in Christianity, do you? Most of them either thought they could get rich quickly, or thought they were defending their country against heathens.'

'So we need a new set of heathens?'

'Exactly. We need an opposition. An identifiable enemy.'

'Bit aggressive, wouldn't you say? You're painting a picture of Munro and Woeters as part of the military.'

'Not really. They'll justify it as defence. They're simply giving in to the inevitable. You know what it's like. Families split; groups create factions; nations divide. Every structure we've got has a tendency to polarise. It's just being transferred on to a bigger stage.'

'You didn't watch much cricket, did you?' laughed Alex in response.

'I suppose not,' smiled Paine. 'But seriously, why else would the Vatican offer us such banal press statements on the pope's visit? Why so little detail on the archbishop's illness? What else is there we don't know? There's a political element in all this. I can feel it in my bones.'

Alex looked closely at her husband. He had become more and more animated as he delivered his opinions, his face flushed and contorted as he spoke.

'You've a good nose for this sort of thing, Robert, but you may have let your imagination run away with you. I don't see how you can jump from the pope's visit to some notion of a major religious conspiracy.'

'Neither do I!' laughed Paine. 'I told you it was a hunch. But there may be some evidence.'

'Such as?'

'I've spent some time sifting through the papers recently. Taking notes. Times, places, movements, that sort of thing.'

'Of whom?'

'Leaders of the various Christian churches. I tell you, Alex, when you start to put the bits together it makes an interesting picture.'

'And?'

'And there's a pattern. Similar locations at similar times. No formal press statements but it places the Archbishop particularly, in some very strange locations. It can't be coincidence. I'm sure there have been meetings going on between these men for over a year.'

'Anything else? It's not much to go on.'

'I don't know, Alex. The only thing I can't work out at the moment are the missing gaps.'

'What missing gaps?'

'It's been bloody difficult to calculate, but as far as I can see the majority of these men seem to go missing for anything between one and two weeks. No reports, nothing.'

'So did the pope and the archbishop. They were both ill.'

'That was coincidence, I'm sure. They can't all have been ill. There's something else, I'm sure. Something to do with the meetings.'

'But you can't really be sure, can you?'

'Not without Thomas Costello's help. I still think he knows more than he's prepared to say.'

'Can you contact him?'

'Yes, I can. But I'll have to be careful. If there is a cover-up going on, someone, somewhere, isn't going to be too pleased to find me ferreting about. It wouldn't do a lot for Thomas either.'

'Bed?' asked Alex abruptly. It was not a sexual invitation. The day's fresh air and her husband's revelations had left her exhausted and she was now finding it difficult to respond to Paine's exuberance.

'In a while, Alex. I'd like to think through my letter to Thomas. Whilst the whole thing's fresh in my mind. You go up. I won't be long.'

'How did we get here, Robert?' asked Alex as she stood by the open door.

'What do you mean?'

'I don't know really. I feel it's getting out of control, running away with us somehow.'

'Maybe. We'll see. The cork's out of the bottle, I'm afraid.'

'I think I'll have a long soak.'

'Good idea.'

Alex Paine left her husband at the table and climbed the stairs to the refuge of the bathroom. He listened to his wife's footsteps above him, the running hot water and the flush of the lavatory. They were the commonplace sounds of domesticity, a symbol of their familiarity, but at the same time confirmed their independence. His old job on the *Times* had required many overnight trips, even weeks away, covering inter-governmental meetings or election campaigns. And yet he never felt so detached from Alex as when he was in the same house, hearing her movements from a distance. They seemed to act as a reminder of her individuality, her separateness from the rôle of mother and wife. And in the same moment he thought again of Isobel Griffin.

There had been no hiding Isobel's letter. Alex remained inquisitive about the Hawaiian stamp even after the distraction of a day's shopping with Rachel, and Paine had submitted to her request to see the contents. He had watched as Alex read through the script, fearful of her reaction. He remembered her asking why the letter should 'ruffle feathers' and how he had passed it off as no more than a teasing gesture. Disturbingly, Alex made no further comment, not even a reaction to Isobel's chaotic married life. It was a sure sign that Alex preferred blissful ignorance to raking through the mud of any past relationship. The ensuing silence displayed her knowledge of Paine's false claim to platonic friendship.

But he remained convinced by his own defence. Paine felt guilty and yet there were no grounds for remorse. The emotional ties had been broken 30 years ago in a night of cold passion which confirmed their friendship but destroyed any romanticism. During his marriage to Alex he had remained faithful, an irreproachable husband. And yet now, as he sat alone thinking of Isobel, he was still consumed by a sense of intangible betrayal, unable to construe his own feelings.

Paine left the kitchen and crossed the hallway into his study. He left the room in darkness, apart from a small table lamp which cast its light on to his desk. Quickly switching on his word processor he began to write.

18th July 1999

Dear Izzy,

You were right about my being a poor letter-writer and I apologise for the delay. I'm glad to say that you weren't right about my being as bald as a coot. Certainly a bit thinner on top – but no coot!

It was good to hear from you. As you say, it's been too long. It sounds as if you've had quite a time, Izzy. I'm truly sorry about your marriage, it must have been a really rough patch. These things are never easy. Given the divorce statistics, it's a miracle Alex and I have managed to hold out for so long. With any luck we're past the crisis period by now, but you never know what's round the corner.

Yes – I have heard from Thomas and like you I was a little shocked by his openness and 'baring of the soul', as you put it. I can't begin to tell you what's happened during the past few weeks. Let's just say it's been interesting. At least we managed to meet up – two-thirds of the trinity! It was unfortunately cut short by the pope's illness. You perhaps saw something about it in the press – that's if you get papers in exotic Hawaii. He's apparently recovered now and, if my guess is right, charging ahead with his reforms. I know you say you're not interested in 'religious stuff' but I suspect this new pope could have a major effect – even on heathens like us! Have you heard any more from Thomas? Do let me know if he gets in touch again. You never know, one day the three of us might get together. I'm not really a nostalgia man but it would be fun, I think.

How's the job going? I quite envy you – doing something 'real'. I seem to have spent a life writing about other people's achievements whilst Thomas looks after souls. It's a bit difficult to measure the outcomes or contribution of either occupation. At least you can look up into the sky and say 'that's mine!' I've enjoyed my time in journalism but the results are hardly tangible. And despite all my travelling – I've never been to Hawaii. I'm told it's very beautiful – surely you can find some time to explore? Seems a waste if you can't.

I'm to become a grandfather at the end of the year. A grandfather! That will stop you writing! It's hard to adjust to the notion really. I might have a few grey hairs but I can still only see myself as a fit and healthy teenager. The body seems to move forward while the mind goes on hold – they make strange bed-fellows. But it will be a new chapter. A grandson or grand-daughter (Rachel won't tell us which) – whatever it is – will be born into a new millennium. Exciting – but can you imagine saying you were born at the end of the twentieth century? Our grand-child will be studying our lives as history – a depressing thought.

I've just realised how insensitive I'm being. I'm really sorry you were unable to have children. I don't know how strong your maternal instincts are, but to be honest I was always rather frightened of becoming a father. It's not an easy world any more, and it's very difficult finding a balance between protectiveness and letting your children find their own feet. Perhaps boys aren't so bad. Not politically correct I know, but I think we probably gave Peter a longer leash than Rachel. Peter's been in Australia for nearly five years now and we tend not to worry so much these days. Rachel's quite close to home and I still fuss over her as if she's still at school. Parenting has got a lot going for it – but it's not all good and mostly exhausting!

Can I ask you a small favour, Izzy? I know I haven't really given you much detail of Thomas's visit – it really is very complex. To cut a long story short (to use your own expression!) I've recently given up my post at the *Times* and am just about to start writing a book. I can't go into the reasons for this sudden change, but in many ways it's all wrapped up with Thomas, and even you, Izzy. Without going into detail, this whole business with Thomas has fired my imagination and I'm sure there is a story to be told. What I haven't got access to is the American press. Of course I can have papers sent over and I've still got some contacts in New York. But at the moment I would prefer not to declare my hand and I really need an ear to the ground.

I'm taking the chance that you'll be returning to California quite soon. I think you said that your trips to Hawaii were only short term? If you do go back, could you do something for me? I can't really tell you why at the moment, but I'd like you to scan the press (even some past editions) for *any* reports of meetings between religious leaders of the Christian churches – probably over the past few months. Perhaps you could also see if there's been any hint of their going absent for short periods without explanation – unlikely, but worth a look. I'd be especially interested if there are reports of informal visits to England or Italy.

I realise it's a bit of a shot in the dark, and you probably think I've begun to lose my senses. But if you can help me out, Izzy, I'd be really grateful. I promise to explain the whole thing one day. I'll send you a signed copy of the book!

I'm sending this to Hawaii. I hope it gets there!

With love,

Robert.

PS. Put that cigarette out!

Paine glanced back through his letter. He was tempted to delete his section on children and grand-children, still unsure how Isobel might react. But even after all these years he knew that she was not the motherly type. She had always said that her use of contraception was to avoid children rather than stop her becoming pregnant. In Isobel's mind these were two completely different conditions.

Switching off his light, Paine left his study and crept up to the bedroom. He changed quietly as Alex slept, her usual light and steady breathing the only sound in the darkened room. As he pulled the covers carefully back, his arm brushed against the alarm clock which was always placed on the bedside table. It hit the floor with a dull thud and rattled against the metal frame of the bed.

'Robert?' asked Alex, still half-asleep but disturbed by the noise.

'Go to sleep. It's only me.'

'What time is it?'

'About one-thirty.'

'Did you write to Thomas?' she murmured.

'Got it started,' lied Paine. 'I'll finish it tomorrow.'

10

The temperature of the city was almost unbearable. Despite his many years in Rome, Thomas Costello had never really acclimatised to the searing heat of late summer. He had been raised in the temperate climate of England and his body retained its memory.

Since his hurried return from London, the Vatican had resumed its face of stability. To the outside world the Catholic church had regained its balance, the pope was restored to good health and the world's clergy, beyond Rome, had adjusted to the new papacy. Yet, within the confines of the Vatican and known only to a growing number of senior churchmen, the turmoil continued. Woeters' quiet steps had turned into a sprint for the ecumenical line, creating a growing disquiet amongst those privy to his intentions. So far, these potential objectors had attempted no veto and remained faithful to the pontiff.

But pressure was growing, the chattering *trattorie* of Rome were seething with rumour and clandestine alliances. Giovanni Oliveri had remained Costello's ear to these furtive gatherings and kept him well-informed of possible opposition. The editor of *Osservatore Romano* was incensed by the growing censorship of information and the restriction of his freedoms as a journalist. He remained a good Catholic, realistic about the need to maintain confidentiality in the interests of the church. But he made it quite plain to Costello that he was now receiving pressure from unseen figures in the Curia, determined to block the pope's radicalism. It needed little of Costello's imagination to reveal the source of this coercion.

Cardinal Eugenio Cellini continued to cast his shadow over the papacy, manoeuvring carefully behind the scenes and still nurturing his personal ambitions. He remained the puppeteer, pulling the strings of his supporters and monitoring their responses, yet maintaining a safe distance from the consequences.

Soon after his return from London, Costello had confronted Cellini about the leaks of information to the English press. He knew it was probably a pointless gesture but felt that at last Cellini had exposed himself to justifiable criticism. But, as he suspected, the cardinal dismissed Costello's accusations as fanciful nonsense and made it quite plain that a mere bishop had no right to disparage him in such a manner. Cellini had insisted on a retraction of the claim and Costello was forced to submit, despite his assured knowledge that the cardinal's stamp on the affair was clearly visible.

Costello rose from his desk and pushed the window of his office as far as the hinges would allow. It seemed to make no difference. The air was still and heavy with the midday heat which cast a haze over the distant city. The river was barely visible, and the grassed areas just beyond St Peter's Square were parched and brown. A small number of water sprinklers tried to flick life back into the ground, leaving small circles of green amongst the brittle lawns. Costello mopped his brow as he had done all morning, the beads of sweat returning within an instant, and his handkerchief damp with perspiration.

Robert Paine's recent letter still lay on his desk, a reminder of his visit to Lambeth Palace and his friend's apparent lack of trust. It had been nearly three weeks since Paine had written to lay out his thoughts about Munro's collusion, the defence against Islam and the supposition that Woeters was trying to pull the Christian churches together. It had thrown Costello into a frenzy of doubt and a questioning of his renewed allegiance to Woeters. But what had upset him most of all was Paine's inferred conclusion that Costello was not really declaring his own hand. Robert had accused him of complicity in a friendly and inoffensive manner but it was clear that the allegation was not made lightly.

He had not responded and still felt unsure if there was anything more to say. Paine's notion of the pope and archbishop joining forces to defeat Islam seemed absurd, and yet Costello knew that his friend was unlikely to engage in vacuous thinking. It was also unnerving to hear that the British press was coming under similar pressure to that being exerted on Oliveri. What was certain, however, was that the journalist has misjudged Costello's involvement and knowledge. When he had spoken of the pope's loss of belief in Catholicism, it was an assumption built on no more than the rapid pace of change which had been halted so dramatically by the pope's collapse. He knew no more than he had already revealed.

But Paine's letter had alerted Costello. Over the past few weeks he had had the chance to reassess his own knowledge, and try to determine if he had in fact become blind to the obvious. The early days of Woeters' papacy had been understandably chaotic. The sudden death of the late pope, Costello's involvement in Woeters' election, and the obligation of the the new pope to grant a succession of audiences had perhaps blurred the prefect's senses.

His time had been limited, but in those few spare moments Costello acceded to Paine's request and had begun to scrutinise all of Woeters' appointments over the past few months. Even this morning, battling against the heat, he had spent time examining the dates and minutes of recent meetings, vainly hoping for some pattern to reveal itself and lend weight to Paine's convictions.

A picture had emerged but any conclusions could only have been conjecture. As he would have expected, there was evidence of a succession of church leaders having paid official visits to greet the new pope. Each meeting had been carefully minuted, a transcript kept on record for future reference. Even the requests for private conversations were not an unusual occurrence. There were many instances when the audiences were treated by the various dignitaries as confessional opportunities. On the majority of occasions Costello had been present, often encouraged to join the discussion, and as he sat once more at his desk he found himself embarrassed by some of his own statements.

As almost a second thought, Costello returned to the files and began to note the lengths of the various meetings. It soon became obvious that the pope's conversations with the protestant church leaders and elders of the numerous denominations had been protracted affairs. In itself this was not exceptional, as discussion of doctrinal issues often extended beyond the set limits. But it was the regularity of their extension which captured Costello's interest. Was it likely, as Paine had inferred, that Woeters had used these audiences to promote a church union on a scale never before imagined? Was it possible that he had not been informed of earlier contacts? Just as Westgate had suggested, it would now seem that Munro and Woeters had been communicating long before the trip to England. There was now little reason to dismiss the idea that other contacts had already been made.

The expected call to the pope's apartment came soon after matins. Costello gathered his papers together, welcoming the chance to leave his own office and enjoy the coolness of Woeters' air-conditioned chambers. He entered quickly and without hesitation.

'You are well, Holy Father?'

Costello had developed a pattern of address which satisfied Woeters and himself. There was an agreed formality in his arrival and departure, the use of first names reserved for their discussions.

'Extremely well, Prefect. My head is quite clear and I thank God for each day.'

'Indeed,' smiled Costello.

'You look hot, Thomas,' observed Woeters, watching Costello mop his brow yet again.

'I haven't the privilege of air-conditioning, Johannes,' laughed Costello.

'The trappings of office,' responded Woeters kindly. 'Do we have a lot to cover?'

'Not really, Johannes. Mass at three and dinner with the French ambassador at eight. Unless there is some unexpected crisis, your time is your own.'

'Then we must use it wisely, Thomas.'

'You have something in mind?'

'I have, Thomas. And I shall need your help.'

'In what way?'

'Organisation, Thomas. I intend to call a Third Vatican Council.' Woeters watched Costello carefully as he voiced his intentions. 'You are surprised?'

But Costello had not reacted as Woeters might have expected. Instead his expression showed no more than relief, as if some huge burden had been lifted from his shoulders.

'You have no option,' responded Costello finally.

'Meaning?'

'May I be frank, Holy Father?'

Costello's return to a formal address signalled his intent.

'Of course. You must speak openly.'

The prefect shuffled in his seat, preparing himself for the truth he was about to deliver. He looked directly at Woeters trying to assess the pope's readiness and the reality of his request for candour. He chose his words carefully.

'You are moving very quickly, Johannes,' said Costello, attempting to prompt a response.

'Go on, Thomas. You have my trust.'

'Vatican III seems your only option. You may or may not know, but Rome is almost bursting with rumour and I fear there are men who would gladly see you brought down.'

'I am sure!'

'They must be confronted, and in open debate. My own sources suggest that some of the gossip is almost hysterical. They seem to have you marked as a man intent on destroying Catholicism.'

'And their reasons?'

'As I say, Johannes, it's really the pace of change. Your

pronouncements on fallibility, women priests, changes in the Eucharist, the dissemination of power from Rome – I could go on, the list seems inexhaustible. They feel that even the seven sacraments are under threat.'

'But I have, as yet, made no official statements.'

'There lies the root of the problem, Holy Father. Your congregation is beginning to guess what is in your mind and they are drawing their own conclusions. Speculation is a powerful weapon.'

Costello paused to let Woeters absorb his accusation.

'You have great insight, Thomas. And you read my mind perfectly,' answered Woeters. 'It's time to clear the air.'

'And Vatican III will serve that purpose?'

'That is my hope. You must understand, Thomas, that I have no wish to impose my ideas on the church. The Holy Spirit remains the final arbiter, but I do have a duty to lead and advise. The Petrine ministry is one of service not of dictatorship. As St Irenaeus said: "I am called only to preside over the assembly of charity, not to demand its application."'

'And you can carry your cardinals?' asked Costello, relieved at Woeters' humility.

'With the help of God's other servants.'

'Your meetings?'

'You are aware of my discussions?'

'I am, though I can only guess at their content.'

Woeters rose from his chair and began to pace the room, his hands pressed together beneath his lips. Costello watched as the pope's fingers silently tapped out his thoughts. He turned back to his prefect.

'I under-estimated you, Thomas,' said Woeters in a resigned manner. 'Are the SPCU aware of this?'

'Not as far as I know,' answered Costello, surprised by the question.

The Society for Promoting Christian Unity had grown in strength during the papacy of Pope John XXIII, successfully reducing the power of the counter-reformation movement in the Vatican. But under successive popes of the late twentieth century their influence had been diminished by the growing conservatism encouraged by John Paul II. They had been forced towards a concentration on matters of established doctrine within the battlements of Catholicism, their rôle as unifiers of Christianity no more than tokenism.

'I must renew their spirit,' said Woeters. 'I have much to tell them. And to tell you, Thomas.'

Costello sensed the gradual loss of his own inhibitions. He wanted desperately to unburden his soul and tell Woeters of his part in his election, his correspondence with Paine and his temporary loss of faith in the pontiff's motives. The pope was seemingly on the point finally of explaining his actions and taking the prefect into his confidence. Thomas Costello felt wracked with guilt and overcome by a sense of betrayal. He knew he could no longer indulge in deception.

'May I ask you a question, Johannes,' said Costello, his voice hesitant with apprehension.

'Please,' answered Woeters, with a small wave of the hand.

'Has this anything to do with Islam?'

'With Islam?'

Costello once again watched Woeters' response with great care. He noticed a slight widening of the pope's eyes, a hint of reluctance in his response.

'Am I correct in thinking that your desire for unification is motivated by the growth of Islam?'

Woeters remained noncommittal.

'An interesting notion,' he smiled. 'What led you to such a thought?'

It was the opportunity he had craved. In the space of the next ten minutes, Costello tried to explain all that had happened over the past few months. Woeters remained silent apart from the occasional reassurance or request for explanation. Within minutes, Costello's stumbling admissions had become a torrent of confession and self-condemnation. His exposure to sanction increased by the second, and Woeters' expression gave no clue as to his possible reaction.

'You are a loyal servant, Thomas. You must not be concerned,' said Woeters kindly, as Costello became silent.

'You are not offended?'

'Not at all, Thomas. We all need people to confide in. There is God's will in your actions.'

'I pray there is.'

'And Robert Paine, Isobel Griffin. They are good people?'

'I trust them implicitly, Johannes. Why I wrote to them in the first place remains a mystery. I felt driven to it.'

'You said you dreamt of them?'

'I did. But we dream of many things. It shouldn't have led to betrayal.'

'You are too hard on yourself, Thomas. There is God's purpose in all this, I am sure.'

For a few moments the two men sat quietly, any earlier tension now diffused by Costello's revelations. There was no sign that the pope intended to end their meeting and it was obvious that he wished to seize this moment of affinity.

'You see Islam as a threat, Thomas?' asked Woeters, raising himself higher in his seat.

'In some respects I suppose I do.'

'Are they not God's children? Just as we are?'

'Of course.'

'But you still think your journalist friend has a point?'

'I think he may be confusing the realm of religion with the immorality of politics.'

'It is part of my task to maintain that distinction. Do you agree, Thomas?'

'Of course, Johannes. Faith is born in heaven, politics is man's construction. But we can't divorce ourselves from our own creations. I hope God resides in all our institutions.'

'His hand is there, Thomas.'

'But you have no fear of Islam?'

'It is not my path, Thomas. But I must respect the path of others.'

'And your drive towards unity? If it is not motivated by building defences against Islam, why are you pressing ahead with such urgency.'

'In preparation, Thomas, and as a defence against ourselves.'

'Forgive me. I don't follow. In preparation?'

'It was an ill-chosen word. What is important is that we break down the barriers between all the Christian churches and present a united front. Free of dogma, free of our history and free of self-interest. It is vital that we reduce and reform our faith to the simplicity of glorifying God and following his commandments. We cannot afford disunity in such a purpose.'

'And you have made this known to other church leaders?'

'I have their full and unconditional support.'

Costello was fighting to retain his objectivity. Their conversation had proceeded as a rapid exchange, leaving little room for pause and deliberation. But the idea that the reformed churches could suddenly agree this compromise was difficult to absorb.

'Forgive me, Johannes, but that isn't possible! You can't have dismissed centuries of conflict in a matter of months.'

'It is not only me, Thomas. We came together, already in agreement. Our only problem is the declaration of our intent.'

'Vatican III?'

'Precisely.'

'They will attend? It's unprecedented!'

'So was the birth of Christ,' said Woeters, a gentle smile crossing his lips and diffusing the growing tension.

'I take your point,' answered Costello, slightly surprised by the pope's flippancy. 'But isn't that a problem in itself? Belief in immaculate conception, the Blessed Virgin Mary herself, surely they are all major stumbling blocks to unity?'

'It is an act of faith, Thomas, as well as a matter of faith. Think back to the Lutherans. Why did they come into existence? It was really no more than a protest. The very word "protestant", as you are well aware, has its roots in the rejection of the abuses and immoderation of mediaeval papacy. Remove that intemperance and how do the Lutheran denominations define themselves? The Reformation was not a creation of a separate church which claimed its own truth but simply a reform of an existing truth. The barriers between us are really not insurmountable. Like the ancient myths, they have assumed a truth which never existed. They are no more than the author's creation. They can be unwritten. Trust me, Thomas, they will be unwritten.'

Costello listened carefully to Woeters' delivery. He had spoken with great certainty, as if a conclusion had already been reached, and as if dismissive of opposition. It was plain that Woeters, despite his recent illness, had accelerated his reforms at a greater speed than Costello could have imagined. What remained unexplained was why there was such a coincidence of unity amongst the protestant denominations, even amongst members of the eastern orthodox church who had remained vehement in opposition to papal supremacy. Questions flooded into Costello's head but Woeters' movements suggested that their meeting was drawing to a close. Costello chose his final question with care.

'And your own position, Holy Father? Will you continue to be the focal point of the Christian church?'

Woeters smiled once more, the delay in his response suggesting that Costello had touched on the heart of the issue.

'Again, Thomas, I must ask you to have faith in my actions. I can only say that the papacy has little importance. I can say no more than that. You have my word that in time it will all become clear. But we have not reached that moment.'

'I see,' stuttered Costello, almost incapable of response.

Woeters could see that Costello was shaken by his answer and reached over to take the prefect's hands in his own.

'Have faith, Thomas. We are doing God's work. I must rest now.'

'Of course.'

Woeters rose from his chair, still holding Costello's hands.

'You will accompany me to mass? I would like you to be with me this afternoon.'

'I would be honoured, Johannes.'

'Come to my rooms at two-thirty. We will process together.'

Thomas Costello stepped out into the Vatican corridors, immediately confronted by the stifling heat of the August afternoon. There was a little time before mass and he returned quickly to his office. Having checked through his papers and dealt with a series of minor memoranda, the prefect headed once more into the sultry corridors, in search of the reviving sunlight of the Vatican gardens.

Unlike his daily walk across the river, Costello now stepped slowly, breathing deeply to control his racing mind. The avenues of manicured box hedges provided welcome shade, the small fountains which dotted the gardens giving an illusion of cooler spring days. Flanked by the ancient walls of the old Leonine city, Costello reflected that little had changed in the last 400 years. The gardens, like the Tiber, had witnessed the lives and deaths of successive popes and the birth of the Reformation. As he strolled through the labyrinth of flower-bordered pathways, Costello wondered what new episode of history was about to be enacted. There seemed no doubt that if Woeters' ambitions were realised, then the time-worn city walls and gnarled trees would be present at the conception of a new epoch in Catholic faith.

But what else might they witness? Costello still struggled with his seed of doubt. What pieces were still missing from the pontiff's jigsaw? He had admitted to his meetings and discussions with the protestant denominations, his plans for unity and his intentions to convene Vatican III, but had stopped short of a complete exposition. There was more. Costello knew there had to be more.

He sat for a few minutes on one of the small wooden benches, struggling yet again to piece together the obscure puzzle. Shaded by a large olive tree, its trunk twisted and bent with age, Costello continued to mull over his conversation with Woeters, searching for revelation. It was noticeably quiet, only the distant hum of city traffic disturbing his thoughts. Even the birds which usually dived and swooped over the garden had taken to the shade, preserving energy for their evening song.

Costello heard the voices from a distance, their words indistinct but noticeably impassioned. He strained to catch their meaning but the hedgerows and trees, heavy with summer leaf, dulled the clarity of his hearing. He listened hard as the voices approached, still unable to make any sense of their excitable chatter. Looking to his left a small cluster of figures emerged into the sunlight, their faces masked by the glaring sun.

'Prefect,' came a voice from the centre of the group. 'You are well, I hope.'

Costello blinked towards the sound of the greeting, searching for recognition. As his eyes adjusted to the strong light the figure came closer.

Cardinal Eugenio Cellini stood before him, still exuding the false piety which Costello had always found so repellent.

'I am well, thank you,' responded Costello, offering no continuation to their conversation.

'The Holy Father has unleashed you?' asked Cellini contemptuously.

Costello only smiled briefly in response and glanced round at the small côterie of priests. They had broken into sycophantic laughter, a sign of their approval of Cellini's sardonic comment.

'You are extremely busy, I hear,' continued the Cardinal.

'There's always much to do,' answered Costello, volunteering no detail of his work.

'So I understand,' said Cellini pointedly. He turned without further comment, his followers still amused by the short encounter and babbling like adolescent schoolchildren.

There had always been a degree of tension between the two churchmen but even this short conversation suggested it had reached new proportions. Cellini's mockery had brimmed with resentment, his look displaying a flowering of his hatred for Costello. In those few moments it became plain that the cardinal knew of Costello's involvement in Woeters' election and perhaps the extent of the pope's ecumenical designs. Cellini had many powerful contacts, especially in the ultra-conservative Curia, which derided any notion of unification. The cardinal was still mustering his forces and Costello now realised the urgency of arranging Vatican III at the earliest opportunity. Cellini remained a tangible threat to the pope's design.

It was almost two o'clock by the time he re-entered the Vatican buildings and hurried up to his own small apartment. Showering quickly, Costello changed into his vestments and arrived at Woeters' rooms in good time. Though he had accompanied the pope to mass on many occasions, the renewed openness and friendship between the two men gave this particular occasion an added importance. Since his appointment to the prefecture he had sensed an inner disquiet, generated by his doubts of Woeters' motives. Now, although still perplexed, he felt a new understanding had developed, a restored sense of purpose.

'The Lord be with you,' said Woeters in a whisper as they waited to enter the basilica. He touched his prefect gently on the arm with no more than a brush of his fingertips.

'And with you, Holy Father,' answered Costello, flattered by this moment of friendship and intimacy.

He watched as the door swung open into the transept, the choir's voices relieving the anticipation of the gathered congregation and heralding the pope's entrance. The sound of the canticle resonated in the silence, the purity of their song thrown high into the domed roof.

As the procession passed through the sacristy towards the central aisle, Costello was aware of the ripple of the congregation, rising and falling in a moving swell of genuflection. Woeters returned their show of respect, casting an affectionate smile of acknowledgement from one side of the aisle to the other.

The high altar lay before them, its ornate and twisted

columns supporting the elaborate canopy, guarded at each corner by Michelangelo's bronzed angels. The smell of incense filled the air, the odour of spirituality spreading out from the cortège and demanding veneration.

Costello had ascended the steps of the high altar many times, yet his response never altered. Looking down the basilica, towards the distant portico, he had to steel himself on every occasion, fighting his own sensations. The grandeur of the building seemed to touch his soul, its walls exuding God's power and compassion. He knew the danger of such emotions which could cloud his intellect and logic, and yet he revelled in man's ingenuity in constructing an edifice of such beauty.

Woeters took his seat before the linen-covered altar, the six white candles flickering their light onto the starched cloth. As the pope began the liturgy, Costello listened to the congregation's automated responses, their heads bowed in prayer, dulling their voices into incoherence.

'*Misereatur tui omnipotens Deus, et dismissis peccatis tuis, perducat te ad vitam aeternam,*' continued Woeters.

Costello looked again as the people's 'amens' flooded the basilica. He prayed silently for their sincerity and asked for his own forgiveness.

Unusually, Woeters had elected to act as celebrant for the *Missa Solemnis.* On many previous occasions, he had given the much-sought-after duties of the high mass to a selected member of his household, whilst his own participation was limited to the blessing. But today, and with Costello's help, he had decided to lead the service alone. It had become Woeters' habit to celebrate mass with much greater frequency than his predecessors and on each occasion Costello had noticed a perceptible change in the congregation's reaction. The silence during the consecration was always present but when Woeters acted as celebrant there seemed to be an added element. It was difficult for Costello to discern the contrast, to isolate any added distinction, but what was always conspicuous was the air of calm and a stillness which seemed to infect the worshippers, as if transfixed by the Holy Father's presence.

As the consecration of the blessed sacraments came to a close, Woeters turned and faced into the basilica. Holding the Host high above his head, he offered his final prayer.

'"Behold the Lamb of God, behold Him who takes away the sins of the world."'

His voice was strong, its power and certainty carrying deep into the heart of the basilica. Costello moved forward to usher the the priests and acolytes towards the Holy Father. They knelt in line, striking their chests rhythmically and declaring their unworthiness. Costello walked with him, offering the paten as Woeters distributed the holy communion to the kneeling communicants.

'The body of Christ,' he said softly as each hand stretched out before him.

'Amen,' came the responses, their heads bowing lower as they took the Host.

As Woeters came to the third priest, Costello was surprised to see the pontiff reach out and touch the praying figure gently on the arm. It was the same gesture he had made as they had waited to enter the basilica.

'The body of Christ,' he said once more.

'Amen,' answered the priest, his head rising slightly. 'May the Blessed Virgin Mary forgive me,' he added.

There were only two shots, each one echoing its delivery along the length of the basilica. Costello had no time to respond, and yet every detail was to be etched on his memory. The movement of the hand inside the vestment, the priest's eyes filled with tears and uncertainty, the tremor of his body as he pulled the trigger, the gun no more than inches from the Holy Father's chest. Before anyone had the chance to react, the trembling priest placed the gun in his mouth and pulled the trigger once more, his body thrown violently backwards by the splintering bullet.

Costello remained still, his own body paralysed by the moment. He was aware of figures running forward, cries and screams filling the basilica which only seconds before had been silent in prayer. Looking down towards the fallen priest, he searched the man's bloodied face for recognition and reason, fearful to turn and see the results of his actions. In his heart he knew Woeters must be dead, but as hard as he tried he could make no movement to confirm his fears.

A hand took his arm, its touch demanding a response. His knees crumpled beneath him and as he slumped to the floor he finally turned to face the blood-spattered altar. Woeters lay silent, his face peaceful but drained of any colour, his white robes stained red, the bright crimson ring spreading slowly across his chest. Costello reached out, his fingers seizing the pope's hand in his own. It gave no response, the coldness of the skin delivering its morbid confirmation. The high altar was now in a state of bedlam, people shouting instructions, forcing back the voyeurs who had laid siege to the altar steps. Costello remained on the floor, his hand still grasping the stricken pope. He began to cry, at first silently, his tears dropping to the crimson carpet and lost in its deep colour. But he could contain himself no longer and his body shook uncontrollably, responding instinctively to the events he had witnessed. The quiet weeping became the violent sobbing of a frightened child, uninhibited by any consequence and consumed with a terror of the unknown. His hand remained firm, clasped tightly to its only certainty.

11

Bishop Thomas Costello fought to make sense of his situation. Forcing his eyes open and glancing to his left, a small clock on the wall told him it was 7.30. The room was still lit by sunlight but gave him no clue as to the real time of day. He felt thirsty, his mouth dry with sleep, and his limbs ached as if his body had been beaten by some unseen assailant. His eyes closed once more and he rocked his head from side to side, desperate to regain consciousness, yet caught in his own exhaustion.

'Thomas?' came a voice from his right.

Costello felt his hand being gripped, gently but with enough pressure to persuade him into recognition. The unseen fingers stroked the back of his hand as he showed signs of waking.

'Johannes?' replied Costello in a whisper.

The voice at his side did not respond but simply squeezed his outstretched hand more tightly.

'Johannes?' pleaded Costello with greater urgency.

His mind was a confusion of senseless images, each fleeting picture eluding his grasp and frustrating his attempt to hold on to reality. Gradually the face of Johannes Woeters began to dominate his thoughts and he gripped the unseen hand with all the force he could muster.

'Johannes!'

He could feel his body shaking and his quiet whisper had become a tortured cry.

'Thomas. Thomas. Try to be calm. It's Ciro. Your friend, Ciro.'

The aging priest looked in pity on the prefect's anguished face, his soothing voice filled with a natural compassion.

'You're in hospital, Thomas.'

‘In hospital?’ answered Costello, his eyes opening once more.

‘They had to sedate you. You were not at all well. Do you remember what happened?’

Fr Ciro Ferrara was now standing, and bent over to comfort his trembling friend.

‘Is there water?’ asked Costello, raising himself slowly on to his elbow.

Ferrara poured the drink quickly and as Costello sipped the iced liquid his expression signalled his confrontation with the truth. A single tear ran down his face and remained trapped in the bristle of his chin.

‘The Holy Father?’ he asked with a look of resignation.

‘He is dead, Thomas. I am sorry. May God rest his soul and grant him eternal peace.’

‘God puts us to the test, Ciro,’ cried Costello, his eyes now filling with tears.

‘We can only have faith,’ answered Ferrara, smiling gently and brushing the prefect’s ruffled hair with his long and wrinkled fingers.

Costello closed his eyes once more and prayed silently, still unable to staunch the tears which came yet again. He tried to recall the events in the basilica, which by now were beginning to flood back into his memory. But there was no order to his recollection, only a series of disconnected sounds and images, each detail compounding his growing depression and sense of guilt.

Ferrara remained silent, giving his friend the time to come to terms with the awful realities. Costello suddenly turned to face him, his eyes widened by his realisation.

‘He knew, Ciro. The Holy Father knew.’

‘What do you mean, Thomas?’

‘He knew what the priest was about to do. It was like the recognition of Judas. I’m certain of it.’

Costello thought back to the moments before the shooting and Woeters’ touching of the assassin’s arm as he offered the Host. He related his story to the old priest, searching for detail as he spoke. Ferrara took his hand once more.

'Are you sure, Thomas? It could be no more than coincidence. The Holy Father would have moved away. He would have done something to prevent his own death, surely?'

'I don't know, Ciro. I just don't know.'

'You make it sound as though he entered the basilica intent on martyrdom. It hardly seems credible.'

'I know. It's nonsensical. But I swear, Ciro, he knew. The Holy Father knew he was about to die.'

'You'll raise it at the enquiry?'

'Not without evidence, Ciro. If the priest had survived, perhaps. But not now. Has he been identified?'

'He has. Alberto Gasparri. A minor figure in the CDF.'

'A doctrinalist?'

'A fervent traditionalist as far as I know. But from my limited enquiries no hint that he was mentally unbalanced. I hate to think what's going to come out.'

'You'll make your own investigation?'

'I will, Thomas. I shall do my usual rounds of the dark corners of Rome.'

The door of Costello's room opened. A young nurse, perhaps no older than 25, approached the prefect's bed.

'You are awake, Bishop. How are you feeling?'

'A little hazy, that is all.'

'Be patient. You must get as much rest as possible,' she answered, her confidence belying her age. 'You've been in deep shock. Your body needs time to recover.'

'Is it evening?' asked Costello.

'No, it's morning,' smiled the young nurse. 'You slept for nearly fourteen hours.'

'You have been here all night, Ciro?'

'I thought you might need someone.'

'You're truly a good friend. But you must be exhausted. I'm so sorry, I didn't realise.'

'I'll sleep now and come back this evening. God bless you, Thomas. We'll talk later. You must rest.'

'And you, Ciro. You too. We will both need our strength.'

Fr Ferrara shuffled from the room, his bent figure revealing the tiredness he had tried so hard to conceal.

Costello dozed in and out of sleep, occasionally waking in a lather of sweat as specific memories of Woeters' assassination sprung into consciousness. He was consumed with guilt, reliving his own impotence as the priest had drawn the gun from his vestments and pointed the barrel towards the Holy Father's chest.

Determined to reconstruct the scene, he replayed the moment of the shooting, the two deafening shots and the taut expression of the killer. There was something familiar about his face. The Vatican was such an unwieldy bureaucracy that its members could remain strangers to one another, even those who had served their office for many years. And yet Costello was sure he had seen that face recently, perhaps even engaged him in conversation. But hard as he tried he was unable to place him and gradually he lost his battle against the sedating drugs. He slipped back into a deep but fitful sleep.

'Bishop Costello?' The nurse tapped her fingers lightly on his shoulder. 'You have a visitor. I've said only ten minutes.'

Costello woke quickly, his head now much clearer than during his conversation with Ferrara.

'I'll bring you some breakfast in a while. You should try and eat if you can.'

'Of course. You're very kind.'

Giovanni Oliveri's figure stood framed by the doorway. He walked quickly across to the bed and shook Costello's hand, the smell of stale tobacco filling the sterile room.

'It's a bad business, Thomas. How are you?' greeted Oliveri.

'Better, Giovanni. Better. You haven't given up the cigarettes, I see.'

'I'm sorry, Thomas. I haven't. One day I will.' Oliveri laughed, like a schoolboy who had just been discovered by a senior schoolmaster, his usually deep chortle turned to a childlike giggle by his embarrassment.

'What is it, Thomas?' asked Oliveri. Costello's expression

had suddenly taken on a new intensity and he stared hard at his companion.

'I know where we met.'

'Met whom?'

'Alberto Gasparri.'

'The pope's killer? You knew him?'

'Not really, Giovanni, but our paths crossed only yesterday. Your laughter reminded me.'

'You talked to him?'

'It was hardly a conversation. He was with a group of other priests, hanging onto the coat-tails of a mutual friend.'

'Who, for God's sake?'

'Cellini.'

'Do you mind if I smoke?' asked Oliveri.

'I don't. But you'd better not.'

Oliveri pulled a chair to the side of Costello's bed and blew out a long breath.

'Are you sure, Thomas?'

'Positive.'

'God! Forgive the cliché, but this could blow the dome off St Peter's. You realise the implications, I suppose?'

'I'm aware that it could implicate Cellini, though it would be difficult to prove.'

'I'm not sure you are fully aware, Thomas. There's been a lot happening whilst you've been laid up in here. I know it's only been a day but the wheels are already in motion. You could be talking about implicating the next pope in Woeters' assassination.'

'Cellini! You're not serious, Giovanni.'

'I have never been more serious, Thomas. He's wandering the corridors of the Vatican at this very moment, steeped in mourning and his usual false saintliness. But his strength grows by the second and he's gathering support from many quarters.'

'We must stop him. It's unthinkable.'

'A murderer on the papal throne? He wouldn't be the first. And what can you do?'

'Expose him. Something. Anything,' pleaded Costello.

'Guilty because he was seen in the company of Gasparri? It'll never stick. You might as well accuse St Peter of being in the company of Judas. It didn't make him an accessory.'

'Not the best analogy, Giovanni, and there's many a theologian who wouldn't share your opinion. But I take your point.' Costello raised himself, threw the covers off his bed and swung his legs over the edge. 'Are my things there, Giovanni? I must get back to my office.'

'Your papers are here,' answered Oliveri, reaching for a small, plastic folder which lay in the open top of the bedside cabinet, 'but I'm told they've taken your clothes for forensic examination. You won't remember but they were in a bit of a mess to say the least. You'll see the pictures on the front cover of this morning's *Osservatore*.'

'Can you bring me some clothes, Giovanni? Anything will do. You're about my size.'

'Of course. But is this wise? You're still trembling like a leaf.'

'It's no time for wisdom, Giovanni. I failed to act when Johannes was shot. I will never forgive myself. I at least owe him an attempt to stop Cellini. He'll undo every reform the Holy Father set in place.'

Oliveri returned to the hospital within half an hour, only to be confronted by the nurse and a senior doctor. By some means they had anticipated Costello's intentions and attempted to dissuade him from his rash behaviour. But it was a pointless request, the prefect waving away their advice with uncharacteristic bluntness. His head spun with confusion and his legs, weakened by the sedation, could hardly take his weight as he stepped into Oliveri's clothes. Within minutes he was stumbling towards the hospital's exit and out into the bright sunshine.

Despite Oliveri's attendance, Costello demanded to walk unsupported and he staggered towards the Vatican offices oblivious of the growing crowds and speeding traffic. On more than one occasion Oliveri was forced to pull him back from the kerb as Costello ignored his friend's warnings. He was a man driven by fear and remorse, with little interest in his own safety.

Oliveri saw him to the main entrance, keen to get back to his own office and monitor the day's developments.

'You'll call me?' asked Giovanni as the two men parted.

'Of course. Of course. I won't forget your kindness, Giovanni.'

'No payment necessary, Thomas,' smiled Oliveri. 'Just keep me informed. That's all I ask.'

'I suspect we shall need one another. God be with you, Giovanni. You have been a true friend.' Costello turned quickly and disappeared into the labyrinth of the Vatican.

He almost ran through the corridors, slowed only by the numerous guards who now checked every exit and entrance. Once in his own rooms, Costello showered quickly, changed into his own clothes and tried to plan his strategy. If Giovanni was correct, Cellini's progress needed to be stopped in its tracks. There was no time for deliberation. He picked up the phone.

The internal switchboard operator answered immediately.

'Prefect Costello here. Can you tell me who is handling the enquiry?' There was no reason to offer further detail.

'It has gone to the Curia. They've appointed an emergency committee.'

'And the police enquiry?'

'Commander Franco Atzori. He's set up an incident room in the Vatican.'

'You can put me through?'

'Hold the line, please. He has a direct number.'

There was only a moment's pause before the call was answered.

'Atzori,' came the reply.

'Commander. This is Bishop Costello. Prefect to the late pope.'

'Yes?'

'I would like to talk, if that's possible.'

'You have some information?'

'It may be nothing.'

'Let me decide that, Bishop,' replied Atzori curtly.

'Quite. Can we meet? Perhaps my office, in about half an hour?'

'I'll be there.'

Costello was shocked by Atzori's brusque response. It was as if the Vatican city had been invaded by the irreligious, bringing with it the inhumanity of an ungodly world. The commander was obviously not a man of sentiment and seemed to have little respect for status or position. Yet he would serve Costello's purpose.

Tidying his desk for Atzori's arrival, Costello realised that if Cellini were to succeed in his ambitions, then his own position would be short-lived. It was unlikely that such a sworn enemy would tolerate his continuation as prefect, or even a minor role in the papal household. He no longer harboured personal ambition but did fear a detachment from the city which had become a defining part of his life. Over the years he had begun to feel like a native Roman, a man accepted by the ancient culture and comfortable within its walls.

Propelled by his inner fears, Costello left his room and walked the short distance toward the papal quarters, intent on having perhaps his last view of their interior and to feel Woeters' presence.

An armed police officer sat by the door. Alerted by Costello's approach he stood erect, his thumbs resting on his belt to confirm his authority.

'Yes?' he enquired sharply.

'Prefect Costello. I wish to enter the Holy Father's chambers.'

'Pass?'

Costello reached inside his jacket, fumbling for his identity card which he always carried.

'We've been expecting you,' said the officer, scanning the card carefully.

'You have?'

'You're on the official list.'

'I can go in?'

'I'll have to accompany you. Commander's orders.'

They entered together, the room darkened by the drawn curtains. Costello turned on the lights and glanced around the room. He remembered meeting Woeters only 24 hours before, the room exactly as they had left it, the same papers scattered across the desk, an unfinished cup of tea still sitting on the small table by the cold fireplace. A small shudder drew him back.

'I may look at his papers?'

'As long as nothing is taken.'

'Of course.'

Costello walked over to the large oak desk. He had no idea what he was searching for but felt he needed some form of contact with their friendship. Woeters' fountain pen lay on the leather surface, the ink on the nib now dried by its time open to the moistureless air. He held it momentarily in his fingers, trying to gain a sense of the owner's touch.

The policeman wandered through the apartment, his inquisitiveness overcoming his duty, keen to make a personal connection with authority and history. It would be a moment to relate to his grand-children, a chance to gain status amongst his friends and family.

Costello began to sift through the mound of papers which lay in orderly piles, marked with Woeters' pencilled comments. Reaching down to the side of the desk, the prefect rummaged carefully amongst the contents, his hands working quickly through the collection of pens, photographs and prayer books. The white envelope stuck out clearly from the brown, leather-bound book which lay in the bottom drawer. Without lifting the volume on to the desk, Costello slid the edge of the paper quietly from between its sleeves. His own name was printed clearly on its front, the letters printed boldly in thick black ink.

Looking quickly upwards from his crouched position he could see the policeman, still distracted by his chance to pry into the pope's private world. He slipped the envelope into the inner pocket of his jacket and raised the book onto the desk-top. The officer turned as he heard Costello's movements.

'Finished?' he enquired, now tiring of his own investigations.

'Two minutes,' answered Costello.

Hurriedly, he opened the book which had contained his letter and began to flick through the pages of handwritten script. Strangely they were written in English, as if the pope had somehow known that Costello would be the first to be privy to his account of papal history. His eyes searched rapidly for the slightest clue to Woeters' thinking. The diary was detailed in every respect, a meticulous recording of his daily activities. Even in such a short time Costello could see that here was a treasure trove of information. Days, dates, times, and the pope's own reflections scribbled hurriedly along the edges of the page.

Aware of the policeman's impatience, he turned the pages rapidly, searching for the section which covered more recent events. He scanned the neat and assured writing, stopping briefly to take in the detail.

'I'll have to close up now,' interrupted the policeman.

'One more minute,' pleaded Costello, his eyes now hypnotised by the diary's revelations.

He read even more rapidly, each page's disclosure sending him into a frenzy of amazement. The diary was supplying him with the answer to Woeters' evasive and cryptic responses, the true motives for all his actions. He was determined not to miss what may be his only chance, but the young officer was becoming more and more assertive.

'I must insist, Prefect. The commander will lynch me if you stay any longer.'

Costello began to close the book, his hands now shaking and damp with perspiration. The diary slipped from his hand and fell back on to the desk, its pages falling open to Woeters' final entry. It contained only four letters, written forcefully and underlined heavily by the writer's pen. He had never seen the word before. He was unsure if it was a word at all. But there was no doubting its recognition.

Closing the diary once more Costello submitted to the policeman's demands and hurried out of the room aware that he had only a few minutes before his meeting with Atzori. Prior to his entry into Woeters' apartments he had been prepared to give the police commander any information he requested, driven by his desire to hamper Cellini's ambitions. Now he felt rocked by a new uncertainty and an awareness that he must read Woeters' letter before he met Atzori.

Glancing at his watch, Costello knew he had fewer than five minutes. He entered his office, his hands ripping open the envelope as he walked quickly towards his desk and pulled out the single piece of cream-coloured writing paper. Costello checked his watch once more. If Atzori was punctual, which he suspected was likely from such a man, he now had fewer than three minutes. Costello began to read rapidly, struggling to control his own confusion.

My dear Thomas,

You will see there is no date on my letter. Let us just say that it was written some time ago. What is certain is that you will read my words only when I am in God's embrace, sent into his protection by mortal hands.

I ask you to lay no blame, Thomas, and simply entreat you to grant me your prayers. I ask no more than that, though I should perhaps beg for your forgiveness. I am aware that you were, at times, mystified by my actions and that my purpose was not always clear. Indeed I saw your trust falter yet never truly weaken. You remained a true friend, Thomas, and may God bless you for your constancy.

You will have many unanswered questions. Trust in your faith, Thomas. It is not in my power to reveal God's purpose. He blessed me for a short time as His messenger, a brief link to His design, but not as the proclaimer of His truth. This responsibility lies with other men, and women too. Who they will be, I cannot tell you. You may be among them, you may not, I cannot say. But your faith will be tested and you must stand firm, Thomas.

You have perhaps seen my diaries by now. They will answer many of your questions, though not all. I suspect their contents will make little sense to the layman reader and will only confirm their view of me as an adherent to the ecumenical cause. You will see more, Thomas, and at this point I can only leave you to your own conclusions. I gain no pleasure from presenting you with such an enigma but assure you that I too am uncertain of the resolution and can again only beg your trust.

I leave you with only one request. It seems certain that Cardinal Cellini will follow me into the Holy Office. Support him, Thomas. Give him the love and devotion you kindly gave to me. It will be hard I know, perhaps challenging your very instincts and beliefs. But support him, Thomas, he will need your service.

May God protect and keep you, Thomas. You have been a loyal companion and a true servant of your church. Pray for me, as I pray for you.

Your pope and friend,
Johannes.

Costello sobbed quietly, his tears dripping on to Woeters' letter, dissolving his ink-penned words. The prefect, now bewildered by the cryptic nature of the pope's final message, fought to make sense of its contents. He had told him everything and yet told him nothing. The diary revealed the extent of Woeters' intended revolution in the Catholic church and far more than Costello could have ever imagined. Yet there was no reference to the closing entry in the diary, the unfamiliar string of letters which contained no apparent meaning. He felt certain that without an explanation of this word, the mystery would remain unsolved.

But the letter did at least confirm Costello's suspicions. Woeters had known that he was about to die, and he thought yet again of the pope's hand reaching out to touch the shoulder of Alberto Gasparri, the henchman of Cardinal Cellini. Costello wrestled to make sense of Woeters' demands. Why had he instructed his prefect to give allegiance to a man who was so obviously implicated in his murder? There seemed no logic in his request.

'Prefect Costello?'

There had been no knock at the door, no time for Costello to collect his thoughts and hide his emotions.

'Commander Atzori?' responded Costello.

'Yes.'

'Please sit down.'

Franco Atzori hardly waited for the prefect's reply before he pulled a chair close to the desk, throwing his notebook onto its surface with little care for its scattering of Costello's papers.

'You look upset, Prefect. Bad news?' asked Atzori, pointing at the letter which Costello still held between his fingers.

'A private matter. A friend in despair,' lied Costello, taken aback by the commander's immediate questioning.

'You've something to tell me?'

Costello hesitated. It had seemed so easy only a short time ago, the chance to blacken Cellini's name, even to incriminate him in the pope's killing. But it was no longer an option and Woeters' plea for his support of Cellini still rang in his ears.

'Have you or haven't you?' demanded Atzori impatiently. 'I'm a busy man.'

Costello straightened himself in his chair, offended by the policeman's lack of civility. He looked across at his adversary, a rather stunted and stocky figure, shabbily dressed in an ill-fitting dark blue suit, his thick head of black hair and large moustache adding to his air of aggression. Atzori lacked the finesse of a Roman, and Costello guessed he was probably of Sicilian stock, a man who had grown up fighting for his own survival. Now, finally regaining his control, Costello responded with a greater certainty.

'I think it's probably a minor matter.'

'It sounded more than that on the phone.'
'Perhaps. But I've had more time to consider.'
'Consider?'
'My meeting with Gasparri.'
'When was this?'
'Yesterday. In the Vatican gardens.'
'You spoke?'
'We acknowledged one another. No more than that.'
'Who was he with?'

The questions were coming quickly now and Costello could sense Atzori watching his responses.

'A number of priests. I didn't know them.'
'You knew Gasparri?'
'Not at all. Our paths simply crossed as we walked.'
'So why did he greet you?'
'A politeness, I assume. As you would with any other priest.'
'You didn't find it odd?'
'Not really.'
'And you recognised no-one?'
'I'm afraid not.'
'Wouldn't you say that was unlikely, Prefect?'
'The Vatican is a huge organisation, Commander. We tend to operate in very small and tight-knit circles.'

Atzori stopped talking and glowered at Costello, obviously unsatisfied by the prefect's replies.

'That's three times you've denied knowing anything, Prefect. Very symbolic.' Atzori let out a laugh, reflecting his derision rather than the humour of his own remark.

'I assure you, that is all I know,' lied Costello. 'I have no reason to withhold information. You don't trust the word of a bishop?'

'To be honest, Prefect, I wouldn't trust my own mother. You need an open mind in this sort of work.'

'Forgive me. It was a stupid remark.'

Atzori scribbled a note on the open pad whilst Costello wrestled with his conscience. He was a man torn between his natural instinct to be truthful and his unwritten promise to

Woeters. But he was now trapped by his own lies. To retract his statement would only lead to a betrayal of his friendship, compromised by Woeters' letter, just as he had himself compromised Robert Paine only a few months before.

'You were in the pope's apartments, I hear,' interrupted Atzori once more.

'It was my duty. The officer told me I was expected.'

'Against my better judgement. We had orders to allow two members of the household access before we went through his papers.'

'It is an accepted protocol.'

'Even when it's murder?'

'Whenever death is sudden. Whatever the cause.'

'Closing ranks?'

'It's a matter of discretion. Who else has been given access?'

Atzori fumbled with his notebook, flicking the pages rapidly with his nicotine-stained fingers.

'Cellini. Cardinal Cellini. Do you know him?'

'I know him well,' answered Costello, determined to give Atzori no hint of his true reaction. 'Has he already been into the Holy Father's apartment?'

'Not yet. You were the first. Is there anything you can tell me?'

'I'm afraid not.'

'You left it as you found it?'

'Your officer gave me little choice.'

'No choice, I hope.'

'Indeed.'

Atzori left as abruptly as he had arrived. There was no word of thanks, no hint of pleasantry, only the thinly-veiled threat of his return.

Over the next week Costello immersed himself in the duties of his office. Given the very public killing of Johannes Woeters there was no call for an autopsy and the funeral arrangements were made quickly. Costello's old friend

Giulio Palazzini had left copious notes on the plans for the burial of Pope Paul VII and Costello was able simply to repeat the precise instructions. The world's press was in a frenzy, eager for any morsel of information on Alberto Gasparri and determined to turn him into a demonic figure and religious psychopath. What information they failed to unearth was embroidered from their imagination, falsified to add drama to a life which in reality had been marked by no more than ordinariness. The prefect's own enquiries, made with the help of Oliveri, revealed a young priest who had risen to his post in the Vatican bureaucracy only because of his attention to detail. He had been sponsored into the household by an aged bishop who had shared Gasparri's Tuscan origins and who needed a compliant and meticulous cleric. Gasparri had filled the role perfectly, an unambitious, dull-minded man, open to the influence of more powerful clerics. Cellini must have noticed his weakness as soon as they had first met, perfect material for the sycophancy on which the cardinal thrived.

Yet there was no mention in the press, or even in the whispering corners of Rome, that there was any connection between Cellini and Gasparri. The cardinal had covered his tracks carefully, detaching himself from his own followers. Even Oliveri failed to pick up the slightest hint of scandal, and he had the finest network of informers in the city.

It was reported that Atzori's main hope of revealing a conspiracy lay in the gun which was used in the assassination. But it proved a worthless investigation. Forensic tests showed it to be an old officer's pistol dating back to 1942, kept at Gasparri's home since the end of the war. There was no evidence to suggest that the killer had been in alliance with anyone other than the devil himself. It seemed the act of a deranged man, fearful of nothing more than change. Gradually the conspiracy theories weakened as the mourning grew in strength.

For a few days following Woeters' death, Rome had been thrown into a storm of panic, a rudderless ship, sinking in speculation. Costello watched as Cellini calmed the waters and cleverly placated the city with promises of a return to the old certainties. He watched Cellini's manipulation of events with a degree of admiration for his ability to promote his own ambitions whilst denying his wish for power. The retreat into the lost conservatism was well-established before Woeters' body had grown cold.

And Costello could do nothing, his hands tied by Woeters' demands. Oliveri and Fr Ferrara were mystified by his withdrawal from their plan to expose Cellini and constantly demanded Costello's support. Without the influence of such a senior churchman they had little option than to stay silent. Oliveri couldn't risk bringing down the *Osservatore Romano* through some unsubstantiated rumour and Ferrara was too old to take on an establishment that was closing ranks by the second. Atzori's investigations had already been hampered by the Vatican's ability to unite in the face of external interference and Cellini was rapidly closing every door to the outside world.

As the cardinal's promotion to papacy became more and more likely, Oliveri and Ferrara pleaded with the prefect to take action, their demands becoming impassioned as the College of Cardinals began their deliberations. Costello was becoming an outcast, excluded by his part in Woeters' election, Cellini making no attempt to gain his support or to make any contact with his adversary. There appeared no reason why Costello should stand aside and watch his church drift back into the doctrinal stagnation which had blocked the hope of unity for so many years. Olivera and Ferrara felt betrayed. It seemed that the prefect they had once admired as the standard bearer of change had now submitted to the power of the Curia, unwilling to continue their agreement to expose Cellini.

Costello could see their rising despair but could do nothing without breaking the confidentiality of Woeters' letter. He had been ensnared by the pope's insistence on the endorsement of Cellini, a man with whom he shared a mutual distrust. He had become a friend to no-one, trapped by Woeters' demand for his faith and unconditional trust, tied to a conviction that in some way he may be acting out God's purpose. The words of Johannes Woeters had become a prophecy of his dilemma. In only a few weeks he had become a lonely man, his instinctive faith bending under the weight of his isolation.

12

She was a woman who enjoyed her femininity, a perfect mask for the intellect which had created feelings of inadequacy in so many of her lovers. Even now, in her late middle age, her body still maintained its confidence, a clue to its lascivious history.

Isobel Griffin lay alone and naked on the burning sand, content to let the sun beat on to her skin. This was not the pleasure of a naturist communing with nature itself, but of the hedonist wallowing in her own sensuality. The beach was her erotic pleasure, even the grains of sand blown across her body on the gentle sea breeze roused her sexuality. It was her meditation, her yoga, her complete and uninhibited relaxation.

Rolling on to her front, she reached for the packet of cigarettes which lay half-buried under the fine yellow sand. She lit the cigarette quickly, pulling the smoke deep into her lungs as an act of defiance against the clean ocean air.

Hanalei Bay stretched into the distance, its wide and arcing sands seeming to go on forever, the rolling waves of the Pacific breaking on its shores as if trying to share its pleasures. She had taken Paine's advice. After months of living in the isolation of the small compound and grey-walled laboratories, Isobel Griffin had begun to explore the island of Kauai. It had taken many weeks of careful searching before she discovered the seclusion of Hanalei. The majority of Hawaiian beaches milled with American and Asian tourists, many in the first throes of marriage, clinging to one another with the ferocity which defines newly-wed honeymooners. She was aware of her own bitterness but remained contemptuous of the display of such blind affection, whilst detesting her own cynicism. Hanalei was her escape, a refuge from her memories and from herself, the isolation was an evasion of her unhappiness.

The flow of letters from Thomas Costello and Robert Paine had forced her into a confrontation with her own life. They had dredged to the surface her inability to maintain friendships and to accept any long-term intimacy. The end of her marriage to Bill Harriman had been hurtful but also a relief, a chance to retreat into the comfort of a self-centred lifestyle. She gained no satisfaction from her detachment but had grown to recognise the impossibility of change, accepting her fate to remain on the fringes of life. Isobel Griffin often wondered if her passion for astronomy was nothing more than a reflection of her character, searching for meaning beyond earth's confines, an escape from her own realities.

It was Robert Paine's letter, perhaps more than any other, which had stirred her emotions. She appreciated his contact and his sympathies but hated the exposure to her past. More than any other man she had known, Robert Paine had revealed the inner coldness which she detested so much. Their brief affair at Cambridge was the blueprint for her future, a fleeting glimpse into her history of self-rejection. She knew that Robert had seen this inner loathing and it was possible that this intimate knowledge had cemented their long but intermittent friendship.

Her relationship with Thomas Costello had been quite different. They had been close and the trinity could not have succeeded without his inclusion. Despite his faith in the unprovable he remained the rationalist, the arbiter in all their disputes, his sharp mind cutting through the apprehensions of their youth. Yet she had always feared his insight and the unspoken understanding which made her feel transparent in his presence. Unlike Robert, who had accepted her detachment, Thomas Costello seemed to have captured part of her spirit. He was never judgemental, yet Isobel feared the latent threat of emotional exposure. But if she had ever truly loved a man it was Thomas, a man made inaccessible by his youthful insight and, later, through his vow of celibacy. Despite his intuition, he would always be denied access to her genuine desires. He had been, and still remained, her only safe retreat.

Isobel Griffin covered herself as two young wind-surfers came back to shore, the brightly coloured sails of their boards flapping their arrival. She had watched them earlier, dancing effortlessly on the wave-tops and catching the blustering wind which had swept across the bay. Now there was no more than a breeze and she could see the disappointment on the boys' faces. They smiled an acknowledgement as they left the beach, embarrassed to have disturbed her sunbathing. She guessed that they had probably glimpsed her unclothed body before she had noticed their arrival and could see in their eyes that she was considered too old for a flirtatious remark. Isobel could still remember her own adolescent response to middle-aged men, her assumption that their childhood lay forgotten, their memory remote and unreachable. But it had been a false premise. She knew now that every age-worn body was nothing more than the warder to an imprisoned youth.

Safe again from prying eyes, Isobel removed her towel and lay back once more in the bright sunlight. She thought again of Robert and his strange request for information. At first she had dismissed it as no more than the inquisitiveness of a newspaper man searching for yet another exclusive. But Isobel was intrigued by the nature of his questions. She could only guess that there had to be some tie-up with Thomas Costello. As far as she knew, Robert had always been a political man with little interest in religious matters. This sudden fascination with the affairs of the church seemed out of character, a tangent she would not have expected.

Unfortunately, Paine had been wrong about the length of her contract in Hawaii. Her expected return to Goldstone, California had been delayed by further mapping problems with the telescope on Kauai Island. After some major huffing and puffing by NASA over funding, they had granted her a stay of execution and extended her visit until November.

She had been tempted to write to Robert and tell him she could be of no use. But the assassination of Pope Adrian VII had fired her imagination.

The American papers had been full of reports and eye-witness accounts, some even mentioning Bishop Costello. What had surprised her even more was the election of someone called Eugenio Cellini who had taken the title of Pope Pius XIII. It was not until she re-read Thomas's letters that Isobel Griffin realised this was the man that Costello had painted as a threat to the Catholic church. She could only conclude that Thomas must have lost all his influence and was likely to have been excluded from the Vatican hierarchy.

Her analytical mind had been galvanised by the marked parallels between the contents of the letters from her two old friends. It strengthened her resolve to help Robert Paine as best she could. At first she had tried to play the amateur sleuth, begging and borrowing papers from colleagues in the laboratory, and checking through back-copies of the American press which were kept in the library at Princeville. Despite her efforts she produced nothing at all. Paine's instructions had been fairly clear but she could never find any detail in the one or two scant reports which she unearthed in the national press. She had been on the verge of giving up when she remembered Stephen Erlich.

As a sociology professor, there had been no reason for Erlich to come into contact with Isobel. Social scientists and real scientists, as she liked to call them, rarely had the opportunity to meet apart from the occasional formal gathering of the whole university. It was at such an event that Isobel saw her next conquest and Erlich saw his opportunity. Like all her affairs, it was a short, emotionless, but physically satisfying encounter and Erlich had returned to his wife and family, absorbed by guilt but happy to have discovered such unbridled eroticism. And they had parted as friends, Isobel offering no threat of attachment. It had been no more than a short chapter, a passing whim.

But Stephen Erlich had contacts. He had published a

number of academic texts, one of which was considered to be a seminal piece on the religious and cult activities of native Americans. It had little relevance to Paine's interests but Isobel had assumed, correctly as it transpired, that Erlich's work had spread itself much wider since his arrival at Colgate.

She had made contact with him more than a month ago and, by the time autumn began to transform the colour of Hawaii, she had amassed a huge amount of information. At first the news clippings came slowly, but gradually it became obvious that Erlich had the bit between his teeth. He began to send faxes, e-mails and even the occasional church documents marked 'private and confidential'. In addition it had become his habit to add his own comments and observations, filling out the details which had been omitted from the text.

Initially it made little sense and there was no discernible pattern in any of Erlich's material. As far as Isobel could see there had been numerous meetings between church leaders but nothing to suggest that there was any element of secrecy. Reports appeared to be quite open and frank about their purpose, no suggestion that they disguised a deeper truth. Robert Paine had not really implied that there may be a cover-up but Isobel knew him too well, even after all these years. There was little chance that he would give so much energy to something which did not carry the mark of scandal or the smell of intrigue.

For several weeks Isobel Griffin had searched her material for a common factor, for the slightest correlation between events. Instinctively, she subjected Erlich's information to formal experimentation, setting up a series of hypotheses and searching for empirical evidence amongst the growing mass of paper which began to cramp her small study-bedroom. She had all the information requested by Paine, but still felt dissatisfied and convinced that he had set her a task which required far more than the mere collection of dated clippings.

The sun had begun to lose its power, the breeze strengthening and sending a momentary chill through her body. Isobel Griffin checked the beach again and dressed hurriedly. It was a time she enjoyed more than any other, watching the orange globe of the sun descend rapidly into the oblivion of the mountains which flanked the western end of Hanalei Bay. Lighting yet another cigarette she sat quietly, her knees pulled up to her chest, her head resting on her folded arms. She revelled in these moments of solitude. There was no sense of loneliness but instead a strange thrill of having outlived nature for another day.

Whilst sunbathing, she had drifted in and out of sleep, her mind playing with thoughts of Robert and Thomas. But now she was alert and regaining her natural logic. She reached over to the embroidered cotton sack which she always carried with her on her trips to Hanalei. Pulling out the folded papers she shook them hard to dislodge the sand which had crept into the bag and began to read the contents. They had come in the morning post and she had meant to read Erlich's latest batch of clippings whilst she lay on the beach. But the distraction of the sea and the warmth of the air had robbed her of the concentration which had now returned. There was a scribbled note stapled to the collection of papers, the unpretentious writing clear but erratic in style.

> Izzy,
>
> Not sure if we've been barking up the wrong tree. Have marked a couple of passages which might be of interest. What do you think? Let me know if you'd like me to chase it up.
>
> Stephen.

Turning the pages quickly, Isobel searched for Erlich's promised markings. He had used a bright yellow highlighting pen which stood out clearly from the torn pages. Without reading the script she noticed the word 'unusual' pencilled in the margins of ten or twelve of the many cuttings. Separating them from the rest of the batch she laid them out in the sand, using a handful of pebbles to hold the paper down in the stiffening wind.

It was difficult to see why Erlich had found the highlighted sections so interesting. At first glance they appeared to record yet another catalogue of meetings by various denominational leaders, a repeat of all the data she already possessed. Only on the second reading did she begin to see what had alerted Erlich's attention. The meetings he had marked so boldly were not between men who shared a similar creed but between followers of opposing faith.

Isobel's back straightened as she checked and re-checked the cuttings. She knew instinctively that all her digging had finally struck the richest seam, and doubted if Robert Paine even knew of its existence.

Grabbing a scrap of paper from her bag, she began to jot down details of the sections marked by Erlich's pen and it was not long before the information started to take shape. Although the cuttings went back as far as 1996 there seemed to be nothing unusual until the early spring of 1997. From that point there was evidence of a spasmodic but identifiable flurry of activity. She remembered from her initial enquiries that this was also the period which had witnessed an increased number of gatherings amongst the protestant denominations and the Catholic church. Given the growing ecumenical movement this was not unexpected. What she had failed to notice was a parallel set of events amongst Jews, Muslims, Buddhists, Hindus and, even more surprising, between the eastern Confucianists and Taoists. What Erlich had now revealed was an acceleration and opening up of dialogue between all these traditionally separate faiths.

Isobel replaced the papers and reached for her cigarettes. She tingled with apprehension and excitement, her heart pulsing its rhythms through her body. Quickly gathering her towel and bag, Isobel Griffin headed away from the beach towards the rough pathway which snaked up the rust-coloured cliffs. Breathing heavily by now, she struggled through the thick shrubs which had found a purchase on the thin layer of volcanic soil. Tall, single shoots of sugar cane begged for sunlight amongst the dark foliage, waving their survival in the gusting wind.

It was already early evening and only four cars remained in the small parking area which stood at the cliff-top. She saw the two men immediately, their gleaming car conspicuous amongst the more familiar rusting Toyotas and Hondas which careered along the Hawaiian roads. There had been a number of attacks on women during the past few weeks and Isobel remained wary as she approached her car. She clenched her keys tightly, aware that they may be her only defence and quickened her pace as she came closer. The door of the shining black Ford opened suddenly.

'Miss Griffin?' asked the tall bespectacled man, the remains of the sun catching his glasses as he spoke.

Isobel grabbed her car door and jumped in, banging the locks with the palm of her hand before turning the ignition and firing the engine into life.

Both men had now left their car and they stepped rapidly towards her window, waving their hands and calling her name loudly. She was about to reverse when her curiosity overcame her rising fear. It seemed unlikely that two men who attacked women on impulse should know her name. Still in gear, but holding the car on her brake, she wound the window down enough to hear their voices more clearly whilst maintaining her safety.

'What do you want?' shouted Isobel through the small gap.

'Miss Griffin? Miss Isobel Griffin?' asked the tall man once more. She could see the rings of sweat under the arms of his crisp white shirt.

'Who wants to know?'

The two men produced cards and pressed them against her windscreen. She looked at them carefully, comparing the deadpan expressions of their photos with the more animated faces who now looked into her car.

'Can we talk to you?' asked the shorter of the two men. She guessed he was Hispanic, his dark features and jet black hair contrasting with the pale blue button-down shirt, which obviously had not been bought in a cheap chain-store.

'Who the hell are you?'

Once more they pressed their identification cards against her windscreen and waited for her reply.

'Means nothing,' she said. 'What the hell is the DEA?

'A government organisation. You're in no danger. I'm sorry to have frightened you.'

'Shitless,' responded Isobel. 'What the fuck's going on?'

She sat for a moment trying to weigh up the risk she may be taking. They didn't look like rapists as far as she could tell. She hardly expected a sexual pervert to wear a uniform, but these two supposed attackers seemed too clean-cut and professional to pose any real threat.

'So what do you want?' she asked once more.

'You know Stephen Erlich?' asked the tall American.

Isobel opened her door and got out of the car. The mention of Stephen's name was her final assurance that this was no physical assault.

'He's had an accident?'

'No he's fine.'

'So what's the problem?'

'We believe you've been corresponding with him. Is that correct?'

'Is there a law against writing letters?' she responded, turning to check if her bag was still on the passenger seat.

The American smiled briefly but gave no reply, instead offering only another question.

'You're an American citizen?'

Isobel look bemused and reached for her cigarettes, offering the packet to her interrogators.

'If you're who you say you are, you know I'm not. But I've got a valid work permit. Is there a problem?'

'There may be.'

'If what?'

'Let's just say it could be a problem.'

'That sounds like a threat.'

The tall American smiled once more, yet his manner had become humourless.

'I make no threats, Miss Griffin. I only said it could be a problem.'

'And what's it got to do with Stephen, for God's sake?' Isobel was becoming irritated by this man's veiled aggression and edged back towards her car.

'We're talking state security, Miss Griffin. That's all I can say.'

'He's a sociology professor, for Christ's sake. He's hardly going to bomb the fucking White House.'

'We won't keep you, Miss Griffin. It's been a useful conversation. Thanks for your time.'

'Is that it?' demanded Isobel, as the two men returned to their car. The engine kicked into life and they gave no response to her question. She watched them leave, the black Ford turning slowly left on to the main road which led to Princeville and the eastern coast of Kauai Island.

Isobel Griffin slumped into her seat and hammered the steering wheel with her fists.

'Jesus Christ!' she shouted, now seething with anger and resentment. 'So much for land of the free. Bastards! What utter fucking bastards!'

She sat for a few minutes, staring out over the darkening ocean, trying to assess her next move. There was no doubt that she had to make contact with Erlich and Robert Paine. Perhaps even with Thomas Costello. But Isobel Griffin was confused by the whole affair and her usual rationality had escaped her. There seemed no reason why an innocent correspondence with Stephen Erlich should end up being a matter of state security. It seemed ridiculous. The information she had just uncovered was pretty explosive stuff as far as it went, but it hardly represented an attack on western civilisation. From the little she knew about various world churches and different faiths, the breakdown of religious barriers would be welcomed by most politicians. Sending their messenger boys to warn her off Stephen Erlich made no sense at all.

Her journey back to the observatory at Wailua gave her a chance to regain her thoughts, yet, hard as she tried, it seemed impossible to make a link between Erlich's letters and the over-reaction of the American government. Only an hour earlier, she had been thrilled by her discovery, assured that she had unearthed the answers to Robert Paine's questions, excited by the prospect of helping him with his book. She had even been amused by the fact that Robert might give her a credit for her investigations. But as she approached the lights of Wailua she was filled with doubt about the value of her revelation. There had to be more. There was something missing, some unresolved element in the growing mystery.

Specks of rain appeared on her windscreen as she pulled up outside the low, grey-brick building and Isobel stood for a few seconds letting the raindrops spatter on to her face. It was almost pitch black, only the lights from a small number of rooms illuminating the gravelled area of the car park. She entered quickly, eager to shower away the fine grains of sand which had lodged in her hair and feet. As she strode down the corridor of the main block, towards the staff bedrooms, Isobel noticed the light under her supervisor's door. Without knocking, she entered the book-lined office.

'What's the forecast, Albert?' asked Isobel, carefully stepping across the paper-strewn floor.

Albert Quinon turned from his computer screen, his large frame filling the swivel chair which creaked under his overweight body.

'Hi, Izzy. Good day?'

'Interesting.'

'God, you look burnt. You want to be careful.'

'Fell asleep as always. I never learn, Albert. What's happening?'

'Doesn't look good. This wind's blown in some fairly thick cloud cover. You might be in for a night off.'

'I'm knackered anyway. I hope it rains for a week.'

'Unlikely,' smiled Quinon. 'Want some coffee?'

'Maybe later. I'm going to clean up first. I've still got half the beach with me.'

'Want me to get at the difficult bits?'

'I'd frighten you to death,' laughed Isobel. 'Give me a shout if the weather clears.'

Within minutes, the high-pressure shower head was pulsing water on to her body, stinging her shoulders as it found the small patches of skin she had failed to protect. She watched the brown grains of sand snake their way across the shower floor, reluctant to leave their new-found territory as if fighting to avoid being driven into the plug's black hole. For more than ten minutes Isobel let the water revive her tired body, intentionally blanking from her mind anything other than the physical sensation.

Afraid to rub her sunburnt skin, she wrapped the towel around her dripping figure, lit a cigarette, lay back on her unmade bed and tried to reconstruct the day's events. It was only a matter of seconds before she began to see some of the implications of her harassment by the two American agents. Turning on to her side she reached out to the bedside table and the sliding drawer which contained her private papers. The cigarette hung from her mouth, the smoke stinging into her eyes as she leant over the table and rummaged through the chaos of pens, keys and papers. Her passport had become jammed at the back of the drawer and she pulled hard, tearing its edge in her hurry to check its contents.

The small, laminated card lay in the passport's covers, her unflattering photograph staring back at its owner. Pulling her bedside light closer. she searched for the relevant dates, her eyes only confirming what she already suspected.

Lying back once more, Isobel pulled hard on her cigarette. In all the years she had worked for NASA her papers had been renewed as a matter of course, without request and within two months of their expiry. It was already October and she now realised she had heard nothing from the personnel section in California. She had no more than two weeks before she would be forced to leave the country, her divorce from Bill Harriman robbing her of any claims to permanent residence. Despite all her years in the US, she had never laid claim to citizenship, unwilling to sever completely her ties with the past.

Startled by her realisation, Isobel dressed quickly, grateful that her post did not rely on her appearance. Her hair still dripping, she returned to Quinon's office intent on action.

'Coffee still on offer?' she asked.

'Sure is. I thought you'd hit the sack.'

'I may have a problem, Albert. You might be able to help.'

'Fire away.'

Albert Quinon had become as good a friend as Isobel was capable of having. Even though he held a more senior position, he was at least 20 years her junior, often ribbed by his colleagues as a rising star in astronomy. Although a French-Canadian, this obese bearded scientist had cut his teeth in England. His parents had left Canada after the failure of the French separatist movement, which he talked about endlessly, often slipping into the language he loved so dearly. From his early twenties he had made a startling impact, his many publications on the supernova remnants of the Crab Nebula spawning a whole array of doctoral theses and groundbreaking research. And like Thomas Costello he presented no emotional threat.

On their first meeting Isobel suspected that Albert was probably gay, though his occasional sexual teasing gave her some doubt. After a short time it became obvious that Quinon had little real interest in either sex, his scientific mind dominating his existence and providing him with all his physical and mental requirements. Within weeks they had settled into each other's company, content to share nothing more than their intellect.

'Do you mind if I smoke, Albert?' asked Isobel, as Quinon poured the coffee from the percolator which permanently simmered in the corner of his office.

'No, go ahead. Come on, what's the problem?'

Isobel Griffin took the cup, filling it to the brim with cream and a large spoonful of sugar.

‘That’s an abomination,’ mocked Quinon.

‘You always say that. Typical bloody Frenchman!’

‘*Oui. D’accord.* And proud to be so.’

Sipping the coffee carefully, Isobel pulled her chair closer to her supervisor.

‘You haven’t heard anything about my permit have you, Albert?’

‘Your work permit?’

‘Yes. It’s due to run out in two weeks.’

‘And they haven’t replaced it? I thought that was automatic.’

‘So did I. I’ve never had a problem before.’

‘And this time?’

Isobel hesitated, loath to give Quinon any details of her contact with the men who had threatened her.

‘I think there may be. Could you check for me?’

‘Of course. I’ll ring NASA in the morning.’

‘Thanks.’

‘No problem. Is there any reason they wouldn’t renew it? You haven’t been sleeping with the president, have you?’ chortled Albert.

‘There’s desperate, and there’s desperate,’ laughed Isobel, punching Quinon on the arm.

‘Wish I could help,’ retorted Albert quickly, faking serious injury.

‘As I say. There’s desperate, and . . .’

‘Yeah. Yeah. I know,’ interrupted Albert, now shaking with laughter. ‘I’ll check it out first thing. Promise.’

They sat together for another hour, discussing Quinon’s latest work on radio emissions and Isobel’s attempts to solve their constant problems with optical distortions. It was one of many nights they had spent together, Isobel always marvelling at the depth of Albert’s knowledge. But by midnight her eyes were growing heavy, the day’s sea air finally invading her lungs, making her body heavy with tiredness. Leaving Quinon to his private passion, she dragged herself back to her room and, without undressing fully, dropped on to her bed, falling asleep in an instant.

But it was not the oblivion she had hoped for. Albert's constant supply of caffeine disturbed her sleep, her mind racing with the images of contorted dreams, all slipping from her memory as she woke, angered at being denied a longer rest. Turning to look at her clock, Isobel Griffin swore as she saw it was only 7.30, her mind now too active to sleep any longer. Raising herself slowly she reached for her cigarettes and wandered over to her desk, flicking on the lamp which cast a circle of yellow light onto the table's surface. Her old fountain pen and paper came easily to hand and Isobel began to scribble out her fax to Stephen Erlich.

> To: Stephen Erlich. Prof. Sociology. Colgate University. New York State.
> From: Izzy Griffin. Wailua Observatory, Kauai, Hawaii.
>
> Thanks for info., Stephen. Unusual as you say. Interesting. Any problems? Let me know by return. Take care. Izzy.
>
> PS. By the way, my dog's fine – please answer by return.

Isobel knew nothing about the dark world of espionage. But she did remember seeing an old Humphrey Bogart movie where he alerted Lauren Bacall to danger by including in his letters something plausible but uncharacteristic. It all seemed a little theatrical but somehow she guessed that Stephen may well be under pressure and she did not want to make matters even worse. She hoped that her reference to a non-existent animal might make him realise that she too had been approached and threatened. If there was one thing Stephen Erlich had learned about Isobel during their short affair, it was that she hated dogs, of any description.

It was 9.30 by the time she had showered yet again and had taken breakfast in the sparse and dingy canteen. The office fax machine had whirred her message to Stephen in seconds, and she left instructions to be told as soon as a response came back. Isobel collected her mail and walked slowly to her laboratory, sifting through the various letters for anything out of the ordinary. Noticing Albert Quinon's office was still open she stuck her head around the door to find him still at his desk.

'You haven't been here all night have you, Albert?'

'Grabbed a couple of hours. Something interesting came up.'

'In the nebula?'

'Yep.'

'I don't suppose you . . .'

'Yes, I have. Only a few minutes ago. I was about to ring you.'

'And?'

'Sure you haven't been sleeping with the president?'

Isobel looked hard at Quinon's expression. He had made the same joke the night before but this time there seemed little humour in his comment.

'Why do you ask, Albert? You've got bad news, haven't you?'

Quinon remained impassive, not sure how to continue.

'Come on, Albert. What did they say?'

He coughed nervously before replying.

'No extension. Non-renewable. That's all they would say. No explanation. No nothing.'

'You asked them for an explanation?' asked Isobel, now hanging on his every word.

'Point-blank refusal. Said you had to leave the country by the end of October. I couldn't believe it, Izzy.'

Isobel Griffin slumped into the chair beside Quinon's desk and exploded with anger.

'The shits! The complete and utter shits! Who the fuck do they think they are!'

Albert stood beside Isobel and placed his hand on her shoulder, surprising her with his gentleness.

'Don't know, Izzy. But they weren't kidding and they sounded very heavy.'

13

The grey blanket of a November morning hung over the distant city, the rain-spattered window only adding to its drabness and claustrophobia. Isobel Griffin spread the warm flannel across her tired face, trying to fight off her body's demand for sleep. She waited for the stillness, the inevitable hush she had heard so many times before yet always detested. The piped strains of Vivaldi filled the air, its comforting rhythms drowned by the silence which had descended on the cabin, over 300 gamblers having wagered their life on man's technical ingenuity. For many years she had harboured a desire secretly to replace the optimism of Vivaldi with the dirge of a Bach mass and observe the melting bravado of her fellow travellers.

The hubbub of noise returned as the wheels bit into the runway, the roar of the engines confirming their safe arrival. Excited children and expectant tourists scurried for their belongings whilst exhausted businessmen sat impassively, awaiting their next ordeal.

Isobel let the plane empty before gathering her hand luggage. She stepped into the bright lights of the terminal and the long corridors which led to the baggage reclaim. Surprisingly, her luggage came through quickly and she loaded the three large cases on to the trolley and hurried towards the customs check. She was desperate to have a cigarette and felt irritated that Europe had succumbed to American puritanism.

The relief of the exit was only seconds away when the customs officer stepped out to block her progress.

'Anything to declare?' he asked politely but firmly.

Isobel stopped, angered at his threat to delay her intake of nicotine.

'I thought this was the green channel,' she answered, making no effort to disguise her sarcasm.

'Where have you travelled from?' he continued, refusing to respond to her aggression.

'New York. Is that a problem?'

'Perhaps you would open your cases, madam? We won't detain you longer than necessary.'

Isobel could hardly contain her exasperation and snapped back her reply.

'Jesus Christ! Come on. I've just been on a plane for eight hours. I'm knackered, thirsty and bursting for a cigarette. Is this really necessary?'

'Just procedure, madam. Please open your cases.'

Isobel watched as the customs official began to rifle through her belongings, the chaos of clothes and papers reflecting her present mayhem. She felt embarrassed by her exposure, the assault on her personal belongings making her feel like a colonial refugee.

On the top of her smallest case lay three large brown envelopes, containing all the recent correspondence she had received from Stephen Erlich. Before leaving Hawaii she had taken care to seal the contents, tying the packages together in a neat, string-held bundle.

'The envelopes?' demanded the officer.

'Papers. Just papers.'

'I'll take a quick look, if I may.'

'Do I have any choice?' responded Isobel acidly.

Her anger was now turning to suspicion and she watched carefully as the official sifted through the mass of paper. After her expulsion from America, Isobel was beginning to see shadows in every corner, convinced that she was at the centre of some licensed conspiracy. Her fingers tapped out her disapproval on the surface of the table, her anxiety growing as the customs man seemed to be reading a selection of the documents.

'That's private material,' she said curtly. 'If you've quite finished I would like to go.'

He began to re-pack her belongings, his fingers running

along the side and base of her cases as he replaced their contents.

'Holiday?' he asked, his tone now more friendly.

'No,' answered Isobel, unwilling to offer any further information. 'May I go now or are you intending to subject me to the indignity of a strip-search?'

'That won't be necessary, madam. I'm sorry to have delayed your journey. Enjoy your stay.'

Isobel Griffin gave no response, hurled her bags back on to the trolley, and headed for the exit. She took great pleasure in defying the notices, purposely and with great exaggeration lighting a cigarette before she left the customs hall.

It was this symbol of obduracy which alerted Robert Paine to Isobel's arrival. He could see the indignation on her tanned face the moment she came into view. Her dark tousled hair, now streaked with the greyness of middle-age, seemed to accentuate her indignation, the smouldering cigarette which hung from her lips adding another clue to her obvious rage. Paine hesitated before making himself known and watched her movements as she headed towards him. It had been nearly 30 years since he had seen her and yet she still displayed that curious mixture of coldness and pure femininity which he had rarely witnessed in another woman.

'Izzy!' shouted Paine, as he pressed up against the thin metal barrier. 'Izzy!'

Isobel Griffin stopped and turned her head towards him, trying to locate the vaguely familiar voice.

'Izzy!' called Paine once more, now waving the white cardboard sign which bore her name.

He noticed a faint smile as Isobel raised her hand in recognition and approached him slowly.

'You look like a taxi driver, Robert. Did you think you wouldn't remember me?'

'I was afraid it was you who might not recognise me,' laughed Paine.

They stood together, unsure how they should mark their

reunion. Paine took Isobel's hand, intent on offering the embrace he had planned but now nervous of her response. She could sense his faltering approach and put her hands on Paine's shoulders.

'Still the schoolboy, Robert!' teased Isobel. 'Even old wrinklies are allowed to kiss, you know!'

Paine was relieved by Isobel's directness, and taking her in his arms kissed her gently on both cheeks.

'Sorry,' whispered Paine as they separated. 'I wasn't sure . . .'

'It's been a long time, Robert,' smiled Isobel, noticing the slight flush in Paine's face.

'You're looking good, Izzy,' answered Paine, now more relaxed by Isobel's approach.

'You're a lying bastard, Robert. I'm old and crumpled. Especially after eight hours on that bloody plane.'

'Rubbish. You look as good as ever.'

'You're an old smoothy, Robert. Shall we exchange compliments?'

'No need, Izzy. I never could face the truth.'

'Really, Robert. You're looking disgustingly youthful. A bit more weight than I remember, but it suits you.'

'Enough bullshit,' laughed Paine, taking hold of the trolley.

'End of bullshit,' smiled Isobel in agreement. 'Where's the car?'

Though it had been an early landing, the journey back to Richmond was difficult, the rush-hour traffic building as they approached the outer city. Within minutes of leaving Heathrow, Isobel's head began to nod, the smooth motion of the car inducing the sleep which had eluded her on her flight from New York. By the time he pulled into the drive it was approaching ten o'clock and his passenger had slumped forward, oblivious to the passage of time. Paine tapped her gently on the shoulder.

'Izzy, we're here,' he said quietly.

He watched as Isobel Griffin began to stir, rubbed her eyes and tried to make sense of her surroundings.

'Sorry,' she said apologetically, shaking her head and stretching her arms as she yawned loudly. 'How long have I been asleep?'

'Not long. Come on. Alex has had to go out but I know she's made up your bed. Why not sleep for a few hours?'

'I was going to try and stay awake,' said Isobel as they entered the house. Paine's labrador greeted them as they carried the cases into the hallway.

'I'll wake you at two o'clock. Promise. Upstairs, second on the left. You've got your own bathroom so you won't be disturbed.'

'You'll wake me?'

'Two o'clock. On the dot. I'll bring you a cup of tea.'

'Heaven.'

'Have you got everything you need?' asked Paine, ready to carry the luggage up to her room.

'I'll just crash, Robert. We can sort the cases out later. Do you want to see Stephen's stuff?'

'The letters?'

'Yes. They're on the top of my small case. You're welcome to go through them if you want. See what you make of them. It's only the most recent stuff. I couldn't bring it all,'

'The earlier letters?'

'Burnt them. It seemed safer.'

'Safer?'

'You'll see.'

Isobel trudged wearily to the top of the stairs, turning momentarily to look down at Robert. For an instant, and without speaking, they exchanged a smile which bridged their 30 years of friendship. Yet it disappeared as quickly as it had arrived, Isobel, as always, fearful of her own emotions.

Paine unzipped the case and pulled out the large brown package, surprised at the amount of material that Isobel had amassed over the last few weeks. Having cleared the early breakfast debris from the kitchen table, he laid the papers out, checking the date of each document to organise them into some sort of chronological order. Isobel had sent him a brief note to let him know that she had stumbled on some useful information, but had given no details. The main aim of her letter had been to inform Robert that she was being thrown out of her job and needed somewhere to bed down for a few days when she returned to England.

Alex had taken it surprisingly well, carefully disguising the resentment and fear which secretly gnawed at her stomach and threatened her rationality. Since Robert's growing obsession with the intrigues of the Catholic and protestant churches, she had seen such a revival in his spirits that she was determined to give her support whatever difficulties it might throw up. Isobel Griffin was one of those difficulties but she was prepared to gamble that she represented no more than an imaginary complication and not a real threat to her stability.

It had been almost three months since Paine had written to Isobel. In that time he had tried hard to gather together his own evidence but without much success. The British press had focused all its attention on the assassination of Johannes Woeters and there seemed to be an assumption that, with the election of Eugenio Cellini, the ecumenical movement was about to be put on hold. He had received the briefest of notes from Costello and the occasional phone call, especially during the new pope's election. But he had sounded a defeated man, tired and worn by Woeters' death, and apparently doomed to exile in the obscurity of some minor Vatican office.

Paine was still convinced that Costello was holding something back, some element in his knowledge which he was unwilling or unable to reveal. It had left Robert Paine in a state of frustrated limbo, limited to following a series of redundant trails. Until the unexpected arrival of Isobel's letter, it appeared that the scent had gone cold.

But now, as he sipped his coffee and pored over Erlich's correspondence with Isobel, he could feel his journalistic instincts returning, an excitement which renewed his determination. Like Isobel, he was unsure what exactly he hoped to find but he sensed that somewhere amongst these papers lay the key to a tangible breakthrough and a real exposure of the truth.

For more than two hours Paine examined Erlich's papers, trying hard not to be distracted by the notes and markings which the academic had added to the text. He was searching for something, anything, that might hint at the missing factor.

It was almost one o'clock by the time he heard Alex returning.

'How did it go?' asked Paine as Alex came through the door, laden with heavy plastic bags.

'She thought it was a touch of bronchitis. Given me a course of antibiotics.'

'How do you feel now?'

'A bit tired, but better now that I know what was making me feel so awful. Isobel arrive OK?'

'She's asleep. Horribly jet-lagged. Said I'd wake her at two.'

'I knew she was here.'

'The cases?'

'The smoke. You can smell it as soon as you come through the front door. Just what I need for my bronchitis. What are all the papers?'

Paine ignored her jibe, and shuffled the papers towards her. 'It's all the material that Erlich sent from Colgate. It's a real eye-opener, Alex. He's marked up all the significant sections but I think he's missed some of the less obvious detail. It's bizarre, I tell you.'

'In what way?'

'Let's wait until Izzy comes down. I'd like to hear her story first, but I'm sure we're on to something.'

'You sound excited, Robert,' said Alex. She approached the back of her husband's chair and placed her arms around his neck, kissing him lightly on the top of his head.

'I'm bloody excited, Alex. God knows what can of worms we're about to open.'

'Don't forget we're taking Rachel to the hospital later. I know it's difficult, but you did promise you'd come.'

'I haven't forgotten, Alex. Of course I'll come. We can talk over dinner.'

'You know what Rachel's like. Still daddy's little girl, though she'd never admit it.'

'And I love it,' laughed Paine. 'Would you like some coffee? I've just made some.'

'Later. I'll take Toby for a walk, I think. I could do with some fresh air.'

The labrador heard his name and began to race around the kitchen, his yelps increasing as Alex took his lead from the hook on the back of the garden door.

'Want to come?' asked Alex.

'I'd like to but I'd better keep reading, and Izzy might wake before we get back.'

'OK. I won't be long.'

Paine glanced at the clock. He had barely half an hour before he had to wake Isobel and he returned quickly to Erlich's papers. By now he was making notes, just as Isobel had done on the beach at Hanalei. But they were more detailed, his journalistic experience allowing him to construct an intricate matrix of cross-referenced times, dates and content. He guessed that Isobel's natural intellect had revealed some of his own conclusions but doubted that she had seen the relevance of the concealed, yet equally important, sub-plot.

As promised he made tea, carrying the small tray up to Isobel's room and tapping gently on the door.

'Room service,' called Paine at first quietly. But there was no response and he called again, this time with a little more force.

'Room service!'

'Robert?'

'Who else?' chuckled Paine.

'Come in. It's fine.'

He pushed the door open and entered the room, darkened by the closed curtains. Isobel lay on her front, the straps of her brassière almost fluorescent against her ebony skin.

'What time is it?' she murmured.

'Just after two. How did you sleep?'

'Wonderful. I could sleep for ever.'

'Sleep on if you want. It's no problem.'

'I daren't, Robert. My clock will be haywire. Pull the curtains and I'll take a shower.'

'Don't fall asleep again.'

'I won't.'

There was no sound of movement for another ten minutes and he was about to return when he heard the shower being turned on and Isobel's steps creaking across the floorboards of her room. Toby bounded into the kitchen, his mud-spattered coat evidence of the walk with Alex.

'Did you wake her?' she asked, drying her rain-soaked face with her hands.

'She'll be down in a minute. She's just taking a shower. Good walk?'

'Just what I needed.'

They sat together and awaited Isobel's entrance, both aware of their unspoken apprehension. Paine could feel his irrational guilt returning, almost like a child in fear of being found out by unforgiving parents. What he feared most of all was the possibility that he would fail to confirm his platonic claims, that he would be unable to conceal a more complex history. He heard Isobel's footsteps coming down the stairs and smiled at Alex just as the door opened. Paine stood and turned to greet her.

'Better?' queried Paine.

'Much,' answered Isobel, looking across the table to Alex.

'Alex. Isobel,' said Paine hurriedly.

The two women approached and shook hands, Alex surprised by Isobel's firm grip.

'I've heard a lot about you,' said Alex with a warm smile which relieved Paine's anxiety. 'I'm sorry. That's an awful cliché!' she added

'It's good to meet you,' answered Isobel, responding to her welcome.

Alex had only seen pictures of Isobel, in Robert's old

college photographs, but standing before her now there was no doubting that she was confirming all her instincts. She was much older, as they all were, but the sensuality that Alex had gleaned from the faded pictures was still in evidence. It had little to do with her dress sense. If anything, Isobel looked rather manly, her old faded jeans and simple shirt lacking the femininity that Alex had expected. But her sheer animalism oozed from every pore, more obvious to the rival than the ally, a sexual distinctiveness that perhaps only women can sense in one another.

Though not privy to their thoughts, Paine was well aware that Alex and Isobel's outwardly polite exchange masked a frantic assessment and a search for the strengths and weaknesses of their opponent. He stepped in quickly, afraid of their conclusions.

'You've a lot to tell us, Izzy. Have some lunch and let's hear your news.'

'You've been through Stephen's papers, Robert?' asked Isobel, pulling her gaze away from Alex.

'I have, Izzy. But that can wait till dinner. We want to know why you were suddenly ditched by NASA.'

Alex and Robert Paine sat quietly as Isobel ran through the events of the past few weeks, her contacts with Stephen Erlich, the encounter with the American agents and her subsequent loss of her work permit. Paine knew that she wouldn't have gone quietly and listened as Isobel explained how she had battled with the authorities and pulled every string she could lay her hands on. It had soon become obvious that the decision had been taken elsewhere, beyond the control of her contacts at NASA. Keen not to lose Isobel's expertise, Albert Quinon had tried hard to pull rank, throwing his considerable physical and academic weight into her cause, even at one stage threatening to resign if the matter wasn't resolved. But it had come to nothing. Stephen Erlich had failed to respond to her fax and appeared to have gone to ground. Isobel eventually attempted to phone him direct, taking a chance that she would expose his involvement.

Again she had no success, the university clearly having been briefed to declare that Erlich had taken a short sabbatical and was out of the country. By the time her old work permit had expired she had been left with no option but to pack her bags and leave, the pill having been sweetened by the guarantee of generous severance pay and an assured pension. Whoever was behind her dismissal obviously did not mind paying for her removal.

'That's when I wrote to you, Robert. They gave me no bloody choice!'

'And did you have any more approaches?'

'Nothing.'

'So what's all this customs business?' asked Alex. 'Robert tells me you were asked to empty your cases.'

'That's right. Maybe I'm being neurotic. There's probably no connection.'

'But you say this customs chap showed particular interest in Erlich's papers?'

'I'm sure he did.'

'So who put him up to that?' queried Paine.

'God knows. But I feel the bastards are trying to stitch me up in some way. What a nightmare!'

'And all my fault,' said Paine apologetically. 'I'm afraid this wouldn't have happened without my letter.'

'More bullshit,' laughed Isobel. 'It's fate. Don't you remember my first letter? God knows how, but we've been driven into this position. Thomas thought the same.'

'He said the same to me. I remember it well.'

'You probably think we're all going potty,' said Isobel, directing her comment towards Robert's wife.

'It had crossed my mind,' laughed Alex, grateful to be included in the conversation. 'But you haven't told us what you made of Erlich's material,' she added.

'We'd better leave it till dinner, Alex,' interrupted Paine. 'We're supposed to pick Rachel up in ten minutes. Will you be all right, Izzy? We'll only be a couple of hours.'

'I'll be fine.'

'Make yourself at home,' added Alex. 'There's plenty of

papers, magazines, even good old British TV if you want to relax for a while.'

'That's kind. Thanks. I'll be just fine, really.'

Isobel heard the car leave the drive as she made herself some fresh coffee and relaxed in the warmth of the kitchen. Alex had left the morning papers on the table and she browsed through the headlines, dismayed to see that understatement no longer dominated the broadsheets. Despite all her years in America she had never failed to be irritated by the sensational and inconsequential content of their media, and the replacement of erudite professional journalists with amateur hacks. It seemed that the British press was being dragged into the same abyss of mediocrity.

For the next half hour Isobel tackled the *Times* crossword but became gradually depressed by her rusty logic. As a student she remembered competing with both Robert and Thomas, only ever failing on one occasion when the cryptic clues had an ecclesiastical theme. She smiled as she thought of Costello's delight at finally defeating his female opponent, savouring the moment by passing her the completed crossword as they waited for the start of a race. The two men had laughed so much that they were almost incapable of pulling their oars through the water. But she was out of practice, and she tossed the paper to one side, annoyed by its reminder of her advancing years.

Erlich's correspondence still lay across the table and Isobel could see the efficiency of Robert's approach to his reading. He had left his notepad next to the pile of papers but his notes had been scrawled hurriedly and hard as she tried to decipher his writing, they made little sense.

She began to wander through the house, attempting to absorb its atmosphere, to gain an insight into Robert's marriage. Lighting a cigarette, Isobel left the kitchen and crossed the hallway into the large sitting room, immediately aware of the absence of stale smoke which she had always associated with her various homes. The pastel shades and neatly laid out furniture made her feel uneasy, the chair cushions so regular in shape that they offered no invitation.

Searching for an ash-tray, Isobel approached the large bureau which stood at the side of the large stone fireplace. On its surface stood Paine's history, a collection of framed photographs mapping his progress from student to expectant grandfather. Alex had been an attractive woman in her youth and Isobel could see why Robert had fallen for the young journalist. She knew his wife lacked her own sexuality, but as she held the photograph towards the standing light she could see in Alex the stability which Robert always needed.

Without warning, Isobel felt a tear trickle slowly down her cheek. She was looking at a world which she had always wanted yet had been incapable of achieving, a life which might have been hers if she had been dealt a different set of cards. Placing the photographs back in position Isobel hurried from the room, unwilling to confront her inadequacies for a moment longer.

The phone began to ring as she stepped back across the hallway. Unsure whether to respond, Isobel hesitated before running back into the kitchen and lifting the receiver.

'Hallo?' she answered uncertainly.

'Alex?' came the short reply.

'I'm sorry, she's out at the moment. Can I take a message?'

'Is Robert there?' asked the voice once more.

'He's out as well, I'm afraid. Perhaps I can get them to call you back. Whom shall I say called?'

There was a long pause before the caller spoke again.

'I'm sure I know that voice.'

'You do?'

Isobel felt unnerved by the enquiry and yet there was something in this man's delivery which sounded vaguely familiar.

'That's not you, is it, Izzy?'

'Yes it is. Who the hell is that?' answered Isobel becoming more suspicious by the second.

'It's Thomas. Thomas Costello.'

Isobel felt her grip tighten on the receiver and she dropped into the old wooden chair which nestled against the kitchen wall.

'Good God! Thomas?'

'It is. Really. You sound shocked.'

'You can say that again. I was just thinking of you. Remember the crossword?'

'My only triumph?'

'You've got it! If it's any satisfaction, I've just given up on today's teaser. Lost my touch.'

'It comes to us all, Izzy. How are you?'

'Unemployed, but good. And you?'

'I'm well. Difficult times, but well.'

Isobel could tell he was lying. She recognised his voice but the sparkle had gone, his delivery flat and lacking the vitality she had once admired.

'They've gone to see their daughter,' answered Isobel changing the subject quickly. 'She's due in a couple of months. Did you know?'

'Yes, Robert told me some time ago. What are you doing there, Izzy?'

'Long story, Thomas.'

'You may be able to tell me.'

'Where are you?'

'Still in Rome.'

'But you're coming to England?'

'It's a possibility. I'll let you know.'

'I hope so. It would be wonderful to get together again. Like old times.'

'We'll see,' answered Costello, his tone still cheerless and lacking any vigour. 'Can you do something for me, Izzy?'

'Fire away.'

'Ask Robert to record tonight's news. I've no access to a video recorder here and there's something I'd like him to check. Could you do that for me?'

'No problem. Any particular bit of the news?'

'The whole thing. I'm sure you'll be carrying the same main stories as the Italian networks. At least I hope so.'

'What's it all about, Thomas?'

'Tell Robert I'll ring him around ten. I'll explain then.'

'Anything else?'

'I'd love to hear your news, Izzy, but I've got to go. I'm taking a mass in a few minutes. We'll try and talk later.'

Isobel replaced the receiver and reached for her cigarettes, opening the back door to let the smoke swirl out into the cold and damp November air. Toby saw his opportunity and rushed past her, barking at the feeding birds as he raced off towards the distant copse. Feeling subdued by Costello's obvious depression Isobel stood quietly, drawing comfort from her cigarette but puzzled by her friend's request.

Toby returned quickly, scampering past her legs and shaking his wet matted hair against her jeans. He wagged his tail affectionately but gained no response. Sensing her rejection, he padded across the floor to his basket, pleased to have escaped the rain which now lashed against the kitchen windows. Isobel picked up the paper once more, determined to complete the crossword which had defeated her earlier. Grabbing a pen from the table, she climbed the stairs to seek the comfort of her bedroom, avoiding the sterile sitting room which contained too many ghosts, too many reminders of what might have been.

Robert Paine knocked even harder.

'Izzy? Are you awake?' he shouted. There was a sound of movement behind the door and Isobel Griffin peered around its corner as she turned the handle.

'What time is it?' she murmured.

'Seven-thirty,' smiled Paine, amused by the bleary eyes and dishevelled figure which stood before him. 'Alex is all ready to serve dinner. Hungry?'

'Give me five minutes, would you?' answered Isobel wearily. 'I hate this bloody jet-lag.'

'No rush. We're eating in the kitchen. Take your time.'

Isobel hurriedly washed, adjusted her hair and threw on a little make-up to hide the grey rings which had appeared below her eyes. She felt like death as she entered the kitchen and even worse when she saw Alex's fresh-faced vibrancy.

'Wine?' asked Robert.

'Leave the bottle,' laughed Isobel. 'I need all the help I can get.'

'I looked in earlier,' said Robert as he filled her glass. 'How did the crossword go? It obviously sent you to sleep.'

'How do you know that?'

'It was still lying in your hand as you snored away.'

'I don't snore!'

'Wrong,' teased Robert. 'The windows were rattling!'

'How's the appetite?' asked Alex, saving her from further embarrassment and carrying a large dish of pasta on to the table.

'Like my body, reviving slowly,' quipped Isobel, her mind gradually clearing with the help of the ice-cold wine.

Alex played the perfect hostess, attending to Isobel's every need, and displayed her skill at maintaining a natural flow of conversation. Until the alcohol began to loosen their tongues the exchanges remained polite and guarded, the transmission of facts uncluttered by opinion. But before long there was a noticeable easing of tension, especially when Robert began to question her about Erlich's letters.

'Shit! I nearly forgot,' exclaimed Isobel. 'Thomas rang. Just before I fell asleep.'

'Was there a message?' asked Alex.

Isobel gave them the details of Costello's call and his request to record the evening news. She could see the excitement in Robert's face, the contact from Thomas adding to her own arrival and the possibility that the knot was about to unravel.

'I'll set the recorder. We can watch it later,' said Paine making no effort to disguise his elation. 'We've got to get back to your opinion on Erlich's material.'

Minutes later Paine hurried back to the table and began quizzing Isobel about the American churches, constantly probing for detail and evidence. Alex listened quietly, impressed by Isobel's ability to formulate the information in such a calculated fashion. There seemed little emotion in her delivery, only the analytical style which had always been a characteristic of her work. Even the account of her discovery of meetings between different faiths was presented in a similarly cautious manner.

'It's a lot bigger than I thought, Izzy. I looked through Erlich's evidence and came to the same conclusion as you.' He reached over to the end of the table and pulled over the three large, brown envelopes. 'But I think you may have missed something,' added Paine as he sifted through the sheaves of paper.

'Such as?' asked Alex, determined not to become isolated and forgotten.

'The constant illnesses,' answered Paine, becoming more animated by the second. 'Look, I've listed them all out. I tell you, it's way beyond coincidence. I can't believe how blind I've been!'

'To what?' pressed Isobel, scanning Paine's notes.

'That's the problem, Izzy. It's looking me in the face and I can't make sense of it. But what I do know is that there's been a whole host of church leaders and senior figures from other faiths who have been out of commission for five or six days.'

'Like Woeters and Munro, you mean?' queried Alex.

'Precisely.'

'But with what?' interrupted Isobel.

'God knows. If you look at Erlich's stuff, it's the one ingredient that's missing. Since Woeters and Munro got ill there's been a complete blanket on any medical detail.'

There was a sudden silence as the two women tried to absorb Paine's idea. Isobel began to read his notes, her natural instinct being to validate his claims with evidence, whilst Alex tapped her fork on her plate quietly, searching intuitively for an answer to her husband's claims. She looked across the table unnerved by Paine's impassioned expression.

'You don't think you've let your imagination get the better of you, do you Robert?' asked Alex.

'That's why I became a journalist, Alex. No imagination!' laughed Paine.

'True,' mocked Isobel.

It was a moment which Paine had hoped for, a feeling of camaraderie replacing the initial unease which he sensed when they had first sat down to dinner. Looking across at the two women who had played such a major part in his life, and who now sat chatting easily together, he was filled with a renewed certainty.

'Go on through. I'll bring the coffee,' he offered, rising from the table.

Isobel went ahead of Alex, intent on claiming a seat with its back to the bureau and its array of photographs. Paine stepped forward and pulled Alex back just as she was about to leave the kitchen. He kissed her gently on the mouth.

'What's that for?' smiled Alex, surprised by his sudden affection.

'Everything,' whispered Paine. 'Check the video is on would you?'

It was 10.15 when Costello rang, his voice agitated and frantic in its urgency. He wasted no time with the usual pleasantries.

'Did you record it?' he asked immediately.

'Got it all. We haven't seen it yet. What's the problem, Thomas?'

'Can you play it back whilst I'm on?'

'Of course. Hang on, I'll just rewind,' answered Paine, responding to Costello's obvious stress. 'It's Thomas,' added Paine, cupping his hand over the mouth-piece and turning towards Alex. He fumbled with the remote control and began to play the tape.

'OK. It's on, Thomas. What am I looking for?'

'There should be a piece from Israel. See if you can find it.'

Paine pressed the fast-forward, occasionally checking the various news items. After a short time he could see the map of Israel preceding one of the reports.

'Got it. What now?'

'It should be a report on the chief rabbi. They think he's dying.'

Paine listened to the newscaster's introduction which confirmed Costello's suggestion.

'Yes, you're right. Now what?'

'The Italians had a report from outside the main hospital. Are you getting the same?'

'They're probably network pictures. Hang on, I'll see.'

He watched as the report from Tel Aviv unfolded on the screen, a series of interviews and studio comment. At the very end came the pictures he had been asked to observe. He re-wound the tape and held the hospital pictures on the freeze-frame.

'Still there, Thomas? I've found it. What am I looking for?'

'A man, Robert, and not a Jew.'

'That gives me lot of scope.'

'You can't miss him. A tall shambling figure carrying a black bag. I only saw him for an instant, climbing the stairs to the hospital entrance. Thinning, sandy-coloured hair and angular face.'

Paine ran the tape forward frame by frame, watching the mass of rushing figures who came and went behind the reporter. From the left of the screen came the head he was looking for. Carefully pressing the remote control button he edged the figure forward, gradually revealing a perfect match for Costello's description. In a second he was gone, and he rewound slowly, manoeuvring the image back into the centre of the screen, freezing the figure into full view.

'I see him, Thomas. Fits your description exactly. Who is he?'

'I hardly dare tell you, Robert.'

'Take a chance, Thomas. Come on,' urged Paine, now desperate to share Costello's knowledge.

'It's John Laidler,' answered Costello softly.

'John Laidler?' queried Paine.

'Remember Lambeth?'

'Yes. Go on.'

'He's the consultant who operated on Johannes Woeters.'

'You're sure?'

'Positive,' answered Costello, leaving no doubt in his certainty.

'What the hell is he doing in Tel Aviv, Thomas?'

'You tell me, Robert. But I'm going to find out.'

'You're actually going there?'

'I feel I have to.'

'When?'

'I can get away within forty-eight hours.'

Paine felt unable to respond and covered the mouth-piece with the palm of his hand. He stared across to the quizzical faces of Alex and Isobel, searching for their support. It was clear that Costello had adopted his own obsession and if he knew as much as Paine suspected, there must be good reason for his sudden action. He lifted the phone once more.

'Give me a call in the morning, Thomas. I need time to think.'

14

'The Azarim?' queried Costello. 'Is it easy to find?'

'Half-way along Dizengoff Street,' came the reply. 'David tells me it'll take you about five minutes in a taxi.'

'Ten-thirty?'

'I'll be there.'

When he had first arrived, the white pavements outside the café had shimmered in the winter sunshine. Within minutes of taking his seat, Thomas Costello was forced to edge his chair under the protection of the canopy, as the rain began to beat on the greying pathways which lined the busy street. Even the local people seemed surprised by the sudden change as they scurried for the shelter of the coffee-houses and shopping arcades. It was almost December, yet there was still a warmth in the air, a contrast with the biting winds which had blown across Rome the day Costello had rushed to the airport at Ciampino.

Stretching his hand out, he let the rain cascade on to his palm, enjoying the pounding of the raindrops which sent small rivers of water running up his unprotected arms. Small, laughing children, admonished by their parents, ran in and out of the sudden storm, happy to enjoy the coolness of the first real winter rain and stamp their feet in the growing number of puddles. He was tempted to follow their example, urged on by a desire to let the downpour wash away his growing anxiety.

The coffee came quickly, and he sat quietly watching the old men at the adjacent table arguing over their game of backgammon, black trilbies shading their brown leathery faces. The rain grew more intense, as if a tropical storm were about to hit the city, and he pulled his chair even further back as huge droplets bounced from the pavement towards his feet. Before long Dizengoff Street was awash, a river of dust-filled water spilling debris from the nearby market into the affluent café district.

He felt exhausted by his journey, drained by his decision to take such a dramatic leap and, for once follow his instincts. His natural logic had been abandoned, and whilst he desired the truth he feared the possible outcomes. But he was now a driven man, aware that he had no choice but to cast off the apprehension which had dogged him since Woeters' death, dismayed that the real picture still remained obscure and clouded by the assassination.

The familiar figure splashed towards him, his body bent against the rain, a newspaper held above his head the only protection against the torrent of water.

'God, I'm soaked! I expected to be sunbathing,' exclaimed Robert Paine, throwing himself into the vacant seat beside Costello. 'Where did that lot come from?'

'I'm told it's normal at this time of year,' answered Costello, standing to shake Paine's hand. 'Do you want coffee?'

He raised his finger to beckon the sheltering waiter and turned towards his friend, who was trying to dry his hands and face with a paper napkin.

'It's so good to see you, Robert. I don't think I could have managed on my own.'

'I can't believe I'm here,' laughed Paine. 'Alex thought I'd gone crazy.'

'How was your journey? From what you said on the phone it sounded terrible.'

'As crazed as the traveller. Not a seat free on the direct flight so they shipped me through Paris, Milan and Cyprus. Didn't get into Tel Aviv until two this morning.'

'You must be exhausted,' said Costello sympathetically. 'It's all my fault, I'm afraid.'

'My choice, Thomas. You made no demands. I felt I had no choice.'

'I was just thinking the same thing. No sense to it really. How's Izzy?'

'About to move on. Canary Islands, of all places. She'll be gone by the time I get back. It's a pity really. She and Alex were getting on surprisingly well.'

The rain stopped as quickly as it had arrived, the waiter wiping down the tables and shuffling the chairs back on to the pavement's edge. The temperature rose immediately as the sun burnt out of the sky once more, sending small plumes of white wispy steam rising from Paine's rain-sodden shirt. They edged into conversation, unsure how they should unravel each other's stories, but both eager to gain more information. At first they circled around the main topic, Paine passing on news of Isobel's expulsion from America and the sudden offer of a new job in La Palma. The call had come only an hour before Paine had left for the airport and Isobel had jumped at the opportunity.

'Albert Quinon fixed it up apparently. I don't know him but Izzy tells me he's a leading light in astronomy and has contacts all over the world. Sounds a good man. From what Izzy tells me he's proved to be a good friend to her through the whole episode.'

'I'm so pleased,' answered Costello. 'In many ways I feel just as responsible for Izzy as I do for you.'

It was the opportunity Paine had waited for, and he began to explain the train of events which had led to Isobel's problems with the American authorities. So much had happened in a short time that it was difficult to present the facts in any sensible order. Costello remained silent as Paine described his own search for evidence and the eventual revelations from Stephen Erlich.

'Now you can see why I jumped on the plane, Thomas. Your news about the chief rabbi and John Laidler's sudden emergence really whet my appetite. As I say, it was my decision and in all truth a fairly selfish one. God knows where it will lead but I'm too intrigued to stop now.'

Costello sat quietly sipping his bitter café hafuch, mulling over Paine's information. He had been presented with another piece of the jigsaw and yet the picture was still incomplete.

'One thing I must ask you, Thomas,' added Paine, interrupting Costello's thoughts. 'I'm still not sure why Laidler is such a big player in all this. If the chief rabbi has got a similar problem to Johannes Woeters, doesn't it make sense for the Israeli authorities to use his expertise?'

'Possibly,' mumbled Costello, uncertain how to construct his response.

'I mean, we could just have forked out a large amount of money for nothing more than a wild goose chase. Without being offensive, Thomas, I doubt if it's money you can really afford to spend.'

'It's not a wild goose chase, Robert. I'm certain. I don't want to sound melodramatic, but you said yourself that you felt you had no choice.'

'True,' answered Paine resignedly. 'But you're not telling me everything, are you, Thomas? I can feel it. There's something else.'

'Trust me, Robert. That's all I ask. What did David have to say?'

Paine shrugged his shoulders before replying, sighing his resignation to Costello's guarded response.

'He reckons Laidler's still in the city but hasn't located him yet. He's going to join us as soon as he can.'

'Do you think he'll find out?'

'He's optimistic. It's been difficult but he's chasing a contact at the hospital. With any luck he'll be talking to them now. We'll just have to wait and see.'

'Laidler's the key, I'm sure.'

'Maybe. We'll soon know. What's happening in Rome? Cellini waving the big stick?'

'If only it were that simple, Robert. To be frank, I'm quite mystified by his actions. He's not really running true to form. It's very odd.'

'In what way?'

Costello began to catalogue the events which had followed Woeters' death and the expected pogrom of Vatican staff which began soon after Cellini's election. It had left Costello on the fringes of power and reliant on the eyes and ears of his old friends, Ciro Ferrara and Giovanni Oliveri. He had even considered retirement but was determined to do all in his power to halt Cellini's inevitable conservative reforms. His dismissal from the prefecture had robbed Costello of almost all his authority, but he had maintained a number of allies within the Curia. They shared his fear of Cellini's retreat into what he proudly boasted were the old ways of the mother church.

Robert Paine listened intently to Costello's story, trying to piece together the information and relate it to his own investigations. He allowed his friend to pour out his experiences, only interrupting occasionally to prompt Costello into detail.

'But you say it didn't happen?' he asked.

'Initially it did, Robert. But on this occasion the storm came before the lull.'

'You should have been a journalist, Thomas,' laughed Paine, raising his hand to call the waiter.

But there was no humour in Costello's eyes, blind to Paine's teasing joke. His expression betrayed a deeply troubled spirit, burdened by anxiety.

'Within three weeks he asked me to resume the prefecture,' said Costello suddenly.

'He did what?'

'Asked me to come back. It was extraordinary.'

'You took it? I thought you were sworn enemies.'

'I couldn't, Robert. It would have been like selling my soul and I still have my suspicions about his part in Woeters' death.'

'But you considered it?'

It was probably Cellini's offer which had finally thrown Thomas Costello into his present despair. Caught between his allegiance to Johannes Woeters' memory, and the equally strong temptation to retain his influence in the Vatican, Costello had been emotionally ravaged by his dilemma. What had made it even more problematic was that Cellini became an illusive target for Costello's resentment. In the first few days of his papacy he had gained support through his astute and pious mourning, building alliances between the warring factions. But soon came the tirade of invective, a block on Woeters' reforms which was justified by Cellini's conservative rationalism.

At this point Costello had no doubts about his desire to escape the clutches of a man he despised so much, and any offer of the prefecture would have been rejected without a second thought.

'Are you saying it didn't last?' prompted Paine.

'I can only say he ground to a halt. It was astonishing.'

Both Olivera and Ferrara had come to Costello with the same information. His friendship with the two men had been strained by his unwillingness to expose Cellini, but the bond between them was never fully broken. They could see that Costello had been disabled by circumstance. After great deliberation, they continued to act as the bishop's eyes and ears in the streets of Rome. The restaurants, cafés and, most notably, the influential Santa Marta Club were again buzzing with rumour, the Vatican village once more enlivened by gossip. The wagging tongues carried the message that Cellini had gone into retreat, had begun to soften his line, and there were even whispers that he was now giving credit to the former pope's reconstruction of Catholicism.

It was at this point that Costello was requested to resume his post as prefect to the Holy Father, and the apparent change in Cellini's stance had thrown Costello into a frenzy of indecision.

'But you resisted?' asked Paine.

'It was only hearsay, Robert. I wanted to believe there had been some transformation but I couldn't betray Johannes on no more than speculation. It was dreadful, Robert. I was torn between the forgiveness I have preached all my life, and a sense of duty to my conscience.'

'And Cellini's reaction?'

'Kindness itself. No hint of the insincerity which I'd expected. I can tell you, it was very hard to reject his offer, almost impossible.'

'But you did.'
'I felt I had no choice.'
'It's a recurrent theme, Thomas.'
'Sorry?'
'Having no choice in our actions. You could give free will a bad name,' laughed Paine.
'It's always been a difficult concept. Even for a Catholic bishop.'
It was the first time he had seen Costello smile since they had first met and he seemed more relaxed having unburdened himself to his old friend. Yet as quickly as the lightness had arrived, it disappeared in a mask of anxiety and Paine seized his chance, his journalistic instincts still sensitive to such changes of expression.
'There's more, isn't there, Thomas?' he asked quickly, determined not to let the moment pass.
Costello paused, the smile momentarily returning as he shuffled uneasily in his seat.
'You know me too well, Robert.'
'I didn't become a newspaper hack for nothing. What is it, Thomas?' His tone had become insistent, demanding a reply. 'It's why we're in Tel Aviv, isn't it?'
Costello drew his chair closer to the small metal table and leant forward towards his friend.
'To some extent,' he answered quietly.
'And?'
'And you're right. Until you told me about Izzy and her contact with Stephen.'
'Erlich,' interrupted Paine.
'Yes. Stephen Erlich. Until then I was concerned that you'd think I was losing my senses.'
'Go on.'
'He started to get headaches.'
'Who?'
'The Holy Father.'
'Cellini?'
'Yes. From what I could gather it was exactly the same pattern as Johannes. Passed off as stress, but getting worse.'

'And this came at the same time as his supposed change of heart?'

'Precisely.'

'And then you saw Laidler on the news bulletin?'

'Exactly.'

Paine could feel the blood draining from his face and he took a long deep breath to fight off the light-headedness which had made him feel suddenly dizzy.

'Why didn't you tell me on the phone?' spluttered Paine.

'Until the news from Izzy, I don't think I had even started to see the implications. As I say, I assumed you would think I was being absurd to draw any parallells.'

'Far from it, Thomas,' answered Paine, leaning back in his chair and once more breathing deeply. 'God, I'm not surprised you were so insistent on coming to Israel. I daren't think what we're about to uncover. What the hell's going on, Thomas?'

Before Costello could offer a response, his eye was distracted by a squat, casually-dressed figure approaching their table, his dark blue shorts and bright yellow shirt giving no clue to his occupation, and yet he seemed vaguely familiar.

'David!' called Paine, as the man drew closer. 'Any luck?'

'I think so. I've fixed up a meeting in half an hour if that's OK.'

He had the dark, swarthy features of many of the men Costello had seen since his arrival in Tel Aviv, a short but athletic figure whose large, jet black moustache gave him a doleful appearance which did not match his obvious vitality and enthusiasm.

'I'm sorry, David. This is Thomas. Thomas Costello.'

'Hi. David Reisman,' said the man, reaching forward to shake Costello's hand. 'Recognise you from the papers.'

'The papers?'

'Woeters' shooting,' answered Reisman.

'Of course. Can I get you a drink?'

'I'm fine. We'll have to get going really. It's on the other side of town.'

Costello watched the Israeli as he chatted to Paine and

gave him details of the proposed meeting. His heavy American accent had come as something of a surprise but he realised it was a voice he had heard before.

'Weren't you the reporter outside Benyamin hospital?' he asked, interrupting Reisman's conversation with Paine.

'For my sins,' laughed Reisman. 'I do some network stuff for NBC. Helps pay the bills.'

'Is there anyone you don't know, Robert?' teased Costello.

'Old friends from New York,' answered Paine, giving Reisman a friendly slap on the shoulder. 'Happy days, David. Some good stories.'

'Another day,' beamed Reisman. 'You ought to get going.'

'You're not joining us?' asked Paine.

'Can't, Robert. I've got two stories to file before three o'clock. I'm really pushed.'

'Sarah will recognise us?'

'You'll recognise her. She'll be in a nurse's uniform, she's coming straight off her early shift.'

'How will she know us?'

'She'll soon spot your pale faces and stuffy clothes,' laughed Reisman. 'Come on, I'll get you a taxi.'

The two men sat tensely as the car sped northwards through the back streets of Tel Aviv, their apprehension increased by the driver's apparent lack of fear and his complete disdain for traffic signals. Paine spent the time explaining to Costello how he had sought out Reisman after seeing the television news. The woman they were about to meet was a nursing sister at Benyamin hospital and a close friend of Reisman's wife. Recently divorced and a single mother of three young children, she was glad to accept the money that had been offered for her information.

'She's not been bribed, surely,' asked Costello, disturbed by Reisman's under-hand approach.

'Let's say a token gift,' smiled Paine as the taxi entered the affluent Herzliyya district, a distinct difference from the squalor of the Lod suburbs he had encountered on his arrival early that morning. 'Look, that's it, I think. Over there on the left.'

He told the driver to pull over and clambered out on to the pavement, Costello close behind. The aging sandstone frontage of the Dan Arcadia hotel provided a distinct contrast to the high-rise developments which dominated the Tel Aviv skyline. As they entered the foyer, Paine commented on its colonial feel, the array of leather club chairs an anachronism in such a modern city which had only blossomed in the last fifty years. Large fans circled above their heads, whirring quietly over the hubbub of conversation and smoke-filled air. Quickly laying claim to a table within sight of the main entrance, they waited for the nurse's arrival, Paine watching the door carefully for any sign of their informant.

There was little conversation between the two men as they stared towards the large, ornate wooden doorway, their tongues tied by anxiety and excitement. Costello glanced at his watch.

'What time do you make it, Robert?'

'One-thirty. She should have been here.'

'Do you think she's coming?' asked Costello nervously.

'We'll give her till two. I don't know what we do then.'

'Ring David?'

'Could do.'

They sat for another 20 minutes, still concentrating on the entrance, both men fascinated by the constant flow of staff and customers who gave life to their stylish and elaborate surroundings. Each table seemed to be engaged in barter and discussion, business deals being negotiated over coffee, beer and olives. Even a small group of bearded and black-suited Hassidim had taken over a corner of the room, their animated discussion rising above the general murmur of conversation.

'Mr Paine?' came a voice from behind their chairs.

Robert Paine turned his shoulders and looked towards the man who had called his name.

'Yes?' he answered instinctively. 'We were expecting . . .'

'Yes, I know who you were expecting, Mr Paine. She won't

be coming. And you're Mr Costello?' asked the tall blond figure, turning towards Thomas.

There was something rather threatening in the young man's tone. He asked his question precisely and courteously, but there was little warmth in his delivery.

'Bishop Costello,' answered Thomas, emphasising his title.

'Quite,' responded the stranger.

'Where's Sarah?' asked Paine, beginning to feel uneasy about this unexpected approach.

'Unavailable, I'm afraid.'

'Unavailable? What's that supposed to mean?' demanded Paine, now irritated by the man's manner.

'It means unavailable, Mr Paine. That is all. We'd like a quiet word, if that's OK.'

'We? Who's we?' snapped Paine.

The man bristled at Paine's tone and straightened himself to assert his authority.

'It's of no concern. Please come with me. There's a car waiting outside.'

'Not until you tell me who you are. I'm going nowhere. Stay where you are, Thomas.'

Costello had begun to rise from his seat in response to the man's demands, unused to Paine's bravado and becoming wary of a public scene.

'We've done nothing wrong, Robert. Let's discuss it outside.'

'Sound advice, Bishop,' added the stranger. 'I have men all over the hotel, Mr Paine. I suggest we avoid any commotion. You have nothing to fear. We just want a few words.'

Robert Paine glanced towards Costello and back to the young man whose expression suggested there was little point in refusal.

'Can I make a call?' asked Paine.

'Later,' answered the man bluntly.

Given his youthful consumption of gangster novels, Paine had expected to be thrown into some sort of black limousine driven by a bullet-headed chauffeur who looked menacingly in his rear-view mirror. The unremarkable white Peugeot which waited outside the hotel was almost a disappointment and hardly worthy of such intrigue. But once they entered the car, the sense of threat rapidly returned. As soon as the door was shut they were cast into semi-darkness, the windows providing no view to the outside world. A glass screen separated them from the driver, and this too was so heavily tinted that it was only possible to distinguish the vague shape of their captors. Paine tried to open the door as the engine started.

'Locked from the outside, Thomas,' he whispered to Costello.

'Quite correct, Mr Paine,' came a voice from the front seat. 'Just sit quietly. It's not a long journey.'

Paine looked towards Costello and placed one finger across his lips. Reaching inside his trouser pocket he pulled out a pen and began to mime the actions of writing. Costello responded immediately and without speaking handed Paine a small guide map of Tel Aviv.

'What do we say?' wrote Paine, handing the paper back to his friend.

'The truth?' scribbled Costello. 'We've nothing to hide.'

'Sure?' wrote Paine, and Costello nodded his approval. 'Good luck,' added Paine, pointing to the words with his finger.

Costello reached over and held Paine's hand, squeezing it slightly in reassurance, his palms damp with perspiration. Robert Paine smiled his response and then tried to concentrate on the movement of the vehicle. At first it seemed that the car had driven directly away from the Dan Arcadia and appeared to take no real turns off the major road, which he knew ran due south towards Jaffa. He glanced repeatedly at his watch trying to gauge the distance travelled through the streets of Tel Aviv. He listened closely for any sound which might give an indication of their position and after 20 minutes he guessed they had been hugging the coastal road. He grabbed the pen once more.

'Think we're near to St Peter's monastery,' he scribbled quickly.

Costello shrugged his shoulders. If Paine was correct they were driving back along the very road Costello had taken earlier that morning on his way to meet Robert Paine. The Franciscans at St Peter's had given him lodgings for the duration of his stay, whilst Paine had been given a room by David Reisman in the northern suburbs of Herzliyya. Paine had studied the map of Tel Aviv quite closely, just to get a picture of its layout and to locate where Costello was staying.

'Try to remember,' wrote Paine once more.

But it was too late. For the next 15 minutes the car seemed to be turning in continuous circles, bumping over cobbled streets, smooth tarmacked roads, and along a series of rough tracks. By the end of their journey Paine had completely lost all his former orientation, and as they pulled to a halt he realised that any attempt to pinpoint their location had become entirely pointless.

'This way,' instructed the tall, blond man, who had still offered them no identification.

The two men blinked as they left the darkness of the car and stood in the grey but bright confines of what appeared to be a small underground car park. They were ushered towards the stairs and into a small lift whose doors were already open, as if awaiting their arrival. Paine watched as the man pressed the number five, which illuminated as his fingers touched the button. No words were exchanged as the familiar whirring of the lift glided its way to the fifth floor.

Paine could feel a heightening of his senses as they stepped out into the long carpeted corridor, his eyes alert and soaking in the minutiae of his surroundings. Like the car which had brought them, the building was far from what he had expected. As far as he could see they had entered another hotel, the room numbers clearly visible on all of the doors within sight.

'Room 527,' said the man curtly. 'Someone will be with

you in a moment. Please wait. There's a drinks cabinet if you require one.'

'Might as well make ourselves at home,' said Paine as the door closed behind them. 'Drink?'

'Water, if there is any,' replied Costello nervously. 'What happens now, Robert?'

'God knows, Thomas. Check the window. See if you recognise anything.'

Costello shuffled across the room and pulled back the curtains.

'Shuttered,' he said with a sigh.

'Not surprising, I suppose. We'll just have to go with the flow, as Izzy might say.'

Before Paine could pour the drinks, the door opened once more and the two friends turned instinctively as they heard the key.

'Mr Paine. Bishop Costello. I'm glad you could come.'

'We had little choice,' answered Paine sarcastically. 'Who are you?'

'Forgive me. Myron Jakobowits,' he answered walking forward to offer his hand. 'Apologies for the little melodrama, but we too had little choice. Please sit down.'

Both Costello and Paine were surprised by the man's manner. Jakobowits was a tall but heavy man, his paunch clearly visible beneath the blue linen jacket and white open-necked shirt. Paine guessed he was probably of a similar age to themselves, but his full head of grey, crinkled hair could have put him anywhere between 50 and 65. Despite his gentle demeanour and unquestionable politeness he had an air of authority which was immediately evident. The moment he walked into the room he commanded attention.

'You will have questions,' continued Jakobowits.

'We assumed it was the other way round,' answered Paine.

'In time,' smiled their interrogator. 'I perhaps owe you the courtesy of explanation.'

Costello was happy to let Robert Paine lead their discussion, aware that his friend was perhaps more accustomed to such confrontation and had a natural talent for eliciting information. He listened closely as Paine fired questions at Jakobowits, demanding clarification and detail. It became a battle of wits and it was not long before Costello became aware that Paine was losing the contest. The Israeli proved a highly skilled communicator, able to say a great deal without ever committing himself to the precise reason for their apparent abduction. From the few responses which were given, Costello began to realise that, for some unknown reason, they had fallen into the hands of the Israeli security services. It was also apparent that there was little chance of ever making contact with Laidler, or their contact at Benyamin hospital. Any detail of the chief rabbi's illness was being kept under very close wraps.

'Where's David Reisman?' asked Paine, aware that he was making little progress.

'At his desk, I would think,' answered Jakobowits.

'You threatened him?' pressed Paine.

'I would prefer the word persuade.'

'Is there a difference?'

'There is a difference,' laughed Jakobowits.

A knock at the door interrupted their conversation and Jakobowits raised his large frame, annoyed by the intrusion. They listened to the short, whispered conversation before the Israeli turned back into the room.

'Bishop. Do you mind if we speak to you alone for a moment?'

Costello hesitated, looking for assurance from his friend.

'Don't go, Thomas. Stay where you are,' demanded Paine.

'Please don't make this difficult, Mr Paine. I assure you, neither of you is in any danger. We simply request a word in private.'

'I'll be fine, Robert,' interrupted Costello. 'Don't worry. I'm sure it's nothing.'

Paine tried to assess the situation, quickly realising that there was no point in resisting the demands. If there had been any doubt about the authority of Jakobowits it was soon dispelled by his request. This was a demand and not open to negotiation.

'No choice again, Thomas,' he said, grasping Costello by the arm.

'So it seems, Robert. Don't worry.'

Paine heard Costello's steps outside the door, accompanied by what he thought were two other people.

'Where are you taking him?' he asked.

'Only next door, Mr Paine. I assure you again. He is in no danger.'

Once alone, there was an immediate reversal of rôles. Jakobowits began to trace Paine's involvement with great precision, even touching on his relationship with Isobel Griffin.

'How do you know about Izzy?' demanded Paine, surprised by the depth of the Israeli's knowledge.

'It's our job, Mr Paine,' came the terse response.

He could hear the dull thud of his own pulse, its rhythms quickening as Jakobowits probed for answers. Whilst he had the company of Costello his fear had been deflected by his wish to protect his friend. But now he was isolated and unable to control his growing panic. He sensed his bravado leaking from every pore in his body, his shirt soaked in apprehension. There was no physical threat, but like the anaesthetised patient he anticipated the striking of a nerve. It was the fear of the possible; the fear of the known.

Jakobowits required every detail, from Costello's initial contact to the assassination of Johannes Woeters, and on to Paine's information from Stephen Erlich. Judging by the lack of surprise, it soon became evident that his interrogator was only using Paine to confirm his knowledge rather than uncover any new information.

'And what did you hope to gain by contacting John Laidler?' continued Jakobowits.

'A pattern, perhaps. We weren't really sure,' answered Paine truthfully, sticking to his agreement with Costello. He fought to maintain an authority in his voice but was angered by the uncontrolled tremor in his delivery.

'I see,' continued Jakobowits. 'I have only one more question, Mr Paine.'

'And we are free to go?'

'Perhaps.'

'Ask away.'

'What do the letters a-i-t-u mean to you, Mr Paine?'

'I'm sorry?'

'Let me repeat them. A-i-t-u,' he repeated slowly, laying emphasis on each syllable and vowel.

'It's a word?' queried Paine.

'What does it mean to you?' responded Jakobowits insistently.

Paine was totally bemused by his interrogator's demands and could offer him nothing more than a slightly nervous giggle, his laughter distorted by his increasing tension.

'Absolutely bugger all. I've no idea what you're talking about.'

'One moment,' answered Jakobowits as he rose once more from his chair and quickly left the room.

Left alone in the sparse hotel bedroom, Paine felt trapped and suddenly aware of his vulnerability. He doubted if anyone apart from the Israeli authorities had any idea where he was and he had no guarantees that Costello was still in the building. The phone provided no relief, its long tone confirming that it could offer no escape. Rushing to the window he tried to peer through the faded green slats of the shutters, but could only see glimpses of the clear, blue sky above the city. He was aware of his body beginning to tremble when the door opened once more.

'You wish to re-think your answer?' demanded Jakobowits.

'I tell you. The letters mean nothing,' pleaded Paine, unnerved by the Israeli's abruptness.

'Bishop Costello suggests they do.'

'He said I know what they mean?' shouted Paine incredulously.

'Not in so many words, Mr Paine. Let us say by inference.'

'Bullshit! You're making it up,' laughed Paine. 'Either let us go or ring the embassy. You've no right to keep us any longer.'

'You can go, Mr Paine. But there will be a small delay.'

'How long?'

'Three days. Your tickets and baggage will be waiting at the airport.'

'Three days! Three days!' exclaimed Paine. 'You've no bloody right.'

'I have every right, Mr Paine. Please relax and enjoy our hospitality.

'We'll let you have a change of clothes. If you require anything else, you need only ask.'

'And Thomas?'

'Bishop Costello will be joining you in a moment.'

True to his word Costello entered the room soon after Jakobowits had finally left. Paine could see the distress etched on his pale, drawn face. He knew he should give sympathy and comfort to a man who was obviously giddy with fear and distressed by the Israeli's interrogation. But Paine felt only anger, towards his situation, towards the skilful Jakobowits and, most of all, towards Costello.

'You've got some talking to do, Thomas.'

'I know,' stuttered Costello. 'I'm sorry.'

'Forgive the Anglo-Saxon, Bishop, but what the fuck do the letters a-i-t-u mean? I think it's time you gave me the whole story.'

'No choice again, Robert. Forgive me.'

The three days of their imprisonment passed quickly at first. Consumed by conversation they had little time to wallow in the tedium of confinement, both friends eager to drain every last detail from one another's experiences. And in this short time, Costello began to regain his former strength, his energy renewed by the unburdening of truth. At last, he could share his concerns, released from the necessity to conceal his suspicions. It struck him as an irony that it had taken imprisonment to give him the freedom to regain his inner calm. Paine had listened carefully, his anger subdued by Costello's obvious predicament. There were so many potential strands to Woeters' death, the illnesses of church leaders, and the eccentric development of Cellini's papacy that it was difficult to locate a common thread.

Yet all their conversations led back to 'aitu', this strange collection of letters which meant nothing to either man but which they instinctively knew must be the key to their unresolved problem. Somewhere in this puzzle sat Laidler, the surgeon whose contact they were now being denied. The very fact that the Israelis were so keen to prevent this meeting told its own story. Costello remembered vividly that it had been Laidler who had first mentioned 'aitu' when he had operated on Woeters.

What this still left unanswered, was why a series of unintelligible letters, first whispered by an ailing pope in the centre of London, should end up on the lips of the Israeli security services. It took Costello and Paine only a short time to come to the same conclusion.

'The rabbi. The chief rabbi. It's the same pattern, isn't it, Thomas?' exclaimed Robert Paine rising from his bed.

'Exactly, Robert. And if my guess is correct it was the same for Archbishop Munro, maybe even Cellini.'

'And who else? That's the big question.'

'Your missing American clergy? Disappearing for short periods, with no explanation?'

'Erlich's evidence?'

'Precisely.'

'But it doesn't really explain the meetings, does it, Thomas?'

'There's Woeters' diary.'

'Go on.'

Bit by bit, Costello searched his memory for the detail he had seen as he searched through Woeters' papers. Early in their conversations he had told Robert Paine of the final entry in the diary, the heavily underlined letters of 'aitu' and the enigmatic note which he had discovered in the folds of book. But he had hesitated in describing the other contents until Paine had heard the rest of his story.

'The meetings weren't limited to the Christian church, Robert. I only had a short time, but from what I was able to see we're not only talking about cross-denominations but cross-faiths.'

'The chief rabbi?'

'The chief rabbi and many more.'

'Such as?'

'Muslims, Buddhists, Hindus, Taoists. You name them, they were there.'

'Just like Erlich's evidence in the States?'

'Exactly. But at a slightly higher level, wouldn't you say?' smiled Costello, his voice heavy with irony.

'God! You're not joking, Thomas.'

'I'm not, Robert. But you don't think I'm being fanciful? I'm terrified of promoting some imaginary conspiracy theory.'

'That's what Alex said,' laughed Paine. 'She thought it was a leap too far.'

'So did I until we met Jakobowits,' answered Costello, returning Paine's laughter.

'Quite,' chuckled Paine.

'But why the secrecy, Robert? Why the involvement of Israeli and American security? These are religious matters. They hardly threaten the state.'

Paine had few doubts in Costello's obvious intellect, but his confinement in the walls of the Vatican had left him with a certain naïvete and an under-estimation of man's natural aggression.

'You haven't thought it through, Thomas. Can you imagine the reaction of the various fundamentalists if news of some collusion leaked out? Think what might happen in Tel Aviv, Jerusalem, even Northern Ireland, Pakistan, India. The list is endless. There'd be riots, complete bedlam. It's a short step to all-out war.'

'In the name of religion,' said Costello sombrely.

'Initially, maybe. But it would soon escalate into nationalism. Read your history books.'

'But why would Woeters, Munro and all the others take such a chance? They must have realised the implications.'

'"Aitu," your four little letters, Thomas. Whichever way

you turn, it comes back to that. My hunch is that Jakobowits knows the answer. All he wanted from us was confirmation of our ignorance.'

For the next two days and nights the two men played and replayed their memories, searching for that one shred of evidence which might reveal the truth. Jakobowits had kept his word, confining them to their room but constantly delivering drinks, meals and even the western papers. All their smallest requests were met without question, and they resigned themselves to sitting out their enforced imprisonment. As the time passed, their trust for each other grew, the factual exchange of life stories moving rapidly to admissions of their weaknesses and unfulfilled ambitions, the reflectiveness of middle-age, and the reassessment of their personal histories. The past became their focus, an escape from the uncertainty of the present.

Once they had exhausted their tales, they began to fill their time by playing mind games, trying to remember the names of old friends, university staff, even the porters and kitchen staff at Trinity, giving each other extra points for the most obscure memory. It maintained their spirit and by the time Jakobowits made his final call their broken friendship was repaired, unified by what had now become an open and common purpose.

The afternoon of the third day saw their sudden release. A flurry of activity outside their room gave them only a few moments' warning. Seconds later, they were bustled into the lift and down to the waiting car, the same white Peugeot which had played its part in their abduction from the Dan Arcadia. Jakobowits was already waiting.

'Your flight's at five,' he said casually. 'We have plenty of time.'

'We're both going to London?' asked Costello, wary of Jakobowits' relaxed manner.

'You can transfer once you're there, Bishop. The ticket will take you on to Rome.'

'What's the catch?' demanded Paine.

'The catch, Mr Paine? I don't follow.'

'Why let us go? You must know we'll contact Laidler.'

'How's your daughter, Mr Paine?'

'My daughter?'

'Heavily pregnant, I hear. Our congratulations.'

'What's Rachel got to do with it?' asked Paine anxiously.

'You're an intelligent man, Mr Paine,' answered Jakobowits pointedly.

Robert Paine felt the sweat glistening on his forehead. It was a cold December morning yet his body was fired by a sudden panic.

'And you're a complete shit,' answered Paine angrily, slumping back into his seat.

15

'Not in,' said Paine, replacing the receiver. 'Probably popped out to see Rachel.'

'Are you sure she won't mind my staying?' asked Costello, struggling to manoeuvre his trolley towards the exit.

'No problem, Thomas. She'll be delighted to see you. Come on, we'll grab a taxi.'

There was a biting wind blowing down the grey concourse outside the terminal, and they were relieved to find the waiting queue of black cabs.

'Richmond,' called Paine, through the open window of the nearest taxi. 'I'll direct you when we get close.'

Both men felt jaded after their long flight from Tel Aviv, remaining silent as the driver picked his way through the evening traffic. They had been given no opportunity to use a phone until arriving back at Heathrow, and Paine was concerned as to how Alex had handled his sudden disappearance. Whenever away from home, it had become his habit to call at least once every couple of days. He knew that Alex was bound to be concerned, especially when she had a deep-seated suspicion of all middle eastern countries. She had refused to travel beyond the Mediterranean since the day they had been married.

It had been Costello's intention to return to Rome and check on Cellini's progress but Paine had persuaded him to break his journey. He had no wish to break up the bond which had at last been re-established, and he knew that their access to Laidler probably depended on Costello.

'Third on the right,' instructed Paine, as they neared the house.

'Ready for Christmas, gents?' asked the cabbie, reminding his passengers that a generous tip was expected.

'Hardly given it a thought,' answered Paine, shuffling through his pocket for loose change. 'Pull in here, would you?'

As the two men approached the house, the light from the hallway was clearly visible through the stained-glass arch which formed the mantel of the doorway.

'Alex!' shouted Paine as they stepped into the hallway. 'Alex!'

'Still not back?' asked Costello.

'Apparently not. No sign of Toby, either.'

'Perhaps she's taken him for a walk?'

'Not at this time of night. Where the hell is she?'

'There's probably a rational explantion,' Costello assured him.

'I hope to God there is. Let me take your bags. I'll show you to your room.'

Grabbing Costello's cases he began to trudge up the steep staircase, his legs heavy with fatigue. He had been in the house only a matter of minutes but already he sensed the remnants of anxiety in the silent rooms. The building not only looked empty but smelled empty. There was no scent of Alex, no hint of her presence. Paine felt like a stranger in his own home.

'Give me a second, Thomas,' said Paine. 'I just want to check something.'

His heart was pumping rapidly as he raced down the landing towards their bedroom. Throwing open the door he strode quickly across to the wardrobe which filled the whole of the wall on the far side of the room. There was a moment's hesitation as he paused to take a deep breath, arming his lungs against the coming revelation. Seconds later he snatched the handle and threw the doors open. As soon as he glanced inside, his movements became more frenetic, almost running across the bedroom to the other cupboards and dressing table which stood by the window. He began pulling at the drawers, leaving them open like an amateur burglar, his speed increasing as each one delivered its disappointment.

'Thomas!' shouted Paine, now desperate for support.

'What is it, Robert? Are you all right?'

Paine was sat on the edge of the bed, head in hands, as Costello entered the room.

'She's gone, Thomas. Almost everything's missing.'

'You're sure?'

'She's left a few bits and pieces, Thomas, but most of her stuff isn't here.'

'Why? There must be an explanation.'

'Only two I can think of.'

'Rachel?'

'Possibly. But why take most of her clothes?'

'And the other?'

'Jakobowits,' answered Paine, with an emphasis which exposed his anger. 'If that bastard's harmed Alex or Rachel, I'll . . .'

'You're jumping to conclusions, Robert,' interrupted Costello, putting his arm around his friend's shoulder. 'Let's check the rest of the house.'

Paine should have guessed, but the shock of Alex's disappearance had robbed him of his usual reasoning. The note was clearly visible under the black pepper-grinder, centred on the empty kitchen table. It was where they always left notes for one another. He grabbed the small piece of paper quickly and scanned its contents.

'What does it say?' queried Costello.

'Look for yourself,' answered Paine, a small smile crossing his lips.

Costello took the note, which contained only four words.

'"Toby's got the answer?" What does that mean, Robert?' asked Costello, bemused by Alex's cryptic message.

'Come on. I'll show you. Take the torch, I'll just go and grab a spade.'

Costello followed as Paine left by the back door and headed into the garden, his movements quick and certain despite the darkness. They stopped briefly as Paine collected the spade from the wooden shed and took the torch from his friend's hand. As Costello's eyes became accustomed to the dark night sky he could see they were heading for a small wooded copse at the the end of the lawn. Paine seemed to have no doubt about where he was heading and he stopped only a few yards into the trees. He handed the torch back to Costello.

'Shine it down here, would you, Thomas?

The spade hit the ground with a dull thud, its edge cutting deep into the turf beneath the silver birch. He asked Costello to move a little closer as he scraped away the loose soil, exposed by his digging.

'Here we go!' he exclaimed triumphantly.

Costello shone the light towards Paine's hands. He was holding what seemed to be a tiny hinged tin, its surface splattered with mud yet quite undamaged.

'Let's get inside,' said Paine.

They hurried across the lawn and back into the warmth of the kitchen, the box held firmly in Paine's grip. Taking a kitchen knife he prised open the top and pulled out the damp folded paper. Holding it close to the light he read the message out loud, savouring the reassurance of every word.

> Robert,
>
> I hope I'm doing the right thing. It seems a crazy thing to do, but David R. was *most* insistent and said we had to get out. Should I have trusted him? He sounded very agitated. Forgive me if I've made a huge mistake. Don't worry about Rachel, she's with me (Roger's on a trip to the Far East – we'll find a way to contact him). We'll be fine. Hope you're OK. Join us when poss. Gone to see the ospreys – got the key – hope there's some heating! Love you.
>
> Alex.
>
> PS. Isobel called from the Canary Islands. Wants you to contact her urgently. Have left her number in the bureau – left hand drawer.

'Uncle Jamie's! God I love that woman, Thomas. I'd never have thought of it.'

'Uncle Jamie?'

'Left me his cottage up in Scotland. They'll be safe there, I'm sure.'

'And the note? How did you know where to find it?' asked Costello, struggling to keep pace with his friend.

'Toby's treasure trove. Buries everything there,' laughed Paine. 'I'd love to have seen the dog's reaction when Alex started digging up his secret store.'

'What now?'

'Let's get some sleep. Tomorrow we'll chase up Laidler.'

'Is that wise?'

'I've got to see it through, Thomas. As long as Alex and Rachel are safe, we might as well go for it. I'm damned if I'll be bullied by Jakobowits.'

'You'll ring Alex?'

'I doubt there's a phone at the cottage. It would be dangerous in any case. Too easy to trace.'

'And Izzy?'

'I'll ring her first thing. I'll use the phone box on the corner.'

It was well after ten o'clock by the time Costello woke. He had slept fitfully, his rest disturbed by a strange bed and the unaccustomed sounds of the house. Each creak from the wooden floorboards, every gurgle from the pipework, seemed to be magnified, shaking him from his exhaustion. At three in the morning he had paced the room, distracting his racing mind by flicking through the old magazines which lay on the bedside table. But eventually his body had succumbed to sleep, his dreams a chaos of emotion.

The smell of newly-made coffee wafted up the stairs as he left his room and headed for the kitchen.

'Sleep OK?' asked Paine, as Costello entered.

'Eventually. Took a long time. To tell you the truth I felt so tense it was almost impossible.'

'Me too, Thomas. It's been a difficult time and this morning's news doesn't make it any easier.'

'You've already called?'

'Izzy and the hospital. Thought I'd better get on with it. Coffee?'

'Please. What's the news, Robert?'

'Izzy or the hospital?'

'Laidler. Are we going to see him?'

Paine poured the coffee as he answered.

'If your imagination isn't on fire already, Thomas, it soon will be. Do you know where he's gone?'

'Tell me.'

'Teheran, Bombay and Tokyo.'

'Dearest Lord!' exclaimed Costello. 'I'm surprised they told you.'

'I tell you, it was like speaking to an answer-machine. Whoever handles the calls had been given a pre-prepared speech.'

'You said you were one of his patients?'

'I could hardly say I was a newspaper man,' laughed Paine.

'I suppose not. So what's the official line?'

'A lecture tour. A bloody lecture tour!'

'How convenient. And Izzy?'

'Even stranger. I'll give you the details later but she wants me to go out to La Palma.'

'When?'

'Immediately. I've never heard her sound so excited, Thomas. She was almost hysterical.'

'You're going?'

'I've got to see Alex first. I want to make sure she's all right. You'll come?'

'I should get back to Rome.'

'Stay, Thomas, stay. I really think we need to stick together.'

The taxi arrived at twelve o'clock. It had given Paine just enough time to ring the airport, book two seats on the shuttle, and secure the house.

'Wapping,' demanded Paine as they shuffled into the cab.

'Wapping?' queried Costello, surprised by the request.

Robert Paine was still aware of the threat from Jakobowits and realised that David Reisman would not have rung Alex unless there was an authentic risk to his family. He knew nothing of espionage or security services but common sense told him that he must make some effort to conceal his destination. Throughout the journey he glanced behind, looking for any sign of being followed but knowing that he was unlikely to have much chance against professional surveillance. But he had to try, however amateurish his method.

As soon as they reached the *Times*' offices, Paine hurried Costello into the building, waving his press card at the commissionaire. Instead of climbing the stairs to his old office, Paine stayed on the ground floor and hurried through the large perspex doors which led to the print rooms. Costello simply followed, aware that his friend was in familiar territory and seemed to know exactly what he was doing.

Once through the giant print presses which now lay silent, waiting for the demands of the next edition, Paine stopped at a small office next to the emergency exit.

'Dave?' he asked, putting his head round the door.

'Mr Paine!' came the reply. 'Haven't seen you for a while. What you up to, then?'

'Can you call me a taxi, Dave? *Pronto*?'

'Hang on.'

Costello stood outside, listening to the conversation.

'Old friend,' said Paine, turning back to Costello. 'One of the few to survive since the Fleet Street days.'

'Five minutes, Mr Paine. Usual spot,' came the voice from the office.

'Come on, Thomas. We'll wait outside. Thanks, Dave. I'll buy you a beer. If anybody asks for me, tell them I'm in a meeting with Finlay,' shouted Paine, as they pushed their way out into the cold December air.

Robert Paine was still on edge as they collected their tickets and walked down the long corridors towards the departure gate. He felt hunted, a fugitive waiting for a hand to touch his shoulder. Whether he had managed to lose any possible followers, he could not be sure. As far as he could see there was nothing suspicious about any of his fellow travellers and yet every glance and returned stare filled him with anxiety. Not until the engines fired into life did he begin to relax. If he had unwanted company, there was nothing more he could do.

It was only an hour's flight to Inverness and the plane was soon banking steeply over the Moray Firth, the black shapes of oil rigs sitting like giant spiders on the water's surface. Paine pointed out the distant snow-capped peaks of the Cairngorms as they made their final approach. It was a view which flooded his mind with childhood memories, bolstering his confidence with its familiarity.

The baggage came through quickly, the calm of the small Scottish airport a sudden contrast to the mayhem of Heathrow. Within minutes they were out of the terminal and into the ice-packed car park, the lines of hire cars already sparkling with frost.

'Is it always this cold?' asked Costello, as they climbed into the car.

'This is warm, Thomas,' laughed Paine. 'Wait till we get up into the mountains.'

There was no obvious climb away from the shore, but the driving sleet soon gave way to flurries of snow which began to build up on the edge of the wipers which were struggling to keep the screen clear. Once through the small resort of Nairn, now bleak and unwelcoming with its rain-swept streets, they headed south towards Lochindorb. The occasional car sped past in the opposite direction, the depth of snow on its roof confirming the worsening weather. The light faded quickly, and by the time they approached Grantown-on-Spey the car's headlights made the snow-fall look like a blizzard.

The progress was slow. Paine remembered making the same journey in under an hour and yet they had already been on the road for over two hours. Costello was surprised by Paine's skill in manoeuvring the car on the treacherous surface.

'Quite a talent,' he observed, as his friend successfully fought the spinning tyres.

'Good memory, that's all,' responded Paine, leaning forward to peer through the smeared glass of the windscreen. 'I'm just going to stop for a moment. Hang on, I won't be long.'

Costello watched as Paine trudged through the banks of snow towards a hotel entrance, its lights casting an orange glow on to the glistening pavement. Christmas decorations hung from every window, but not one token gesture to the Christian message was evident amongst the gaudy, twinkling, white lights and brightly-coloured baubles. Though his companion reappeared within minutes, Costello could feel the temperature dropping rapidly, the heater no longer pumping warm air into the waiting car. Paine returned, carefully stepping on the icy path and blowing into his chilled hands.

'Sorry, Thomas. Bit longer than I thought. I should have left the engine running.'

'I'm fine,' answered Costello. 'How much further?'

'Half an hour at the most.'

But it was almost an hour before Costello saw the sign for the Boat of Garten, its letters almost obscured by the icicles which had formed over its surface. He guessed that in a very short time the roads would be blocked, and even now the blizzard was beginning to create drifts, large white tongues of snow eating into their path.

'I'll park by the old station,' said Paine, as they entered the village. 'We'll have to walk from there, the track will be impassable by now. Grab your case.'

They were ill-prepared for such a walk. Their coats and scarves gave them some protection against the cutting wind, but the snow edged above their light city shoes, numbing their feet with every stride. Both men breathed deeply as they bent into the squall, gasping as they began to ascend the path's sharp incline. Paine stopped, now panting heavily as he rested against the dry stone wall which bordered the stony track.

'All right, Thomas?' shouted Paine.

'Getting old,' answered Costello. 'Nearly there?'

Paine was about to continue when he became aware of a momentary drop in the wind, and in that sudden lull he heard the sound which would answer Costello's question.

'Listen, Thomas. Hear anything?'

Costello tried hard to switch his attention from the cold. It seemed to have been absorbed into every joint of his body and was now beginning to dull his senses. But he could hear something, a sound so powerful that it was able to battle against the growing storm.

'A river?' he responded.

'The Spey,' shouted Paine. 'Just listen to it!

Even in the darkness, Costello could see Paine's excitement, the child re-surfacing from the confines of his tired body, his tone of voice and very movements reflecting his anticipation.

'There's no sound like it, Thomas. Come on, we're nearly there.'

Within a few more steps they could see the lights of the cottage, the pale yellow beams flickering as the surrounding trees were jostled by the wind. Pushing open the wooden gate, its timbers now rotten with age, Paine hurried towards the front door and pressed the latch with his aching fingers. Surprisingly, it gave way to his pressure and he stepped into the warm air, the snow which had drifted against the entrance falling on to the old carpet as he stepped forward.

Paine heard the familiar bark as Toby, alerted by his movements, rushed towards the door, and as he entered the room the labrador threw himself forward, his tail beating out his welcome. The heat of the open wood-fire filled the room, its flames sending a glow across the ill-lit room, the air heavy with the comforting smell of burning logs. On the old velvet-covered chaise-longue lay Rachel, her distended stomach rising and falling in rhythm with her breathing. The two men stood quietly for a moment, frightened to disturb her deep sleep. Gradually she began to stir, her eyes opening slowly as Paine knelt by her side.

'Rachel,' he whispered.

'Daddy?'

'Yes, it's me, darling,' answered Paine, kissing her gently on the forehead. 'Where's Alex?'

'In the bath,' she answered, her response still restrained by sleep. 'What time is it?'

'Ten-thirty. Are you all right, Rachel? I'm so sorry about all this.'

'I'm fine, Daddy, don't worry.'

'You're very brave,' answered Paine, hugging his daughter closely.

Costello realised that his presence had not been noticed. He watched as Rachel returned her father's embrace and gave way to her emotions. Tears streamed down her face as she began to sob uncontrollably, her outward bravado melting in her relief. Costello stepped back to the entrance. He was afraid to interrupt their moment of intimacy and found himself fighting a growing sense of envy. It was a display of love he had never had the chance to experience.

Hearing the steps running down the stair-well he stepped forward once more. Alex flew into the room, still tying her bath-robe as she ran towards her husband.

'Robert!' she screamed, joining him at Rachel's side and throwing her arms around his neck. 'Thank God you're all right. We've been so worried. Have I done the right thing?'

'Apart from leaving the door open,' he laughed.

'The windows don't close either. Seemed no point.'

Paine almost lifted her from the floor and cradled her in his arms, their affection for one another confirmed by their embrace.

'You've been wonderful, Alex. Just wonderful.'

He pulled her close yet again and as he held her warm body he noticed Rachel glancing towards the door, her expression a mixture of surprise and embarrassment. Paine turned his head towards Costello.

'Forgive me, Thomas. Come in. Come in. You look frozen.'

They talked into the early hours, driven by their curiosity. At first their conversation had been difficult, Alex and Rachel thrown by Costello's arrival and each one keen to fire their own questions, to make sense of the growing chaos. Alex was still terrified that she had over-reacted to David Reisman's call, but after hearing Paine's account of Tel Aviv she became gradually reassured.

'Who's looking after you, Rachel?' asked Paine.

'There's a midwife in the village, Robert,' answered Alex. 'Mrs Foresythe. She's wonderful, a real character, but knows what she's doing.'

'She's close?'

'Only a few minutes' walk. She's even got a mobile, believe it or not.'

It was a room that lent itself to the sharing of tales, its stone-flagged floor scattered with an array of time-worn furniture and threadbare Persian rugs. Faded pictures of distant relatives hung from the uneven walls, refusing to submit to their new owners. Yet there was an almost tangible peace in his uncle's old home, a sense of calm which had been left as a final inheritance. Paine had been aware of this tranquillity even in the moment he had stepped excitedly through the front door. There was a welcoming quiet which seemed to cloak the whole building, just as the snow now blanketed the ground outside. He felt his own tension disappear as they continued to exchange their stories.

From what Alex said, Paine realised that David Reisman must have rung her soon after they had been abducted from the Dan Arcadia hotel. Perhaps it had only been a hunch, but he knew that Reisman had worked long enough in Israel to know how men like Jakobowits chose to operate. Even Paine realised that a veiled threat was a real threat. It was obvious that Reisman had taken a genuine risk.

'Your note about Toby was quite brilliant Alex. I told Thomas you should have joined MI5,' laughed Paine, as Alex brought in some hot soup.

'All thanks to cheap spy novels,' answered Alex. 'And pure

fear. It's amazing how the mind works when you feel threatened.'

Alex pulled the large metal guard in front of the fire, pushing the smouldering embers into the back of the grate.

'Come on. We ought to sleep. You must be exhausted. We can talk again in the morning.'

'What's the forecast, Alex?' asked Paine.

'Clearing, I think. We should be all right. I think we've had the worst. For the moment at least.'

'Have we a bed for Thomas? I didn't think to ask.'

'You'll have to share, I'm afraid, Robert. There's only two bedrooms and I'd like to keep Rachel with me. The baby's getting lower and lower.'

'Don't fuss, Mummy. It'll be ages yet,' complained Rachel in mock disapproval.

'That's what I said when your brother was born, and he nearly arrived in the Tate Gallery,' laughed Alex. 'Come on, you need your rest. Show Thomas where he's sleeping. I'll be up in a second.'

Alex waited until she could hear Rachel's steps on the floor above. She turned to her husband and kissed him gently on the lips.

'What happens next, Robert?' whispered Alex.

'In what way?

'How long are we here for? I'm really worried about Rachel.'

'Did you contact Roger?' asked Paine, avoiding a direct response to her question.

'Through the firm.'

'You've heard from him?'

Alex glanced towards the stairs, wary that Rachel might suddenly reappear.

'Nothing. Not a thing,' she whispered. 'Rachel doesn't show it but she's terrified he won't be here for the birth. Your description of this Jakobowits character doesn't help, either.'

'I'm not surprised.'

'Did you see her face when you described your own abduction?'

'She thinks Roger might be some sort of hostage?'

'It's possible, isn't it? I don't know what to think any more.'

'We'll get through, Alex,' answered Paine, unconvinced by his declared certainty.

'And what if Rachel needs emergency medical help, Robert? What happens then?'

'Then we have no choice. Whoever might be looking for us won't have much trouble.'

'So when does it end?' Paine watched the tears begin to well in his wife's eyes. 'How do we know when we're safe?'

Paine shrugged his shoulders as he searched for a response, trying hard to conceal his growing despair.

'We don't, Alex. Not until I've finally come up with the answers. I honestly don't know why we're considered such a threat. That's half the mystery.'

'So we're going to have a Scottish grand-child?'

'Looks like it, Alex.'

'Chip off the old block, Robert,' smiled Alex, recovering her composure and kissing him once again. 'Let's get some sleep. I'm exhausted.'

Soon after their arrival at the cottage, Alex had managed to re-light the rusting farmhouse Aga. It must have been over 40 years old but still performed its duty like a trusted retainer. The smell of frying bacon had brought Costello downstairs, his stomach rumbling with hunger.

'Sleep well?' asked Alex.

'Does Robert always snore that much?' laughed Thomas.

'You should have heard him when he smoked,' she chuckled. 'Is he up?'

'He left about an hour ago. Said you'd know where he'd be. Didn't you see him?'

'I only woke at eight. But I know where he is,' she smiled. 'Hungry?'

'Very.'

Robert Paine searched the sky, vainly hoping for just one glimpse. He recognised the futility of his behaviour but he was no longer driven by logic, but by the emotions of infancy. The storm had cleared leaving a crisp bright morning, the clear blue sky bringing the distant mountains into stark relief. Water splashed onto his face like icy needles, the spray from the river's torrent rising high into the air as it cascaded over the grey, granite boulders. He had slept badly, eager for the day to come, excited by the chance to relive his childhood by the river's edge.

The snow had begun to melt rapidly and the Spey was now in full flow, crashing its way down to the sea some 50 miles away. As he had done some 40 years before, he cast small sticks into the foaming water, watching them bob and struggle for survival in the rapid currents, the eddies and whirlpools which cast the fragile twigs into a crazed and frantic dance. As they disappeared he would throw another, trying to judge its progress in the swirl of the ice-cold river, stopping every few seconds to gaze up into the cloudless sky.

He felt compelled to stay, as if there were a task to complete, a need to find some symbol of conclusion. He had walked down from the cottage with a desire which had suddenly become a necessity, intent on clutching at the straws of reassurance. There was no reason in his actions and yet he revelled in its absurdity. He had known such moments before. Prior to his finals at Trinity he had refused to go into his exams until he had tossed a coin to show three successive 'tails'. Often it would take more than 15 minutes to produce the required result, but until that moment he would not set foot in the exam room. It was not superstition, but like his present experience a need to confirm the closure of a chapter, to signify its end.

He searched the skies once more, his eyes darting across the dark horizons of the heather-covered hills. And then it appeared, at first only a solitary speck in the distance, climbing high on the light wind which rose from the valley floor. His body stiffened, transfixed in disbelief, checking again and again as his eyes watered in the cold, morning air. But as it came closer he knew there was no doubt. The white mottled plumage caught the light as it dived towards him, the sleek lines of its wings propelling its flight with the grace and elegance he had seen in no other bird. It swept over his head silently but at great speed, its head bent slightly downwards as it searched for prey amongst the snow-covered fields. Paine swung round to follow the osprey's progress only to see it disappear into the gloom of the shaded hills. It had been only a fleeting glimpse, yet it was all that he had wanted. Rising from the river's edge, Paine began his walk back to the cottage, stunned by the unexpected, but exhilarated by his discovery.

'You saw it then?' smiled Alex as he came through the door.

'How do you know?'

'It's written all over your face,' beamed Alex. 'You look like a dog with two tails,' she added.

'What a wag.'

'Very funny,' laughed Alex once more. 'Breakfast's ready.'

'I shouldn't have,' said Paine, almost in a whisper.

'Shouldn't have what?'

'Seen the osprey. They're supposed to migrate in the winter. It was a real surprise, Alex.'

'But a good one.'

'Bliss,' smiled Paine in response. 'Rachel up?'

'Still sleeping. She gets very tired despite all her stoicism.'

Costello sat drinking coffee as Paine tucked into his full breakfast, their conversation inevitably returning to Jakobowits.

'I don't see how he can find us here,' said Costello.

'Unless we press on with the enquiries he has no need to,'

answered Paine as Alex delivered some more toast on to the table.

'You're going to stop?' asked Alex.

'Don't see how we can. It may all depend on Izzy now. She's about the only contact we've got left. If we ring anybody else our cover's completely blown.'

'So how do we contact Izzy?' asked Costello.

'I sent a fax to her last night. From the hotel in Grantown. With any luck we might get a reply this morning. I'll go down there soon, the roads should be clear by now.'

'You left our address?'

'No. Don't worry. Just the fax number at the hotel.'

'It's still a risk.'

'One I had to take, I'm afraid.'

Within half an hour Paine had walked back down the lane towards the railway station, the track now running with water as the snow melted in the morning sun. Billowing clouds of steam rose high into the air as the old engines strained to build the pressure in their aging tanks, black soot speckling his face as he approached his car.

Apart from the occasional patch of ice which had remained shaded by the trees, the road was almost free of snow and it took him only a short time to re-trace his journey back into Grantown. The traffic was light and he was able to park easily by the old bakery which stood adjacent to the Glen Shiel hotel.

'Can I help you, sir?' asked the young receptionist.

'Hope so. My name's Paine. Robert Paine. I left your fax number with a friend. Are there any messages?'

'I'll look for you. One moment, please.'

'Mr Paine?' came a voice from behind.

He swung round slowly, his mind immediately turning to Jakobowits and his fear of exposing his family.

'Yes,' he answered cautiously.

'Gregor McInlay,' said the man, offering his hand. 'You're in Jamie's cottage? And expecting a grand-child, I hear.'

'Word travels fast,' said Paine, still wary despite the man's heavy Highland accent, and uncomfortable with the possible menace in McInlay's reference to Rachel.

'It's a small community, Mr Paine. That's the way around here.'

'And you are?' asked Paine directly.

'Your uncle's solicitor. I handled his estate. Perhaps you remember my writing to you when your uncle died?'

'Vaguely. Who else knows?' queried Paine.

'Who else?'

'Who else knows I'm here?'

'The whole village, Mr Paine. We've been waiting to see who would take the place over.'

'You don't happen to know if anybody has been asking for me, do you?'

'Not as far as I know. Why do you ask, Mr Paine?'

'We just enjoy our privacy,' lied Paine, now irritated by the interruption.

'Mr Paine?' interrupted the receptionist. 'Your message.'

'Thanks.'

Grabbing the flimsy paper Paine shuffled to the end of the desk, out of sight of the prying McInlay. He glanced down at the contents, a look of puzzlement crossing his face as he studied its message. It was almost entirely black, the image only punctuated by a small number of irregular white spots.

'Is your fax working properly?' he asked, turning back to the young woman.

'There are two pieces,' she smiled, reaching over and pulling the pages apart.

'I'm sorry. Of course,' answered Paine, hurriedly removing the top copy and reading the note.

> Robert,
>
> Hope you're OK. If this doesn't make you come nothing will. Taking big risk. This place is like Fort Knox. Found out about your little 'word'. Is it important? Grab a plane and let me know. I'll meet you – there's an airport at Santa Cruz de la Palma. I have to show you

something – to do with 'black' page – no time to waste.
No dithering Robert – just come.

Izzy

'Bad news, Mr Paine?' asked McInlay approaching him once more.

'What?' answered Paine abruptly.

'Forgive my saying so, but you look rather startled,' said McInlay piously.

'News. Just news. Nothing important,' answered Paine aggressively. He turned quickly towards the exit, now certain that fate was driving him back to Isobel Griffin.

16

'You are joking, Robert?' protested Alex. 'You're not seriously going to leave us just when your daughter's about to give birth?'

'I've got to, Alex. Izzy's fax hardly gives me any choice.'

'Izzy, Thomas, Jakobowits, Reisman! It's all I seem to hear these days. To tell you the truth, Robert, I've had enough. I'm sick of the whole thing.'

Paine reached over and put his arm round her shoulders.

'Don't,' said Alex abruptly, turning away from her husband and covering her face with the high collar of her jacket. 'Don't,' she repeated.

Toby rubbed his head against her legs. As if sensing her mood, he let out a series of whines, nuzzling against Alex until he gained her attention.

Their walk had been filled with silence, every unspoken word building a dam which stemmed their emotions. Alex's outburst was the inevitable breach, her anger and panic only subdued by confusion.

'I suppose you're going to accuse me of being an over-reacting, irrational female,' said Alex, turning back towards Paine.

He turned in response, expecting to see an expression of anger, a show of aggression. But what he saw was fear, the look of a wounded animal, a submission which failed to match her words.

'You're an intelligent woman, Alex. The last thing I would accuse you of is irrationality. You know that, you always have.'

'And my emotions, Robert? Is an intelligent woman allowed to have emotions?'

'In my own way, I've always loved you, Alex. You know

that.' He responded quickly, trying desperately to tease out the hidden agenda.

'Maybe.'

'Maybe? I never thought you doubted me.'

The silence returned, strengthened by their incomprehension, fearful of the path they were about to take and intimidated by the journey.

'It's not about Rachel, is it, Alex?' asked Paine after a few moments.

Alex leaned against the dry stone wall and looked directly at her husband as if determined to justify her response.

'Of course it is, Robert. This whole thing's become obsessive. You can't leave it alone, can you? What's happened to your sense of priorities, for God's sake?'

Aware that Alex was about to vent her anger, he offered no reply. As she paused, Alex Paine snatched a small stone from the wall's top and hurled it down towards the stream. She turned on him again.

'You race off to Tel Aviv. You disappear. We run off to Scotland like hunted animals. Your daughter's almost hysterical with fear when she should be relaxed and well cared for. Even her husband's disappeared. The only saving factor is that her father suddenly reappears. And then what happens? He announces he's flying off to the Canary Islands. How the hell do you expect me to feel? What do you want me to say? "Off you go, dear. Don't worry about us. Have a wonderful time. Go and solve your little problem." Is that what you want, Robert? Is that what you really want?'

'It's not been easy for any of us, Alex.'

'Save me the platitudes, Robert. I'm talking about your commitment to your family. The safety of your family, come to that. How long do you search for this Holy Grail of yours? And at what cost? There's got to be a limit somewhere.'

'But we're so close, Alex,' answered Paine, jolted into response by his wife's accusations.

'You. You are so close, Robert. Not me. Whatever great revelation is waiting for you in the Canary Islands has nothing to do with the health of my daughter. You're on your own now, Robert. I haven't the time or the energy to support you any longer. If Isobel's got the answer, all well and good, but it's just not my concern.'

Paine shuffled uneasily, unsure whether he should take the next step, but certain that he had to resolve his battle with Alex.

'It's about her, isn't it?'

'Her?'

'Isobel.'

There was no reply, her lack of reaction an answer in itself.

'You don't like her, do you?' he continued.

'You make me sound like a child,' answered Alex quickly, without looking towards him.

'I'm sorry. I didn't mean to. But she is a problem.'

'Not really.'

Her qualified response was enough to confirm Paine's suspicion. He risked the final move.

'You don't trust her?'

'You slept with her, didn't you, Robert?' said Alex, in a matter-of-fact manner.

'Yes.'

He answered without hesitation, feeling he had rehearsed this moment since the day they had married.

'Recently?'

'Christ, no! Years ago. At college. Before we met.'

'No "quick one" for old times' sake when she stayed with us?'

'Come on, Alex. That's a cheap jibe. I would never do that to you. I swear on our grand-child, there's nothing, nothing between us. There never was.'

'But you admit to sleeping with her?'

'Once. Years ago. It meant nothing. It was a big mistake. A big mistake for us both.'

'Meaning?'

'Meaning it should never have happened. I was no more than a substitute for someone else.'

'Who?'

'No one you'd know.'

He moved closer and took Alex in his arms, brushing her windswept hair with his hands before kissing her gently on the forehead.

'I always assumed you knew,' he said quietly.

Alex grew less rigid, but was still taut with the fear of revelation.

'Denial was easier than reality,' she answered.

'So what brought on the reality? Isobel's visit? Something I said? Something I did?'

'No need, Robert,' smiled Alex. 'Old lovers bear scars. Put them in the same room and the scars reappear. We used to call it chemistry.'

'It was so obvious?'

'As a tattoo on the nose.'

'And you minded?'

'Only when I'm vulnerable.'

'And you're vulnerable now?'

'As strong as tissue paper. Battling against sensuality, intelligence and big breasts is hardly what I need at the moment.'

'There's no battle, Alex,' laughed Paine, relieved to see the familiar smile returning. 'There isn't a contest.'

'But you're still going, aren't you?'

'Only if I'm sure you're safe. I promise.'

Anticipating his wife's reaction, he had waited until the morning to tell Alex the full details of Isobel's fax. He needed time to reassess, to draw breath after his return from Tel Aviv. The accusations of having lost his priorities had struck home. He felt trapped between his desire to see an end to the whole business, and his instinctive need to protect his family. With Rachel about to give birth he knew that if he didn't leave in the next few days, his chance would be gone.

'Do we need anything?'

'Only milk and bread. I'll go into Grantown this afternoon. We can stock up for the week.'

It was still cold, an easterly wind biting into their faces as they walked towards the village. But much of the snow had now cleared, the roads and pathways sparkling with the dawn frost. The small incline made them snatch for air, white plumes of breath billowing from their mouths as they reached the top of the hill.

'I'll grab some papers. See you back here in ten minutes? I'll take Toby.'

The newsagents reminded Paine of his youth, shelves heavy with jars of delight, a treasure trove of jellied sweets and roughly-broken toffee. The sugary smell had been absorbed into every crevice, the old wooden counter rubbed smooth by generations of excited small hands. Toby sniffed the air with obvious pleasure.

'Any back copies?' asked Paine, searching for change.

'I'll have a look. Anything in particular?'

'Anything.'

He glanced along the shelves as the shopkeeper shuffled into the store room. The headlines seemed dominated by a recent train crash in London, the tabloids still preferring the trivia of petty scandal. There was something frightening about their normality, something alien in their banal delivery.

'Couple of *Telegraphs* and *Daily Mails* if that's any good,' interrupted the newsagent. 'Any good?'

'Fine. Thanks.'

As he was paying, Robert Paine caught sight of the pile of local newspapers stacked high on the counter's edge. Two faces dominated the front page, their faces blurred by poor printing but immediately recognisable.

'Bad business,' said the old man, noticing his customer's startled expression. 'Know them?'

'Sort of,' answered Paine, skimming through the report. 'I'll take a copy.'

Alex was waiting by the grocery store as he ran down the pavement.

'Let's get back,' he said.

'What's the matter, Robert? What's happened?'

'I'll tell you on the way. Come on. Let's go.'

He thrust the local paper into Alex's hand and began to stride out towards the cottage, almost running as they began the descent towards the river.

'Who are they?' asked Alex breathlessly. 'Slow down, for God's sake, Robert. I can hardly keep up.'

'McInlay and his daughter.'

'The solicitor?'

'And the hotel receptionist. The one who gave me the fax.'

'You didn't tell me they were related.'

'I didn't know. Not till now.'

'It was only an accident. These things happen.'

'In the middle of nowhere? Forced off the road? High speed car?'

'They're both dead?'

'She died instantly. McInlay lasted a few hours.'

They had reached the gate when Paine grabbed the paper and pushed it inside his jacket.

'No need to tell Rachel,' he said.

'Why not? She knows nothing about them. It's just local news.'

'I hope so. I certainly hope so.'

Alex grabbed his arm, pulling him back as he reached for the door catch.

'You don't think there's a connection with us, do you, Robert? You're not thinking about Jakobowits again, are you?'

'God knows, Alex. But who can tell? We just can't take the chance.'

Costello greeted them as they entered, his hands blackened by soot, his clothes covered in splinters of wood.

'Thought I'd clean out the fire. Make myself useful,' he said, clearly embarrassed by his lack of practical skills. 'Made rather a mess, I'm afraid. Do we have fire-lighters or anything?'

'It's fine. I'll do it, Thomas,' smiled Alex. 'Nice of you to try. Has Rachel stirred yet?'

'I don't think so.'

'I'll go and check.'

'Sit down and look at this,' interrupted Paine.

He handed Costello the local paper and waited for a reaction. It only took a few seconds before he gained a response.

'You're sure these are the same people, Robert? I waited in the car if you remember. Never saw either of them. Is it important?'

'I don't know, Thomas, but it makes me feel uneasy. McInlay knew where we lived and his daughter probably told him about Izzy's fax. It wouldn't take much for an interested party to put all the pieces together.'

'But why start looking for us in the remote highlands of Scotland? Where would they start?'

'Easy when you think about it. Family tree, church records, register of wills. It wouldn't be very difficult for any organisation that employs even a half-decent computer operator. Probably take them about half an hour to tie us in to this place.'

'So why kill McInlay? There'd be no reason.'

'Don't know. Warning shot? Reminder of their power. I've no idea.'

'Or just an accident? They do happen, you know, Robert. Aren't you getting a bit carried away? There's not a ghost in every shadow.'

'Maybe you're right. But I'm almost sure they know we're here.'

'Then why leave us alone if we're such a threat? What do we really know? We've nothing more than circumstantial evidence. We know everything and know nothing.'

'Laidler?' asked Paine, his mind racing ahead of Costello's cold logic.

'Exactly. We never got near him. If we had, I could understand the threat. But we're isolated. Ineffectual. We're no longer a problem.'

'And Izzy?'

'She's the only reason I can see for receiving such a

violent warning. You can't go, Robert. You really can't go. You'd be risking your whole family.'

'The sword of Damocles?'

'I'm afraid so, Robert. We're imprisoned by the possible.'

'Or probable?'

'That's the beauty of menace, Robert. There are no certainties.'

'Jesus! What the hell do we do now?' It was all that Paine could muster in reply. He was seething with indignation, frustrated by his impotence and trapped by an imposed imagination.

'I'm going to clean up, Robert. It'll give you a chance to think.'

Paine sat for a few minutes, doing no more than stare blankly into the unlit fire, its lack of life a solace to his mental bedlam. He wished it were as easy to extinguish his own turmoil. Reaching over for the papers, he sought the comfort of the trivia he had always despised, the consolation of normality.

'Anything interesting?'

Alex had crept into the room, her stockinged feet making no sound on the stone-laid floor.

'Not really,' he smiled in response. 'How's Rachel?'

'Tired, but OK. I'm going to take her some tea. Want some?'

'Love some. Thanks.'

'No great dramas then?'

'Nothing. The world's gone very quiet. Almost becalmed.'

Paine continued to flick through the papers as Alex stoked up the Aga, heaving the huge kettle on to one of the rusting grey hobs. Droplets of water sizzled as the cold metal thumped on to the burning surface.

'Takes you back, doesn't it? he said, without turning to look.

'Too damned far,' laughed Alex.

The newspapers were scattered across the floor's surface, each one discarded in disappointment. Despite their supposed refuge, Paine knew that he was searching, ransacking the contents for any scrap of information that might help him to solve his dilemma.

'You can always do the crossword,' teased Alex as she put the tea at his side. 'You're obviously not impressed with the storylines.'

'There's not even a test match being played,' laughed Paine.

'Then it really is serious.'

Alex disappeared upstairs only to return a few moments later. She noticed that Paine had gathered all the papers together in one pile and was sifting through the pages once again.

'Found something?' she enquired.

'Nothing. And everything,' he added pointedly.

'Sorry?'

'You know I said it had gone quiet?' He didn't wait for a reply. 'It's dead. Completely dead.'

'I don't follow.'

'Nothing's happening, Alex. Nothing.'

'You're still not making sense.'

'Look for yourself. Parliament in recess. The UN in recess. Not an international conference to be seen. Not one world leader doing a damned thing. They've all gone into purdah. It's crazy.'

'Christmas?'

'It would explain some of it. But not a total shut-down.'

They both heard the click of the gate at the same moment.

'Expecting someone?' asked Paine. 'The midwife?'

'Not till this afternoon.'

'Wait there,' he whispered.

Before he could reach the door he heard the thud of a fist on its surface. But it was not the explosion of sound he had expected. Instead the knock was rhythmical and familiar, holding no trace of danger. He opened the door slowly.

'Mr Paine?'

'Yes?'

'Sorry to disturb you, but your post box is jammed.'

The postman looked embarrassed by Paine's hesitation and quickly held out the two letters.

'For me?' asked Paine. 'Who from?'

'I just deliver them, Mr Paine,' answered the postman, bemused by the question.

'Of course. Forgive me. I wasn't expecting . . .'

'I'll be on my way then,' interrupted the young man turning quickly towards the gate.

'Thanks,' mumbled Paine apologetically.

He had always enjoyed receiving the morning's post. Throughout his life it had acted as a symbol of worth, a sign that the world acknowledged his presence and valued his contact. Even the incessant junk mail provided an element of recognition. But the two letters he now held gave him no comfort. They were no longer tokens of membership, but messengers of exposure and dangerous isolation.

'Somebody knows we're here,' said Alex, her voice wavering as she began to realise the implications. 'Who are they addressed to?'

'One for me. One for Rachel.'

'Who from?'

'Give me a second.'

Paine examined the surface of each envelope, trying to reveal a clue as to their content.

'There's no date, no postmark. English stamps. But not even franked.'

'Neither of them?'

'Not a thing,' he answered, playing with the letters in his hands, switching them back and forth as if making a choice in a nightmare gameshow. 'Rachel's?' he asked.

'We can't risk letting her open it. Not in her condition. God knows what it contains.'

'Open it?'

'We'll have to. Do it carefully.'

Paine walked over to the kettle, passing the envelope through the mist of steam. The flap gave way easily, its edges puckered by the hot vapour. Reaching inside, he pulled out the single sheet, unfolding it as if handling gold leaf. His eyes raced towards the signature.

'Roger,' he said quickly.

'Read it. Read it out loud,' pleaded Alex, her eyes transfixed by the letter.

Paine moved closer to his wife, still fearful that Rachel might appear at any moment.

'Read it,' pleaded Alex once more.

He glanced towards the stairs and turned back to the letter, his hands shaking as he began to read in a guarded whisper.

'"My darling Rachel,"' he began.

'No address?'

'Nothing.'

'Go on.'

'"Forgive me, Rachel. I'm safe. I'm well. All is fine,"' continued Paine. '"I hope to leave Tokyo in the next few days. We'll be together very soon. Unavoidably detained but will explain. Don't worry. You are quite safe where you are. Love you more than ever. Roger."'

'That's it?'

'Look for yourself.'

Alex read and re-read the letter, feeling cheated of detail.

'It's so short,' said Alex, angered by its brevity. 'He could have been more specific. It tells us nothing.'

'It tells us everything,' answered Paine. 'He knew we were in danger.'

'He'd have guessed that. I contacted his firm. Remember?'

'So who told him the hunt was off?' queried Paine.

'Jakobowits?'

'Doesn't really matter. Someone in the know, that's for sure.'

'Getting us to drop our guard?'

'This is hardly a fortress, Alex. We've never really had a defence against them. Thomas was right. Without Laidler we don't really pose a threat.'

'I hope you're right. I'll show Rachel. She needs to know.'

'Shall I seal it again?'

'She'll understand.'

Alex Paine ran up the stairs to deliver her news, leaving her husband staring at the second envelope. It had lain, almost forgotten, as they had engaged in the small intrigue of opening Rachel's letter. Paine examined it once again. For the first time he noticed its striking resemblance to Roger's hurried note, the same buff envelope and carefully crafted writing of the address. He tore open the flap and began to read. Like his son-in-law's letter there was no date and no address.

> Robert,
>
> I feel responsible for throwing your family into turmoil. I had to take a decision and felt I could not afford to hesitate. You must trust me. There was good reason. You are safe now. Perhaps we are all safe now. 'And what rough beast?'
>
> Shalom,
>
> David Reisman.

'A letter?'

Costello stood at the foot of the staircase.

'Reisman.'

'Reisman? How on earth . . .'

'Not sure. No address. No date. Completely out of the blue,' interrupted Paine. 'See for yourself.'

He handed the letter over and watched Costello skim through the lines.

'There was one to Rachel as well,' interrupted Paine.

'From Reisman?'

'Roger. Different words but the message was almost a carbon copy.'

'Same ending?'

'You mean the rough beast?'

'Yes.'

'Not as far as I can remember. I'd have noticed, I'm sure. It was a strange thing to say. Is it important?'

'I doubt it,' replied Costello with a dismissive waft of the hand.

'It sounds vaguely familiar. Auden, or maybe Eliot?'

'Yeats,' answered Costello, with complete certainty. 'You should go,' he added suddenly. His expression was one of command rather than suggestion.

'Go?'

'To Isobel. To La Palma. I'll look after things here.'

'You seem very sure, Thomas.'

'I am. Go. Go as quickly as you can.'

17

The make-shift buildings of Santa la Cruz reminded Paine of the airport at Inverness, no more than a sprawling coffee shop where the planes were incidental to the exchange of information and local gossip. It had taken him seven hours to reach this small rugged island and his eyes stung with tiredness as he scanned the faces which waited against the small rope barrier. Though it was late December, the early morning sun was already warming the air. The heavy tweed coat which had given him protection against the highland winds now slowed his movements, its weight uncomfortable on his shoulders.

There was no sign of Izzy. She had always been notorious for her inability to to be punctual, but after the urgency of her message Paine was surprised by her absence. He could do no more than wait and he slumped onto the hard wooden benches which lined the walls of the cramped waiting area. Porters and taxi drivers milled around him, their rapid Spanish voices and sunburnt faces a reminder of his sudden flight from Scotland.

He realised the approaching figure had something to do with Isobel the moment she ran through the door.

'Mr Paine?' asked the woman breathlessly.

Paine nodded. She was a young, elegant woman, probably in her early thirties, her jet black, shining hair cascading over the brightly-coloured sari.

'Indria Khumar,' she added, offering her hand. 'Isobel sends her apologies. She sprained her ankle, I'm afraid.'

'She's OK?'

'Fine. But can't drive at the moment.'

There was hardly the hint of an accent in her voice and Paine guessed she had been brought up in England.

'Forgive the dress,' laughed the young woman. 'It's my day off. I call it my ethnic day – reminds me I'm off duty.'

'I'm sorry to have dragged you out,' answered Paine.

'No problem. The car's just over the road. It's only a half-hour journey. You'll enjoy it,' she added. 'There are some wonderful views.'

Paine was not disappointed. Indria gave a running commentary as they began the steep climb away from the shore and through the dark pine forests which stretched into the distance. The incline increased rapidly, forcing Paine into the back of his seat as Indria fought with the crunching gears of the battered Ford pick-up.

'To the right,' shouted his driver as they shuddered over the pitted surface of the road. 'Tenerife.'

He could see the island's distinct shape, its mountains reaching upward from the stark horizon.

'The big one is Pico de Teide,' called Indria. 'It's nearly 4000 metres at its highest point. Quite a sight, isn't it?'

'Wonderful,' answered Paine. 'Ever climbed it?'

'I have. But not in a sari!' laughed Indria. 'We'll be at the Caldera soon. Wait till you see that.'

He was relieved to see Indria drive with such certainty. Within minutes they appeared to be on a narrow ridge, the land falling away into the depths of a deep canyon, the ocean now far below them, small fishing boats no more than specks on the water's surface. He fell silent as Indria manoeuvred the truck carefully along its edge, the tyres skidding on the loose stones of the clay-coloured track.

And then he saw it, the giant dome silhouetted against the clear, blue sky, like some ancient temple torn from its original foundations.

'The Herschel?' asked Paine.

'You know it?'

'I've seen pictures. It's far bigger than I imagined.'

It was only another ten minutes before they pulled up outside the collection of single-storey buildings which lay at the base of the telescope. The hobbling figure of Isobel

Griffin stumbled towards them as Indria finally came to a halt.

'Fucked up this time,' were her opening words as they embraced briefly and headed inside. 'Good journey?'

'Long,' smiled Paine. 'I hope this is going to be worth it, Izzy.'

'It will be,' she answered, her tone abrupt and without her usual humour.

'It's not been easy.'

'I know,' replied Isobel dismissively. 'Want something to eat?'

'Please. How's the ankle?'

'To be honest, bloody awful. Come on, I'll show you to your room.'

Isobel led the way, her steps obviously painful as they made their way along the corridors, the white-painted walls flaking with neglect. He could sense her tension and her face seemed strained, the lines deeper than he had seen them only weeks before. She retained her femininity but her appearance was dishevelled, her shoulders hunched and lifeless.

The canteen was almost empty as they took their seats by the large metal-framed window, away from the other small groups of staff who chatted noisily over their breakfast.

'You OK, Izzy?' asked Paine once the coffee had been served.

'Just the ankle,' she answered sharply. 'It's a bit wearing and bloody painful.'

'Nothing else?'

'Eat your breakfast.'

'So what's going on, Izzy? Time for some answers.'

'Tonight,' answered Izzy abruptly.

Paine was becoming irritated by her short responses and could not hide his annoyance.

'Tonight? Tonight! Come on, Izzy, I've just flown for God knows how many hours and you're still keeping me on tenterhooks.'

'I'm sorry. But it can't be sooner. I have to be sure.'

'You mean I've come all this way on a hunch? Jesus Christ, Izzy. I've just left my wife and my pregnant daughter in the middle of a Scottish winter, and you're asking me to wait? I promised to get back as soon as I could. Alex was nervous enough already, without me disappearing again.'

'How did she take it?'

'What?'

'You upping sticks and leaving them in Scotland.'

'Not easy at first. But you know what she's like. Supportive as always. She knows I've got to see this through.'

'Did Indria say anything to you?'

'About what?'

'I'll tell you later. As soon as the light goes it'll all become clear. Trust me.'

'You're asking a hell of a lot, Izzy.'

'I know,' she answered, reaching over the table and taking Paine's hand. 'I don't think this is a wild goose chase, Robert.'

'Have you heard any more from Erlich?' asked Paine, aware that Isobel would not be persuaded.

'Nothing. But Indria's been useful.'

'In what way?'

Isobel Griffin began to detail her sudden call from Albert Quinon offering her a job on La Palma. She told Paine that Quinon was quite insistent that she move very quickly and had even directed her line of research. Indria Khumar had been made available for her skills in calibration exposures, whilst Isobel was asked to concentrate on the analysis of data. Though she hadn't heard a thing from Stephen Erlich since his last batch of notes, Isobel arrived in La Palma still burning with questions. Her brief stay in London had only added to her own desires to make sense of the whole business.

'So where does Indria come into this?' interrupted Paine.

'She's a Hindu. British-born but a practising Hindu.'

'What are you getting at, Izzy?'

'Well, think about it, Robert. What's the strangest thing about all these meetings exposed by Erlich? What's the oddest thing about you and Thomas chasing off to Tel Aviv?'

'Go on.'

'The mystery is, that it just doesn't make sense. Or at least it didn't.'

'Meaning?'

'Meaning that from what you've told me, this whole business started by Thomas getting the frights about ecumenicalism – about the unification of the Christian churches.'

'And?'

'And suddenly we're presented with evidence of meetings between different faiths. Faiths which have absolutely nothing in common. They're divided by belief, by structure, by history. They have nothing to talk about.'

'So why meet?'

'So what do they talk about? That's the big question, Robert. Or at least it was until I talked to Indria.'

'You told her the whole story?'

'No. Just showed an interest in Hinduism and took it from there. No more than that.'

'So what's the story?'

Isobel began to take Paine slowly through her conversations with Indria Khumar. At first she had no idea where they might lead, but gradually a picture began to emerge. Her assistant not only had a deep knowledge of Hinduism but also possessed a working knowledge of many other religions. What Isobel couldn't find was any obvious common link, the one factor which might draw them together.

'But you did?' asked Paine.

'What's the main characteristic of Christianity, Robert?' questioned Isobel in reply.

'Jesus Christ, I suppose. I don't really know.'

'You're right. I know they operate with a concept of the trinity, but essentially it's monotheistic. One God. One supreme being. Same for the Muslims, eastern orthodox, Jews and many others. Obviously their concepts differ but their beliefs have a central core.'

'It doesn't explain the Eastern religions,' interrupted Paine. 'I know little about them, but surely their whole way of thinking is so different that there could be no common bond? What the hell would a pope and a Buddhist monk have to discuss?'

'That's exactly what I asked Indria,' answered Isobel, her eyes now sparkling with a renewed energy. Paine listened spell-bound as she began to relate her discussion.

'Take Hinduism for a start, Robert. They do have a notion of one central spiritual being. An aatman, I think she called it. No physical sense, no gender, nothing tangible. But it's something with which Hindus feel they can connect. Just as Christians have denominations, prophets, leaders who interpret the bible and their own history, so the Hindus have swamis. Some of them are even thought of as incarnations. Indria tells me that these avatars, as they're known, are considered to be sons of God – deliverers of the world when needed.'

'You're saying that Christ was a . . . what did you call it?'

'Avatar.'

'Avatar,' he repeated slowly.

'Precisely. And Krishna. And, believe it or not, Gautam Buddha.'

'But I thought Buddhism was atheistic? It's simply about a sense of being. There's no notion of a supreme being.'

'Exactly. But there is a sense of otherness, a sense of potential bliss.'

'Nirvana?'

'Yes.'

'And the rest? What about Taoism, Confucianism, the old tribal religions?'

'Different concept, different interpretation, same core,' answered Isobel excitedly. 'They're all an attempt to explain existence. Each as valid as the next and none of them wrong. Simply different conceptual models.'

'So a pope would talk to a swami about interpretation? So what's new? You're telling me nothing.'

'Maybe.'

Paine could feel his irritation returning. She had presented an interesting idea but hardly enough to justify abandoning his wife and daughter. His patience was being tested by what seemed an intentional ambiguity. He pushed harder.

'Come on, Izzy! There's got to be more to it than that, for God's sake.'

'I think there is, Robert,' she answered firmly. 'In fact, I'm sure there is.'

'And?'

'Tonight, Robert. I'll call you about eight. We'll have a meal and go up to the laboratory.'

'You can't tell me now?' appealed Paine, growing more and more agitated. 'About the black paper? About the word? Anything?'

'There's a lovely walk along the ridge. You can see the other two telescopes from there,' answered Isobel, avoiding a direct reply. 'I'd join you if I could. Give me a call if you need anything, I've got to go and do some work.'

'Maybe later, Izzy,' he answered, resigned to her refusal. 'I think I'll grab some sleep first. Where do I find you?'

'Put a call over the tannoy. I'll hear it in my office.'

He had only intended to doze for a few minutes when he first lay on the bed. His internal clock had been thrown into mayhem by the long flight from Inverness, punctuated and disturbed by a need to change planes in Paris and Madrid. His body ached for the relief of sleep, his mind begging for the oblivion which only unconsciousness would offer. The wish was granted quickly, the warmth of his room tempting him to submit. Within minutes, Paine had fallen into a deep but fitful sleep.

The sound which finally woke him left no question of its urgency. At first the light tapping noise hardly registered, but gradually its insistency could not be avoided. The knock on the door became more rapid, hammering out its message with increasing force. Paine struggled to wake himself as he heard the voice calling outside his bedroom.

'Mr Paine! Mr Paine! Are you awake?'

He glanced at his watch as he dropped his legs on to the floor and approached the door. It was already three o'clock and he realised he must have slept for over five hours.

'Yes?' he murmured. 'What is it?'

'It's Indria, Mr Paine.'

He opened the door wide to find Indria standing in the corridor, her face flushed with excitement.

'I'm sorry to wake you,' she said, 'but I thought you'd like to see this.'

She handed him the flimsy grey paper as Paine rubbed his eyes and asked her to come in. He sat on the edge of the bed, his head still dizzy from the sudden awakening, his eyes trying hard to focus on the printed message.

'Pass my glasses, would you?' asked Paine. 'They're just on your right. On top of the desk.'

Indria reached over and handed him the thick gold-rimmed spectacles, her face still beaming with anticipation as Paine began to read.

'Good God!' he exclaimed, poring over the paper. 'When did this come in?'

'About five minutes ago,' replied Indria. 'Congratulations. You must be delighted.'

'A grandfather!' exclaimed Paine. 'I can hardly believe it.'

'You're glad it's a boy?'

'Anything. As long as it's healthy.'

'I wish my father had felt the same,' she laughed. 'I think I was a disappointment until I got my Ph.D.'

'Different cultures,' smiled Paine sympathetically.

'I suppose so.'

'I must get back, Indria. When's the next flight? Do you know?'

'There's the regular flight to Madrid at eleven tomorrow. It's the one you arrived on.'

'Nothing sooner?'

'Nothing, I'm afraid. I'll fix the booking if you like.'

'Thanks. That would be a help. Let me know if there's a problem.'

Indria stood and unexpectedly kissed him lightly on the cheek, the perfumed smell of her hair startling Paine as it brushed gently across his face.

'I'm so happy for you,' she said as she opened the door and swept out of the room.

'Thanks,' he called, still surprised by her open display of affection.

By the heading on the fax, it was clear that Thomas must have gone down to the hotel in Grantown as soon as he had the news. His message confirmed that Rachel and the baby were safe and well but Paine was now frantic to see them all, to embrace his daughter, to hold his grand-son, to comfort Alex. He felt a long way from home and angered that he had missed the moment.

Glancing again at the message, he checked and re-checked the scribbled note, fearful that he may have missed a detail, a hint that something was wrong, some indication that Thomas was hiding an awful truth. But there was nothing. Even in those few lines, the tone of celebration was clear and not the faintest suggestion of deceit. Yet even then, it was impossible to shake off the worm of doubt which he knew would plague him until he got back to his family.

'Robert?'

Isobel Griffin entered, not waiting for a reply.

'A grandfather, eh? You old bastard!' she said, embracing him warmly as he stepped forward. 'She must have been early.'

'I should have been there, Izzy. I should have been there,' repeated Paine, holding his head in his hands.

Isobel could see his anguish and tried to deflect his growing anger and self-pity.

'Has he got a name?'

'Thomas didn't say.'

'And it went well?'

'He said the midwife was very professional. It all went very smoothly by the sound of it.'

'Lucky girl.'

'I suppose so.'

'I'm sorry, Robert. I've really screwed things up for you.'

'You weren't to know, Izzy. Indria's fixing up a flight for me first thing tomorrow.'

'Yes, I've just seen her.'

'So it's got to be tonight, Izzy. No choice. Whatever happens I'm catching that plane in the morning.'

'I know, Robert. Don't worry,' stressed Isobel. 'You'll understand. I promise.'

He was thinking more clearly as he strode out along the rough pathway which led away from the observatory. The wind swept up from the bleak valley which lay far below, the light cloud sending shadows scurrying across the granite rocks which rose steeply to the mountain's summit. As Izzy had suggested, he could see the squat dome of the Isaac Newton telescope, and to its left the smaller Kapteyn observatory. They stood like grey sentinels, guarding the pathway to the giant sphere of their larger brother. Though the Herschel dome was lost amongst the peaks of La Palma, its rounded shape dominated the landscape, somehow threatening nature itself. As he turned to look back, Paine imagined explorers in a thousand years' time discovering this object and assuming it was some ancient idol, worshipped by all who approached.

Leaving the track, Paine scrambled over the rocks, carefully picking his way amongst the granite boulders which must have lain in the same position for many millions of years. Clambering up on to one of the larger stones he let the warm winter wind beat into his face, the ground directly in front of him falling away rapidly into the distant valley. The sea was still visible from this position but only as a thin, green line which merged into the horizon. He sat on his haunches, letting the sun warm his face as he once more began to think of Alex and Rachel and what the night might bring.

He sensed that Isobel was about to deliver the final part of the puzzle and whilst he was fired with excitement he also feared the consequences. Bit by bit, it was beginning to make sense even though there were still many questions left unanswered. What had unnerved him most about Isobel's theory was that it failed to explain any connection between the contacts made by Woeters and the illness which had apparently afflicted some of the world's senior religious leaders. He knew that Isobel had made great play of the American meetings and the fact that there may have been a succession of discussions about the interpretation of belief. But as he had complained, this was not new ground; there had to be another factor.

As he looked out over the barren mountains of La Palma, trying to make some sense of all the evidence, he began to take his final steps towards the solution. He realised that the mass of detail had once again blinded him to a simple truth. The escape to Scotland, the threats from Jakobowits, and Rachel's pregnancy, had fogged his imagination. All it needed was an ability to cast off logic and free himself to accept the impossible. And as it had done before, all his questions came back to those four simple letters, repeated by Woeters as he lay in his bed at Lambeth. The four letters he had underlined in his diary just before his death. 'Aitu' was the key, but until now he had no idea how to locate the lock. Who guarded the door? Who had imprisoned the truth? Why had they found it so important to conceal reality?

Robert Paine leant back and closed his eyes, blanking every thought from his racing mind, willing the solution to fill the empty void.

And it was Laidler who stepped into that darkened room, the tall wiry frame and angular features which had been frozen on the television screen when Costello had called from Rome. Thomas had described him so vividly that Paine could see him clearly, stepping in that unco-ordinated manner along the corridors of St Thomas's hospital, the crumpled suit and artistic hands gripping a small brown file of papers. It was Laidler who had first mentioned 'aitu', Laidler who had been seen in Tel Aviv, Laidler who was on a supposed lecture tour in the far east, Laidler who had contacts with Lambeth Palace, with Jakobowits and the Israeli security services. Laidler was the door-keeper.

Paine sat up with a start, small beads of perspiration forming in his hands, his forehead damp with tension as he scrambled back along the track in search of Isobel.

He put out a call as soon as he returned and she reached his room within minutes.

'It won't be dark for another couple of hours,' said Isobel as she entered Paine's room.

'I know that, Izzy. Can we eat early? I need to talk to you.'

'If you like. The canteen's open in a few minutes.'

Isobel asked about Paine's walk as she hobbled along the corridors, occasionally grabbing his arm for support. It was only six o'clock and they were the first people to arrive.

'In the corner,' directed Isobel. 'No-one sits there. It'll give us some privacy. This place will be packed in half an hour.'

'Some wine?' asked Paine, hoping it might loosen Isobel's tongue.

'Why not?. The local stuff's quite good. And cheap. Mind if I smoke?'

Isobel lit the cigarette without waiting for Paine's consent. He looked almost manic by now and she wanted to arm herself with all the props she could find. She blew the smoke to one side as she prepared to listen to Paine's story.

'So what is it, Robert? Rachel? Alex? You look very tense.'

Even though they were still alone in the bleak canteen, Paine drew his chair closer to the table and began to speak in no more than a whisper.

'It's Laidler,' he said.

'What about him?'

'You remember all the stuff I gave you about Tel Aviv. Laidler outside the hospital, then his disappearance from London?'

'Go on.'

'What if he was treating exactly the same complaint in all these religious leaders? What if they all had the same mysterious tumour as Woeters?'

'That's no more than you'd guessed already,' interrupted Isobel. 'I thought Thomas and you had come to that conclusion before you left Inverness?'

Paine hesitated in his reply as the waiter brought the wine, the young waiter filling their glasses with surprising confidence.

'The chicken,' said Paine looking up from the table.

'Me too,' added Isobel.

He waited a few more seconds until the boy was out of ear-shot.

'We *had* come to that conclusion, Izzy. But we didn't take the next step.'

'Which was?'

'You're not going to like this, Izzy.'

'Try me.'

Paine inhaled deeply before replying, glancing round as a few more of the staff began to filter into the room.

'What if all these men were operated on by Laidler and woke up saying the same thing – regardless of their native language.'

'Saying what?'

'"Aitu", Izzy. "Aitu".'

Paine watched for Isobel's reaction, looking for that one look which might reveal her knowledge, one sign that she held the missing piece. And he wasn't disappointed. Her reply lacked her usual assurance, her voice shaking with the hesitancy she tried so hard to conceal.

'How can you come to such a conclusion, Robert. You've no evidence.'

'Jakobowits?'

'Jakobowits? What proof does he offer?' asked Isobel, her face now strained as she waited for Paine's reply.

'Why ask about "aitu" if he hadn't heard it himself? Why should Laidler mention it to him?'

'Supposition. Bad science,' answered Isobel, regaining her composure.

'Maybe. But how do you account for some obscure little word coming up in two cities thousands of miles apart? And both linked to religious leaders.'

'Of different faiths,' observed Isobel.

'Quite.'

There was a long pause as Isobel Griffin tried to digest Paine's theory. He noticed her hand visibly shaking as she raised her cigarette to her lips.

'God knows, Robert. I've no idea.'

'You're lying to me, Izzy. You bloody well do know and I deserve an answer.'

Isobel drew hard on her cigarette and filled both their glasses, her eyes casting around the room, anything to avoid direct contact with her friend. Finally she turned to look him square in the face.

'I am not lying, Robert. Believe me. Until you confronted me with this idea I was clutching at straws. Just like yourself.'

'And now?'

'Now I'm frightened.'

'Frightened?'

'Shitless.'

'So what's "aitu"? You've got to tell me now.'

'As soon as it's dark, Robert. I told you. I need one final check.'

'God. You're bloody impossible, Izzy.'

'I know. It's my most redeeming quality,' she smiled.

Her tease broke the intensity of their conversation. They sat eating their meal mainly in silence, watching the light slowly fading outside the large window which looked out over the mountains of La Palma. The wine gradually had its effect, easing the former tightness of their exchanges. By the time the coffee had been served it was almost dark and she could see the anxious anticipation returning to her friend's expression.

'Before we go, I ought to tell you something, Robert.'

'Another revelation?'

'You could say that,' laughed Isobel.

'What is it?' he smiled in response.

'Let's say I was hoping to renew an old friendship,' she said, grasping his hand as she spoke.

'You wanted to . . .'

'Seduce you,' interrupted Isobel. 'To tell you the truth I hoped you might fuck me senseless.'

'You have a way with words,' smiled Paine, quickly looking round to see if anyone had heard Izzy's outburst. 'I'm flattered. But it sounds as if you've changed your mind.'

'Rachel, I suppose. I knew there was no chance once the fax came. It would have stretched your loyalty a bit far, I guess.'

'Who knows, Izzy. I don't know what to say.'

'Nothing would be fine, Robert. It was a crazy idea.'

'But why? Why after all this time?'

'You tell me, Robert. Some kind of catharsis, I suppose. Re-live old times. Regain our youth.'

'We weren't much good the first time, Izzy,' laughed Paine, squeezing her hand gently.

'That's the point, Robert. Really shitty, isn't it?'

'Just the way it was. Better left to history.'

'You haven't heard the worst yet.'

'There's more?'

'Are you sure you want this?'

'Might as well.'

Isobel lifted her glass and gulped the remaining wine, her voice now slurring slightly as she spoke.

'It was Thomas who really turned me on. Thomas bloody Costello. Can you believe it, Robert. I fell in love with a fucking Catholic priest!'

Paine could see Isobel losing control, her eyes welling with emotion as she made her final admission, the alcohol robbing her of any inhibition. He raised his hand to her face, gently wiping away the tears which now ran down her cheeks.

'I know,' he whispered. 'I always knew.'

'And Thomas? Don't tell me he knew as well.'

'I'm afraid he did, Izzy. It nearly tore him apart. You tested every ounce of faith in his body.'

'And lost,' murmured Isobel, now blowing her nose and fighting back the tears.

'He told me he had no choice,' smiled Paine sympathetically. 'He was caught in a triangle of his own.'

'Weren't we all, Robert. What a fucking mess.'

'I suppose it was.'

'Let's go,' she said suddenly. 'I need some air.'

They walked slowly towards the start of the ridge which Paine had crossed earlier in the day. The sky had darkened by now, the mountains slowly disappearing in the fading light.

'Hold me, Robert. Would you? Just for a moment.'

He stood at her back and wrapped his arms around her waist, her body responding to his touch and leaning back into his chest. Paine pulled her hair to one side and kissed her on the neck. She glanced back and smiled silently, gripping his arms in her hands.

'Why now, Izzy? Why the admissions?' asked Paine.

She turned towards him.

'You're about to find out, Robert. Come on. Look at that clear sky. It's perfect.'

Isobel Griffin swung open the metal, panelled doorway which gave access to the dome, the stale smell of the interior reminding Paine of a prison he had once visited as a junior reporter. A series of bare concrete steps led up to a number of steel platforms which sat below the main body of the telescope. He had expected a larger version of the simple equipment he had seen as a child, but what he saw now resembled nothing he had seen before. How the skies could be monitored with such an instrument was impossible to see. Instead of the long sliding metal tube he had anticipated, Paine was confronted with an object which looked more like a miniature oil rig. Four grey tubular stanchions supported the main barrel of the telescope which disappeared into the darkness of the towering dome.

'Welcome to Autofib 3,' said Isobel, positioning herself by a bank of computer screens.

'Autofib 3?' asked Paine.

'Optical fibre telescope,' she answered by way of explanation. 'Too difficult to explain. Take a seat.'

There was a noticeable change in Isobel. Minutes before she had given way to emotion, given way to the heady wine. But now she was alert, professional and obviously in command. Paine watched her, admiring her expertise as she went through the procedures, responding quickly to the messages which flashed on to the screens.

'It looks new,' he observed, moving closer to her side.

'That's how it all started, Robert. It was only commissioned the day before I arrived.'

'It works?'

'I'm the only one to produce images so far. You're about to be the second.'

'The black paper?'

'From Autofib 3. Want to do the honours?'

'Sorry?'

'Press the yellow button,' she said, pointing to a bank of switches in front of his seat.

The response was immediate. High above Paine's head came the faint but distinctive hum of movement, growing louder as the machinery strained to divide the half-mooned canopy. Gradually the night sky crept through the widening gap, and as his eyes adjusted he began to see the star-filled panorama, their flickering lights bright and unobscured in the pitch-black heavens.

'God, it's magnificent, Izzy,' exclaimed Paine, his neck bent backwards as he looked up through the open roof.

'I never tire of it,' smiled Isobel. 'It's my playground,' she added wistfully.

'Some playground,' laughed Paine. 'What next?'

'We line it up at the target, capture the image, bounce it over to Cambridge and they bounce it back as an image.'

'You're joking!'

'I'm not. It's all automatic, of course. A series of satellite links and back it comes. Easy really.'

'You've lost me already. What's the target?'

'Crab Nebula.'

'A star?'

'Sort of. It's hard to explain. Have you heard of a supernova?'

'Well, yes. But I've no idea what they are. Carry on. You can explain later.'

He was determined not to delay Isobel's work and he watched her playing with her giant toy, each small adjustment of the telescope signalled by a whirring response high above their heads. He could see the images changing on the green-tinted screens, their message obscured by a haze of electrical interference. It was difficult to see how Isobel could make any sense of the information, yet she worked with great certainty, her hesitations only momentary as she revealed her expertise.

'Over here,' she said suddenly. 'It only takes a few seconds.'

She led him across the concrete floor to a large printer which stood, isolated, in the far corner of the laboratory.

'The image?' asked Paine.

'It's coming now.'

The paper began to curl out into the tray, stopping occasionally as if drawing breath and resting between signals. Isobel grabbed each sheet as it spewed out from the machine, studying the detail with a small eye-glass which was now strung around her neck. The printer stopped suddenly, its green and red lights dimming as it came to the end of its work.

'You're about to get your answer, Robert. I need some light.'

Paine could feel his heart pumping as he followed Isobel into a small office which lay adjacent to the laboratory. She almost ran towards the desk, shining the reading lamp on to the collection of papers, her fingers tracing quickly across their surface. They looked very similar to the fax he had received in Scotland, almost totally black yet filled with minute blotches of irregular white dots.

'Pass me the ruler, would you?' asked Isobel.

'This?'

Isobel nodded without turning, snatching the instrument from his hand and laying it across one of the papers. It reminded him of the slide-rules he had been forced to use as a child but had never understood. But Isobel was again in full control. She slid the ruler back and forth, often stopping to make quick calculations on a small white note-pad.

'Jesus Christ!' she shouted, throwing the pencil on to the desk and leaning back from the table.

'What is it, Izzy?' asked Paine quickly. Her look of concentration had now been replaced by an expression of fear, an air of panic which Paine felt he could almost touch. 'What is it?' he urged.

Isobel lit a cigarette and turned towards him.

'Where do I begin, Robert?' she pleaded.

'At the beginning. And slowly,' answered Paine, his voice deliberate and calming.

Isobel began to clear the desk, leaving only one printed sheet in the centre of the table. Reaching into a drawer she pulled out a large brown envelope and pulled out five more pieces of paper. Carefully she arranged the prints, checking the dated headings as she spread them across the surface.

'Look at the third one, Robert. Recognise it?'

He bent over the table, peering closely at the blackened paper.

'Not sure. Is it the one you sent me?'

'It is, and only five days ago.'

'They all look the same to me,' added Paine, glancing across the table.

'Look in the centre. The larger dot with the fuzzy edges.'

'Is that the Crab Nebula?'

'That's what I thought it was.'

'And now?'

Isobel reached over to the last piece of paper.

'Notice anything?'

Paine looked again.

'It's different. Not quite the same shape.'

'Even simpler, Robert,' she answered, lighting another cigarette. 'It's bigger. Much bigger. And . . .' Isobel hesitated, her voice now shaking as she spoke.

'And?' urged Paine.

'And it's heading our way, Robert. Heading our way at a speed which defies every law of physics. I tell you, it blows Einstein's theories right out of the water.'

'What the hell is it?' asked Paine, looking closely at the image and trying to make sense of Isobel's claims. 'A meteorite or something?'

Isobel began to laugh hysterically, her face flushed red with colour.

'If that's a meteorite, I'm Joan of Arc,' she giggled.

'Bigger than that?'

'A little,' she answered, laughing once more.

'How much bigger?' demanded Paine.

She swivelled round in her chair, the humour now absent from her expression, her words delivered slowly and deliberately.

'At a rough estimate, I'd say we're talking anywhere between two to four million miles in width, and probably the same in length.'

'Million!' exploded Paine, rising from his seat. 'Two to four million? You can't be serious, Izzy.'

'I wish I wasn't.'

'My God!' exclaimed Paine, now pacing up and down the office, his body shaking uncontrollably.

Their conversation had come to an abrupt end and Isobel sat in silence, chain-smoking and staring blankly at the wall. Paine had no response. Her message was too much to contemplate. There was no frame of reference, no possibility of anchoring his thoughts.

'Cigarette?' asked Isobel, offering the packet to her friend.

'Why not?' answered Paine in a whisper.

His head spun as the smoke surged into his lungs and he

slumped back into his chair, the dizziness weakening his legs.

'Who else knows, Izzy?' he asked finally.

'Just me, and, I suspect, Albert Quinon. I think he knew what was going on. This posting was his final favour.'

'No-one else?'

'I didn't think so. Not until you told me about Jakobowits.'

'He knows?'

'My guess is that every government in the fucking world knows. They're just terrified of mass panic. It's no wonder they threatened your family.'

'And threw you out of the States.'

'Exactly.'

Paine stubbed out the cigarette, annoyed by his own weakness.

'How long?' he asked simply.

'Two weeks, maybe three at the most.'

'And there's nothing we can do?'

'Nothing.'

Isobel stood up and put her arms around Paine, knowing what was coming next. She could see the desperation in his face as he stirred himself for the final question.

'And "aitu"?' he asked.

'No more than a word, Robert. The final explanation in four simple letters.'

'So it is a word?'

'African, of all things.'

'African? Come on, Izzy, for God's sake. What is it?'

'Remember I took a year off after Trinity?'

'Voluntary service?'

'To work with the Maasai. It's the only unselfish thing I've ever done.'

'So what's the connection?'

'The language, Robert. The ancient Maasai language.'

'You're telling me "aitu"'s a Maasai word?' His eyes widened as he spoke. 'Are you sure?'

'I am now, Robert. It all makes perfect sense,' answered Isobel, kissing him lightly on the lips.

'Tell me,' asked Paine gently, and almost terrified of her response. 'Tell me.'

She held him once again and he could feel her warm tears on the side of his face. Her body trembled as she answered, each word delivered slowly and punctuated by her growing fear.

'"Return", Robert. "Aitu" simply means "return".'

18

'*In nomine Patris, et Filii, et Spiritus Sancti.* Amen.'

Thomas Costello took the small bundle gently in his arms and raised it slowly above his shoulders, bowing his head in prayer as he offered the child to God.

After a moment's pause he dropped on to one knee, cradling Rachel's son as he leant forward towards the water's edge.

'I baptise thee in the name of the Father, and of the Son, and of the Holy Ghost.' The baby's head turned away with a cry as the ice-cold water trickled down its forehead, the tiny droplets glistening in the frosted sunlight.

Costello spoke softly, his voice barely audible against the river's torrent, the small group huddling together as the bishop offered his final prayers. Stepping forward, they kissed the child in turn, Rachel sobbing quietly as her child was returned.

'Thank you, Thomas,' said Paine, as they turned to walk back to the cottage. 'It means a lot to Rachel. And to Alex, oddly enough.'

'But not you, Robert?'

'I don't know, Thomas. There are still so many unanswered questions.'

'They're about to be answered,' smiled Costello.

'I know. I only wish I had your faith.'

They continued up the path, their feet crunching on the ice-covered ground. Alex and Rachel had walked ahead, keen to protect the baby from the biting cold.

'You've told them?' asked Costello suddenly.

'Not yet, Thomas. I know I will have to. I just haven't found the right moment.'

'Of course.'

'You knew about Reisman's letter didn't you, Thomas? It was Yeats, wasn't it?'

' "And what rough beast?" '

'Yes.'

'There seemed no point,' answered Costello simply.

Alex was waiting at the gate when they finally clambered up the rough track towards the cottage.

'Anyone for a walk?' asked Alex.

'You two go,' answered Costello. 'I'll stay with Rachel, if you like.'

'Sure?'

'Really.'

'Toby!' shouted Alex, into the house.

The labrador rushed out, his tail wagging its approval as they set off towards the village.

'You haven't really told me about Isobel,' said Alex after a few moments.

'Maybe over dinner,' answered Paine, taking his wife's hand.

Alex stopped abruptly as they reached the brow of the hill.

'Look at the sky, Robert. It's so clear. Almost translucent. I've never seen it like that before. It could be God's own light.'

Paine pulled Alex towards him and kissed her gently on the mouth.

'Perhaps it is, Alex. Perhaps it is.'